Dirty Tricks

A Novel

by

Rita M. Bleiman

PublishAmerica
Baltimore

First printing

ISBN: 1-4137-6078-3
PUBLISHED BY PUBLISHAMERICA, LLLP
www.publishamerica.com
Baltimore

Printed in the United States of America

From the Author

I am always asked if this novel is autobiographical. The short answer is no. But I have taken a character—Gloria Warren—who is not me, and put her on the path I followed in the 1960s. I grew up in Dallas, have crummy hair, never felt I fit in, saw John F. Kennedy just before he was assassinated, got involved in local and state politics and eventually moved to Washington, D.C. But after that, all similarities come to an abrupt end. The story is fictitious and I invented all of the characters. Nor are these characters composites of folks I knew. Any resemblance to any person living or dead is purely coincidental.

Many people spent hours helping me with this book and I would like to thank them for their time, effort and direction. From Texas, I am grateful to Dave McNelly, Dwayne Holman, Dave Moss, Betsey Wright, Lydia Chandler, and the Honorable Oscar H. Mauzy. From Massachusetts, I owe much to Jay Neugeboren, Jonathan Harr, Steve Berrien, Tanyss Martula, Carol Edelstein, Rene Schultz, Bret Averitt, Penny Cuninggim, Lida Lewis, Bill Dwight, Carol Schweid, Sue and Geof Woglom, Linda Kopf, Ronnie Janoff-Bulman, Marjorie Hess and, of course, to Bruce Bleiman, my harshest critic and most enthusiastic supporter.

In researching this book, I studied 1966 and 1967 issues of *Newsweek*, *The Texas Observer*, and *Cosmopolitan*. I also read *Molly Ivins Can't Say That, Can She?* by Molly Ivins; *The Gay Place* by Billy Lee Brammer; and *The Establishment in Texas Politics* by George Norris Green.

Spring 1966

Veronica gave me the wig just before Senator Vic Davis flew into Love Field, and I believe that was the beginning of all the trouble that followed. My drab, shoulder-length hair was thin and fine and refused to hold any style other than a droop.

Veronica's auburn hair was naturally golden: she colored it, saying the blond field was too crowded. When it was time for a touch-up, it seemed as if she had a halo rather than roots. In spite of the fact that each morning she woke at five to set it in wire rollers, and then fell back asleep under her bonnet dryer for ninety-minutes, she had no split ends. After twenty minutes of teasing and spraying, Veronica's hair cascaded nonchalantly down her long neck and across her perfect shoulders. She was the most natural-looking ex-beauty queen you'd ever meet.

"If you gave yourself more time," she said as I staggered past her that morning, with a coffee mug in one hand, and towels I planned to use for an ironing board in the other, "you could be a knockout."

I glanced in one of Veronica's mirrors—she'd practically wallpapered the place with them. While the front of my hair fanned up and out like a peacock with clipped feathers, the back stuck to my skull in such a way that, from the rear, I resembled an onion.

"Right!" I snorted.

I wasn't what you would call ugly: in fact, people mostly thought I was cute, though beautiful was never a word they resorted to. When I was a kid, grownups called me Tweedy Bird because I had large, wide, blue eyes, a tiny nose and a bow mouth. They meant it as a compliment, but because everyone laughed when they said it, I assumed they were making fun of me. My hair was the color of a grocery sack, but I had an oval face and my complexion was clear: I was probably good raw material. Where I lost it was in the packaging. When it came to teasing hair, Phyllis Diller and I were on a par, and I never seemed to have time to put on make-up, even when I didn't have much else to do.

"Most of my friends would kill for your waist," Veronica, always the cheerleader, said.

I had a high rib cage that created a disproportionately small waistline. My measurements were 35½–19–36. Naked or in a bathing suit this was an asset, but under more respectable circumstances it was an affliction. Mine was a body that didn't dress well. Because when people looked at me, they assumed my waist was average sized—say twenty-five or twenty-six—their mind completed the equation by assuming I had a ninety-eight-inch butt. Though I wore a size six and weighed 109, sales people always directed me to the twelves and co-workers forever mentioned the latest fad diet they'd spotted in some magazine. Next to all the Twiggy-look-alikes, I felt like Moby Dick's steady.

"Can you do my hair today?" I yelled out from under my bed, where I had crawled to plug in the iron. Whatever I planned to wear was always somewhere in the laundry chain.

"My bus'll be here in ten minutes. I'll just have time to throw in a few rollers. You'll have to comb it out yourself."

I grabbed my blouse, which was lying on my closet floor and arranged it over the towels. Veronica rushed back with her supplies. While I ironed, she sectioned my hair and, after Aqua-netting the inside of the roller, curled my locks around it and clipped it in place. It took three minutes.

"I hope you don't make me late again," she said.

Veronica led stretching and toning classes at a phony little health club called *A Stretch Over Thyme*. It was located in a second floor unit of a block-long strip mall not far from SMU. The exercise leaders—goddesses, they called them—wore black leotards with purple, Grecian-looking togas draped over their left shoulders. As far as I could tell, from those few times I went there to meet Veronica, membership was restricted to people who didn't need it

Because of its proximity to the college, the strip mall was a kinky little place that included an intellectual book store catering to the furrowed-brow set; craft and pottery co-ops run by the artists; a head shop where you could buy cigarette papers that looked like tiny America flags, or pornographic playing cards; a pharmacy, where condoms were prominently displayed; a vegetarian restaurant run by a religious sect, whose members wrapped themselves in gauzy fabric as if they were mummies; a dilapidated movie theater that showed a different vintage double feature each night; and a plant emporium that specialized in exotic plants and herbs. The plant emporium was directly under the health club, thus its name.

"Shit!" I yelled. A spot—mustard or something—right in the middle of my blouse. "Veronica, do you have some kind of big brooch?"

Veronica stood back and sprayed my rollered hair until the lethal fog became so thick you would have thought the Angel of Death was scouting the place for firstborns.

"If you just went to a little trouble, you could be very pretty." She cocked her head and studied me. "What you need is a wig."

That evening when she got home, she carried a huge, black, cylindrical, vinyl case.

"I bought you a present." She unzipped the box and opened the top half, revealing an intricately styled wig perched on a featureless Styrofoam head. "It's the Donna Reed," she said.

She had managed to match my dull color pretty well, except that the wig had more luster. It was chin length and styled in a complicated pageboy, with feathery bangs. Veronica bobby-pinned my own four strands of hair up before expertly pulling the wig in place. I could not believe the transformation. With plastic curls I was not half bad.

"See how pretty you are?" Veronica cooed. "I'll have ta be on guard when you're around Hunter from now on."

Hunter was Veronica's fiancé. Sort of. She met him at one of the Greenville Avenue clubs two years before. Everyone said he was handsome, though he was a little sticky for my taste. He thought he was a big deal because he was a driver for the Executive Transportation Service, a firm that hauled out-of-town big shots around in brand new Grand Prixs. Whenever Hunter drove someone important, he'd talk about him—it was always a *him*—for weeks, using his first name, as if they'd become close friends. Hunter was supposedly madly in love with Veronica and wanted to get married just as soon as possible. Unfortunately, he lived with another woman. This other woman, who was the Executive Secretary to a corporate VP, more or less supported Hunter since it turned out that the visiting dignitaries Hunter drove around were disappointing tippers. He promised Veronica he'd move out when the timing was right—in other words, when his metallic silver Corvair was paid off.

Because she could never see past biceps, Veronica always latched on to what could only be called appealing scum. I, on the other hand, who had too much respect for myself to spend an evening conversing in grunts, usually ended up alone. Oh, lots of guys asked me out. Once. It embarrassed me that at twenty, I was still a virgin, but I was usually humiliated by the losers who found me attractive. Guys criticized me for being unfeminine just because I slouched, read the editorial page of the newspaper, insulted people, and repaired my skirt hems with staples.

The wig could not have come at a better moment. My big break was looming. I was a clerk at the Freedom Mutual Insurance Company on Lemon Avenue, where I typed policy numbers on forms. But my passion was politics.

The first presidential election I followed was Stevenson vs. Eisenhower. I was in kindergarten. My father, a construction worker, supported Stevenson. When I asked him the differences between Republicans and Democrats, he said, "The Republicans are for rich people. The Democrats take care of the working man." This meant, I believe, that if the Democrats won, the morning after the election there would be a bundle of money on our front steps. Election eve I had trouble falling asleep, but the next morning the second I opened our front door, I knew Eisenhower was President. Disillusioned, I dropped out of politics until high school.

I was sixteen years old and less than a block away when Lee Harvey Oswald shot President Kennedy. Like everyone else in the city, I had gone downtown early to claim curb seating along the parade route. I ended up on the corner of Main and Houston—just before the School Book Depository—and after waiting there for hours, I first heard, rather than saw, the motorcade. Well, I didn't hear the *motorcade*, but the crowd. It started as a low roar and built to a thunderous clamor as the hysteria tumbled down the street toward me. Whipped into a frenzy, I screamed and yelled, jumped up and down, and waved my arms over my head.

Then, as if by magic, as the President's car approached, it slowed—or maybe it didn't, maybe it was my imagination. But it *seemed* as if the motorcade slowed. And Jackie, who was waving politely to the swarm of fans, *seemed* to look right at me. And as the limousine pulled past, she turned her head back slightly as if to keep me in view. I remember standing there, paralyzed, with my mouth open and both my arms raised over my head, prepared to jump yet again in the delirium that had overtaken me, overtaken all of us there. But when her eyes fell on me and held me, I froze, perhaps my feet were not even on the ground, perhaps I had jumped at that moment and hung there suspended, I can't say for sure. But I knew then that politics was my calling.

In spite of my father's labor ties and my newfound friendship with Jackie, I wasn't positive which party I belonged in, so—and here's where some of my later problems hatched. I started hanging out with both the Young Democrats and the Young Republicans. These two groups could not have been more dissimilar, except for one shared trait: no one in them was young. The average age was about thirty. At sixteen, I was an oddity.

At first the Young Republicans awed me. Their socials were exactly what I pictured myself presiding over someday. The women were genteel and expensively dressed and the men, though they had that short, well-groomed look you tend to associate with Southern Baptists, all seemed rich and confident. By contrast, the Young Democrats was a small, motley collection of misfits, most of whom were Unitarians. The first meeting I attended, which took place in an elementary school classroom, happened to be their election night and perhaps because there were so few of us there, I ended up Treasurer.

"I'm not real good at math," I warned.

"That's okay. We don't have any money." Herman Tedley was probably thirty. With his curved spine and potbelly, not to mention his slightly nasal Alfred Hitchcock voice, he was the oddest grown-up I'd ever come across.

Unlike the YRs, who had something social going on almost each week, the YDs met monthly in the school and simply sat around complaining about the war, the grape growers, and Governor Connally. When I gave the treasurer's report each month, I simply said, "We're still broke," and only I seemed concerned. I felt sad that the YDs had such a dreary existence and started nagging that we should have a bake sale or something. The others said if I wanted to raise money that was fine with them, though they couldn't care less. What did I know about fundraising? I was a junior in high school.

Just as Herman was my advisor at the YDs, Anna Tyson filled that role at the YR meetings. I asked her how they raised money.

"We ask for it," she replied.

"Just *ask* for it?"

"Yes, of course."

"Who do you ask?"

"Whom. Whom do you ask?" She corrected me. "We ask business leaders. Professionals. Elected officials."

"How do you know if they are Democrats or Republicans?"

"It doesn't matter. Everyone in Dallas supports a two party system. It helps, too, that we list them as contributors in our publications."

The YR roster included the office addresses of its members, most of which were downtown. Playing hooky one day, I called on about twenty of those listed. I didn't realize you needed appointments so sometimes I had to wait around a while. But, eventually a confused-looking man would stray into the reception area, frown and ask, "Did you want to see me?"

"Yes sir," I would answer, jumping up, "I wondered if you'd be willing to make a contribution to the Young Democrats?"

The executive would cast a worried glance toward his secretary, who would have stopped typing to watch.

"The Young Democrats?"

"Yes, it's important we support a two party system."

"Ah," he would reply and usually accompany this with some sort of gesture, such as running his hand through his hair or adjusting his belt or slapping his pockets searching for a cigarette. "I mean, how much we talking about?"

"For twenty-five dollars, we'll list you as a contributor in our newsletter," I assured him.

"I can manage that, I guess."

The secretary would handle the details.

By the end of the afternoon, I had collected five hundred dollars and felt as if maybe I had a future in fundraising. Then I stopped at the last office on my list. The man, an insurance executive named Dexter Peddy, started quizzing me.

"The Young Democrats?" he snorted, "I thought they were just a pack of queers and malcontents."

"No sir, not at all," I assured him, but this made me nervous: it sounded as if he'd maybe attended one or two of our meetings. Eventually he wrote me a check for a hundred dollars and handed it to me along with his business card. "Always willing to help a fellow democrat," he said. I glanced down at his card.

Dexter Peddy
Democratic County Chairman

As I stood there, gaping at what surely must represent an enormous scandal—the Democratic County Chairman listed on the roster of the Young Republicans! He ambled toward his office. Pausing at the door, he turned back to me.

"I'd like to see that newsletter when it comes out."

Shit! We didn't *have* a newsletter. But I had the goods on this guy. Stopping at the first pay phone I could find, I called Herman. Much to my chagrin, he told me it was common knowledge that Dexter Peddy was a Republican as were many Democratic precinct chairs and office holders. This seemed unethical if not downright illegal. But Herman told me that Texans, like many Southerners, still fumed about Lincoln freeing the slaves and so, many ultra right-wingers alleged Democratic leanings. Also, since the Democrats generally won statewide races, if the Republicans wanted any say in who held office, it was crucial to vote in the Democratic primary. Herman added that Dexter Peddy hated the YDs and was always looking for an excuse to destroy their charter. In other words, I was now newsletter editor.

I had never written anything more than book reports and never got more than a C on any of those. For days I couldn't eat or sleep and spent my time devising ways to kill myself. Then, as if by magic, as I was leaving homeroom one day, someone handed me a copy of the high school newspaper. Of course, I'd seen it around for years, but had never bothered reading it. So, during study hall, I flipped through the four pages of flattering blather about the twenty most popular kids. That didn't seem so difficult.

For the next two weeks, in an effort to track down gossip, I went to as many political events as I could get rides to. My usual chauffeur was Billy Anders, a buyer for a local store and President of the liberal-led Democratic Men's Club. Luckily, he lived two blocks from me so he was always willing to give me a lift. Most of the blurbs I came up with were mildly entertaining. I've always had a talent for puns and so I made up a few jokes that way, like when I read that the Democratic Women served fish at their luncheon, I said, "Those democratic women sure have sole!" Stuff like that.

But the clip that catapulted me into the spotlight concerned a "Meet the Candidates Coffee," at a home in Oak Cliff. Larry Bergen, a conservative Democrat who was running for State Senate, was the guest of honor. His speech was kind of clever in that after he expressed his views on any one of several hot topics, he'd close that part by saying, "Don't tell me about labor unions, 'cause I been there." Or "Don't tell me about war, 'cause I been there." When, toward the end, he touched on the mentally ill, he said, "Don't tell me about mental institutions, 'cause I been there."

"Bergen Admits to Stint in Asylum" was my lead story. Though my article admitted that the headline was a joke, it turned out to be a little close to the truth. Peddy was furious and the tone for our future relationship congealed.

Throughout those months of leading a double life, I devised a method to help me decide which group I should ultimately side with. Whenever a controversial issue stumped me, I would ask my mentors what their feelings were. For instance, when I asked Anna why the YRs were against social security, she said, "Because people should put money away for their retirement. Why should the taxpayers support people who didn't plan ahead?" This made sense to me, but when I asked Herman, he said, "But if you only make $50 a week and can barely feed your four kids with that, how could you put money aside?" I couldn't argue with that, so I repeated it to Anna. "You shouldn't have four kids if you can't afford to feed them, should you?" Although that, too, made sense, it also made me feel uncomfortable.

"Why," I asked on another occasion, "were the YRs in favor of keeping the poll taxes?"

"Because there's nothing more dangerous than an uninformed voter," she said.

To this Herman said, "Why would you assume that the poor are the uninformed?"

Though I longed to align myself with the glamour of the YRs, I eventually realized that, deep down, I was what they would call "a slimy liberal Pinko." And so, after eight months of mugwhompery, I leaned to the left and fell off the fence.

By 1966, I was President of the Dallas County YDs and the newsletter had become so popular that it was frequently quoted in the *Dallas Times Herald*, the less conservative of our two newspapers, and strangers occasionally sent me tips on things they were too timid to repeat themselves.

For example, two weeks before Veronica bought the wig, a courthouse informant sent me confidential documents about a prominent, outspoken John Bircher who had participated in, if not led, two of Dallas' more famous spitting matches. The first took place in 1960. As Lyndon and Lady Bird crossed a downtown street, jeering protesters surrounded and spat on them because they resented his decision to run with JFK. The second occurred less than a month before the assassination. While leaving a speech at Memorial Auditorium, U.N. Ambassador Adlai Stevenson was mobbed by right-wingers who viewed the UN, like fluoride, as a communist plot. These incidences, along with the assassination, caused the press to label Dallas *the City of Hate*.

Anyway, the John Bircher's wife had filed for divorce. The proceedings revealed that he liked to dress up in her clothes. Now, this had not bothered her for twenty years of marriage, but as he neared fifty, he had put on a few pounds and was stretching out the waistbands of her good knits. Local newspapers would not have touched this story and I suppose the informant assumed I would. The papers hadn't been in my possession twenty-four hours before I got a call from Peddy.

"All right," he started in, not asking how I was or anything, "I know what you have."

"Who's calling, please?" I asked.

"You know darn well who this is and listen here, you print any of that filth in your rag and I'll see that you're tossed in jail every time you so much as jaywalk."

"Peddy! How nice to hear from you."

"I mean it this time. There's a limit to what decent people will sit by and watch you print about upstanding citizens. You wanna write trash, why don't you write about those worthless, irresponsible beatniks in the Young Democrats—"

"They're called Hippies now. You're dating yourself. The really bad ones are Yippies—"

"Don't change the subject."

"Oh, right. The newsletter. I just sent it to press, but—Wait a minute. I have a copy here." I rustled the *Dallas Morning News* around. "Somewhere. Here it is. Now, let's see...what story could you mean? 'Political Paranoia Raises Funds?' Did you see that show, Peddy?"

Political Paranoia was an annual parody put on by members of the Democratic Women, which was pretty much the brainchild of an outrageously funny housewife named Ann Richards. Peddy would have never been caught dead at one of the shows.

"Don't waste my time."

"Sorry. Let's see. 'Middle-Age Spread leads to divorce?'"

"You send that out, I'll make your life miserable."

"Can you speak a little louder? I'm not sure my recorder's picking all this up."

"I've never found you funny, Gloria, so save your jokes. What do you want?"

"Is this a bribe?" I was stunned. He'd never treated me this seriously before.

"It's a favor."

"I want to be convention secretary," I blurted out. I had never really even considered the possibility before but now that I'd said it, I realized it was exactly what I wanted.

"You're not even old enough to be a delegate."

"I can take shorthand and type. I know all the issues, most of the people. I'd be perfect." Unable to stand still, I started pacing back and forth as far as the phone cord would allow me to maneuver.

"You have to be a delegate!" he shouted as if I were blind.

"Well," I sighed. "That's all I want." There was silence and I worried he'd hung up on me again.

"I'll see what I can do," he said as he slammed the receiver down. Peddy was corrupt, but I assumed there were limits even for him.

I was wrong. The next day he called to say he had worked something out.

* * *

While Veronica was fitting the wig in place, I got the call saying that Senator Davis was flying into Dallas that night and that an effort was underway to scrounge up bodies to greet him. A moderate State Legislator from Sumner, he was one of thirty-two men salivating for Governor Connally's job should he not seek an unprecedented fourth term in 1968.

I had never met Vic Davis, but I had heard an interesting story about him. Supposedly, when Kennedy and Johnson were running for the Democratic nomination for President, Davis headed up the Texans for Kennedy Committee, a move viewed as political suicide in Texas. When Kennedy won, Davis reaped the consequences of this stand. Connally, the most powerful man in Texas hated him; but Kennedy, the most powerful man in the country found him impressive. Rumor had it that when the Kennedys came to Dallas the President planned to announce the appointment of Davis to the White House legal staff. Senator Davis and his wife were asked to sit at the head table with the President. But, the President never made it to that particular head table. And once Johnson was President, it was open season on Vic Davis. The Establishment tried to sabotage his last election, but even against all that money and power, he got sixty percent of the vote. His constituents loved him.

Ty Whittaker was the liberal choice for governor. An undertaker from Sweetwater, he had shown enormous potential four years earlier when he nearly won a three-way race for Attorney General. Though he received the most votes, it was not enough for outright victory and he was trounced in the resulting runoff. However, his respectable showing made him the liberal star.

Unfortunately, during the intervening years, Ty Whittaker experienced several bizarre tragedies—which began when his son tried to beat the draft by eating forty-five hard boiled eggs just before his physical (a ploy that not only allowed him to skip Vietnam, but also made him temporarily blind and caused his body to emit a sulfur-like odor for over a year) and ended when he found his wife and the embalming fluid salesman going at it in one of the Big Tex coffins just before the Mayor's wake. These and several less dramatic but equally embarrassing episodes eroded his standing in his hometown and made him the butt of a series of tasteless, but amusing jokes. Eventually, all this caused something in him to snap because suddenly he claimed that he had visits from Mary Magdalene. No one really believed this but his face took on a sanctimonious aura, he started speaking in parables and his feet smelled suspiciously like Evening in Paris.

In spite of this goofiness, the liberals clung to him as their only chance for victory. His advisors never let him out of their sight and for the most part, Ty Whittaker behaved as if he were normal. Because there was a chance he could win and because some liberals worried the "cause" would suffer a magnificent blow once the electorate got a whiff of his eccentricities, there was a move among some moderate liberals to back Senator Vic Davis who, with his charisma and intelligence, might triumph in a crowded field.

* * *

We gathered in a VIP lounge off one of the concourses. I was barely inside the door before Estelle Harris, a Black woman who had recently been named Democratic Woman of the Year, cornered me.

"Gloria, honey, you're just the person I wanted to see."

"Estelle! Congratulations."

"Thanks, honey. Now listen, I was wondering if you'd like to help us go door to door next month to register voters."

"Sure."

"Here," she said, handing me a clipboard. As I studied the sign up sheet trying to remember what my commitments were for May, someone swatted me on the butt.

"That's some little ass you're gettin' on you, Gloria," Chick Flower said. He was with his sidekick, Lance Wallace.

Chick and Lance were State Representatives and were often called Tweedle-Dee and Tweedle-Dum, because you almost never saw one without the other. Politically they had their differences. Chick was a moderate conservative who coveted Establishment approval, while Lance had labor ties.

Chick was about five-six and had bumpy wheat-colored hair that he oiled up gangster-style. His clothes seemed just a little big, as if he'd been incarcerated and lost weight on the food, but then got released and was stuck with his old clothes until he could find respectable employment. For reasons that defied logic, he considered himself a ladies' man and was always flirting. Lance Wallace, was much better looking. He was five-eleven, stocky and had dark hair, Bryll-creamed to such an extent that it looked like patent leather. His eyes were bright blue and I suspected tinted contacts were involved. His teeth were square and white—like Chicklets.

Chick and Lance routinely opposed each other's bills and ridiculed each other's votes, but they had the two W's in common: whiskey and women. Like me, they showed up at everything, so I'd been running into them for years, though aside from the occasional obligatory pass, I was as invisible to them as air. With their flies metaphorically at half-mast, like boy scouts, always prepared, they were constantly on the make and usually a little tight, even in the mornings.

"You supporting Senator Davis?" I asked Lance.

"Oh, hell no! Labor'd kick my butt up 'tween my shoulders if I didn't endorse that idiot, Whittaker. I just came for the free booze."

"Well, I hate ta disappoint you, pal," Chick cut in, "but the booze ain't free."

"Are you shittin' me?" Lance said. "Damn, I coulda gone to that Red Cross thing. Gotten me a Bloody Mary: they're weak, but you can get as many as you want."

"Well, you start feelin' sober, you can always drink your piss," Chick said.

"You have ta drink a hell of a lot of piss ta even get a buzz on," Lance informed him.

"Gloria, honey!" Chick said, leering, "How old yew now?"

"Seventeen," I lied.

"Well, you give me a call in a year or so, okay?"

"Sure. If my phone's working."

"Wait a minute," Lance said. "Haven't you been seventeen for near about five years?"

"No. Just three."

Chick whacked Lance's arm. "An angel of mercy just appeared," he said, nodding toward the door.

"Who's that?" I asked, studying the elderly man who stood there, scanning the crowd.

"President of the Chamber of Commerce, who'd like nothin' better'n ta try'n buy a few votes."

They approached him, shook hands, exchanged jokes, and in no time, ended up at the bar, where the Chamber guy treated. Once they left, I realized I'd never given back Estelle's clipboard. She was across the room now, cornering someone else.

"Estelle," I said when I reached her, "I'm going to have to get back to you on this when I'm looking at my calendar."

"That's fine, honey. I know I can count on you."

"Will you be at the convention—" I started, but stopped when applause broke out across the room.

I looked up and froze. Perhaps the most gorgeous man in the world was making his way through the gauntlet toward the front of the room. Senator Davis was over six feet tall and his navy suit, white shirt and red tie looked as if they'd been steam pressed two seconds before he walked into the room. His thick, unruly flaxen hair was long for a Texas politician: it actually grazed his collar. In spite of his blondness, his skin was tan—as if he were from California. He had a dazzling smile with almost perfect teeth: one of his incisors slightly overlapped the tooth next to it, but oddly, this flaw added to his appeal. Most noticeable about him, however, were his hazel eyes, a shade so pale that they matched his hair. Riveted, I watched him smile and shake hands as he made his way to the speaker's podium. I followed, Zombie-like.

Since he was not on a raised platform and since I was only five-three, I eased myself to the periphery of the crowd so I could see. I assumed it was my movement that drew his attention my way and so I didn't, immediately, think much of it. But he glanced at me and then quickly did a double take, smiling before he went on with his speech. I gasped at how that moment startled me and I could tell that I was blushing, which really pissed me off.

But then it happened again. When he had to wait for the crowd's applause to subside, he turned toward me and, I believe, he winked. In all fairness, these things did sometimes happen to me because I was so young. (Most of my activist contemporaries had chosen more radical means of expression, such as Students for a Democratic Society and the Weathermen.) I assured myself that this was all that was happening here. But then I noticed that whenever I glanced toward him, we made the kind of eye contact that's not that easy to break off. It actually made me lightheaded. After a while, it seemed so brazen that I worried others would notice. Confused and embarrassed, I eased myself behind a tall man so that I could not see or be seen.

After his speech, we formed a reception line to introduce ourselves. I slipped to the back of it, jittery about speaking to him. As the line advanced, Senator Davis kept glancing toward me while he spoke to others. I felt as if my feet were stuttering. No doubt, by the time I reached him, I'd be all tongue-tied and squirrelly.

Trying to appear unconcerned, I folded my hands primly in front of me, allowing the strap of my purse to skid off my shoulder. My bag crashed to the floor scattering my wallet, keys, and God knows what else across the linoleum. While I stooped over, herding things back into captivity, the man in front of me stepped on a Tampax, lost his balance, staggered backward and grabbed the nearest thing for support.

The nearest thing was my wig.

It could have been worse, I suppose. He could have pulled it all the way off and screamed with horror. But I found no consolation in that when I saw that the pageboy curls were where the bangs had been. I beat it out of there as if someone had just fired off a tear gas canister.

Rather than wait for my ride, I shot down the hallway, twisting my wig in place. I didn't have enough money on me for a cab and I wasn't familiar with the bus lines that ran to the airport, so I scooted up to Mockingbird Lane and stuck out my thumb.

By the time I reached the apartment, I was exhausted and more than a little miffed to see that there was a small party going on. Veronica and Hunter were lying on the sofa in each other's arms; Jo Beth, Veronica's other best friend, was sitting on some guy's lap. The lights were low and the stereo whispered romantic tunes from the Hundred and One Strings Orchestra.

"Hi, Gloria," Veronica called, but Hunter just looked at the floor with a tight-lipped expression on his face. Jo Beth nonchalantly buttoned a crucial button on her blouse.

"I don't believe you know Larry Lynch," Veronica continued, indicating Jo Beth's date. "Larry, this is my roommate, Gloria Warren." Even though Larry had his hand halfway up Jo Beth's skirt, he checked me out as if I were auditioning for a position as a stripper. I considered being polite, but I didn't see the point, so I marched over to him and extended my hand. This surprised him so much that after a moment of indecision, he stood, dumping Jo Beth on the floor, and shook hands with me.

"Oh, what do you know?" I said casually, "Your fly's down." I have no idea whether this was true or not, but the room chemistry sure changed.

"Wanna catch the news?" I asked, flipping on the television and collapsing into one of the chairs. The apartment was all mine within ten minutes.

Once I was alone, I stared at the wall and daydreamed about Senator Davis. Panic set in as I realized that the more I thought about him, the less well I could remember what he looked like. I'd planned to pick up one of his brochures, but the wig business short-circuited just about everything. When I tried to imagine what it would have been like to talk to him, to stand next to him, to touch him—even just to shake hands—my stomach tumbled around as if I'd just jumped out of an airplane.

* * *

I called in sick the Friday of the State Convention, and got a ride to Austin with Billy Anders. But when I tried to register, my name was nowhere on the delegate list and Peddy was mysteriously missing from action.

"Gloria, what the hell you doin' here?" Lance Wallace asked as he approached, pinning his delegate badge to his jacket.

"Have you seen Peddy?" I demanded.

"I'm sure the sombitch is around somewhere but, I sure ain't been lookin' for him."

"Where's Tweedle Dumb?" I asked.

Lance nodded toward the convention room door where Chick was making eye contact with some woman's nipples.

"What on earth do they see in him?" I said, dumfounded that the woman actually seemed thrilled by this attention.

"You don't find Rep. Flower charmin'?" Lance asked.

I gave him a look.

"How 'bout me? Ya find me charmin'?" He flashed his teeth.

"You remind me of every cool guy I knew in high school," I sneered, as diplomatically as possible.

"Well, high school was *fun*, wasn't it?" He squeezed my arm. "See ya inside, Gloria."

I staked out the lobby nonstop but didn't spot Peddy until Saturday afternoon, long after they'd sworn in the convention officers.

"Peddy! You son of a bitch!" I shouted, when he finally surfaced.

Like most hawks, the closest Peddy had ever come to military service was the high school band. But you'd never know it from looking at him. He wore his dirt-colored hair in a flattop, with the sides shaved so close that after every haircut he probably needed a transfusion. His shirts, which were always white, were tapered to show that he had not one ounce of fat on his body. This man did not enjoy himself.

"Gloria. What are you doing here?" I gave him an incensed look. "Didn't you get my message?"

His face was so innocent that I knew he'd screwed me even more than I thought.

"I called your office Friday around ten and left a message that things hadn't worked out. That you should stay in Dallas."

"You called my office? Friday morning?"

"They claimed you were sick, but I told them I'd tried your place and there'd been no answer—"

Denied access to the convention floor, there was nothing for me to do but hang out in the hospitality suits or by the pool. I bought *The Adventurers* at the gift shop and passed the time reading Harold Robbins while working on my tan. To my surprise, the book turned out to be a sizzler, with "good parts" in almost every chapter, and the chapters were never more than six pages long.

By Sunday I was burning—physically and psychologically—so I planned my revenge. I changed from my bathing suit to a colorless, cotton sleeveless shift and sandals, which I believed would make me blend in with the walls. Then I stationed myself in the lobby and watched the delegates prepare to leave.

Billy was meeting with members of Texas Liberal Democrats in one of the hospitality suites. He invited me to join them, but I declined. Instead, I circled the lobby like a ravenous shark until Charlotte Flynn, the convention secretary, abandoned her Samsonite to gush over a departing delegate. A canvas bag, bulging with papers, sagged against her makeup case. Bending beside it, pretending to adjust my shoe, I slipped my arm through its straps and heaved it up when I stood. In the Ladies Lounge, where I had stowed my overnighter, I stuffed her bag inside my own and locked it away. After that, I sat in the lobby, my feet curled under me, reading my book.

"Gloria, honey. What yew readin'?" Lance Wallace asked.

"Nothing you'd be interested in," I said without looking up.

"Why's that?"

"Has some big words."

"Hell, I know some big words," he said.

"Like what?"

"Fornicate."

"What else?" I asked. He glanced toward the ceiling as if searching his brain.

"Let's see," he said. "I knew another one, too. Hey, Flower!" he shouted across the room. When Chick looked up, Lance hollered, "What's that other big word I know?"

"Fornicate," Chick said.

"No, the other one."

"Masturbation," he said.

"Right! Masturbation." He grinned as if he expected a gold star.

"Don't you worry people are going to question why you two hold office?"

"Hell, no one from my district's here," he said. Then he reached over and squeezed my knee. "Some of us gonna grab a beer across the way. Wanna come?"

"Can't," I said. "My ride's going back to Dallas soon."

"I'll give you a ride. Might not be for a while, but—"

"Thanks. I've seen how you drive. Particularly after a few beers."

"Be your loss," he said, standing.

I returned to my book as he ambled away. "Hey," he called to someone else, "how yew doing, Senator?"

I glanced up. Lance was shaking hands with Senator Davis. The glare from their teeth was blinding.

"Some of us heading across the way to grab a beer in a bit. Wanna join us?" Lance asked him.

"God, I'd love to, but," he checked his watch, "I'm leaving Austin soon."

"Too bad. I was tryin' to talk Gloria, here, into joinin' us, but she declined. Bet she'd change her mind if you were going."

I could have killed him.

Senator Davis smiled at me. "Well, that's an awfully flattering thought, but I'm sure not at all grounded in reality."

I repeated that sentence several times in my mind. I wanted to remember it correctly later.

"You know Gloria, don't you, Senator?" Lance said.

"I don't believe we've met," he said stepping toward me and holding out his hand, "but weren't you at Love Field last week?"

As I tried to untangle my feet so that I could stand, my sandal strap caught on the chair's arm and I was almost pitched forward onto my face. Luckily I caught myself, but my book went flying toward Senator Davis's feet. I leapt up to retrieve it not knowing that he was bending over to get it for me. When

I rose up, the back of my head smacked his chin and our hands both flew to our injuries.

"Oh, God, I'm sorry," I shouted. My eyes watered instantly but it was hard to know whether it was from pain or humiliation.

"You okay?" he asked, but before I could answer someone across the room called to him and he turned away. "I need to talk to him," he said when he looked back. "But, are you okay?"

"Yeah. Sure." I said.

Lance put his arm around me as we watched him walk off. "Gloria, honey, you certainly know how to make an impression."

"Drop dead!" I said.

It was another hour before Billy finally returned. The lobby had emptied some, but there were still clumps of hangers-on hashing and rehashing. Lance and his pals had left and Senator Davis must have used another exit because I hadn't seen him since our collision.

"Gloria," Billy called, "you don't mind if we give someone a ride to Dallas, do you?" I glanced up. Senator Davis was next to him. "By the way, Vic, have you met Gloria Warren?"

"We bumped into each other a while ago," he said, smiling and massaging his chin.

"I'll bring the car around," Billy called out as he headed for the door.

Senator Davis was looking directly at me with no expression on his face.

"Wait!" I called out to Billy, my heart suddenly pumping, "I'll go with you."

Since I knew the Senator would commandeer the front seat, I crawled into the back. Billy and I waited at the entrance for thirty minutes before he emerged holding hands with a tall, slender, regal-looking woman. I stopped breathing as I watched her ash blond hair and the skirt of her dusty pink silk shirtwaist flutter gracefully in the breeze. She wore strappy white sandals with three-inch heels that accentuated her delicate ankles. When they started our way, I felt hot…trapped somehow.

They both leaned toward the passenger's window and joked with Billy, though I had trouble following the conversation. At one point, Mrs. Davis glanced back at me and I quickly turned away. Aware of how guilty this made me appear, I forced myself to look back. Our eyes locked. I smiled and nodded. She smiled, too, but only with her mouth.

"You have room for Estelle?" Senator Davis asked.

Sure enough, Estelle Harris was right there with them, but I hadn't even noticed her.

"Of course. Hop in, Estelle. Sorry *you* can't go with us, Penny," Billy said to Mrs. Davis.

"Well, the kids are beginning to think they're orphans." At the mention of "kids," her eyes cut back to me. She knew.

But what was there to know?

Senator Davis kissed his wife good-bye and then opened the front door, for Estelle.

"Oh, Vic, don't you want to ride in front?" she protested. "I need to talk to Gloria about the voter drive anyway." But he didn't appear to hear her as he climbed into the back with me.

Overwhelmed and intimidated by his closeness, I opened my book, even though I could never read in cars without getting horrible headaches.

"What are you reading?" he asked, as we pulled into the traffic.

"Just a novel," I said, clearing my throat.

"Does it have a title?" He leaned over and pushed the book toward me so that he could read its name on the spine. "Oh, that's the one about Porfirio Rubirosa, isn't it?"

"Who?" I asked, mortified that he, of all people, might know something about this smut.

"Rubirosa. The South American playboy."

"I didn't know that." God was he cute.

"Now you do."

"Yes. Thank you."

"Any time. Is it good?"

"What?"

"The book."

"It's...just, you know, a book."

"Here's a list of the folks who'll be at the coffee," Billy said, passing him a manila folder. Senator Davis settled back in the seat, scanning the pages. He glanced at me. I quickly looked away.

"I've marked the names of folks you've already met and made comments to jog your memory so you'll recognize them right off."

From the corner of my eye, I saw him turn back to the first page. He squirmed around in his seat as if trying to make himself comfortable; as he did, his knee rested against mine.

"Excuse me," I mumbled, as I jerked away, but he didn't appear to hear me.

"This woman," he said, suddenly leaning over the front seat, "you have an asterisk but I don't recognize the name."

"It used to be Cooper, but she's divorced. Now it's Julia Poston. Ring a bell?"

"Julia Poston?" Senator Davis focused on an imaginary spot just beyond the dashboard.

"About thirty-five, attractive, black hair, lots of makeup," Billy supplied.

"Is she real tan?" the Senator asked.

"That's Julia. Anyway, she's divorced now and loaded, and though her politics are a mystery, her ex-husband's right-wing as hell and she's doing whatever she can to embarrass him."

Senator Davis settled back in his seat and as he turned the page, his knee again leaned against mine. I eased away but his leg followed. I believed this might be intentional and I didn't want to insult him by acting as if I thought he had cooties, so I just sat there trying to concentrate on something other than the warmth from his leg. All at once, he flipped the pages back to the beginning.

"God, I'm hogging the whole seat," he said pulling his legs back to his side of the car. "I'm sorry." Embarrassed, I glanced down at his papers.

"You want to look at this?" He passed them to me.

There were five pages. I didn't know anyone listed. These were money people: good for hefty contributions but nowhere in sight when envelopes needed stuffing. Next to each name was a physical description and a rundown on their professional status. A sentence followed that either encouraged or discouraged discussion of certain topics. I wanted to flip through and find the blurb on this Julia chick but Senator Davis was reading over my shoulder.

"Can you give me any pointers about these people?" I knew this was not a sincere question, but I answered anyway.

"I don't believe I know any of them."

"Well, I guess you'll get to meet them," he said. His shoulder touched mine and I longed to melt against him.

"Oh! I'm not going to this coffee."

"No?"

"No." With effort I looked out my window.

"Billy!" Senator Davis called out a while later. "Is the air conditioner working?"

"We're freezing up here," Billy replied.

"Do you think it's warm back here?" Senator Davis asked me.

"No. But the sun's coming in your window."

"So, it is," he replied, glancing over his shoulder.

"Maybe if you took off your shirt—*I mean jacket*!" Blood stampeded to my cheeks. He stared right at me. For several seconds.

"That's an excellent suggestion," he said, struggling to pull his arms out of his coat. Normally, I would have helped, but I didn't dare touch him.

Instead, I tried to read my book. He reached out and touched my shoulder. Cutting my eyes toward his hand, I froze as if a wasp had landed on me.

"You're a little burned," he said.

I wondered what it would be like to kiss him.

I had a hunch I was going to find out.

"Anything you need to do before this coffee, Vic?" Billy called out.

"I don't know." Senator Davis rubbed his hand over his chin. "Maybe I should shave. You think I should shave?"

"It's up to you," Billy answered.

"I'd hate to look like Nixon."

"You might get more money that way," Estelle laughed.

He continued to stroke his face as he looked back at me. "What do you think? Should I shave?" I shrugged and he reached for my hand and rubbed my fingers upward against the stubble on his face. "Is that too rough?"

I could feel his breath on my palm. I glanced guiltily toward the front seat and pulled my hand away. Billy was entertaining Estelle with a story about some convention in Ft. Worth where the conservatives were so fearful the liberals would get a microphone that a man in the balcony stood guard with a drawn pistol.

"Your birth stone?" he asked, picking up my hand to study my $12.95 JC Penny gold-filled ring.

I nodded. With his thumb, he caressed first the stone and then the top of my hand. I tried to swallow but couldn't and watched as my fingers closed over his hand.

We both knew I was going to sleep with him.

Just before Waco, Billy pulled into a Lone Star Donut shop.

"I need some coffee," Billy said.

"I'll get it," Senator Davis said as he jumped out of the car.

Estelle and I decided to hit the ladies' room. Once inside the shop, we saw Senator Davis talking to the proprietor—an obese woman with a gray, Dutch-boy haircut—about every aspect of donut-making. She seemed to be spewing out her life and he was listening as if this were the most fascinating tale he'd ever heard, asking her relevant questions about the equipment and ingredients she used. On our way back to the car, she was offering to show him the kitchen.

When he returned, a good twenty minutes later, we were all a little peeved at the delay. He carried a large white paper bag full of coffees and donuts.

"Damn, Vic. What took you so long?" Billy asked, firing up the engine.

"I met a very interesting woman inside." Billy and Estelle exchanged knowing looks. "Her grandfather built that shop. With his own hands. It's been in the family for over eighty years. Used to be a full bakery, but they started losing money. So, she bought a Lone Star donut franchise about—"

"Vic! Who cares?" Billy interrupted and Estelle giggled.

"I thought it was kind of interesting."

Estelle twisted around in her seat and smiled at him. "Is she going to vote for you, Vic?"

"I believe so," he smiled back.

When we reached Dallas, Billy announced that he was skipping the coffee because he wanted to see his kids before bedtime. He suggested that Senator Davis drop him off and keep his car until the next afternoon, when he (Senator Davis) would hop the puddle-jumper back to Sumner. Senator Davis volunteered to take Estelle and me home after the coffee, if we wanted to attend.

* * *

I was considerably underdressed for the coffee. The men wore jackets and the women modeled elegant sundresses or hostess ensembles. Everyone was tan, healthy, and perfectly groomed. Surprisingly, no one sneered at me: no one seemed to even notice me. At first, I shadowed Estelle, but the third time she was introduced to a group and I wasn't, I made myself scarce, rambling around pointlessly, hoping I didn't seem like a tourist as I gawked at all the opulence. Eventually, I stationed myself in front of a bizarre painting not so much to study it but to make it seem as if I had something to do.

""Edvard Munch," someone behind me volunteered.

"What?" I asked, pivoting toward the voice.

The man standing there resembled David Niven with somewhat handsome, underfed, aristocratic looks. He threw his head back and held his champagne glass out at mustache level as if he hoped a bird would perch on it.

"It's by Edvard Munch," he explained.

"I see," I mumbled.

"The focus of the painting, you've probably ascertained, is these three females in the foreground. The one to the left, in white, represents the virgin, sweet and pure; on the right, in black is the widow, sour and ugly. This woman," he gestured toward the middle one, dressed in red and dancing with a man, "is the seductress. See how her hair and dress reach out to snag her partner? Munch felt all women fell somewhere in this group." We both studied the painting again. "Where do you see yourself?" he asked.

"Myself?" I said.

"Well, you're clearly not the widow, so you must be either the virgin or the seductress."

"Well, I'm wearing beige," I said.

"So you are," he replied. Then he walked away.

I slipped into the next room, where things only got worse. Senator Davis sat on a sofa, conversing with a woman who could only be Julia Poston. She had Cleopatra hair and eyes and wore a green and blue paisley dress that stuck to her body as if she'd just been pulled from the pool. The neckline plunged: more than her bank account was bulging. Senator Davis beamed like a lovesick adolescent.

I decided to call a cab, but though I meandered from room to room, I couldn't find a phone. When I stumbled into the kitchen, a startled waiter gawked at me as if he mistook me for a roach.

"May I help you?" he asked, though his voice implied he meant, "What are you doing here?" For reasons I cannot understand, rather than asking to use the phone, I asked where the ladies' room was.

The powder room, as he called it, was as large as a classroom, with pinkish marble walls, makeup mirrors, a sunken, clover-shaped bathtub and a shaggy white carpet deep enough to mow. When my eyes strayed to the mirror, I realized that my wig was slightly off-center, mascara tracks were under my eyes and my shift had horizontal wrinkles all the way to my knees. I resembled a weary accordion. I decided to leave; to slip outside and just walk. Even in this neighborhood there had to be a Seven-Eleven. Once I found it, I could call from there.

"Just a minute," I yelled when someone tapped on the door.

I flushed the toilet, so no one would suspect I was just hiding. Immediately I regretted that. Did I really want these people to think I had to pee? Veronica spent hours in public restrooms combing her hair, touching up her lipstick. But because the behavior was so alien to me, I had flushed the toilet. And probably everyone, including Senator Davis, heard it and wondered who had done such a sordid thing in such a pristine house.

Julia Poston smiled and nodded as she displaced me in the powder room. A delicate fragrance followed her in. As the door shut, I closed my eyes and inhaled deeply, but by then the scent was gone. I knew I should move on—how weird would it be if she opened the door and found me still standing there - but I lingered. What I hoped to gain or learn was unclear, but some force held me in place. My anxiety levels crept up, as if I were about to read someone else's personal mail or listen into a private phone conversation. I stared at the door, knowing I would have no explanation if it suddenly opened.

My gasp was almost a shriek when someone touched my arm.

"There you are."

I spun around.

"Hey," Senator Davis whispered as his index finger made its way from my elbow to my shoulder. My stomach jumped around recklessly. "I'm going to leave in a few minutes. Is that all right with you?"

Before I could answer, the art critic appeared, "Vic, can I give you a ride to your hotel?"

"Thanks, but I have Billy's car. Besides, I have to give Estelle and Gloria lifts. They've been with me since Austin."

"You shouldn't have to bother with that, Vic. Pete can run them home ..." He snapped his fingers while leading us to the foyer where a waiter appeared. "Pete, could you..."

"That's all right," Senator Davis interrupted, "Gloria has some files I need to pick up tonight"

My head jerked toward him. Files?

"Besides it's on the way."

I waited in the foyer while Senator Davis said good-byes. I was sure no one would think it rude if I didn't pay my respects. Eventually, Estelle joined me.

"Well, these people are real live wires, aren't they?" I whispered.

"Didn't you enjoy yourself, Gloria?"

"Did you?"

"Oh, my, I was the toast of the party. Seems everyone's domestic help has quit and they all wanted to know if I knew someone dependable and honest who'd work for minimum wage."

"What assholes," I laughed. "They all seem to like Senator Davis though."

"What's not to like? He's a sweet guy."

After a while, I grew impatient and ambled toward the living room to see what was holding things up. He was with Julia again, holding her hand as if to shake it, looking deeply into her eyes. Both had sticky smiles on their faces.

Ten minutes later, we were in the car. Quickly claiming the back seat, I let Senator Davis and Estelle chat up front. It did not surprise me when he dropped her off first. He walked her to her porch and gabbed for a while before returning to the car.

"Please move up front," he said, opening my door. "I don't mind driving people home, but I hate to feel like a chauffeur."

My heart thudded as I made the move, terrified I'd do something memorable, like trip over the curb or whack my head on the car door and knock my wig into the gutter.

"Are you in any hurry to get home?" he asked, glancing into the rearview mirror as he eased away from the curb.

I had to say "no" twice before any sound came out.

* * *

He opened the door to his motel room with his right hand and with his left made an "after you" gesture. I stepped inside and waited. He flicked on the lights. I stayed by the door while he dropped his suitcase on the luggage stand. He glanced back at me and smiled. I smiled at him but didn't move. He had said he needed to make some calls, but he didn't go anywhere near the phone. Instead, he walked toward me until he was standing by my side. I looked straight ahead. He slipped his fingers under my shoulder strap and eased my purse off my arm. I watched as if it were imperative that I remember exactly where he put it, as if the room were so cluttered, I might have difficulty finding it later. He slowly leaned toward me, not touching me anywhere except when his lips brushed mine. My brain must have blown a fuse, because I just stood there with my mouth open, clutching my hands in front of me.

He pulled back and we just looked at each other for what seemed like a week. Then, he circled my neck with his right hand and bent toward me. We kissed with an almost violent enthusiasm until he tried to run his fingers through my hair.

"It's a wig," I murmured when he jumped away. I was sure he would suddenly decide those calls couldn't wait another second. But instead, with a quick motion, he tossed it to the floor, unconcerned that after ten hours in a wig, without it, I resembled a ringworm host.

He kissed me roughly while tearing at my clothes, and before I could blink, I was naked. Only then did he step back to look at me.

"You're even more beautiful than I thought," he whispered, as he carefully unbuttoned his shirt. I stood by, shivering slightly, while he emptied his pockets onto the counter and then retrieved a hanger from the closet for his suit, all the time staring at me.

Not familiar with proper etiquette for such occasions, I studied the floor until I felt his arms slip around my waist. He pulled me to him as he kissed me and the chill I had felt earlier vanished. The golden hair on his chest was spongy against my breasts. He kissed me over and over again, pulling me closer to him each time. Just standing there required so much energy that my legs shook as if I'd hiked a mountain. I wondered if he had forgotten we were both naked.

When my knees buckled, he eased me to the bed. I was panting like a dog in August, but he seemed in no particular hurry. Every guy I'd dated couldn't wait to get his hands on my breasts and here I was in a motel room, almost blind with lust, and all he seemed interested in was my mouth. He pulled back some and just grazed his lips over mine. Luckily, I was lying down because I thought I might faint.

I had wanted to be cool with this, but the odds of that remaining possible, were slipping. I rolled over on my side and pushed myself against him, hoping that he would get the hint. He ran his hand down the length of my body and back up again to my breast. Pushing me onto my back, he kissed my nipples several times before he sucked them so hard that I actually cried out. This did not seem to surprise him as much as it did me.

"I've never done this before," I whispered, suddenly nervous about the pain and blood that I'd heard accompanied the first time. I was willing to endure the pain, but it dawned on me that a married politician might not be thrilled for the cleaning staff to find bloody sheets in the morning. He probably deserved to be warned, though I worried he'd back out once he knew.

"I know," he said, but I don't think he really believed me. In spite of the sexual revolution, women still often pretended to be inexperienced. Even Veronica's friend, Jo Beth, sometimes claimed that she was a virgin, and she had a child.

It surprised me how easily it happened. There was a pressure that made me jump a little but it was hardly painful. At first, the pleasure I felt was more mental than physical. I couldn't believe I was so close to this man—this incredible man. I could feel the warmth of his skin from my face all the way down to my feet. It was as if I possessed him, if only temporarily, and that idea created a sensation of … of what? Redemption, maybe. If this man—this gorgeous, powerful, older, married man—could find me desirable enough to risk the works for, then every rebuff in my life—from males and females—was trivial by comparison. I was actually grateful for all those rejections that had allowed me to remain virtually untouched until that moment. For this, I knew, would remain vivid to me for the rest of my life, no matter how short-lived it might be or how badly it might one day end.

Suddenly, I became aware of a warmth bubbling out from my stomach, down my legs, across my chest, through my arms. Urgency overwhelmed me and I raised my hips higher to him as if I were afraid he would somehow get away. My orgasm lasted forever and I kept crying out in spite of the fact that he kept saying "Shh. Shh." Finally, he put his mouth over mine to drown out the sound and then he started coming. He thrust himself into me roughly and bit my neck and shoulders. I worried I would never catch my breath.

"Jesus!" he said. "You've never done that before?"

I just shook my head.

"I can't imagine what you'll be like when you know what you're doing." He rolled over onto his back and rubbed his eyes with the heels of his hands.

"I wasn't *lying* to you," I said.

His eyes darted in my direction before he rolled toward me again. "I'm sorry you think that's what I was implying." A strand of my hair stuck to my lip and he lifted it and brushed it aside. "I just meant that you were sensational. It was a compliment."

"I only told you in case there was, you know, blood or something. That's all. It's no big deal otherwise."

"Of course, it's a big deal!" He ran the tips of his fingers over my lips, "They say you never forget your first lover. I'm honored. Now, you'll never forget me."

"I probably wouldn't anyway."

"You flatter me."

"Do you remember your first time?" I asked.

"Of course. She was a very bored hooker in La Grange."

I laughed.

"She ate an apple the whole time. A golden delicious."

We both laughed.

"You're sweet," he said a little later.

"Even my parents don't think I'm sweet," I said.

Just because I was a virgin at twenty didn't mean that I felt strongly about saving myself for my husband or that I never had any opportunities to get laid. Neither was true. Except that I wanted to be First Lady, I had no real interest in getting married. From a very young age, I had a premonition that marriage would, well, ruin me. I saw myself depressed, fat and alcoholic, wearing those little snap-up housedresses you see in the Sears catalog. I wanted to be someone. Sometimes, I hoped to be a femme fatale, amassing hundreds of lovers, many of whom would be famous and powerful. And, though I was often overlooked, living as I did, in Veronica's wake, there were guys who liked me. But I wanted the first time to be special.

"Do you want me to take you home now?" he asked. "Or can you stay here tonight?"

"I can stay," I blurted out and then, in order to sound nonchalant, I added, "if you want me to." I couldn't believe I was going to get to stay all night. Somehow, sleeping with him seemed even more important than sex.

"Well, I wouldn't have presented it as an option if I didn't want you to, would I?"

"I don't know." I had an unlimited assortment of insipid comments at my disposal.

He dialed the phone by his nightstand and after a moment said, "Could you give me a call at seven-thirty?" As he hung up, he said, "I have an important meeting in the morning so I'll have to give you taxi fare." Then he pulled on his trousers and went back to his car to retrieve my suitcase from the trunk.

* * *

I woke up sometime during the night. My back was curled against him—I could feel the hair on his chest between my shoulder and that sensation caused a tickling in the pit of my stomach. His arm rested across my waist. I snuggled in closer to him. He must have been awake, or a light sleeper, or maybe he could do this sort of thing in his sleep, because in one easy movement, he pulled me toward him and slipped on top of me. I was mortified that I had not brushed my teeth, but this didn't appear to bother him. My body felt sore and sour and sticky and I worried that he would find me repulsive. But he didn't seem to.

The next time I opened my eyes it was dawn. We were lying apart, but his left hand covered my right. I propped myself up on my elbow and looked at him. The thick, bleached hair on his chest and arms contrasted with his skin, which was the color of oak furniture. Ropey veins stood out on his arms. He had long, thin fingers, with buffed nails. His wedding ring was a plain, thin band. He had a small white scar on his left shoulder and a triangle of beauty marks on his neck. The stubble on his face was darker than I would have imagined and even more pronounced now. His hair—. I caught my breath: he was watching me.

"You can look," he said. "You can do whatever you want." He touched my chin with his index finger. "Hi," he said.

We stared at each other for a while until he moved us so that I was on my back looking up at him.

"So, Gloria, what do you think of sex?"

"It's nice," I said.

"Nice! You thought that was *nice*?"

Clearly that was the wrong answer. "What's wrong with nice?"

"The weather's nice; a flower's nice. But last night was a hell of a lot better than nice." As if talking about it turned him on, he started kissing my shoulders and neck. His leg rubbed up and down on mine before it slid between them. "Did you like making love to me?" His voice was husky.

I nodded.

"I loved making love to you," he said.

"You did?"

"Didn't it seem as if I did?" His erection was right there and I held my breath waiting.

"I guess," I said. His face was hovering over mine and he was so beautiful.

"Want to take a shower with me?" he asked.

"Right now?" I said and my voice was almost shrill.

"Now," he whispered crawling on top of me, "or in a few minutes. Whichever you want."

"In a few minutes," I said.

* * *

"Too bad you have to work today," he said when we were recovering. "I'd like nothing better than to do this all day."

"I could call in sick," I suggested.

He grinned at me. "Could you?"

I nodded.

"That's awfully sweet and very tempting. But I have a lot of money riding on my meeting."

He kissed me one last time and then got out of the bed. I watched him walk away from me. He had moderately broad shoulders but very narrow hips. His legs were long, with bulging calves tapering to slender ankles. As he flipped on the bathroom light, an automatic exhaust fan revved up. I heard him turn on the faucet and I could tell he was brushing his teeth.

The phone rang. Once. Twice. I glanced at my watch. It was seven-thirty: the wake-up call. He stayed in the bathroom: the vent fan must have drowned out all other noise. I wasn't sure what to do, but I suspected I shouldn't answer the phone.

"Senator Davis?" I called, but he didn't answer. The phone rang again, so I got out of bed and slipped on his shirt that he'd draped over the desk chair. I tapped on the bathroom door.

"Who's there?" he called out playfully.

"Senator Davis?" I said, pushing the door. "Your phone's ringing."

Once he turned off the water, there was dead silence, except for the phone and the exhaust fan. He opened the door all the way and glared at me. He'd draped a small white towel around his waist.

"What did you say?" he asked, which seemed stupid because he had to realize by now that his phone was going nuts.

"Your phone," I said, stepping away from him. "It's ringing." Still, he just stared at me as if confused about how I'd gotten into his room.

"What did you call me?" he asked, ignoring the phone. He seemed angry, offended even. I didn't say anything but just glanced toward the phone. "Did you call me Senator Davis?"

"I believe so," I said watching his feet.

Suddenly, he hurried toward the phone as if needing to catch it before the hundredth ring.

"Yeah!" he barked. "I'm up. Thanks." He slammed the phone down and glared at me. I felt as if I'd been caught in some shameful act. Finally, he looked away. "It was just the wake-up call," he said. "But thanks for not answering it."

"Sure," I said, relieved to have done something right.

He walked back to me and, slipping his shirt off my shoulders, ushered me toward the bathroom. "Come on," he said, "let's take a shower." As he turned on the faucet, he added, "Call me Vic."

I had considered calling him Vic and, in retrospect, it was stupid not to have. But at the time it seemed presumptuous. I never called important people by their first name until they told me to. Granted, I had never slept with any of them before and clearly there was some leveling out that took place once that happened, but I didn't understand that at the time. I'd never taken a shower with a man before, either and I was a little confused about how to act, especially now that things seemed a little bumbling.

The shower was really a bathtub that could work either way. Vic stood toward the controls while I slipped to the opposite end. The water was gushing over his head and into his face causing him to shut his eyes. It was cold where I was since only an occasional drop or two hit me. Vic squirted shampoo onto his hair and lathered it up. When he finished, he hooded his eyes with his hands so that the soap would drain off toward the back of his head. For the first time, he looked at me.

"Why are you way over there?" he asked. I shrugged. "Come here. I'll wash your hair."

I stepped toward him and he squeezed shampoo over my head and massaged the soap in. Once he rinsed my hair, he reached for the soap and washed my body. After my front was sudsy, he slipped his arms around me to lather up my back and as he did so, he pulled me against him and kissed me. My skin felt slippery against his. Then he handed the soap to me. At first I was a little inept. I don't know why touching him seemed so different standing up in a lit room, but it did. The soap kept slipping out of my hands and banging to the tub, but finally I managed even to wash his penis, which was huge by then.

When it became so steamy that it was hard to breathe, he turned off the water and eased me out, never taking his mouth from mine. Soaking, we slipped to the yellow tile floor of the bathroom, which was as inviting as a glacier. He lowered himself to me and pushed both of his legs between mine and then pried them as far apart as he could. Before I knew what was happening, he slithered down my body until he was between my legs. I grabbed his hands and tried to pull him back up, but he shook them off. When he kissed me, he was disgracefully on target.

* * *

I wrapped a towel around myself and watched him smear shaving cream over his face.

"You have amazing eyes," I said.

"You like my eyes?" He stopped to smile at me. I nodded. "What do you like about them?"

"They're very...dramatic."

"Dramatic? Oh, I like that."

I slipped behind him and leaned against his back, wrapping my arms around his waist and running my fingers over his chest.

"You're going to make me cut myself," he said.

"Oh! We wouldn't want to scar that face, would we?"

He pivoted toward me. "Are you being fresh?" he said. When I laughed, he rubbed shaving cream over my cheeks and nose. "Now get out of here. You're too distracting."

In the other room I stood by the picture window overlooking an ugly highway where clumps of asphalt had ruptured and jutted out from the rest of the pavement. Suddenly, in glaring sunlight, things seemed more complex than they had the night before. I worried that I had made a big mistake. As I watched cars jockeying for position during the rush hour, I deflated. I've never dealt well with ambiguity: I like to know where things stand. But, there I was, full of his semen, as close to being in love as I'd ever been, and I had no idea if I'd see him again. Oh, there was no doubt I'd see him—at political gatherings, or airport press conferences, or conventions—but would he ignore me, or would I see him circling someone else? Nothing he had said the entire night hinted that he planned to continue this. I was beginning to feel like a casualty of friendly fire. It wasn't that I resented being used: I was afraid I wouldn't be used again.

When he emerged, he was tucking a red striped shirt into his slacks and I was struck again by how gorgeous he was.

"God!" he said, stretching his back, "I'm sore. Are you sore?"

"Maybe a little," I said. My body felt as if it had been strip-mined.

"Well, you're young," he said. "How old are you, Gloria?"

"Twenty."

He was threading his belt though the loops in his pants and he froze, and I thought, for a moment, that he was angry about something.

"When will you be twenty-one?" he asked, turning away from me and scooping up some change from the dresser.

"Are you worried that after all this work I might not be old enough to vote for you?"

"What an impertinent thing to say." He slipped his wallet into his back pocket. "I could be your father." He was about to turn away again, but stopped. "You look sad. Have I made you sad?"

"Why would I be sad?" I struggled to maintain eye contact.

"There might be reasons." After a moment, he sighed and approached me. He stood there staring down at me. My part must have been crooked because he picked up a strand of hair and moved it to the other side, like I was graduating. "You okay with this?" he asked.

"With what?" His closeness made my head spin a little.

"With what happened? With us?"

"*Us*?" Had he really said *us*? Like we were going steady or something?

He laughed out loud. "Clearly my worst nightmare has just come true. I practically kill myself for some woman and in less than twelve hours, she's forgotten all about it."

"I could never forget you." What a loser I was. Everyone knows you don't admit that shit to guys.

"No?" he asked, stroking my cheek with his thumb.

"Well," I started in, trying to regain some dignity, "you told me I wouldn't. You know, because you were the first...you know."

"The first man who ever made love to you?"

"Yeah," I shrugged. "Something like that."

"I'd like to make love to you right now," he whispered and instantly I felt a quickening between my legs.

He leaned over and kissed me very gently. My bones felt as if they were disintegrating. At any moment, I might ooze to the floor. He pulled back and looked at me.

"If I get back in bed with you, it will cost me thousands of dollars." He seemed to weigh the pros and cons of the dilemma. "Maybe I should just hire you as my personal secretary. Then you'd have to travel with me. Would you like that?"

Was he kidding? "Sure," I said.

"It'd mean you'd have to leave Dallas, and maybe you don't want to—"

"I'd move," I said.

I'd planned to leave Dallas for years. Only I always thought I'd wind up in D.C.—I even had a list of Senators I'd agree to work for. There were five of them. They were all young, liberal, attractive and potential Presidential candidates: Ted Kennedy, Ed Muskie, Walter Mondale, Birch Bayh and Philip Hart.

"Well, *if* it happens, it's *months* down the road. Think about it, thought." I stared at him: he seemed serious. Finally, he turned away. "I *have* to go." He started for the door and then stopped "My plane doesn't leave until three, if you promise to wait, I'll be back by noon."

Once he left, I sat on the bed to watch The Today Show and spotted a dark brown stain on the bottom sheet. For a horrible moment, I believed I had started my period, but then I realized what it really was. I studied the stain closer. So, that's what all the fuss was about.

When I opened my suitcase, I found Charlotte Flynn's bag inside. I had forgotten all about that. In addition to the minutes, I found handwritten resolutions, subcommittee rosters, Robert's Rules of Order, and a lunch-sized paper bag of campaign buttons. "LBJ for the USA." Well, better with me than out on the street where they might do some harm.

* * *

Vic called at noon, saying things were taking longer than he'd imagined and it didn't look as if he would be able to get back. I decided I might as well make an appearance at the office.

Anticipating that Peddy's call on Friday aroused suspicions, I went to some trouble to make myself look sickly. My hair had dried naturally, which gave it the frizzy, fly-a-away look you see so often at bus depots. Luckily, the hotel had a room of small lockers where, for a dime, you could store your possessions for as long as twenty-four hours. I took Charlotte's minutes with me and each time I passed a trash can, I threw away one page, playing "He loves me, he loves me not." When it was apparent that the last page would end on "he loves me not," I tore it in half so I would have a good ending. At a convenience shop, I bought some make-up in mime white. In spite of all this preparation, I hadn't made my first personal call before Lonnie Mossman, my supervisor, buzzed me.

"Where were you Friday?" she asked as she opened what was obviously my file, and glanced nonchalantly through the pages.

"I was sick. Didn't they tell you?" I was playing for time.

"I did get your message, Gloria, but when I called your apartment, no one answered."

Lonnie Mossman was a large woman: not fat, just large, as if maybe she'd once been a man. Nothing about her relaxed. Every hair was in place; her posture was perfect; her makeup never faded, even on humid days; her blouses never wrinkled or came untucked; her shoes never scuffed; and, most amazingly, her fingernail polish always matched her outfit, and her outfits ran the spectrum of the Crayola Super Fun Box.

"Well, yes ma'am. That's because I was feeling so rotten that I went to stay at my mother's." It's like inspiration how these things come to me.

"Ah. Well, I guess that would explain it, except for one nagging item." She tapped her pencil point on her desk. "See, I got this call from—" she looked at her notes, "Dexter Peddy. Ever heard of him?"

I nodded.

"Well, he led me to believe that you had gone to Austin—"

"Yes, ma'am. See, I was planning to go to Austin, but then, like I said, I, ah, got sick, so I went to my mom's instead."

"Ah." She held the pencil in her mouth, the way a Spanish dancer might bite a rose, and studied the note. "This gentleman—" In spite of myself I snorted. She glanced up. "Mr. Peddy," she corrected, "was kind enough to give me the name of this Austin hotel." I really owed Peddy one for this. "Can you guess what they told me when I called Friday?"

"Yes ma'am." Neither one of us said anything for a while until finally I cleared my throat. "Shall I pack up my desk?" I asked.

"No," she replied, crumpling the note about Peddy and tossing it in her trash can. Then she closed my folder and clasped her hands together, resting them on the file. "I'm not firing you. Not that you don't deserve it." I couldn't think of a response. "This isn't the first time this has happened, is it?"

"No ma'am."

"There was that time you said your grandmother broke her leg and you needed to help her. I remember how—" she paused, "—puzzled I was when I saw you on the evening news, waving a sign at some rally. Then there was—"

"I know I've done this several times—"

"Three. That we know of. What should I do with you, Gloria?"

I shrugged, but kept quiet.

"You have friends in high places," she went on. "Mr. Sweet has asked that you be promoted to his secretary as soon as Jeannette leaves to have her baby."

Mr. Sweet was the head of the claims department and he and I had always liked each other. He was about fifty-five years old and only a little taller than me. A Stevenson Democrat, he would come around my desk to talk about "those Republican bastards" at least once a week.

"He believes this job is not challenging enough for you and I'm inclined to agree with him. The promotion would mean a significant increase in both pay and responsibility. And, of course, you would have your own office. However, I cannot recommend the move at this time. What I'm willing to do is give you six weeks to shape up. Six weeks. I want you here every day and I want you working on Freedom Mutual projects. Not this." She pulled out the mimeo sheets I'd used to type up the YD newsletter. "Do you think you can do that, Gloria?"

I shrugged.

"Well, your future here depends on it."

"Yes ma'am."

"That's all," she said, lifting her phone to make a call. I didn't leave, so she stopped, the eraser-end of her pencil aimed at the rotary dial. "Is there something else, Gloria?"

"Yes ma'am. Can I have those mimeo sheets?"

She almost laughed, but instead she hung up her phone and gawked at me. "Any work done in this office on our equipment is the property of Freedom Mutual," she said, and then, with some effort, she tore the sheets in half and tossed them in the trash.

* * *

By the time I got home, my mood was rotten. Loaded down with my suitcase, our mail, the sack of LBJ buttons and the *Times Herald*, I pushed open the front door. As I turned around to kick it shut, my equilibrium shifted and before I could adjust, the sack slipped from my arm and a million buttons scattered for cover like roaches surprised by a midnight snacker.

"Son of a bitch!" I shouted.

"Speakin' of ravin'." I recognized Jo Beth's snotty voice before I realized anyone was home.

"Well, if it isn't Madame 'Not-so-Nu,'" I replied.

"Hi, Gloria." Veronica lounged on the sofa, a makeup mirror propped expertly on her knees, her implements of beauty scattered on the coffee table. "Tell us all about the convention."

That was the last thing I wanted to do with Jo Beth there.

"Did you hear? Someone dug up Oswald." I said, mainly to change the subject. I scooted buttons under the sofa with my foot.

"Oh, my God!" Jo Beth's hands flew to her face as if she were a relative or something.

"Why would anyone do something like that?" Veronica didn't even stop applying mascara: she found politics boring.

"They wanted to kick his ass for killing the wrong man." I'd heard the joke fifty times at the convention, but it still cracked me up.

"I don't think those Connally jokes are funny," Veronica said when I finally got control of myself. She patted a cotton ball into loose face powder and then dabbed it over her eyelashes, turning them frosty.

"I have to go drain," I said, just to annoy Jo Beth, and made my way to the bathroom.

"She is *so* crude," she complained as I shut the door.

Even though Jo Beth was pretty much a slut, when it came to urine, she thought anything more descriptive than tinkle was obscene. She was always cutting me down just loud enough for me to hear. While neither of us was in Veronica's league, Jo Beth thought she was hot stuff. She had long, frazzled, bleached-blond hair that looked as if she had just gotten out of bed, which was more than likely the case. Though she wasn't fat, she had big boobs and hips and bought her clothes a size too small so they'd still fit her when she lost those ten pounds.

When I returned to the living room, Veronica was applying the second coat of mascara. The powder and the cotton ball fibers added a quarter of an inch to the length of her lashes. She would repeat this until her lashes reached her eyebrows.

I flipped through the mail and noticed there were five applications for the YDs. A month ago I persuaded the membership to place an ad in the newspapers. Because we had no listing in the phone book, it took a pretty determined person to track us down if they wanted to join. Normally, one could just contact the Democratic County Chairman, but when our treasurer called just to see what would happen, Peddy told him there was no such group. We hoped to run someone—probably me—for State Vice President at the next convention and the number of votes we would have then depended on the size of our membership.

Actually, and he'd croak if he knew this, Peddy gave me the ad idea. We ran into each other at a City Council meeting in the fall and when I complained that he had omitted us from a brochure about local political organizations, he snarled, "You want new members, take out an ad in the newspaper." As a result of this, we had so far netted twenty-three new, paid-up memberships.

"Do my eyes look even?" Veronica asked Jo Beth.

"Yeah, they look fine. Hey, I got more information on that business college course."

"You gonna do it?"

"I dunno. It'd sure take up lots of my evenin's...not ta mention the money."

"I can think of better ways ta spend my cash."

"Still, court reporters make a hell of a lot mor'n we do."

Jo Beth worked at Sanger Harris Department Store—appropriately in bedding. But she found it boring—she only met housewives—and wanted to transfer to men's furnishings.

"Jesus!" I said, even though Jo Beth didn't give a hoot about my opinion. "Your plans change every time you get drunk and read the ads in matchbook covers."

"If I was thirty and over tha hill," Veronica mediated, "maybe I'd think about it. But, frankly, Jo Beth, what man wants ta marry a *business* woman."

"True. Junior used ta always say, 'If a woman ain't soft enough, a man'll just have ta find another spot ta rest his head.'"

Junior was Jo Beth's ex-husband and it was no secret that she still had the hots for him. Neither Veronica nor I had ever met him, but I knew he was probably one of those skinny little slimy guys with greasy hair, a jutting Adam's apple, and a tattoo on his forearm that said, "Eat me." When she talked about him, which was all the time, she got this sappy, faraway expression on her face.

"He always had such a fine way of puttin' thangs, ya know? Hand me that fingernail file, would ya, honey?"

Veronica passed her the emery board and the two of them worked away at self-improvement. I lugged my suitcase to my room, hoping to get my wig back on its stand before it resembled my own hair.

"Still," I heard Jo Beth going on, sniffling a little to compose herself, "if you're fixin' ta marry Hunter, yew should probably be prepared ta keep him in the manner he's become accustomed to...if ya know what I mean?"

I froze. It was rare that Jo Beth and I shared an opinion.

"I don't think that's funny," Veronica snapped. "Besides, what he's accustomed to isn't so great...I hear she has a space between her front teeth."

"Still, she pays the bills. She could probably fix that space if she didn't have Hunter."

"Maybe someone ought ta mention that to her," she giggled.

"Maybe someone ought to mention it to *you*," I said, heading to the kitchen for a Dr. Pepper.

"I don't recall anyone speakin' ta you," Jo Beth hollered. "See what I mean?" she whispered to Veronica, obviously referring to an earlier conversation. "She was in there listenin' ta our conversation."

Veronica ignored both of us. Instead, she held up two tubes of lipstick. "Which will be best for tonight—red or pink?"

"How about the brown?" Jo Beth offered.

Veronica began the painstaking task of applying the beige lipstick to her perfect mouth.

"Is that tonight's paper?" Jo Beth asked, pointing to the *Times Herald* I had dropped on the table earlier. Before I could answer, she scooped it up and began tearing through it.

"Horoscopes are in Section C," I offered.

"Jo Beth's wantin' ta buy a car," Veronica said.

"What's wrong with yours?"

"Nothin' serious. I mean, it still starts and all. Just sometimes the brakes don't work."

"That seems serious."

"No. If I slam it inta neutral, it stalls out. I can always stop it that way."

"What kind are you looking for?" I asked.

"Something flashy." Surprisingly, her lips didn't move when she read. "Darn!" She threw the paper on the floor.

"Nothing?" Veronica asked.

"Nothing I'd buy," Jo Beth replied. "If I could have one wish, it'd be that I'd find an ad readin' '1966 Mustang Convertible, Candy Apple Red, Five Hundred Dollars!' I'd take out a loan so fast your nose would bleed." She stood abruptly. "I should be gettin' along."

She jiggled her way across the room and I followed her to the door.

"I'll come by for you," Veronica said.

When she was safely outside, I flipped the dead bolt.

"Just in case she tries to get back in," I explained.

"Why do you hate her?"

This was a rhetorical question. Veronica knew exactly why I hated Jo Beth and it had nothing, really, to do with her looks or her attitude. All my life, I had been surrounded by, first girls, and later women, who looked and acted exactly like her. That's why they were called common. What I had against Jo Beth was her daughter, Dusty.

After Veronica and I moved into the Saracen, a complex for "swinging singles," Jo Beth practically had multiple orgasms. She spent entire weekends with us, prancing at the pool and gyrating at the club. She begged the management to let her move in, but kids and wives were strictly forbidden. So, she unloaded Dusty and leased a one-bedroom apartment.

"It's none of your business," Veronica replied, reading my mind. "Besides Dusty's better off with her grandmother."

"And Jo Beth is better off in a singles complex."

"She might meet the right man here and be able to give Dusty a real home again."

"There are no 'right men' in this place."

"So, was convention secretary everything you hoped it would be?"

"I wasn't convention secretary."

"But I thought you and that guy had an agreement."

"He pulled another fast one. Then to make it up to me he gave me a ticket to this luncheon on Thursday. Hundred dollars a plate. This Senator from the Midwest is speaking. Peddy said he could care less about seeing him, so that must mean he's good."

I slumped on the sofa and leafed through the classifieds: I might need a used typewriter now that the office was on to me. But before I found anything promising, a hundred-watt idea came to me.

The phone book was under a mountain of debris on my desk. I pulled it out and flipped through the pages until I got to the "P's". Then I ran my finger done several columns before I found what I was looking for. Not wanting to take the time to write down Peddy's home number, I tore his page out of the directory and put it by the phone. Then I drafted a note. Veronica was concerned enough to stop primping.

"What are you fixin' ta do?"

When I was happy with my composition, I called the *Dallas Morning News*.

"Hello. Could Ah please have tha classified office? Thank yew."

"Gloria?" Veronica warned.

"Hello, Classified? This is Mrs. Dexter Peddy.Ah'd like ta place an ad. Ye'us, Ah can hold."

"Is this going to be against the law?"

"Okay! I'd like tha ad ta read: '1966 Mustang Convertible, Candy Apple Red. $500.00. Must leave town quickly.'"

I gave her the Peddy's phone number, but before I could hang up, she asked about the bill.

"The bill?" I repeated, feeling annoyed that a perfect plan was running into such a stupid snag.

"I see that you have a business account with us, Mrs. Peddy. You want me to just put it on that?" the woman suggested.

"Great! That would be...great." I hung up seconds before I burst into hysterics.

"One of these days you're gonna get in *big* trouble," Veronica said.

* * *

We were quiet at dinner. I had felt fragile most of the afternoon: questioning my judgment—something contrary to my philosophy. Whenever I thought of Vic, which was about every fifteen seconds, my stomach plummeted, as if I were at the edge of a cliff. I was disappointed that he hadn't called again to say good-bye, but then he never asked for my phone number: a bad sign, I believed. It would have been nice to talk to him. To hear his voice. To know that he thought of me. Instead I was just moping around. Waiting for nothing. If this was the side effect of sex, I couldn't imagine ever doing it again.

Normally, I would have talked things through with Veronica: she was a well of wisdom when it came to other people's love lives. But, because of who he was, I wasn't comfortable confiding in anyone. Then there was my job. I was going to have to figure out a way to take some time off Thursday for that luncheon without getting my butt fired.

"Where are you and Jo Beth going tonight?" I asked, feigning an interest I didn't have.

"To the club. Wanna come?"

The Club was a nightspot attached to our apartment complex. Local rock groups performed there on Fridays and Saturdays. During the week a jukebox howled until midnight so that the Saracen Studs could be assured of getting laid without making commitments too far in advance.

"No, thanks. Is *he* going to be there?" My voice was snotty and I regretted that. I didn't want to take my bad humor out on Veronica, but evidently she was cranky too, because she snapped right back.

"Why can't you try to be nice to him?"

"I can't trust a man who looks in mirrors more than I do."

"Well, that probably eliminates most of 'um."

"We can't all be Miss Dallas." Veronica hated that I considered her greatest accomplishment grounds for ridicule. "Has he found an apartment yet?"

Veronica tossed the uneaten half of her sandwich onto her plate, knocking her knife noisily to the table. "It's not like they're married or anythin'," she snarled as she carted her dishes to the sink.

The phone rang.

"It's for you," Veronica said, holding the receiver out to me.

My heart soared as I reached for the phone, but it was only Greg Monroe, one of the Young Democrats. A Psychology major at SMU, Greg was not only active in local and statewide campaigns but also volunteered at The

Draft Information Center. The DIC encouraged potential draftees to get arrested for political behavior in the hopes that the military would not want to draft left-wing troublemakers.

"Have you seen tonight's paper?" Greg asked. " Peddy set up a committee to find a replacement for Henry Dunlop's seat."

Henry Dunlop, who had died suddenly a month ago, was one of the few liberal State Representatives from Dallas.

"I think he has a right to do that, Greg."

"He does, but half the people on the committee aren't even from Dunlop's district."

"Of course. Because Dunlop's district is liberal."

The idea of a conspiracy cheered me some. We considered options before choosing our usual solution: a resolution condemning Peddy. By the time I hung up, I was a little high. God, I loved that shit. Too bad I couldn't get a full-time political job. I thought about Vic's offer, but strangely, that depressed me. If he hadn't even asked for my phone number, how was he going to hire me?

"Veronica!" I said, whirling around, "let's move to D.C."

"What on earth for?"

"I don't know. I just keep thinking it'd be a good place for me. In the right environment, I think I could, you know, accomplish something. Become someone. Who knows? Maybe I could end up secretary to the President of the United States. Wouldn't that be something?"

"Too many coloreds there for me," she replied.

"You know, sometimes I wonder why I live with you." I scanned the newspaper for the article Greg had mentioned.

"Maybe ya won't have to for long. Maybe Hunter 'n me'll be gettin' married or something."

I glanced up: she was at the mirror, wiping lipstick off her front tooth.

"It's a good thing you're so pretty," I said, folding the paper back to the article, "'cause you're dumb as shit."

"Is that right?"

"You should be doing something about your life. Not just growing old waiting for a *loser* like Hunter."

"Bite my butt!" She began to pat her hair as if our argument might have dissolved some of her hair spray. "He is *not* a loser! Besides, maybe I *have* taken matters into my own hands." She fished through her pocketbook until she found a rat-tailed comb.

"Oh, really? What'd you do? Propose?" I dropped the paper on the sofa, stood, and walked over to her. Leaning against the wall, I crossed my arms over my chest. "You know, I don't think you're the only one waiting for him when and if he escapes from his rent-free apartment." Her eyes narrowed as she glanced my way. "I've seen him," I explained. "At the club."

"That's a lie! You never even go there."

"I did once. When you fixed me up with that creep."

"You hate him because he tells you what he thinks of you," she said, aiming the tail of the comb at me. "That you and your big mouth chase off every boy who shows any interest. You're just jealous things might work out for me. And once I leave, Miss Smarty Pants, who have you got left?"

"I chase off every *boy* who's interested in me because that's what they are—boys! And as for you, an ex-beauty queen with nothing to show for her life but a million dollars in cosmetics and a tarnished trophy..."

"Well, that tarnished trophy is one thang more than you'll ever have." Savagely, she plunged the point of her comb through her teased hair and lifted it, adding more height to her do. "You've been a failure at ever'thang. Always waitin' for the big break! Well, I've got news for you. The big break is marriage. That's where the money is! That's where the power is! If ya wanna make it big, Miss High and Mighty, you better give up politics and find a charm school. Because no one—no one!—would marry you. You're a slob and you're obnoxious and—"

"Shut up! Just shut up! You think everyone's like you? Well, they're not!" I considered flaunting Vic Davis.

"Right!" Veronica tossed her comb back into her bag, did a quick inventory of other essentials inside, snapped it shut and started for the front door.

"Do you know how ridiculous it is for someone your age to be working in a health spa?" I thought I'd just hit all the bases. She stopped, spun around and glared at me. "People are changing," I went on. "Women are changing. In ten years these places will evaporate completely. Even in Texas!"

"Well, you'd be interested ta know, that I was asked by WDIP ta audition for Miss Physique."

"Miss what?"

"They're fixin' ta do a TV exercise show and they want me ta be the star."

"That's the dumbest thing I've ever heard!"

"Well, I've turned it down. I plan ta be married before the year is out." I just looked at her. "Hunter *does* love me and I guarantee you, we'll be married."

She slammed the door so hard that the dishes in the sink clattered. I stood right where I was for some time after she left just thinking about the truth of what we'd said to each other.

Though Veronica and I had been inseparable for most of our lives, high school was the first time we got sorted into different categories: winner and nothing. I wasn't quite a looser: not like the kids who stuttered or had oozing acne, but I wasn't anyone who counted, either. Veronica, however, was Most Beautiful, Most Popular, Best All Around, Homecoming Queen, and Most Likely to Succeed all four years at Dallas Central High. To truly understand the social aura of our school, you have to realize that our yearbook gave full-page photos to not only the women who won these titles, but also to the ten runners-up. By contrast the National Honor Society had one group picture that took up a fourth of a page. Although Veronica deserved all of her titles, she won them, not on *her* merits, but as a result of whom she dated. At Dallas Central High, the only identity a girl had came from the guys who asked her out. If football players liked you, you were an in for the top honors at the school. If someone one the basketball team liked you, you had potential, but hadn't arrived yet. During my entire time there, no one asked me out. So, in some ways, I hadn't even existed.

During the Christmas season two years after we'd graduated from high school, I was waiting for a bus when Chris Humphrey pulled up in his Studebaker and asked if I wanted a ride. Chris Humphrey was Dallas Central's star quarterback and Most Handsome. He'd never spoken to me in high school, so it surprised me that he even knew who I was. On the way home, he was completely at ease, the way those kinds of kids always are, and when he dropped me off, he asked if I wanted to catch a movie that weekend. Said he'd always thought I was real cute. Flattered, I jumped at the chance. But later, in my apartment, after I thought about it for a while, I called him up and told him I was engaged.

* * *

When I saw Hunter at the club, he wasn't with another girl: I lied about that. He was alone. My date and I had a little spat, which I'll admit was partially my fault. When he left to dance with someone else, Hunter slipped into my booth.

"What do *you* want?" I had asked, not hiding my contempt.

"You know, Gloria, in this light and after several Margaritas, you're not half bad."

"Why don't you button your shirt?" Hunter's shirts were always open to his navel.

"Does it make you uncomfortable?"

"Sick is the word." I reached for my purse and started to leave, but he blocked my way.

"Gloria," he put one arm on the back of the booth and one over the table, pinning me in. "Why can't we get along?"

"Other than the fact that I have standards, I guess there's no reason."

"Maybe you just haven't seen me at my best." He held my face in his hand and pulled me close.

"I certainly hope that's the case—" Before I could finish, he kissed me, lightly, on the mouth. Stunned, I stared at him and I guess he mistook that for encouragement because he kissed me again, ramming his tongue into my mouth like the reptile he was.

"What do you think you're doing?" I shouted when I was able to push him back.

"Just relax, Gloria, I know what you need." His hand traveled up my skirt and he seemed unconcerned that we were in a place frequented by his fiancee' who was my best friend. The music was so loud that no one noticed us. I felt his fingers sliding under my panties. Finally, I reached for my mug and poured icy beer over his chest.

"You stupid cunt!" he yelled and pushed me back so hard that my head banged into the wall.

Then he stormed out of the club. I wanted to leave, too, but I was afraid he'd be waiting outside. I sat there, alone, for over an hour before my "date" made an appearance and offered to walk me home so that he could come back to collect his dance partner.

* * *

After Veronica left, I flipped through my forty-fives. I wasn't sure if I wanted to cheer myself up or make myself miserable, so I was open. I decided to cut right to the bone and played "Tracks of My Tears" and "Will You Still Love Me Tomorrow" over and over. There's only so long you can do this sort of shit and maintain any self-respect. So, after a while, I snapped on the television and watched *The FBI.* That night's episode—about a drug ring led by a handsome nightclub owner—reminded me of Hunter. I found myself projecting my resentment on to this actor so that when they shot him in crossfire, I cheered. Too bad I couldn't have Hunter shot in a crossfire. Or at least thrown in jail. But those things only happened in movies.

Or did they? Just out of curiosity, I called Information.

"Do you have a number for the FBI?"

It surprised me to learn there was a Dallas office. I thought they were just in Washington. As I dialed, I promised myself I'd hang up when they answered.

But I didn't.

* * *

I arrived early for work the next morning. Crossing the main reception area, I cut through Personnel until I reached the back stairs to the second floor. The peon floor, as I called it, was home to the bookkeepers, file clerks, typists and steno pool. Except for enclosed spaces for our four supervisors, the room was open, noisy, and cluttered with desks, trash cans, file cabinets and a Xerox machine.

I tossed my handbag under my desk and flipped on my machine as I fell into my chair. As usual, five stacks of files waited on my desk. If I worked straight through, I'd finish before lunch. Then the challenge would begin: appearing to keep busy when there was nothing to do.

I could type ninety-eight words a minute. I applied here right after I dropped out of college. They were looking for clerk typists and since any ninny could type policy numbers, they didn't require a speed test, so they had no idea. My co-workers, the other two clerks who performed the same job, were considerably less talented. It took them all day to clear their desk. I wanted to fly though my work just to show Lonnie what a whiz I was, but once my secret was out, they'd transfer me to a more demanding position and I'd be screwed.

Though my pay was little over minimum wage, the job served my purposes. Since I was one of the company bottom-feeders, my desk was in an out-of-the-way corner. Unimportant and unobserved, I handled YD stuff there like that's what I was paid to do. In addition to producing the newsletter, I made fund raising calls, wrote letters to the editor, and composed resolutions. Occasionally I fretted about the ethics of this, but I figured they were getting more than their investment out of me. I could double my income by working for Kelly Girls, but then I'd have no opportunity to promote my real career. So, in spite of its limitations, I was happy enough where I was.

But I also wanted to go to that luncheon on Thursday. Since political luncheons lasted about three hours there was no way I could go legally. If I called in sick again so soon after the Austin fiasco, Lonnie'd surely flip. Vic's talk of a job in the near future gave me some courage. If Lonnie fired me, I could work for Kelly Girls until he came through.

I rushed through my files so I could concentrate on a plan for Thursday. To occupy myself while I thought, I wrote Vic's name over and over until I realized how indiscrete that was. I tore the page up and on another wrote "G.W. + V.D." This stopped me: I never realized those were his initials.

At three, I went to the vending machines and bought an RC Cola and two packages of peanuts. I had this snack every afternoon. Back at my desk, I first took two swigs from the soda and then tore open the first bag of peanuts with my teeth. Funneling my left hand over the mouth of the bottle, I poured the peanuts into the drink. It fizzed up right away and I had to quickly cover it with my mouth to prevent it from gushing all over my desk. My cheeks swelled as if filled with helium. After several gulps, all the peanuts were gone and I dumped the second bag in. Since the soda was half-empty, I had to thumb the top of the bottle and shake the living daylights out of it to get it to foam up properly. I could burp all afternoon if I wanted to.

Once fortified, I tapped on Lonnie Mossman's door. She took her glasses off and placed them on her desk as she nodded for me to come in and take a seat. I planned to just level with her: explain how important the luncheon was and simply ask to take the day off—as vacation time, if necessary.

"On Thursday," I started, but as I looked up into her icy green eyes, I knew the stakes were too high for the truth. If she said no, even quitting wouldn't work, because I'd have to give two weeks' notice. I was momentarily at a loss. I'd have to think quickly of something she couldn't refuse.

"Yes," she encouraged.

"On Thursday, I've been called up for jury duty." I crossed my fingers that it wouldn't occur to her that I was too young for jury duty.

"Jury duty?"

"Yes Ma'am."

"Why are you just telling me now?"

"What do you mean?"

"Didn't you get notified last month?"

"Oh, yeah! Well, that's what's really weird, you know. Because, I guess it got lost in the mail or something, because I, uh, ran into this friend of mine who works at the courthouse and he, uh, you know, said, uh, 'hey, I see you have jury duty Thursday,' uh and I said, 'That's news to me.' So I phoned and sure enough I've been called up. So, unfortunately, I won't be here Thursday."

Her eyes penetrated mine for some time before she said. "Of course, you'll bring in some documentation about that on Friday."

"Oh, absolutely." I had plenty of time to worry about that.

* * *

Thursday morning, Veronica did my hair so I wouldn't have to wear the wig to the luncheon. She really should have gone to Beauty College because when she finished, I looked fabulous. She also let me borrow her Camelot dress. I called it that because it resembled costumes from the musical. It was made of a stretchy electric blue fabric and was fitted to just below the waist. A gold cord belt hugged the hips, tied in front and then fell the length of the skirt. From the belt, the dress flared out into a full skirt that swayed provocatively with the slightest motion. The best part of the dress, and the reason I wanted to wear it, was the sleeves. They were very tight until the elbow. Then, like the skirt, they flared into those medieval sleeves, ending in a dramatic point, which hung three inches beyond my hand. Inside the sleeve were rows of gold rickrack. I was sorry Vic wouldn't be at the luncheon.

Veronica had been moody lately. She seemed preoccupied and was practically mute unless asked a direct question. We had never discussed the argument we'd had Monday night; both of us were much more comfortable just ignoring things we regretted. Maybe what I'd said about Hunter hit home. Or maybe she was coming down with something. On Wednesday, she left the health club early and went right to bed. Or, maybe…maybe she and Hunter had broken up. It was hard to believe she would have kept something like that from me, but when I thought about it, he hadn't been around all week and he hadn't called, either.

* * *

The luncheon started at noon. I decided against taking a bus downtown, because I'd have to walk five blocks and in the heat I'd get all sweaty and my hair would frizz, so I decided to call a cab. While I was on the phone someone knocked. Pressing the receiver against my shoulder, I shouted toward the door: "We don't want any!" Then I continued giving information to the dispatcher. The visitor banged louder, so I covered the phone again and yelled, "Just a goddamn minute!" Jesus! Some people could be so rude. I hadn't hung up before the banging started again. I slammed the receiver down, hoping whoever it was heard it. As I marched from my desk, the heel of my pump got tangled around the phone cord; not only did I almost break my neck, but the phone clattered to the floor, ringing out in pain. As if on cue, my doorbell rang. The idiot just noticed we had a doorbell.

I jerked the door open so hard, I expected him to be sucked into the room by the centrifugal force. Slouching against the doorframe was not a Fuller Brush Man, or a Jehovah's Witness, but a giant, even by Texas standards. He must have been six-four and he had bright red curls that fell to about his chin. But he was no freak: he wore a blue, button-down collar shirt, with the sleeves rolled up, and tan chinos. He had what looked like a slender steno pad in one hand, and several pens poked out of his shirt pocket.

"Uh, hello," he said, "Gloria Warren?"

"Yes?"

"I'm Ian Feldman—"

I knew the name. "From the *Dallas Morning News*?" He was a political writer. I'd even seen his photo in the paper, but he looked normal-sized in black and white.

"Can I come in?"

I stood aside and indicated that he should step in. The sofa was littered with papers and magazines, so I hurried ahead of him to clear a spot.

"Here. Have a seat."

He sat down, started thumbing through his steno pad and then stopped, looked at me curiously, and stood. Running his hand along the cushion, he retrieved one of the LBJ buttons, which were proving as hard to get rid of as Christmas tree tinsel.

"I thought I felt something. What's this?"

"Oh! Sorry. Here. Give me that. These buttons have been a real pain in the…neck."

I tossed the button across the room. Not only did I miss the trash can, but it landed instead in a glass of flat Coke and splattered sugary beads across my desk. I was trying to decide whether it would be classier to ignore the mess or rush over and clean it up, when Ian pulled a folded up newspaper out of his back pants pocket.

"Any chance you read today's classifieds?" He passed the paper to me. One ad was circled. "Particularly this one…"

"Why should I read the classified? I don't need anything."

Shit! The prank had completely slipped my mind.

"Oh! Oh! The want ads! Uh, no, I never have any interest in the want ads. But, uh, let me see." I pretended to read the notice, mumbling key phrases out loud occasionally. "Well, sorry, but I'm not interested in any cars. Besides, I can't drive."

I returned the paper and hurried to my desk where I sopped up the spilled coke with a used tissue that never quite got thrown away.

"Well, this is an interesting ad." He followed me. "See, this is Dexter Peddy's phone number—" He held the paper toward me.

"Dexter Peddy?" I glanced down as if to double-check that fact. Instead I noticed he had freckled arms, something that usually didn't do much for me. But I also noticed that his forearm was bulging and that his veins stood out on his wrist like rope. It made me wonder about the rest of him.

"Exactly."

"Why would I would want to buy a car simply because it belonged to Dexter Peddy? Especially since I just told you..."

I noticed that he was having trouble ignoring things on my desk so I stuffed the page I'd ripped out of the phone book, the one with Peddy's name on it, under some papers. To cover for this, I busied myself tidying up my desk.

"Especially since I just told you I don't drive."

In addition to wadded-up papers, file folders, pencils and a can of underarm deodorant, my desktop exhibited a mug half-full of coffee, the flat coke glass, a bowl that once held ice cream, an open bag of now-stale potato chips and a smaller dish with the cure for baldness growing in it.

"I wasn't showing it to you because I thought you'd want to buy it."

I started gathering up the dishes, but the flat coke glass wanted to stay where it was and I decided not to argue with it at the moment. Clutching the other dishes, I made my way to the kitchen. Ian followed.

"You see, it's not for sale. In fact, this car doesn't even exist."

"Look, I'm in a real hurry," I said, scooting past him.

I returned to the living room and plopped down on the sofa, spreading my arms over the back cushions. The pointed sleeves of Veronica's dress cascaded regally down the cushions. I posed there for a moment until I noticed that I had a hole, about the size of a quarter, in my nylons, right at my knee.

"Shit!"

I jumped up and headed for Veronica's room to find her clear fingernail polish. Ian followed me to her door. It was like having a dog.

"Seems this ad was put in the paper as some sort of a joke. Doesn't the selling price seem low to you?" He was studying Veronica's room as if I had called him in for a paint estimate.

"I don't know anything about cars." It didn't seem right to stay in the bedroom, so I carried the polish back to the sofa. "It seems expensive to me. I'm just a working girl. Sometimes."

"Well, it's not. It's very low. That's the problem."

I dabbed the glaze on the nylons. Considering the size of the rupture, at this rate it was going to take all morning.

"You see," Ian went on, "the Peddys have been harangued with calls from potential buyers."

"Well, tell them to raise the price. If there is such a demand, they must be asking too little for it. I may not know much about cars, but I'm not stupid."

To speed things up, I poured a pool of enamel into my palm and then slapped it onto the hole and held it there a few seconds.

"No, let me explain again. This car doesn't exist."

"So why did they put the ad in the paper?"

"They *didn't*. Someone else did...as a practical joke."

"Who would do such a thing?"

Now my hand was sticky. I looked around for a towel.

"Well, that's why I'm here. Dexter Peddy suggested—rather strongly, I might add—that *you* might know something."

"Me! That's ridiculous." The only thing near was the newspaper, so I wiped my hands on it. "You think I have money to take out ads just to torture a fascist like Dexter Peddy?"

"Well, whoever did this, billed the ad to his business, so they weren't out any money."

"Well, whoever did this sure was clever." The newspaper was now part of my hand. "Ha! Just between you and me, he deserved it. Gee, I wish I could take credit, but—"

I jerked the newspaper and it ripped away, leaving three strips of confetti dangling from my palm. Jumping to my feet, I buckled in pain as the dried polish ripped a plug of skin out of my knee.

"Mr. Peddy said he'd had similar problems with you."

"I'm sure Peddy has a lot of enemies. Have you checked B'nai B'rith?"

He followed as I limped to the kitchen, where I tried to wash the newspaper and polish off.

"B'nai B'rith? No. Why?"

The water didn't faze the polish. When I partially closed my hand, a transparent pocket formed in my palm. I had to scoot Ian aside to reach the silverware drawer.

"Ordinarily I wouldn't tell you this, you being a reporter and all." With a fork, I pierced the bubble and then peeled strips of the polish off my hand. "But I think I can trust you and I know that if I mention my sources were not first-hand, you'll keep it to yourself. I wouldn't want to read about this in the paper. You know, ruin some guy's career. Not unless I was sure this was true, which I'm not, but —"

"What are you getting at?"

I put the fork back into the silverware drawer. "Well, I once heard that Dexter Peddy was a member of the Hitler Youth before he came to this country."

Ian's face broke into a slow, sly smile. He had crows' feet. " Peddy was born here in Dallas." His eyes were very brown.

"That's what the documents say, but those Germans were masters at counterfeiting." Ian's smile was just shy of mocking: he wasn't buying it. "Well, it may not be true. Like I said, ordinarily I wouldn't mention it, but I knew I could trust you to keep it to yourself."

"Oh, mum's the word." He snapped his note pad shut and jammed it into his pocket. "Well, I should get to the office."

"Tell me," I said. "Do you always make house calls like this? Seems a little excessive over something as silly as an ad...especially when you didn't learn anything."

"Oh, no. I usually just call people. In fact, I called your office first thing this morning and they told me you were taking the day off."

"How'd you know where I worked?"

"Peddy told me. Anyway, I just live a couple of blocks away, so I thought I'd stop by on my way to work." He started to leave but then turned back. "To be honest, I was curious: I've heard of you before."

"Really?" It thrilled me to think I was famous. "So, am I as *bad* as you expected?" I practically batted my eyes at him.

"Yeah," he laughed quietly. "You are."

"Well, thanks," I snapped. I wasn't sure, but I thought he'd just insulted me.

"Maybe we'll run into each other sometime." He suddenly didn't seem to be in such a hurry.

"Well, I don't know. I may be leaving town soon."

"Where will you be going?"

"I may go work in Vic Davis's campaign office."

This got his attention. His smile froze and then vanished completely.

"Really?" He took out his note pad and thumbed through several pages looking for something. "Well," he finally sighed, "not if this story hits the paper."

"You mean you're actually considering writing about this?" I followed him. "I had *nothing* to do with it. You're just speculating. Besides it's just a silly joke. Where's everyone's sense of humor?"

"It's called harassment. It's news."

"I had nothing to—" I grabbed his arm and made him face me. "Are you familiar with the libel laws?" I demanded.

"Very. Are you?"

"Look, maybe we should talk this over. This is my first big chance. If you suggest that I had anything to do with it—and I didn't, that's what's so *awful*—it will ruin me!"

He stopped and scratched his chin with his notebook. "Well, I wouldn't want to write about this...ruin someone's career...unless I was sure it was true."

"Exactly! And you're not—sure, that is—are you? I mean...I'm just not that clever."

"Maybe we could discuss this further" he said, "—when you're not in such a hurry."

"That'd be great!" I said, running along behind. "Who knows? Maybe I could solve it for you."

"How about tomorrow?" He stopped at a bright yellow VW and opened the door.

"Fine. Give me a call."

"Over dinner." He put one foot on the floorboard but didn't get into the car.

"What?"

"I'll pick you up at seven." Fishing around in his pocket, he extracted his keys and rattled them in his hand until he grabbed the appropriate one.

"Are you...are you talking about a date or something?"

"Yeah. Something like that." In the sun, his coppery hair sparkled.

"Oh. Sure." I shrugged. "Why not?"

"I'll see you then."

Flabbergasted, I didn't notice Veronica until she rushed past us. "Veronica?" I called after her, but it was too late.

"Who was that?" He stared after her with the same open-mouthed, dazed expression everyone gets when they watch the Fourth of July Fireworks stoned.

I felt resigned. "That's Veronica. My roommate."

"Is she a model or something?"

"No, she's a fiancee'. I mean she works at a health spa."

"What's it like living with someone that gorgeous?"

"It's, you know, kinda like being the flip side of a gold record."

Ian laughed. "Hey, that's very good."

"You want to…meet her?" I asked, glancing over my shoulder toward the apartment. Might as well get this over with.

"No," he said simply, as he stuffed himself into his yellow VW Beetle. "Well, see you tomorrow."

* * *

"Hey, Veronica!" I shouted as I banged the apartment door behind me. "Great timing!"

She had thrown herself across the sofa and was sobbing as if Revlon had just dropped Mischievous Mauve from its lipstick line.

"Veronica? What's wrong?"

"It's Hunter."

"What's he done this time?"

My fury was instant. The guy was such a jerk. It had to come to this. I was just sorry it happened when things were going so well for me. Veronica sat up and dabbed at the outer corners of her eyes.

"No one's seen him all week. He was supposed to be at the club Monday, but he never showed. And he hasn't called or—"

"I told you he was no good. It was just a matter of time—"

"I had one of the weight lifters at the gym call him. That woman answered. Said he was in jail!"

"Jail?"

"She said he was busted late Monday night. By the FBI!"

"The FBI?" My knees gave out and I sort of drifted down onto the sofa. "You mean he really *was* doing drugs!" I whispered.

"No! But they searched the place and found a joint in the guest room. It wasn't even Hunter's! His creepy cousin'd been there the week before. But they arrested him anyway."

"Oh, my God!" At the window I prayed for the taxi to show up. "So what will happen?"

"I'm not sure. Everyone says it's really odd for the FBI ta be involved—"

As I parted the curtains, I saw that my hand was shaking. I clasped it behind my back so she wouldn't notice. My mind revved. When I get like that, I sometimes blurt out things better left unsaid so I took some deep breaths to calm down. I didn't want to incriminate myself. At least not yet. After all, this could blow over and be nothing. Or it could—. I stopped myself. Or maybe it could be a great way to get rid of Hunter. For the good of everyone.

"You should drop him. You don't want someone with a record." I looked her right in the eyes.

"There's something I didn't mention before. I'm pregnant."

I couldn't speak, could hardly catch my breath.

"I thought if I got pregnant, Hunter would—He loves me. I know that. He just needs a push."

"Oh, my God!" Collapsing into a chair, I buried my head in my hands and listened to the refrigerator hum in the kitchen. "You could get an abortion!" I said it before I realized what I meant. "Yes! That's it! You could get an abortion." Not giving her a chance to reply, I continued. "A friend of mine got one in Juarez. She said the guy was good. Did it in his office, even." I hurried over to my desk. "Look, I'm going to call her and get his name..."

"I don't want an abortion. It's too scary. Things will work out."

"How can things work out if he's in jail?"

"We don't *know* that he'll go to jail. Maybe if he gets a good lawyer—"

A horn blasted from the parking lot.

"Oh, great! There's my taxi. Look, I *have* to go. Will you be here when I get back?"

"I'm taking the late afternoon shift."

"We need to talk about this. Why don't you drop by the hotel at two—I'll ride with you to work. We can talk then."

"There's nothing ta talk about. My mind's made up."

"But..." The cabby was leaning on his horn now. "Veronica, I have to go." I opened the front door and waved to the cab. "This luncheon is important, Veronica. If it were anything else, I'd cancel..."

She agreed to meet me at two in the lobby of the hotel.

* * *

The luncheon was in the hotel's second floor ballroom. Not surprising, the majority of those present were strangers to me. Few of my cronies could afford such a lunch. I stood at the entrance and let my eyes wander, for though I didn't know many fat cats, I did follow them in the papers and would be able to recognize some. And who knows? One of two of them might prove to be useful. I was on my way toward this real estate agent whose grinning face dominated his ads in the paper, when I spotted the last person in the word I'd expect to find there.

"Herman!" I shouted. "What are you doing here?"

"I never pass up a free meal."

"A hundred bucks is hardly free," I reminded him.

"Didn't cost me a dime. I got one of Peddy's tickets."

"Wait a minute!" I said. " Peddy gave you a ticket?"

"Yeah. The Democratic Party worried there'd be no interest here in Thatcher Reid and since they see him as a rising star, they wanted to insure a crowd. They gave Peddy fifty tickets and asked him to pass them out. I can't believe you didn't get one."

That son of a bitch had done it again.

"He *did*, but he said it was his ticket because he couldn't care less about coming."

"Well there he is." Herman pointed toward the head table and sure enough, Peddy was right there, next to—

"Oh my God, Herman! Look at the head table."

Herman glanced toward the front of the room, shrugged and turned back to me.

"Don't you see?"

"What?" he asked.

"Next to Peddy. It's Hubert Humphrey. In drag! I need to sit down. Jesus, Herman, why are the liberals always so weird?" I realized almost immediately that when it came to weird, Herman did not exactly have the greatest perspective.

"That's not the Hump. It's his sister. Striking resemblance, isn't it?"

Herman and I talked for a few minutes, until he spotted some guy he needed to speak with and excused himself. Billy Anders was across the room with Chick Flowers and Lance Wallace. Believing Billy might have some updates on Vic Davis, I was about to start toward him when a voice from behind stopped me.

"Your sleeve's in the dip."

Startled, I spun around. "What?" I said.

"Your sleeve. It's sittin' in the dip."

I looked down and sure enough, the point of my sleeve was feeding in the Green Goddess.

"Shit!" I stuck the saturated material in my mouth and tried to suck it off.

"Always prefer a corn chip, myself," he said and in spite of my exasperation, I laughed.

He was not bad looking, but he wasn't my type. Though dressed in a three-piece suit and highly polished shoes, he seemed like a shit-kicker at heart. He was just under six feet and a little heavy—a football player sent to pasture. He had a great smile with chubby cheeks, kind of like Glen Campbell.

"Where's your drink, darlin'?" he asked.

"Oh. I don't really—I'm not old enough to drink."

"Nonsense. I been drinkin' since I was fourteen. What do ya want? I'll get it for you."

"I...I don't drink much. Just beer sometimes. But I don't really like that."

Actually, I hardly ever drank and had never done drugs: another entry in the long list of reasons why I wasn't considered cool. I wish I could say this was because of high moral values, but it just made me too tense to get that relaxed.

"How 'bout somethin' sweet?"

"Sure. I guess." I dipped a napkin in the melted ice surrounding the shrimp and rubbed my sleeve.

A woman at the head table announced that Senator Reid's plane was running late. However, the hotel wanted us to take our seats so that they could serve lunch. The Senator would arrive by dessert.

I looked for Herman but he'd vanished. Billy, Chick, and Lance were just taking seats by the head table. Though I dreaded being so close to Peddy, I didn't recognize anyone else, so I hoofed it to their table, hoping there would be room for me. Luckily, Chick was in the middle so I wouldn't have to sit by him.

"Is this seat taken?" I asked, touching the empty chair next to Lance. The three of them casually glanced over their shoulders at me and then, as if a hurdy-gurdy machine had suddenly hit pop in "Pop Goes the Weasel," they all leapt to their feet.

"It's been reserved for yew, yew cute little thang," Chick Flower said, and then immediately started scanning the room to see if there was anyone more interesting around.

Once I sat down, I realized that when I looked straight ahead, I was staring at Peddy. He glared at me. I smiled as if we were best friends and waved back at him.

"Who's the dish in the hat?" Chick asked Billy.

"She's married," Billy replied.

"Too bad," Chick said, but he continued to leer at her.

Rolls and little plates of lettuce were waiting for us. Since I had skipped breakfast, I was hungry. I grabbed a roll, which was about the size and weight of a baseball. The little pads of butter had melted and kept sliding off the knife.

"I think I need ta freshen' up my drink," Chick said, standing. But he ambled, not toward the bar, but toward the woman in the hat. Mesmerized, I watched. Surprisingly, she didn't puke on him, but instead seemed charmed by his attention.

"How old're you now, Gloria?" Lance asked me.

"You mean, like, now?" I replied.

"Yeah. Now."

"You mean, this minute?"

"Never mind. I've lost interest."

"Twenty," I said.

"Twenty?" he glanced over at me. "My, time flies, doesn't it? Seems like just yesterday you were this scrawny little pain in the ass follow'n us around and now you're all grown up—"

"Wait a minute!" I cut in. "I never followed you around."

"What would you call it?"

"I'm interested in politics. Our paths cross."

Suddenly, Lance's hand was on my knee. I picked up my spoon and whacked his knuckles with it. He jerked his hand away.

"Sorry, I'm a passionate guy," he apologized.

"I'm a virgin," I lied.

"Well, you keep that shit up, you'll be able to make that claim when you're ninety."

"There are worse things, I guess," I said.

"Can't imagine what they might be," Lance replied.

"Well, Lancelot," Chick said on his return, "we're havin' cocktails later and she's got a friend."

"I don't need you fixing me up with her homely friends."

"She ain't homely. There she is. Over there. The one with the mahogany hair." We all looked.

"Think her hair's natural?" Lance asked, grinning.

"I'm sure you could find out. If you asked her." They both snorted like warthogs until Lance glanced my way and sobered up quickly. "What?" he said guiltily.

"Is your name really Lancelot?" I asked.

"Hell, no. Just plain ole Lance. Wanna know how I got it?"

"Sure."

"When I was born, the doctor said to my momma, 'This boy's got the biggest dick I've ever seen on a white child.' So, outta respect, she named me Lance."

This sort of candid revelation is the exclusive domain of Texas politicians.

"Now that's just one hell of a fine story, Wallace," Chick said, "You outta put that in your campaign literature Hell, voters love shit like that!"

Suddenly someone placed a short, fat glass by my plate.

"It's a Mai Tai." The guy I'd met earlier took the chair to my left. I sipped it cautiously, prepared for the worst, but it was surprisingly good.

"How come Ah never seen you around before," the shit kicker said. "Pretty girls don't usually get past me that easy." In kicker language this did not mean that he found me attractive; rather, it meant that he recognized I was female and might put out.

The head table was filling up. In addition to Peddy, Humphrey's sister, and some local officials, Estelle Harris was making her way to one of the seats of honor.

"Ah, shit!" my companion muttered. When I glanced at him quizzically, he nodded toward Estelle and said, "They gotta have 'em everywhere now, don't they?"

"You're a racist?" I asked.

"No. I am not a racist. I just don't think coloreds and whites should mix, is all."

"Oh, thanks for clearing that up."

I turned toward Billy, hoping to move the conversation to Vic Davis, but he, Lance, and Chick were in the middle of some big argument, so I took another drink and, not wanting to look to my left or right, I stared straight ahead—at Peddy. He motioned for me to approach the head table.

"What?" I mouthed and he repeated the gesture. Frowning, I looked at him as if I were trying to figure out what he wanted but just couldn't do it. Things like that really irritated Peddy and I was willing to keep it up for a while, but finally, he just looked away.

"What's your name?" the kicker asked.

"Gloria. What's yours?"

When I turned his way, my head swam a little. Jesus. That drink hadn't felt that strong. One waiter collected our salad plates while another plopped down our main course.

"Hoyt," the kicker said.

I looked at him and raised my eyebrow encouragingly.

"What?" he asked defensively.

"I asked what your name was?"

"And Ah said 'Hoyt!'"

"That's your *name*? I thought you were just clearing your throat."

He laughed and squeezed my knee. "You're not the first to make that bad joke."

Some kind of anemic meat—chicken maybe—was rolled up like a cigar and was puking out this green and yellow stuffing from both ends. On top was a congealed white sauce. A vegetable medley, cooked to exhaustion, rested to the side while an ice cream scoop's worth of rice separated the two.

"So, Hoyt," I said his name as if I were coughing up phlegm, "what do you do?" I had to struggle to keep from making these repulsive snorting noises as I snickered.

Ignoring me, he replied, "Ah'm a law student at SMU."

"Hey, Gloria," someone called. When I turned—carefully, so as not to slip off my chair—I spotted Greg Monroe.

"Did Peddy give you a ticket?" I demanded as he approached.

"Yeah. Sure. He gave everyone one."

"Bastard!" I mumbled.

"I was going to call you tonight," Greg went on. "The Draft Information Center's having a bowl-a-thon for peace next month. You wanna sign up?"

"What do I have to do?"

"Well," he said, handing me a mimeographed sheet of paper that had a short paragraph at the top and them a bunch of blank lines all the way to the bottom. "You agree to bowl three games, but before the tournament, you get yourself sponsors. See," he pointed to the blank lines, "you get friends to pledge so much money per point. Then, after the tournament, you collect the money for the DIC."

"Okay. Sure. Why not?"

After he left, I glanced back at Hoyt. "You want to sponsor me in a bowling tournament?"

"Ah think that if ya had someone fightin' in Nam, ya'd be less willin' to support the traitors of our gummit," Hoyt said.

"What traitors?" Reaching for my drink, I found I'd already drained it.

"The communists givin' aid and comfort to our enemies."

"It's not always apparent, but I believe we do have freedom of speech in this country."

"This isn't about freedom of speech. It's about supportin' your gummit durin' a time of war."

"Oh, did we declare war?"

"You're a quick one, you are. Ah can see you'll be a real challenge for me. But Ah think if ya knew what the Viet Cong were like, you'd feel different about helpin' draft dodgers."

"You know some Viet Cong?"

"Of course not!"

"I just thought that maybe when you were over there, you met a couple."

"Ah was never over there." I looked at him with a shocked, open-mouthed expression. "Ah tried to enlist, but Ah was deferred."

"Section eight?" I have always been very good at this sort of needling, but my implication that he had gone for the loony loophole hardly fazed him.

"Very funny. No! Medical reasons. Psoriasis."

"Jesus! I hope you've had yourself sterilized."

Normally, I can keep a straight face when I'm acting like this, but I found myself terribly amusing and couldn't keep from guffawing and beating my fist on the table. We didn't speak for a while.

Billy, Chick and Lance were discussing gun control and Chick was explaining how we all needed arms so that when the Russians invaded, we could form militia groups and fight them off, just like our forefathers did with the English.

"And you're gonna shoot down their bombers with your goddamn muskets?" Lance asked.

"You all want to sponsor me in a bowling tournament?" I asked. "It's for a good cause."

"What's the cause?" Chick asked.

"The Draft Information Center."

"Count me out," he said.

Lance shook cigarettes out of a pack and offered me one.

"I don't smoke," I said.

"What the hell *do* you do?" he asked, lighting up and blowing a stream of smoke toward the ceiling.

"I'm going to bowl," I said passing him the sheet.

He studied it and reached for a pen in his pocket. "How good a bowler are you?" he asked.

"I don't know. I've never done it before."

Clutching the cigarette with his square teeth, he grinned. "Well, hell then, I'll be generous." He signed his name and pledged a dollar a point.

After Billy Anders pledged a quarter, a commotion across the room distracted us. A sandy-headed, distinguished-looking man was greeting people at the tables.

"That must be Senator Reid," I said to Hoyt as I craned my neck to get a better look. Hoyt made a disparaging noise. "You don't like him?"

"Just another faggy Midwesterner," he answered.

"So, why did you spend a hundred dollars to hear him speak?"

"I didn't. Got a ticket from the County Chairman."

" Peddy! Why would Peddy give you a ticket?"

"He was passin' 'um out at the NRA meeting last night."

I glared at Peddy, who happened to be looking my way. He motioned for me to come up to the head table. I stood quickly, which was a mistake, but as soon as I steadied myself, I stomped up to him.

"What?" I demanded.

"It's nice to see you with that Whitehead there."

I glanced toward the table. Hoyt saluted us with his glass.

"Well, he's a jerk, but his complexion seems fine."

"I've always thought you had potential, if you just hung out with more respectable and responsible adults, instead of those long-haired, foul-mouthed, flag-burning, smelly, fornicating, Pinko perverts."

"Don't hold back, Peddy. You have a problem with the YDs I want you to just speak right up." He sort of snorted. "By the way, Peddy, I understand you accused me of taking out some ad in the newspaper."

"What makes you say that?"

"A reporter told me."

"A reporter's trick. They always say stuff like that. Try to lure guilty people into admitting something. I wouldn't accuse you of anything, Gloria. We're getting along better these days, aren't we?"

"Are we?"

"Oh, I wanted to ask you. Last weekend, the convention minutes vanished. You wouldn't know anything about that, would you?"

"Peddy, I offered to be convention secretary, but you screwed me. Now that you put some incompetent in there and she's lost her notes, you can't expect me to help bail her out."

"She lost the notes, but she still has the tapes."

"Tapes?"

"The whole convention was taped. She'll just have to transcribe it."

Well, shit! When I reached my table, Chick was sputtering about campaign expenses. Half-falling into my chair, I leaned over Lance and got Billy's attention.

"Any news about Vic Davis's campaign?" I asked.

"Hey, don't waste your time with Vic Davis when you can have me," Lance said.

"I'm interested in his campaign," I snapped.

"Right," Lance snickered.

"Never heard it call *that* before," Chick mumbled and they both cracked up.

"Does it ever bother you," I said, "that you're such assholes?"

"Not one bit," Lance replied, "and you wanna know why? 'Cause we are members in good standing of the Texas Legislature."

"And goddam proud of it," Chick added.

"Vic Davis!" Hoyt said, "Now *there's* a joke."

"What makes you say that?" I looked him dead in the eyes, surprised at how civil I remained. Must have been the alcohol.

"Growin' his hair like a girl's. When he raises money, he should just take himself to a barber."

"I like his hair."

"In *my* circle, we think it's only a matter of time before he's caught in bed with another guy."

The absurdity of this left me speechless. I toyed with setting the record straight. Instead, I came up with one of my better lines, though it was a mistake. My tongue twisted and while I meant to say, "What circle is that? The jerks circle." I *actually* said, "What circle is that? The circle jerk." That alone would have left me hysterical, given my mood, but the look on Hoyt's bug-eyed face made the day worthwhile.

He jumped to his feet, outraged, and announced, "Excuse me, folks, I just remembered that I have to be somewhere." He nodded to the others at the table and then to me. "Gloria."

I convulsed into laughter, braying like a mule, when someone tapped me on the shoulder. I twisted around, unable to stop laughing, and spotted a hand extended toward me. My eyes were so teary that everything was a little blurry. I gripped the hand as I looked up.

"Hi, I'm Thatcher Reid."

At that moment, a light flashed, searing the insides of my eyes. When I could see again, Reid had moved on and I realized that a photographer had taken our picture.

"I'll get you a copy of it," Ian said as he straddled the chair vacated by Hoyt. "I told him to take it." He was dressed as he had been earlier, except that he now wore a tweed jacket and had a flowered tie draped over his neck, though it was not knotted. I started giggling again.

"Are you *drunk*?" he asked, lowering his voice some.

I straightened my posture and stopped laughing, "Of course not. I had one drink."

"Feldman!" Lance called out, extending his hand. Ian shook hands with Lance and Chick.

"What's new, guys?" he asked.

"Well," Lance said, "My buddy here's thinkin' about runnin' for speakership next session."

"You going to support him?" Ian asked.

"Hell, yeah. Unless someone offers me more money."

"Rep. Wallace was just explaining to me why his mother named him Dick." I said to Ian.

"Dick? I thought his name was Lance." He was coveting my plate.

"You know, honey, it's people like you could ruin a guy's whole image," Lance said.

"You gonna eat that?" Ian asked pointing to half a roll.

"No. You want it?" He stuffed the whole thing in his mouth. "Want the chicken, too?" I asked.

"I'm not that hungry."

"Here. Have another one," I said passing him the lone remaining roll from the basket.

"Thanks." He dropped the roll in his jacket pocket.

"Hey," I said, reaching for the bowling sheet, "you want to sponsor me in a bowling tournament?"

Ian read the paper quickly before handing it back. "I never take public stands on political issues."

"Are you hatched?" I asked, referring to the Hatch Act which prevented government employees from campaigning.

"No. Just don't think it's good policy." He glanced around, his gaze stopping on the head table. "I hear your friend, Peddy, is thinking about endorsing George Wallace in '68."

"What? You mean he's abandoning the Republicans?"

"If they nominate Rockefeller."

"You've got a great job, you know? You get all the gossip."

"We like to call it news. Speaking of which, I should get back to work."

"Wait! What time is it? I'm supposed to meet someone."

"Two-twenty."

"Oh, no. I'm late. I'm not going to hear Senator Reid."

"You can read about it in the paper. I'm a great reporter."

I started weaving my way through the tables to the exit. I glanced back at Ian twice and each time he waved to me.

* * *

"Well, I was about ta give up on you, girl," Veronica scolded when I reached the lobby.

We crossed Commerce to Elm in order to catch the bus to *A Stretch Over Thyme*. We only had to wait ten minutes. Veronica adamantly refused an abortion, because she felt her pregnancy was all she had in her battle against Hunter's ambivalence.

There were two seats available on the bus. Veronica grabbed the side seat and I sat next to a businessman on the first seat facing forward. Luckily we were close enough to gab but because of the crowd we avoided the hot topic. Three stops later, a large Black woman got on the bus. Her feet puffed out over her shoes like yeasty bread waiting to be punched down.

"Here," I said, standing.

"Thank you," she said, lowering herself to the seat. I grabbed the pole by Veronica just as the businessman I'd been next to grabbed my arm and swung me around.

"You had no right to do that!" he shouted. I couldn't imagine what he meant. "You think I want her rubbing her fat ass against me?" He climbed over the woman, abandoning his seat.

"It's a public bus," I said. "Anyone can—"

"Don't smart off to me, you little brat!" I worried he was going to hit me. I glanced around the bus: everyone watched.

"It's kids like that who're ruining this country," he said as he stormed off the bus.

I was mortified for myself, and for the Black woman. I wanted to look back at her, to establish some connection, to see if she was okay, to let her know we shouldn't give a shit what an asshole like that had to say, but I couldn't. I just looked straight ahead. I had no more courage than that.

* * *

Friday morning, Senator Reid and I were on the front page of the *Dallas Morning News*. I dreaded the scene with Lonnie Mossman so much that my stomach felt upset, but I didn't dare call in sick. A copy of the front page was on my desk with a notepaper clipped to it. "Please stop in my office, LM."

"The only reason you still have a job here is that Mr. Sweet intervened on your behalf again. He pointed out that though your behavior has been irresponsible, there have never been complaints about your work. Which is true. Consequently, I'll give you the chance to bail yourself out: you can work Saturday."

* * *

Veronica got home just as I rejected the last item in my closet. Ian was the first real date I'd had in a long time and I wasn't sure how to dress. I was also ambivalent about the wig: the experience with Vic still caused me to cringe. But in spite of my urgency, the second I saw Veronica guilt gushed through my chest with the heat and force of a broken steam valve.

"What do you hear about Hunter?" I asked, as she led me into her room to explore her wardrobe.

"His lawyer's trying to come up with his bail." She studied a hot pink-print, silk jersey chemise, held it up to me, then hung it back up. "You kinda like this guy, don't ya?" I shrugged. "You're sure goin' to a lot of trouble." She pulled out a bright green mini dress with wide white stripes dissecting the front vertically and horizontally.

"Well, he's the first date I've had that I might have something in common with."

Veronica opened one of her dresser drawers, scattered things around a bit before she located a large green bow attached to a hair clip. Situating me in front of her mirror, she backcombed the top of my hair and trapped the sides and back with the clip at the nape of my neck. It took her a second. She also suggested I wear her spiked heels so that there wouldn't be such a height discrepancy.

"I'm considerin' that TV thang," she blurted out.

"The audition?" I slipped the dress off the hanger.

"It'd pay me a lot of money. I'd get a retainer or something. They remember me from the Fourth of July parade—I guess they read the write-up."

"When you got second degree burns on your ass from sitting on the hood of that car?"

"Yeah. They said I was a real professional. Some people are sayin' I'd have it made."

"Well, then do it." I stepped into the dress.

"I think I will. It would give me enough to get Hunter out."

"Hunter?" I had zipped the dress halfway up, but I stopped. A weight pulled my shoulders down. "Veronica? There's something I need to tell you." She was dabbing a huge facial brush in some powdered rouge. "I did something really terrible—"

"Go like this," she said, sucking in her cheeks. When I did what she said, she brushed streaks across my face. "Give ya some nice contour."

"You know, last Monday, when Hunter got busted?"

"Oh!" she interrupted me, "guess what I found out today?" She turned me around and zipped the dress the rest of the way. "It seems there was an informer in Hunter's case."

"An informer?" My stomach heaved.

"His lawyer says that's the main thing against him. The cops believe that even though there was only one joint, the fact that someone informed shows that he was more involved. That's why bail's so high."

"Really?"

"I just can't imagine who'd do that. Destroyin' someone's life and all."

"I have a little money," I said. "You can have it."

"You'd do that for Hunter?"

"I'd do it for you." I left her room. She followed me.

"If Hunter thought the money was comin' from you, he'd wanna stay in jail." She brushed lint off the back of my dress. "There's only one problem with this audition…" She frowned.

"What's that"

"I may have to sign a year's contract."

"Well, so what?"

"Aren't ya forgettin' somethin'?" She patted her concave stomach.

"Oh, shit." I ran to my desk and flipped through my Rolodex. "I talked to my friend. She said the abortion wasn't as scary as you think. The guy speaks English and everything." Jerking the card loose, I passed it to Veronica, but she didn't take it. "Forget about Hunter. You deserve—Oh! You had a phone call earlier." I scattered papers on my desk searching for the message. "Here: Mr. Whitehead. Who's that?"

"Just some guy I met waitin' for you the other afternoon. He was sweet. In a weak moment I gave him my phone number." She wadded the message up and dropped it in the trash.

"Don't be in such a rush. Maybe you should call him back." I smoothed out the message.

"I'm not in the mood to go out with anyone. Not now."

"Wait! Here's this guy's number. He might be okay. At least you didn't meet him in a singles' bar." Knowing Veronica to be both resilient and fickle, I hoped that if she met another guy, this dilemma with Hunter would vanish. "Go to lunch with him. Explain that you're trying to get over someone and don't want to move quickly..."

Veronica rolled her eyes, but took the phone and dialed the number. My spirits rose instantly. That was it: get her involved with someone new and everything else would work out.

"Hello? Is this Hoyt?" she said into the receiver.

"Hoyt?" I whispered. "Did you say '*Hoyt*?'"

Veronica covered her free ear and pivoted away from me so she could hear him better.

"Wait a minute, Veronica. Ask him to hold for a second! I need to talk to you."

She pulled away again, "What? I couldn't hear ya. My roommate was sayin' somethin'."

Finally, desperate, I yanked the phone away and simply hung it up. Veronica's mouth fell open.

"Uh. I thought this over a little. And, uh, I think it was a mistake to call him."

"It was *your* idea."

"Uh, yes. But, uh, what's this guy going to say when he finds out that you're engaged to a drug dealer and pregnant. He'll think you're a slut! Running around on poor Hunter while he's rotting in prison."

"What's got inta you?"

The phone rang and I grabbed the receiver. When Hoyt asked for Veronica, I told him she'd left for the weekend and hung up.

"I mean, before you go starting God-knows-what with God-knows-who, you should at least have the baby. I don't want you to make a fool out of yourself. That's all. I wasn't thinking. But anyway, I'd stay away from this jerk. Hoyt! What kind of a name is that? Sounds like he's clearing his throat."

* * *

"Whoa, you're *way* overdressed," Ian said, as he walked into the apartment. He wore cut-offs, tennis shoes and a tie-dyed T-shirt. "Don't you have any jeans?"

He slapped a document-sized envelope into my hands and when I opened it, I found a framed 8 X 10 glossy of Thatcher Reid and me.

"Where should I hang it?" I asked him.

"I don't know? Over your desk?" I glanced toward my desk. There was a perfect place right next to the window. "Get me a hammer and a nail. I'll hang it while you're changing."

"I don't think we have a hammer," I said.

"Of course you do! How'd you hang these mirrors?"

"I don't know. Maybe she used a broom handle."

"She didn't use a broom handle. You have to have a hammer."

I ransacked drawers and found a tiny hammer and even located a nail. As I started for my room, Ian was sitting on the edge of my desk measuring off the wall space with his fingers.

"What?" he said when he saw me lingering there.

"I don't want you snooping around my desk," I said.

His mouth gaped open and his hand flew to his chest as if the remark had taken his breath away.

"Who could find anything there, anyway?"

My jeans were under the bed. They were hip-huggers and if I wore them with a ribbed pullover, it was one of my few fashion ensembles that accentuated my waist.

"Hey," he yelled to me, "don't have that many sponsors for your bowling thing, do you?"

"Are you snooping?" I hollered out to him.

"Trust is a rare thing with you, I guess," he called back.

When I returned to the living room, he was sitting with his feet on my desk, reading my newsletter.

"You have a typo right here," he said.

He took me to a barbecue dive about forty minutes east of Dallas. It was a shack, really, in the middle of nothing. Loud R&B music sailed through the battered screen door. The floor was three inches deep in sawdust and newspapers served as tablecloths. We were the only white people there, but Ian seemed to know everyone, particularly Del, the owner.

"Is this place safe?" I asked.

"Hey, I thought *you* were the liberal."

"I have a question," I said later, as we pigged out. "What do you know about this committee Peddy established?"

"Probably just what you do: he set it up and he went outside the district to do so."

"What's he up to?"

"Want my opinion?"

I nodded.

"It's just an opinion—I don't have any facts."

"I never worry about facts," I said.

"I think he wants the committee to appoint him."

Stunned, I sat back in my chair. "I bet you're right."

"Look at the names. Everyone owes him something. Every one of them."

* * *

"How'd you find this place?" I asked when I'd eaten so much I thought I'd pop the button off my jeans and blind someone with it. Ian was still putting it away as if it were his last meal.

"When I was in college and broke, I started scouting out dives. Often, they're real finds. Even though I'm a reporter now and rolling in dough, I still can't kick the habit."

"Where'd you go to college?" I asked.

"I went to UT for graduate school."

"You have a graduate degree?"

"Yes, ma'am."

"How old are you?"

"Twenty-eight."

"Where did you go for regular college?"

He leaned on his elbows and edged toward me. "I'll tell you, if you promise to keep it to yourself."

I crossed my heart.

"Harvard."

We both laughed. Texans were suspicious of Ivy League schools. When a friend of mine—a Princeton graduate— wanted to run for office, he got an associate degree from a community college and listed that, rather than Princeton, on his brochures.

"So, now I have a question?" he said, wiping his mouth with a badly-shredded napkin.

"Shoot!"

"How come you never went to school?"

"How do you know I didn't?"

"I know everything," he said. "I'm a reporter." He ripped two ribs apart. "Know what else I know?"

"What?"

"I know you've got something going with Vic Davis. Del!" he called over his shoulder, "Can we get some more rolls?"

"Who...who told you that?"

"You did."

"I did not."

"You know something else? Yesterday when I came by your apartment, I lied to you."

"How?"

"By implying I had never seen you before when I had."

"I don't remember ever seeing you before."

"Well, I kinda blend in."

It was a funny line, but I was too paranoid to laugh. "Where did you see me?"

"At Love Field, when Vic Davis flew in."

"I didn't see you there." My stomach tightened a little.

"Well, I wonder why?" He ripped another rib free and pointed it at me. "See, I think Davis is a little bit of a prig anyway, but I noticed at Love Field that every time I ask a question, he's staring behind me. So, I glance over my shoulder. And I see you. Staring back at him."

"Of course, I was looking at him. Everyone was—"

"*Looking* is not the word. After everything was over, I tried to find you. I was going to pretend to interview you, but you were gone, which surprised me. I'm sure he was planning to slip away with you. I thought—erroneously, I guess—that you were too smart for him and got the hell out while you could."

"You're right: I left early."

"But somehow, you got back together."

"What makes you so sure?"

"You. You told me you might work for him. He dangles that possibility over the heads of his new conquests. It doesn't take a college degree to know a guy's not gonna hire someone he's sleeping with. Davis couldn't afford such a large staff."

"It's getting late and I have to work tomorrow—"

"You're mad at me." He tilted back in his chair, making the two front legs airborne.

"I'm not mad. Anyone can make a mistake. Even a reporter."

"However, I haven't, have I?"

I stood and walked out the screen door. Ian tossed some money on the table and followed. When he caught up, he draped his arm around my shoulder and walked me to the VW.

"Hey, it's your business," he said opening the car. "You should just know, the guy's a predator."

I slammed my door so fast that I nearly caught his hand. When he took his seat, he tossed the keys on the dashboard and turned toward me.

"I want to go out with you again," he said, "and I sense you're probably not inclined to agree to that just now. So, I have bribes." He pulled tickets from his ashtray. "Oil lobby's giving a big party in Austin."

"I hate the oil lobby."

"Well, eat their food and drink their booze and say bad things about them anyway. That's as Texan as the Alamo! Everyone will be there. What do you say? You might even get to see your boyfriend again."

"He's not my boyfriend!"

"'Course he'll be there with his wife."

"He's *not* my boyfriend!"

On the way home, he asked me what I planned to do with my life, what books I read, and what movies were my favorites as if there was no tension between us. I mellowed and told him about the list of Senators I kept, which now included Thatcher Reid.

"You'd like D.C.," he said.

"Wouldn't you miss me?" I teased him.

"Well, it looks as if I'll be leaving soon, myself."

"Where are you going?" I felt a little betrayed.

"*The New York Times*."

"When?"

"It's unclear, but probably this fall."

When we reached the Saracen parking lot, Ian turned off the motor and we sat there talking. Finally—and I'm not sure why, because I still felt skeptical about him after that Vic Davis bomb—I said: "The oddest thing happened yesterday on the bus."

"What could you have done, really?" he said, after I described the incident. "Other than pray the guy died a slow and painful death…soon."

"I should have done something. Called him a racist or something."

"He already told everyone that."

"I could have said something nice to the woman."

"You think she was going to cheer up because a white kid says 'it's okay'? Believe me, she would have viewed any kind words from you as merely patronizing. And she'd be right."

"How do you know so much?"

"You think Jews don't put up with that crap?"

I thought about this for a minute. "You're Jewish?"

"Gloria! Come on. Feldman. What did you think I was?"

"A reporter."

"You mean it never dawned on you that I was—"

"I never thought about it. Besides, Ian does not conjure up Israel for me."

"A concession to my mother." I just looked at him. "She's Irish-Catholic."

"Does she have red hair?"

"How'd you guess?"

"ESP."

I agreed to go with him to Austin: not just because I could be bought with a high-rolling ticket to a political event—which, of course, I could—but because I kind of liked him. And Vic would be there.

* * *

Within seconds of arriving at my office, the phone rang. I dropped the *Morning News* on my desk and grabbed for the receiver.

"Gloria?" Lonnie said. "I just wanted to make sure there were files on your desk?"

"Yes, Ma'am."

"I wouldn't want you to sit around there all day with nothing to do."

"No, Ma'am."

"Okay. Well, I'll check in with you from time to time to see how things are going."

"Yes, Ma'am."

It was all bullshit. She was just checking up on me.

I had been writing the Peddy press release in my mind ever since Ian shared his suspicions with me, so I wanted to get that done right away. I flicked on the typewriter and started in.

> *THE DALLAS COUNTY YOUNG DEMOCRATS condemn Democratic County Chairman, Dexter Peddy, for his highhanded and criminal tactics in appointing a committee to select a candidate for Henry Dunlop's state legislative seat.*
>
> *EVIDENTLY Dexter Peddy is trying to restrict the selection of a candidate and he is using his characteristic heavy-handed fascist and totalitarian techniques to do so.*
>
> *THE YOUNG DEMOCRATS vigorously denounce the possibility that Peddy himself might well be the preference of this biased and handpicked committee.*

I needed Executive Committee approval, so I called my officers and read the resolution. No one objected. After making copies, I mailed one to the *Morning News* and the other to the *Times Herald.*

Once I finished, I spread the *Morning News* over my desk and read while I sipped coffee. A column on the editorial page, entitled, "The Davis Campaign: There's More to Running for Office Than Kissing Babes" stopped me. Ian did not do editorials, but somehow I sensed his touch. Contrary to my expectations, it did not contain anything about Vic's extramarital activities. Rather, it lambasted him for sidestepping controversial questions: namely the war in Vietnam.

Since I needed to buy a gown, I studied the advertisements. Veronica had agreed to go shopping with me on Thursday when the stores stayed open late. I wanted to look fabulous for the party. For Vic.

I did half my file folders so that if anyone checked up on me they'd see I'd made some progress. Then I went to work re-doing the newsletter Lonnie'd destroyed. Once that was out of the way, I fooled around a while, making phone calls and such. Around eleven, I took a short break. On the way back from the soda machine, I noticed a light blinking in Lonnie Mossman's office, so I stepped in to investigate. Her private line was ringing. After ten rings, it was still going, so answered it.

"Lonnie!" It was a desperate-sounding woman.

"She doesn't work on Saturdays," I said.

"Who is this?" she demanded.

"No one. I just work here and I heard the phone ringing."

"Oh. When will she be in?"

"I just told you, she doesn't work on Saturdays."

"When she shows up, tell her to call Lisa." She hung up before I could say anything else.

Since I was there, I thought I might as well look around. Though I'd worked for her for over a year, Lonnie remained mysterious. No one at Freedom Mutual was as private and aloof. When I'd first come to work, I'd sensed a kinship—believed that we would become friends—but that never panned out. Though virtually everyone on our floor was female, only two of the supervisors were, and most of the underlings resented working for women. Because she was solemn and demanding, people called her a bitch. Granted, I had my problems with Lonnie Mossman. But the supervisor for the bookkeepers—a man—ranted at his workers, called them degrading names, tossed papers in their faces and required that they work right up until the quitting buzzer went off. The rest of us had our desks cleared, coats on and were halfway out the door by then. Everyone respected him. Personally, I liked working for a woman—even Lonnie. Since I spent my free time in what could only be called a man's world, I wasn't all that convinced that men were inherently better at running things. As far as I could tell, a penis was a detriment to just about anything requiring rational behavior. Maybe it was the fact that I was *for* Lonnie that made her indifference so hard.

Behind her desk and to the right was a large file cabinet: to the left, a bookcase. The bookcase was full of manuals, but her file cabinet had her personal records, including her resume. Lonnie Mossman was thirty-seven, from Philadelphia, graduated from Trinity where she majored in math and minored in biology. Her grade point average was 3.68 and she had won a science award her junior year. Her first job was as a receptionist at a medical research institution and after five years there she married Theodore Mossman and relocated to Dallas. She took two years off to have a baby, and then was hired by Freedom Mutual as a supervisor. I never realized Lonnie was a mother: it was easier picturing my parents having sex.

What was odd about Lonnie's office was the absence of anything personal. Everyone else had pictures of family members or boyfriends; trinkets; potted plants; pictures or poems by their children; and whimsical toys that had meaning only to the owner. But Lonnie's desk was as sterile as an operating room. She had a green marbleized pencil cup filled with pens and pencils, an empty two-tiered in-box, and a message spike skewering five messages. I flipped through them. Most were from executives, but two were from this Lisa person and one said URGENT across the bottom. Just for kicks, I dialed the number to see if it was a business, but Lisa answered and I hung up.

She'd locked her desk drawers. I lifted her blotter and the sudden gust of air this created gently boosted some photographs causing them to heave up and then land with a quiet clap back on the desk. One was a picture of a beautiful woman with brown hair and vivid blue eyes. She wore a black leather jacket: its large collar stood up in back, like a thug's. She smiled seductively at the camera. There was a strange little dimple, not on her cheek where most people had them, but under it at the corner of her mouth. A beauty mark on the tip of her upturned nose gave her an impish look. "Love, Lisa," it said. The other two were pictures of a child—first as an infant and then as a toddler.

I was so caught up in my research, that I didn't hear the footsteps until it was too late. Lonnie Mossman was just rounding the corner. Luckily, she was looking at my desk and not her office; luckily, I had been working on company business. I slid out of her chair onto the floor, realizing at once that while I could have made something up about being in her chair, there was not much to say about being under her desk. But I had made my decision and was stuck with it. I peeked through a two-inch space at the bottom of the desk and watched her approach. My mind raced but nothing believable came to me. She walked to her file cabinet and reached behind it, retrieving a set of keys that must have been hanging back there. Miraculously, as she unlocked her desk, she failed to notice me curled up at her feet. From the skinny middle drawer, she extracted some sort of document and, after studying it, carried it out of her office. Looking through the two-inch space, I watched her head for the Xerox machine. It was now or never. I belly-crawled out from under the desk, and peeked around the corner. She was hunched over the machine making copies. The second I reached the hallway, I greeted her, as if returning from the ladies' room.

"Miss Mossman. I didn't know you were coming in today."

"I've scheduled an appointment."

"You had a call," I shouted down the hallway. "Someone named Lisa."

Her face clouded for a second. Then she gathered up her papers and clutched them to her as if she worried I was selling secrets to Fireman's Fund.

Thirty minutes later, a tall, lean, well-dressed man slipped into Lonnie's office and shut the door. Though he was attractive, he had a million character lines in his face, which probably made him look older than he was. He seemed familiar. I *knew* him: or at least I'd seen him before. It irritated me that I couldn't place him and I kept pretending I had to go to the bathroom so that I could walk past her office to get a closer look. Something was definitely up. Lonnie and the man poured over the document she'd copied and once, thought I would have *never* thought it possible, Lonnie seemed to be crying. I was sure she hadn't show that much emotion even in childbirth

I just about drove myself nuts all afternoon trying to place Lonnie's visitor until that evening when Ian called and took my mind off him.

"Hey," he said after ten minutes of chit-chat. "Did you read today's paper?" I could tell he was dying to get my reaction to the editorial.

"I was just reading the *Times Herald*," I replied, fighting to keep from snickering.

"Not the *Times Herald*! Did you read the *Morning News*?"

"I didn't and I feel guilty about that, now that I know you and all. But I had to work today and when I got home my roommate had thrown it out."

"So what'd you think of the editorial?"

"I just told you—"

"That's bullshit. Anyway, the title was mine!"

"I *knew* it was, you asshole!" I shouted and we both burst out laughing.

We went to see *A Man and a Woman* that night at the Village Theater. It was terribly romantic and when the couple finally landed in a hotel room, I found myself daydreaming about Vic. Ian put his arm around me and pulled me over to his shoulder. It was cool in the theater and I was surprised at the warmth he radiated. I leaned against him. Once, he rubbed his cheek on my forehead and I thought he might kiss me, but he didn't.

On the way home, he didn't look at me when he said, "Wanna come over to my place for a while?" I wanted to spend more time with him, but I wasn't sure I was ready to make a decision about sleeping with him and I had a feeling that was going to come up. Generally on dates, I could play the virgin card and most guys respected that. Sort of. But Ian knew better.

"I better just go home."

He didn't respond. When we got to my parking lot, he turned off the key but didn't get out of the car. As he leaned against his door, a streetlight threw a strip of yellow across his face.

"I love your hair," he said. I almost laughed. He ran his fingers down my hair and lifted a section up and let it fall back down. "It's the color of buttered toast and it's so soft."

"All you ever think about is food."

Rather than laugh he leaned over and kissed me, lightly and then more energetically. His mouth was hot. I reached for him, but the "Love Bug" was misnamed, and so it was hard to do much easily.

"Come back to my place," he said.

"No. We can't." I wanted to, but I was feeling a little like a slut. Now that I'd shed my hymen, was I just going to sleep with anyone I found attractive?

"Why not?"

Since I didn't have an answer, I didn't say anything and after a while he got out of the car and walked me to my apartment.

"Don't be mad at me," I said, lingering at my door.

"I'll get over it." Then he walked away.

"You're home early." Veronica was watching television. It was ten-forty-five.

"How come you're not at the club?" I asked.

"Just didn't feel like it. I saw Hunter earlier and it sorta, you know, depressed me."

"I can imagine. Is he all right?"

"I guess. Even in that horrible jump suit, he looked great. God, I just love him so much."

"Did you tell him about the baby?"

"No. I figure he has enough ta worry about right now. You think I should?"

"I don't know. Maybe." Hunter would insist on an abortion. "I guess he has a right to know."

"Yeah. Maybe next time." She walked across the room and straightened debris on one of the end tables. "How was your date? He's awfully cute."

"It was all right, I guess."

"Oh, no. Did you smart off already and send him packin'?"

"I'm not sure." I slumped on the sofa. Veronica glanced toward me, eyebrows raised, waiting for the inevitable request for advice. "Veronica?" I said after a moment, "how do you know whether you should sleep with some guy?"

"Oh, I get it!" she grinned. "He wanted to get laid and you didn't."

"It's not that I didn't want to, it's just—. I mean, *everyone* you go out with must try to—How do you know whether you should or not?"

"Well!" She fluffed up a pillow and plopped down next to me. "My first rule is that I never sleep with anyone unless I truly want to. Now that might sound silly, but it's a good rule. 'Cause you'll find, Gloria, that guys'll use about any trick: guilt, pity, sarcasm, insults. You name it. I had a guy cry once.

It wasn't even like he'd been out lots of money—we'd played miniature golf. Don't ever fall for any of that crud, believe me."

"What if you maybe want to."

"Then, what's the problem? Now that we have the pill, there's nothing ta worry about." She rolled her eyes and smiled. "Unless you decide ta quit takin' it, like me. No one cool thinks it's wrong anymore. That is, not until you break up with some guy, then he'll call you a slut, just like in the olden days. But, sex today is kinda like kissing was in high school: it's probably cheap ta do it on the first date, but after that, who cares?"

"I don't know." I stalled. "Have you ever slept with two guys at once?" I asked.

Veronica slapped her hand over her chest as if she might be having a heart attack. "You mean in the same room at the same time?"

"No. I mean has there ever been a time that you had two, you know, lovers at once?"

"Oh, well, sure. I mean, sometimes that's just good insurance. That way, if you get dumped, you don't have ta pound the dating pavement when you're low."

Someone knocked at the door and when Veronica opened it, Jo Beth breezed in.

"Hi, girl," she chirped. "The club's dead tonight. I don't know where ever'one's at. Thought I'd hit Greenville Avenue for an hour of two. See what's up there. Wanna come?"

"I don't know, Jo Beth. I'm not in a party mood."

"Well, even more reason why ya should get out and dance. Come on. I don't wanna go by myself. I'd look desperate. Besides, I heard that Scott Beardsley was headin' that way and he promised me he'd be at the Saracen tonight. If I show up alone, he'll think I'm chasin' him ."

"Oh, okay. But only for an hour or two, Jo Beth."

"Sure thing."

"Wanna join us, Gloria?" Veronica asked and Jo Beth's body slumped a little.

"No. Thanks. I'll be fine."

"You know what, Gloria? You should glance through some of my *Cosmopolitan* Magazines. They offer some good advice to the liberated *Cosmo* girl."

In spite of my skepticism, once they left, I slipped into her room and scrounged up some back copies. I searched the tables of contents for relevant pieces. Three issues in, I spotted "I've Got Two Lovers and I'm Not

Ashamed," and thought I'd struck gold. Unfortunately, the article was about a *publishing girl* who divided her time between career and husband. Though *Cosmopolitan* courted single women, a lot of articles focused on how to keep husbands from running off with their secretaries. I wondered if Vic's wife subscribed. Just when I had given up the idea that I would discover anything pertinent, I found an article entitled, "Are You a Nymphomaniac?" Since this was a concern, I turned to page forty-three but stopped reading after leaning that the most salient feature of a nymphomaniac was an inability to have orgasms.

After reading all those *Cosmopolitans*, I felt like doing something feminine, so I opened the medicine cabinet where Veronica stored her cosmetics. There were jars and pots and tubes of creams. I found four masques, each a different color. One promised to tighten and firm, the second would moisturize, still another could stimulate, while the fourth would deep clean. I examined my face in the mirror but couldn't determine which treatment I needed. Dipping my index finger into the icy pink one, I painted a flower on my left cheek. Then with the mud one, I sketched a peace sign on the other. I drew a mint green infinity symbol on my forehead and a gold star on my chin. Then I smeared them across my face and immediately regretted it. The shades did not get along and I ended up with this puke-colored goop. Just as I turned on the faucet to rinse it off, the phone rang. Hurrying to my nightstand, I lifted the receiver of my blue princess phone. The illuminated dial was the only light in the room.

"Can I speak ta Veronica?" I recognized Hoyt's voice.

"She's out for the evening."

"Would ya ask her ta give me a call when she gets in?"

"She may be spending the night at her boyfriend's," I said. My face felt as if it had eaten a persimmon and I sounded like someone whose teeth were soaking somewhere.

"Well, then, have her call tomorrow sometime."

"I sure will," I promised, hanging up noisily.

In the bathroom, I looked in the mirror at my now-chalky complexion. I smiled, then frowned, then made a series of stupid faces. When I finished, my face was as scored and parched-looking as a dried out river bed.

I looked like Anna Tyson's husband.

I froze. Anna Tyson, my old mentor from the YRs. Her lawyer husband, Clearance, had just spent the afternoon in Lonnie's office.

When I scrubbed off the masques, I looked exactly the same.

* * *

"I'm doing a story on your press release and I have a quote from Peddy you might want to respond to." It was Jim Drury, the political reporter for the *Times Herald.*

"What's he say?" I asked.

"Let me get it. Okay. 'Gloria Warren reigns over a group of immoral, pot-smoking, flag-burning degenerates'—he wanted to say queers, but I discouraged him,—'and her opinion and that of her so-called organization, should not be of interest to anyone.' Oh, and I'm paraphrasing here, but he added that what you needed was a good...romance, or something like that. Any response?"

"Just say that the real reason we don't want him to leave his current position for the state legislature is that no one could fill his shoes. Each time we've changed County Chairman, we've gone from bad to worse and frankly, there isn't anyone around bad enough to be worse than him."

Both papers carried our feud, but the *Morning News* never called for a statement. I clipped both pieces and put them in my file. I love seeing my name in print. So far I had eight articles. Most were the results of press releases that the YD sent in during my presidency. But sometimes reporters called me for interviews. Three articles included my picture, which was even better. There was the one with Senator Reid; my high school picture, which we included when I became YD President the first time; and a picture taken when I arrived at some meeting and stopped to speak to a district Judge. I'm sure the photographer wanted the Judge, but I was there and that was all I cared about. Sometimes I liked to take all those clippings out and line them up on the floor and just look at them.

Once they interviewed me on television. That was fabulous, except when it was over, it was over. You couldn't clip it out for your scrapbook or file. Couldn't show it to someone later and say, "See, I'm someone. I was on television."

Tuesday, there was a negative article, under Ian's by-line, about a series of votes Vic had cast on minimum wage. The gist of the piece was that he had not always been the moderate he was passing for. Generally, the *Morning News* tried to paint moderates as communists, so this was an odd swerve.

Thursday came and I hadn't spoken to Ian since our date Saturday. I worried that he had changed his mind about taking me to the Austin party and I didn't want to spend a fortune on a dress for nothing.

"Feldman," he said when he picked up the phone.

"Are we still friends?" I asked.

There was a long pause before he said, "Sure, why not?"

"Do you still want me to go with you Saturday?"

"Do you want to?"

"If you want me to."

"What is this, eighth grade? I asked you, didn't I?"

"Yeah, but you seemed in a little bit of a snit last time I saw you. I just thought if you were having second thoughts—"

"I'm not having second thoughts," he snapped. "We'll need to leave around three."

"God, I'm going to have to be dressed up from three on?"

"We can change in the room."

"The room?"

"Did you think we were driving back at two in the morning?" he snapped.

"Aren't we touchy?"

"I'll see you Saturday." He hung up.

I wanted to tell him to forget it: I couldn't afford a dress I'd only wear once anyway. Who'd have thought he'd have so much jerk in him. I dialed his number but then hung up.

* * *

The phone rang just as I walked into the apartment.

"Didn't she call you back last time?" I asked once Hoyt identified himself.

"No, she didn't."

"I'll level with you," I said, "she's in love. In fact, they're talking about marriage."

"Well, she should at least tell me that, don't you think?"

"Absolutely! I don't know where her manners have gone."

"Will ya just have her call me?"

"I promise," I said. But I had my fingers crossed.

I'd barely hung up when Veronica called. "I got some good news and some bad news."

"The good news is?"

"I got the show!" We did all the appropriate squealing and cheering required for such news. "But the bad news is, I can't go shopping with you."

"You're kidding?" I sagged against the wall. It was the end of the world.

"I'm so sorry, Gloria. They need me for publicity shots and costume fittings. They want ta get movin' right along on this."

"What am I going to do?"

"They're havin' a terrific sale at Neiman's. Go to the Mezzanine and ask someone ta help you. They're very good."

"Veronica, they always treat me like I'm a troll."

"Ask for Noreene. Tell her you're my roommate."

Normally, I'd have to sell an organ to buy something at Neiman's. Not only that, but all the employees, even the janitors, knew I was intruding into the world of good taste. I took the stairs to the Mezzanine level glancing over my shoulders, worried security guards would grab me and toss me over the railing, where I would suffer a humiliating death impaled on some umbrella in Women's Notions. My family would spend the rest of their lives paying for the silk and cashmere scarves my blood desecrated.

Once upstairs, I crept to the counter where a clerk worried over paperwork. Not daring to be rude, I waited for her to come to a stopping point. She was about forty-five, with smoke-colored hair styled in a bouffant bubble that looked as if it would remain intact during a tornado. Her tailored suit with rhinestone buttons seemed dressy for work. She wore so much make-up that I suspected the store furnished it free of charge. Suddenly, she looked up and past me, as if beckoned by a noise too high for lower-class people to hear. Then her gaze fell on me and, for an instant, she seemed startled.

"Are you looking for something?" She nervously fingering the beads around her neck.

"Ah...yes ma'am. Is...ah...Noreene around?"

"Goodness no. It's her day off," she replied, as if anyone literate should at least know that. Assuming the conversation was over, she returned to her work. I waited for another moment to ask for help, but without even glancing my way, she gathered up her papers and carried them to a back office.

I decided to try Sanger-Harris instead, but as I started down the stairs, I glanced to the right and spotted Julia Poston holding a sparkling gown in front of her body, examining herself in a mirror. I edged her way, hovering first on one side of a rack of clothes and then on the other, but her concentration on herself never faltered. I found an identical dress and gasped at its three thousand dollar price tag. Following her example, I grabbed a random frock and stood by her at the mirror studying myself.

"Julia?" I said, as if just noticing her.

Tearing herself from her reflection, she frowned as she focused on me.

"I'm sorry. Have we met?" she asked in a slow, husky voice.

"In Highland Park. At that coffee for Senator Davis?"

"Oh, of course," she said, but I could tell she'd never seen me before. She held up another dress and posed. I watched her.

"What did you think of him?" I asked after a while.

"Of whom?"

"Senator Davis."

"Oh," she replied, looking at herself from different angles, "I'd screw him."

Startled by her honesty, I was momentarily struck dumb. "I mean politically," I stammered. "What'd you think of him politically?"

"I'm not interested in politics." She glanced at the dress I clutched. "Going somewhere special?"

"Yes." I held the dress up the way she had been doing. "What do you think of this?"

For the first time she contemplated me in earnest. "I think you'll look a member of the Royal Family in that. Plus I'm not sure you wear a size eighteen."

"Oh, gee. Is this an eighteen? People are so careless about hanging clothes back up correctly."

"What sort of party is it?" She tried on a series of sultry expressions to see which went best with the beaded gown.

"It's some party the oil lobby's having in Austin—"

"That's where I'm going," she interrupted, smiling broadly. "Maybe I'll see you there."

She turned back to the mirror but I just stood there watching her. After a moment, she sighed and glanced back at me.

"Was there something else?" she asked.

"No," I said quickly. She kept staring at me until I felt self-conscious. "Well, bye," I said.

"Good-bye."

I hung the dress on the rack and started for the stairs.

"Hey!" she called out. I turned around. She had followed me. "What was your name again?"

"Gloria. Gloria Warren."

"You...couldn't find a dress?" she said, turning, her arm presenting the vast array of satin and sequins and taffeta and silk. My head jerked toward the sales clerk who was back at the counter.

"Uh...no. I didn't, you know, see anything I liked. I have dresses at home—"

"Would you like me to help you?" she asked.

"Oh, well. I'm sure you're busy and all—"

"I'm not going to beg."

"Yes, I'd like it if you'd help me."

"Okay, you need to tell me two things." She hooked her arm through mine while leading me toward the clothes. "How much can you spend? And what do you hope to accomplish?"

"Oh, I don't know. Sixty dollars?"

"Sixty dollars!" She almost staggered. "Are you wanting a handkerchief or a dress?"

"Eighty?"

She sighed. "Let's look at the sale rack. And what do you want to accomplish?"

"Accomplish? Someone invited me—"

"No. I mean, what are your goals for the evening? A girl always has to have goals."

"I want to look really good."

"Well, no one starts out *wanting* to look like shit. It's just something that sometimes happens. The question I'm asking is, *why* do you want to look really good? Are you hoping to get married or laid? You want to make someone jealous or break up a marriage? What?"

"Well, there's this guy—"

"There's always a guy. How rich is he?"

"I don't believe he's rich at all."

She stopped dead in her tracks. "Then why bother?"

"Because I really like him."

Her body drooped a little. "I remember that. So, he's asked you to this party—"

"No! Someone else did."

"Ah. But he's going to be there?"

"Yes."

"With someone else?"

"Yes." I glanced away.

"His wife?"

"No! He's not married."

"Of course, he's not. Tell me. Have you slept with him?"

I started to lie, but I knew she'd see through me. "Yes," I whispered.

"We'll just have to remind him what he's missing, won't we?"

Tucked behind a partition, against a far wall, were the dresses that had overstayed their welcome.

"What are you?" she asked, scanning me. "A six?" She zeroed in on the sixes and shoved everything else aside. "Glance through these and show me what you like."

"What about this?" I asked, spotting a hot pink mini dress with ostrich feathers along the hem.

"Christ!" she shouted. "That reminds me of something I saw growing up in the projects."

"*You* grew up in the projects?"

"Yes," she said. "Isn't America thrilling?"

We settled on a two-piece dress, made of a black, stretchy fabric. The floor-length gored skirt flared gradually on the way down. The wrap-around top had long sleeves, ending in soft ruffles of the same fabric, which fell over the hands. After it snapped at the waist—which was snug even for me, and was probably why they had reduced the price so much—the jacket fell to mid hip where it ended in another row of ruffles. Its neckline plunged, but the ruffles there concealed most of the flesh. I looked fabulous.

I tried on my dress for Veronica the second I got home and pretended I'd found it on my own. She was astonished. Later, she babbled about the audition and the show and the money.

"The retainer will be enough ta get Hunter out."

My stomach tightening as it always did now when Hunter's name came up. "Well, okay, okay, that's cool. It's your money. Uh, but I want to say something before things get much more out of hand." She was flying from her success and not paying close attention to me. "This isn't easy for me, and I want you to know that I'm terribly, terribly sorry, but—"

"In my heart, Gloria, I know this was the right thing ta do. Besides, there's some hope now." I glanced up. "Accordin' ta Hunter's lawyer, if we could locate that informer and get him ta admit he made a mistake or somethin', Hunter could flea bargain."

"Plea bargain?"

"Yeah. Isn't that great? I tell ya, this is the best news I've heard since all this happened."

"So it would help if the informer came forward and—"

"If the informer just admitted he lied, Hunter *might* get off with probation or something like that."

"What would happen to the informer?"

"Well, he could be tried for perjury."

"Perjury! Jesus Christ! Doesn't that seem excessive?"

"Well, Gloria, you weren't this concerned about poor Hunter and he's innocent."

"Do they have leads?" Suddenly, my finger ached: I had bitten the nail down to the quick.

"Hunter's lawyer suggested a private detective. I told him ta do what he had to. I'd pay him back if it took forever."

"Can't he just ask the authorities?" My stomach churned.

"He did, but they protect their informers—even the scum. Besides, it was anonymous. He found out that much."

I took a breath and covered my mouth with my hand. She stared into space before she continued.

"There's another bright side ta all this. I just betcha now that Hunter's in trouble, she might be ready ta kick him out." She cut her eyes in my direction. "And guess who'll be standin' around waitin' for him?" She beamed and pointed toward herself with both thumbs. "But you were gonna say something."

"Oh, nothing, really."

"It must have been something."

"I...just wanted to say..." I looked at her. She had such a sweet, trusting face. I turned away quickly. "that if things work out...I'll make an effort to get along with him."

She threw her arms around my neck. "Oh, I'm so lucky ta have a friend like you."

As I was hanging up my dress someone knocked at the door. Veronica yelled that she would get it. It occurred to me that my good black heels might need polishing and so I was crawling around in my closet when I sensed someone was watching me. Looking up, I saw Ian looming at my bedroom door.

"Hi." I said, clambering to my feet. Only then did I realize how much I'd missed him. He wore a madras shirt and chinos and had pulled his hair into a pony tail at the nape of his neck.

"Hi."

"I bought a dress for the party," I said, turning to my closet. "Wanna see it?"

"Not right now. I'm kinda pressed for time." He glanced down at his watch.

"You can't stay?"

"No. I've got to—. I have some things I need to do."

"Oh." I tried not to seem disappointed. "You must have come by for a reason."

"Yeah! I almost forgot. Peddy announced who the appointee would be."

"It's not him?"

"Supposedly it was going to be but all the publicity ruined it for him. Congratulations."

"Aw. Too bad."

"I knew you'd feel contrite."

"Who is it?"

"Pete Thornton."

"Never heard of him."

"Well, I thought you'd want to know." Ian picked at something on the door frame with his thumbnail and then glanced toward the living room. I could tell he was planning his escape.

"Let's at least have a Coke to celebrate." I grabbed his arm and led him to the sofa.

"Really, I can't. I have to go." He pulled away.

"Are you mad at me?"

"For what?"

"For stealing your idea?"

"I *gave* you the idea. I knew what you'd do." He reached for the doorknob, but I put my hand over his and stopped him.

"Ian? Are you mad at me?" His gaze shifted from me to a spot just beyond my shoulder.

"No," he said and he bent down and kissed me lightly on the mouth. I just stared at him. "No," he repeated and tapped me on the head with his notebook. "I'll see you Saturday."

I peeked through the curtains and watched him walk down the sidewalk until he vanished into the shadows. Then, I called Greg Monroe and told him about Pete Thornton.

* * *

Greg called Friday: he had dirt on Thornton. Greg and his girlfriend, Rachel, Herman and I agreed to meet at nine at The Hair of the Dog, a seedy coffee house close to the fairgrounds, famous for everything Dexter Peddy associated with us. Greg haunted it since it was a block from the Draft Information Center.

"I'll let Rachel fill you in," Greg said, once we got squared away.

Rachel's radical political beliefs could be grating. She treated me with thinly veiled contempt because I shaved my legs and slept in a bed rather than a sleeping bag. Greg was the only reason she even acknowledged I existed. The last time we'd all gotten together she called me an opportunistic cupcake because I said I wouldn't allow the YDs to be part of anything illegal. (She and Greg proposed pouring sugar in gas tanks of trucks hauling grapes from the Valley.) Rachel had ties with the Weatherman and her rhetoric embraced violent overthrow of the Establishment. It always made me nervous to be around her. She also belonged to a clandestine nationwide group called WATCH OUT, which operated in over thirty states. WATCH OUT's main goal was to gather information on right-wing hate groups.

"Pete Thornton's involved, not only in the John Birch Society, but in the Klan, as well."

From a macramé shoulder bag, Rachel withdrew a Xerox of a grainy photograph, obviously enlarged several times. Some men were clustered in front of a wall-sized rebel flag. The focus of the picture was a fat, balding man holding a crudely painted sign that read "White is Might; White is Right." Rachel assured us he was no problem any more, and no one dared to ask why. But she pointed to a guy just over his right shoulder.

"Thornton!" She announced.

We took turns studying the photograph, but since none of us had seen Pete Thornton before, we could neither verify nor refute her claim.

Our waitress arrived with coffee. I glanced her way and then did a double take. She looked familiar. She had short dark hair and a beauty mark on the end of her nose, making her look a little elfish.

"Have we met?" I asked her.

She smiled at me. "I don't believe so," she said, moving on to the next table.

"Greg," I said, tugging at his sleeve, "She looks familiar. Is she involved in politics?"

"Lisa? Not that I know of."

"She's awfully pretty."

"Yeah, what a waste, huh?"

"What do you mean?

"She's a lesbian."

"Which is *her* business," Rachel said.

"Hey, I'm not making a judgment call."

I looked at the waitress again, still couldn't place her, shrugged and forgot about it.

Rachel extracted another Xerox, "Here's one taken along the Kennedy parade route."

This one showed a mob of people on a downtown sidewalk, obviously waiting for the motorcade. In the center two women held a banner: "Impeach JFK for Crimes Against Whites" Next to one stood the alleged Pete Thornton.

"But he's not holding the banner," Herman said. "Maybe he's an innocent bystander."

"You can tell by his body language, vis a vis the woman to his left—the woman holding the banner—that he's with them."

"We should publicize this," I said.

"Dunno," Herman said. "Shit like this could *win* votes here."

"True," Greg cut in. "But not in Dunlop's district."

"I'll put it in the newsletter," I said after a brief hesitation. Hate groups were scary and I worried I might be putting myself in danger.

"Forget the newsletter," Rachel cut in. "No one reads that fluff sheet. The media has to get involved."

"Excuse me, Rachel," I couldn't believe I was fighting to get myself on a hit list. "A lot of people read that newsletter and it's routinely reprinted in the *Times Herald*—"

"Yes, in their little gossip column that no one takes seriously."

"More people read gossip columns than hard news—" I stopped.

The door to The Hair of the Dog had banged shut and when my gaze jumped that way, there was Ian. With a striking woman. She was tall and thin and dramatically dressed in a colorful flowing skirt and large noisy jewelry. Her dark hair fell to her waist and she glided across the floor like a dancer. Though they walked past us, Ian was so enthralled in something she was saying that he never glanced our way.

Rachel was spewing something—probably at my expense—but I didn't listen. I suddenly felt trivial and frivolous. Maybe the newsletter was a joke, and maybe I'd been kidding myself about Ian.

They found a table some ways from us and he sat with his back to me. No affection passed between them, but she kept smiling and he seemed delighted. Thank God I'd never slept with him.

"What do you think's going to happen in the Governor's race?" I asked.

They all looked at each other and then at me. Clearly, I'd interrupted an ongoing conversation—probably still about Pete Thornton. But I didn't care. Suddenly, I wanted to talk about Vic.

"Connally'll run again," Greg pronounced.

"Maybe not," Rachel said. "He's bored."

"Yeah, but Lyndon doesn't want in-fighting here—not with all the shit he has on his plate."

"Suppose he doesn't run—what then?" I asked.

The waitress brought coffee to Ian's table. His date lifted her mug with both hands as if she were too fragile to manage with just one.

"Too soon to say," Greg said, "but it'll probably get down to Ty Whittaker and Frank Sutton." Frank Sutton was not only reactionary—he was dumb.

"Yuck!" I said.

"And if the liberals start fucking around with this 'let's-support-a-moderate shit' they're going to divide the vote so there won't even be a run-off."

"Now wait a minute, Greg—"

"No, you wait a minute. We got a guy like Whittaker—he votes right on everything. Maybe he's a little peculiar, but he's one of us. Yet, all we do is talk about how it would be better to support someone who's only occasionally with us because he might have a better chance to beat someone truly repulsive. I don't buy it. If liberals can't depend on us, then why should they stick their necks out. The least we can do is go down with them."

"Watch you don't bloody your nose with that knee," I said.

"Unlike you, Gloria, some of us are proud to be called knee-jerks," Rachel said.

"Well, unlike you, I believe we have to compromise to get things accomplished and then you take your winnings and move on from there."

"All of our *winnings* have come from the Supreme Court—not from the State government," Rachel spoke as if she were addressing a five-year-old.

"So why vote at all?" Herman said.

"I don't," she replied.

"Look at Johnson," I said. "If it weren't for the war, Lyndon would be—"

"If it weren't for the *war*?" I knew this would upset Greg. "That's a big if."

"Look at all the social legislation. A liberal could have never gotten that through."

"If it weren't for the war," Rachel's voice was patronizing, "maybe he could have funded the Great Society so that it could live up to its full potential. Kids are dying in an immoral war, the cities are exploding with race riots and all the Johnsons do is plant flowers." She was referring to Lady Bird's Beautification Program.

I opened my mouth to counter, but at that moment, Ian's date reached across the table and kissed him on the mouth. I quickly looked away and suddenly had no idea what we were arguing about.

"I think I'm going to leave, guys," I announced. Everyone looked at me. "I'm tired and I have a big day tomorrow. I think."

"Well, wait until we settle this thing with Thornton."

"Hey!" Herman shouted. "I see someone who can give us some expert advice. Feldman!" he shouted across the room. Instantly, my neck began to ache.

"Who's that?" Greg asked.

Ian looked over his shoulder at our table. Right at me.

"The political writer for the *Morning News*." Herman waved for Ian to join us and, after saying something to his date, he did.

"Like the *Morning News* is going to give this play," Greg snorted. "The newspaper that claimed the censure of Joe McCarthy was a 'happy day for communists.'"

"Yeah, but Feldman's okay."

"What's up?" Ian said, shaking hands with Herman, but glancing gravely at me.

"We have a question about how to get some play in the newspaper on a political scandal of magnificent proportions. By the way, do you know everyone here?"

"I don't think *we've* met," Ian said to Greg and Rachel.

After he introduced them, Herman said, "You know Gloria, don't you?"

"Doesn't everyone?" Ian replied, smiling. I just looked at the table.

"This is pretty grainy," Ian said, squinting at the Xeroxes. "How can we be sure it's Thornton."

"You'll just have to take my word for it," Rachel informed him.

He stared at her for a long minute before he replied, "Yeah, well, I think my editor will need a little more than that to go on." He wrote Rachel's phone number on one of the Xeroxes and then stuffed them into his pocket. "I'll see what I can do," he said.

"Prick," Rachel mumbled as he wandered back to his table.

I had come to the Hair of the Dog with Herman, but he wasn't ready to leave. I'd have to call a cab. I fished through my purse for a coin. The most direct route to the pay phone would have taken me past Ian's table, so of course I went out of the way to avoid that.

I relied heavily on cabs and knew the phone number by heart. However, I misdialed the first time and had to hang up quickly. When I tried to scoop out the returned coin, it slipped through my fingers, hit the ground and wobbled in circles before finally falling down a grate in the floor. I closed my eyes and leaned against the phone to compose myself. It would be necessary to walk past Ian three more times to get a cab. Hanging up the phone, I turned and he was standing there.

"Need some change?" I glanced toward his table; his date was gone—probably to the ladies' room.

"No, I have money."

He pushed a coin into the phone. "What number are you calling?" When I told him, he dialed and handed me the receiver as he said, "I'm sorry, Gloria."

"For what?" I said and at that point the cab company answered so I cold shouldered him and gave them the relevant information. He was still there when I hung up.

"I'll see you tomorrow," he said. I glanced at him and then at the floor and started to walk away. "Gloria?" I turned back. "I'll see you tomorrow?"

"If you want," I said.

Back at the table, I grabbed my handbag, said my good-bye's and stepped outside to wait alone. It was oppressively hot out and clumps of what looked like the cast of *West Side Story* talked and laughed up and down the street. Before I had a chance to worry about them, Ian and his date exited.

"Gloria? What are you doing here?" Ian said, as if just realizing I was on the premises.

"Waiting for a cab," I said. His girlfriend smiled a doe-eyed smile at me.

"We'll give you a ride." He turned to his date. "Gloria's a neighbor. You don't mind if we drop her off, do you?"

"Certainly not—"

"It's okay. The cab will be here any minute—" I started.

Ian slipped his hand around my upper arm; while it seemed a casual gesture, his grip was painful.

"Nonsense. This isn't a great neighborhood." For emphasis, he squeezed my arm a little tighter as he hauled me along with them. Digging my heels in, I pulled back, engineering a little passive resistance. Ian's date crossed her arms over her chest and frowned at us. Luckily for everyone, the cab arrived and, after a brief but acute visual skirmish, he released my arm and we went in opposite direction.

* * *

"Sorry about last night," Ian said when he arrived at three.

"It's your business." I grabbed my suitcase and headed for the door.

Veronica had put my hair in a French twist, but at my insistence hadn't teased it much. I didn't want it to resemble something that had been pulled out of a brush the next morning.

"Here I'll get that," he said, reaching for the bag.

"I can manage."

He opened the hood of the VW and I tossed my stuff inside. Neither of us spoke until we were outside Dallas city limits.

"Why are you taking me to this party?" I finally demanded.

"Because I thought you'd enjoy it."

"Why aren't you taking her?"

"Because I asked *you*. Besides, she's gone home."

"Where's home?"

"New York."

"She just flew in to go to that dive—"

He didn't answer at first and then he sighed and admitted, "She's been here all week."

"I see." I looked out my window.

"You don't really have any right to be mad at me."

"I'm not mad." He could be such a prick.

"By the way, put your seat belt on."

"What if I don't want to?"

"Don't be a jerk. Put it on."

I looked out the window.

"Come on, Gloria. Quit acting like such a brat."

"I don't like you telling me what to do."

"Okay. Please. Would you *please* put your seat belt on?"

Still, I made no attempt to reach for the seat belt. Out of the corner of my eye, I could see him watching me. He swerved over to the side of the road and cut the engine.

"OK. We can just sit here until you decide to grow up."

I calmly pushed my cuticles back with my thumbnail.

"All right," he continued, drumming his fingers on the stirring wheel. "Let's just clear the fucking air and start over. Samara—"

"Oh, *please* tell me her name isn't Samara."

"Do you want to hear this?"

"Not especially."

"Samara and I are old friends from college—"

"From Harvard?"

"She went to Radcliff."

"Well, aren't we impressed."

"Gloria, cool it. Her trip here was planned months ago. Long before I met you."

"So why didn't you mention it?"

"I planned to, but I thought it would be less complicated to avoid you. I was wrong: I apologize."

"You were so confident we wouldn't run into each other?"

"It's a big city."

When I thought about how I'd spent the whole week worrying that he was mad at me, I felt so foolish and humiliated that I couldn't even look at him.

"Maybe you should just take me home," I snapped.

He was quiet for a long time before he exhaled loudly and said, "If I take you home, we'll never get past this."

A Peter Paul Mound wrapper was lying on the shoulder of the road ahead of us. Each time a car passed, it jumped up, as if startled, spin around and then landed only a few feet beyond where it had been.

I fastened my seat belt. Ian glanced toward me, but didn't say a word as he started the car.

* * *

I was relieved that there were two double beds in the room. Ian must have picked up on this because he suddenly turned surly. Throwing his suitcase on the bed closest to the window, he said, "I'm sleeping here. You can do what you want."

While he took a shower, I unpacked and felt uptight about the situation's intimacy. He stepped from the bathroom surrounded by steam with only a towel around his waist.

"Jesus," I said before I could stop myself. "Do you work out with weights?"

"There's a lock on the door, if you need to take a shower," he said, without glancing up.

When I came out, clutching my bathrobe at my neck, he was gone; he didn't return until it was almost time to leave.

"Nice dress," he said curtly.

"Why are you mad at me again?" I asked.

"I'm not mad," he replied, flipping on the television news. "I just realize it's going to be a very long twenty-four hours."

"What's *that* supposed to mean?"

"I think you know exactly what it means."

"You want me to sleep with you?"

"Hey what a great idea. Why didn't I think of that?" He flipped channels.

"Ian, we hardly know each other."

His gaze shot to mine. "I didn't realize that was one of your requirements."

I wanted to slug him, but I just stood there, leaning against the wall, while he watched the news.

* * *

"Hey," he said while we queued up for the valet parking, "You look great." Reaching over, he kissed me quickly. His lips were so soft that I kissed him again and it made my stomach drift a little.

The two-story private club hosting the party was perched on a hillside overlooking Lake Travis. The entrance hallway had yellow stone walls and Mexican tile floors, both of which were so highly polished you could spot all your flaws as you passed by.

On the first floor there were three "smaller" rooms (each about twice the size of my apartment). The first was a library. Jammed book cases lined all four walls and tiny swing-around lamps protruded from the sides of the bookcases, so you could adjust the illumination while you searched for a book. Though it was ninety degrees outside, a fire blazed in the fireplace.

A billiard room was next to the library. The focal point, of course, was the pool table and hanging over it was a ceiling fixture that dangled down like a huge trapeze. From what would be the bar of the trapeze hung two green-shaded lamps over either end of the table. The third room seemed to have no specific purpose, but like the library, the fireplace crackled.

Though guests could use these rooms, the real action was in the ballroom, which took up the entire second floor. The gleaming hardwood floors made dancing possible almost anyplace. A small orchestra, made up of elderly men in powder-blue blazers and black slacks, played Big Band music at one end of the room. Tuxedo-clad waiters circulated with enormous trays of food and drinks. Facing the lake, floor-to-ceiling glass doors lead to the terrace and a breathtaking view.

Once we arrived, Ian abandoned me to gather material for three separate articles: a fluff piece on the party, another on the widening field of gubernatorial candidates, and a third on the oil lobby itself. I was uncertain about where to hang out, but eventually decided I'd be less conspicuous in the ballroom.

Right away I spotted Vic. He and his wife stood with three other couples and he was telling a story, gesturing wildly. Penny was easily the most beautiful woman in the room. She wore a beige, strapless gown with a wide brown sash tied in an enormous bow in the back. It must have been a funny story, because suddenly they all laughed. It was a side of him I'd never seen before and it was strangely jarring.

I ducked behind a clump of people so that he wouldn't notice me and bumped right into Lance Wallace and Chick Flower standing, predictably, within yards of the bar.

"Jesus!" Chick cried. "Lay down, I think I love you."

I sneered at him while Lance twirled me around.

"Let me eyeball you, girl. Have you always had that body?"

I pulled my hand away from him and simply ignored them. "How'd you get invited here, Lance? Aren't you a little liberal for this crowd?"

"Look who's talkin'. At least I can sell out if I want. What do you have to offer?" Then he pointedly looked down the front of my dress. "Never mind, I think I figured that one out."

"I came with a *date*," I said.

Before anyone could respond, this dazzling stick-woman slithered our way. A white sequined gown had adhered to her bones and her shoulders and toothpick arms glistened with silver glitter. Six rows of pearls choked her swan-like neck and her hair was reddish and bouffant. After introducing herself as Anita Mann, she asked Chick to dance and he immediately started licking his lips as if he'd just finished a large platter of fried chicken. Her voice was husky—like a smoker's. I rolled my eyes toward Lance, but instead of panting, as I would have expected, he was watching the ice melt in his drink. Chick practically tripped on his erection getting to the dance floor.

"Just tell me one thing," I started in, once they were out of earshot, "what do they see in him?" Lance doubled over with laughter. "I mean it," I insisted. "She's beautiful."

"Yeah, for a guy," he laughed. I looked at him questioningly. "A transvestite," he clarified.

On the dance floor, Chick was all over his partner.

"How do you know that?"

"'Cause a group of us hired him."

I scanned the room and saw other legislators, grinning like beauty contestants, watching Chick and the woman.

"But isn't Chick going to be pissed when he finds out?"

"Oh, shit, yeah!"

"Well, he might hurt her. I mean him."

"We won't let it go that far. We're keepin' an eye on 'um."

"You know, if you guys put as much effort into solving the State's problems as you do playing jokes, we probably wouldn't have one of the highest poverty rates in the country."

"Gloria, honey, don't get preachy. It's unfeminine. Wanna dance?"

"No way."

"Why the hell not?"

"I don't want you pawing me."

"Now, goddamnit, have I ever laid a hand on you?"

"Yes."

"No. I mean, really laid a hand on you. 'Cause if I'd ever really laid a hand on you, you wouldn't be drooling over someone like Vic Davis."

I gasped. "Vic Davis? You must be nuts."

Lance flashed his square-teeth. "You think I'm blind?"

"That's bullshit," I shouted, but Lance laced his finger through mine and pulled me to the dance floor.

"Come on. Dance with me."

"Okay," I said. "But if you act like a jerk—"

"I'll be a perfect gentleman." We danced two feet apart.

"Is your wife here?" I asked.

"Nope."

"How come she never shows up at any of this stuff?"

"She hates politics."

"So why don't you drop out?"

"Then who would save the world?"

When the song was over, some older guys approached Lance on business and since he forgot I was even there, I slipped away. It only took a minute before I noticed Willie Henderson. Willie was a genuine political operator. We met in YDs—he was with Rice University—but after graduation, he moved on to hardcore politics. His recent resignation as co-chairman for the Ty Whittaker campaign had sent shock-waves through the knee-jerk community.

"It looks like Gloria Warren," he said, "except it looks like a girl!"

"Up yours," I replied.

Once I had a crush on Willie but he never asked me out, though he always flirted with me. He was speaking with an unfamiliar, somber-looking guy.

"But it definitely sounds like her." He turned to his friend, "You can dress them up—"

"Looks like they can't even dress you up," I said, "Where's your tie?"

"In my pocket. Wanna get it out for me?"

"Not on your life. No telling where it's been."

"Gloria Warren, this is agent Jeff Parker. Jeff, Gloria Warren. Jeff's with the Secret Service. Gloria's with the Young Democrats."

Jeff Parker was not bad looking, though he seemed a little bloated with self-importance. He was about five-nine with a muscular body. His light brown hair was short and militaristic and his green eyes seemed mocking and cold.

"Where I come from, the YDs don't look like this," Agent Parker said to Willie. I could tell that he thought this tribute thrilled me.

"They don't here, either. Even Gloria doesn't." Willie felt he had to clarify that.

"So is someone important here?" I asked, ignoring them.

"You might say that," Willie said, "The Governor, Lt. Governor, half the State Senate—"

"No. I mean why is the Secret Service here?"

"Advance team.," Agent Parker said. "Lady Bird's coming home next week."

"Wow! So you, like, get to hang out with her and all?"

"Gloria lusts after power," Willie said.

"Willie," I said, "Look around this room and then tell me—if what you say is true—why I'd be wasting my time with you?"

"You want to meet Lady Bird?" Agent Parker asked, taking a step toward me.

I had been in politics for years and I knew a proposition when I heard one. On top of that, from the corner of my eye, I saw Vic approaching.

"Well, ah, I'm supporting Bobby." I glanced sideways. Vic was back-slapping Willie.

"Senator Davis! How's it going?" Willie said as he shook hands with Vic.

"I hear you left the campaign," Vic said. His skin was bronze.

"Hey, man, don't get me started." We all laughed and Vic nodded toward Agent Parker and me. "Do you know Agent Jeff Parker with the Secret Service?" Willie asked.

I had trouble not staring at Vic and I became acutely aware of my mouth.

"And Gloria?" Willie continued, "You know Gloria Warren?"

"Yes. I do know Gloria," Vic replied. "Hello, Gloria." He smiled casually, but his eyes latched onto mine for a second or two longer than necessary and everything else blurred.

"Senator Davis," I said.

"Vic. Please. Call me Vic." He smiled at the joke.

I smiled too, but I felt completely overwhelmed and knew I should get away as soon as possible. I tried to think of a graceful way to slip off when, to my chagrin, Vic's wife joined us.

"Willie," she said, her taffeta shirt rustling, "what happened with Whittaker?"

Her eyes sparkled with amused expectation. She slipped an arm around Vic's waist and reflexively he put his across her shoulder. I turned away but couldn't find anything to focus on so my eyes ricocheted around like I'd been knocked senseless.

"We have him flying into Houston, right?"

As Willie spoke, I found myself inspecting Penny. In her spiked heels, she was almost as tall as Vic. She had enormous brown eyes, a pert nose and full, shiny lips. Her skin was rosy. My eyes flicked to the side and I saw that Vic was watching me inventory his wife, so I looked away.

"Got three, four hundred folks of all ages meeting the plane. I tell him, 'don't quote from anything, especially not the Bible.' He gets off the plane, and the crowd roars. Things are looking favorable. We sort of relax, thinking we're home free. Then, he walks up to the platform and he extends his arms and says, 'Bring all the little children onto me.' I scribbled my resignation on a bumper sticker and split."

Though I realized the story was funny, it only occurred to me to laugh when everyone else did.

"Well, now maybe you can help Vic," Penny said, smiling at her husband.

"Hey, I can be bought."

Willie grinned at me and I knew he was waiting for me to make a "whore" remark, but there were reasons I didn't want to cast any stones.

"Are you advancing the First Lady?" Vic asked Agent Parker.

"That's right." Agent Parker put his arms around my waist and pulled me to him so that my back was against his chest. My mouth fell open and I looked guiltily at Vic as if somehow I was responsible for what was happening. "I'm trying to get Gloria, here, to help me out but she says she's supporting Bobby."

"Is that right?" Vic said, as if my Presidential preferences were of interest. I stepped away from Agent Parker, and just when I thought things couldn't get weirder, Ian showed.

"Well, this looks like one big happy family?" he said.

His gaze slid from Vic to me and then jumped, self-consciously, to Penny. Penny regarded him curiously for a moment and then jerked her head my way, noticing me for the first time.

"Senator Davis, any chance I can ask you a few questions this evening?" Ian abruptly turned back toward Vic, as if he and I were strangers.

"Sure, Ian," Vic replied, an odd sarcasm to his voice, "my family and I always have time for the press." He put his arm over Penny's shoulder and pulled her to him. "Perhaps you might want to interview Penny, as well." Penny stumbled his way, but her eyes never left me.

"Excuse me," I said and walked off. Agent Parker caught up with me seconds later.

"Hey, seriously. Why don't you come down here next week and help me?"

"I have a job." I kept walking.

"Call in sick. You might find it would pay off."

"How?"

"Well, besides getting to know me better, you'd meet some VIPs—not to mention Lady Bird."

"What would I do if I came down?"

"Oh, just handle whatever comes up." He had this annoying smirk on his face.

"You don't waste any time, do you?"

"I don't have any time to waste."

"Like I said, I'm supporting Bobby." I walked away.

"Wait!" He caught up with me and slipped me his card.

"In case I become President?"

"In case you change your mind. That's my Washington number, but they'll forward messages."

I considered tearing it up and throwing it in his face, but political animals often have to forego the dramatic moment—he might come in handy some day. I stuffed the card in my pocket and walked off.

The scene with Penny freaked me out so much that I just wanted to get away by myself. Jesus! She knew. Fucking Ian. I'd have to stay as far away from Vic as possible. What would I do if she said something to me? Started calling me names here in front of everyone? Home wrecker! Whore! God, what if she had a gun? I decided to look for a quiet corner and just sit there the rest of the evening.

Besides the obvious, the ladies' room also had a lounge where overstuffed chairs waited in front of a battery of mirrors. Shelves of hair spray, hand lotion, tissues, nail files, mouthwash and even perfume sat within reach of each chair.

"There you are! I wondered if I'd see you here."

Julia sat in the corner, touching up her eyeliner. At first, except for some strategically placed sequins, she appeared to be naked. But then I realized that the underdress of her see-through gown was flesh colored, merely giving the illusion of nudity. Jewelry glittered from her ears, neck and wrists, but most noticeable was a ring on her right hand—a huge diamond mounted on a spring, that jiggled with the slightest movement.

"Here," she said, twisting around toward me, "let me see you." Scowling, she continued, "Oh, dear, I should have told you to get one of those push-up bras."

I looked down at myself. "I don't know," I said, "it seems revealing enough."

"There's no such thing as *revealing enough.* Until you're suffocating from your own cleavage, you're always going to have to worry about the competition."

I studied the cosmetics on the counter next to hers and squirted the complimentary perfume in the air. It was harsh and seemed to boil up and drift around, waiting, like cigarette smoke, to assault innocent hair or clothing. "What have you been doing all evening?" I asked, fanning the air.

"Just looking for a future ex-husband."

I laughed. "Maybe this time you'll be lucky."

"I'm always lucky."

"Maybe the next one will be your true love." I smeared on some hand lotion.

"I'm not rich enough for true love just yet."

She brushed rosy smudges across her cheeks. My hands were completely white and greasy and the more I rubbed them together, the worse it got. Julia passed me a tissue from her counter.

"Did you see Vic Davis out there?" I asked, though it made me nervous to say his name out loud.

"Now which one is he?" She outlined her lips with a pencil.

"The cute State Senator from Sumner. I met you at his coffee, remember?" I decided not to sample anything else.

"The blond?" She looked at me, the pencil an inch from her lips.

I nodded.

She leaned back in her chair and crossed her legs. "I can see you and I need to have a little talk."

I just looked at her.

"In a room full of oilmen," she continued, "there is simply no reason to concern yourself with a State Senator."

She held my gaze in the mirror before rummaging through her bag for mascara. "Is he any good?"

I frowned, confused.

"Vic Davis," she said. "Is he any good?"

"Well, he's a moderate. So, he's good on some things and less good on others—"

"I *meant*," she interrupted, "is he good in bed?"

My face almost exploded into flames. "How on earth would I know?" I shouted, glancing around to insure that we were alone.

"How, indeed," she replied. "Know what?" she said, snapping her purse shut. "Why don't we get drinks? It will make this scene bearable."

She led me across the dance floor to one of the bars and ordered a fruity drink for me. It had this adorable paper umbrella popping out of it and when I lifted it up, I found it speared an orange slice and two cherries. I was biting into the second cherry, when I spotted Vic. He seemed captivated by a strawberry blond who had known enough to buy a push-up bra. I hesitated, and Julia glanced back at me inquiringly.

"You can't be worried about *her*," she said, once she saw what I saw. "She's from Fort Worth! Besides she's screwing one of my ex-husbands. See that rock around her neck? He bought it for me before that unfortunate business with Carlos." She held her hand up as if to stop me from interrupting. "Oh, I know what you're thinking: women and their stable help! But let me tell you something." Leaning closer and lowering her voice, she continued,

"Carlos had a penis the size of my arm. You don't turn your back on something like that."

She started toward them but I lingered. Vic had not taken his eyes off the redhead and I was afraid I was about to witness something painful.

"You want him?" Julia asked, her hands on her hips.

"Julia, please. He's married." I watched for Penny the way ocean swimmers look for sharks.

"Was that a joke? Or are you really that naive?" She grabbed my wrist and pulled me toward them. "I can't promise you happily ever after, but I can sure brew up attention for you."

I pulled back but was reluctant to slump to the floor and have her drag me along. "Julia, really—"

"What's his first name again?" she asked.

"Vic. But, listen—"

"Vic. That's right!"

As we neared, Vic eyed us suspiciously. I glanced around the room casually, pretending to search for someone.

"Vic!" Julia cried, as if just spotting an old friend. "You gorgeous piece of beef, you!" I cringed for him, but he smiled back at her. "And Tammi! My God! You look so much better, doesn't she, Vic?" Vic cut his eyes toward me before waiting, silently, for Julia to continue.

"Oh, you're wearing the Huntington Diamond," Julia said dislodging the stone from between Tammi's breasts and examining it. "And where is the little curse that goes with it?"

Vic glared at me with a tight-lipped expression, obviously blaming me for the whole fiasco. Julia caught him watching me.

"How rude of me," she said. "Vic, this is my little friend —" she stopped herself as if realizing she was about to make a horrible faux pax. She even rested her fingers gently on her breastbone and then looked down, shyly. "Oh, but I think you two have..." She looked first at him and then at me. "*Met*. Haven't you?"

Neither Vic nor I dared to speak. I felt a little sweaty.

"Well, we can't stay," she hurried on. " I promised Gloria I'd introduce her around. Look at that face!" Her fingers gripped my jaw and pushed my face up. "Wouldn't it be great if we were that young again, Tammi? Cute little kid like this in a room full of millionaires—she could have her pick, don't you think, Vic?"

"If that's what she wants," he replied evenly.

"I can't believe you did that," I said when we were out of earshot. "He hates me now." I glanced back: Vic was walking off in another direction.

"Don't be silly. These legislative types—especially the cute ones—are like a bunch of busy bumblebees stockpiling pollen. You want him? Make him feel like he made you feel. Trust me. What turns them on is an opponent. And what's great is, there doesn't even have to be an opponent: they just have to *think* there's one." She took a sip of her drink. "And now, and I don't want you to take this the wrong way, I want you to run along and play somewhere."

Bewildered, I looked at her. She sighed.

"When I'm with you, I look my age and that pisses me off."

Deflated, I turned to go but she stopped me.

"Let's have lunch one day, okay?"

"Sure," I replied, but I knew she didn't mean it.

I searched for Ian—surely he'd be free by now—trying at the same time to avoid Penny. A group in the living room was planning some big event, but Ian was not with them. When I stepped in the billiards room, I clearly triggered a silent alarm, because the men gathered around the table became mute and turned in unison to watch me until I backed away. At first I thought the library was empty, but as I was leaving, I heard someone moan and turned back. Chick had Anita Mann cornered and was making his moves. Anita Mann coyly avoided him. Sensing an intrusion, Chick glanced my way.

"Get lost, Gloria," he said.

"Lance is looking for you," I said.

"Screw him."

"He said it was important."

"Well, it's not important to me." With hands on hips, he glared at me. "You can leave now."

"I just want to get a book," I said, pointing toward the bookcases. "You know where fiction is?"

"Gloria? I'm gonna count to three—"

"I'll just be a minute." I snagged a novel and pulled it off the shelf. To my horror, the entire shelf of books fell toward me. It was just a facade. Luckily, it weighed nothing so I wasn't hurt. But the incident startled all of us.

"Let's go, honey," Anita Mann said to Chick. Reluctantly, he followed him out.

Rushing from the room, I hurried to locate Lance before things got much more out of hand with Chick. It wasn't hard: he was by the bar.

"Lance, you better do something. Chick and that woman were making out in the library!"

Lance, who was considerably more drunk than before, thought this was a riot. "I'll go break it up," he promised me. "But first, I gotta get me a camera."

Jim Drury, from the *Times Herald* passed by right after Lance left. "Have you seen Ian?" I asked.

"Yeah. About an hour ago. Out on the terrace with one of the independent oil guys."

Vic passed but appeared not to notice me.

Knowing it was unlikely that he'd still be there, I stepped outside anyway. The terrace curved around the building. Large, round cedar tables dotted the area. The matching chairs were large and lazy looking. No one was around, probably because of the heat, but it was quiet, which was, no doubt, why Ian was interviewing there.

A crimson dahlia, probably from a corsage, was wilting on the ground close to one of the tables. I picked it up and sniffed it, but it had no smell. Twirling it between my fingers, I strolled the length of the terrace until I reach a secluded alcove at the north end, just after the terrace rounded the building. Giving the flower magical powers, I plucked the petals off, saying either Vic or Ian as I threw each over the railing. I didn't hear the footsteps until he was right behind me.

"Where are your admirers?" Vic said.

I swung around, dropping the dahlia into the darkness below.

"Jesus!" I shouted. "You almost gave me a heart attack." I held my hand to my chest and waited for the excess adrenaline to burn off.

He held out his glass to me. "Need a drink to calm you down?" he asked.

"Where's your wife?" I asked once I caught my breath.

"Around." His bottom lip had a small, ragged piece of skin sticking out.

"You're so…tan," I said, after a moment.

"We took a quick vacation. Padre Island."

"Oh. Well. You're…really tan." I glanced around guiltily as if I were selling CIA secrets.

"Why didn't you warn me that you'd be here?"

"Warn you?"

"I don't like surprises." He paused before he added, "Though it's delightful to see you again."

He slouched against the railing and stared at me: he did for eye contact what James Dean did for toothpicks. I couldn't think of a single thing to say.

"So. What happened to your friend, Julia?" he asked.

I shrugged.

"It amazes me to learn you two are such close friends."

"She's nice," I said.

"Is she?"

"Isn't she?" He snorted. "Well, she's been nice to me," I added.

"Introducing you to millionaires?" I didn't deny this, so he continued. "Guess that *is* a little altruistic for her."

"What does that word mean?"

"Altruistic? Philanthropic. Magnanimous. Benevolent. Big-hearted." With each word his voice got more sarcastic.

"You don't like her?"

"Not especially."

"You certainly seemed to at that coffee."

He barked a little laugh and looked away. "And what about 007? Where did he go?"

"Agent Parker? I have no idea. He was leaving."

"You going to come down here and help him out?"

"Of course not!"

"He's not looking for a typist."

"I know exactly what he's looking for, Vic." This was beginning to piss me off.

"He's married, you know."

"How do you know that?"

"I know the look." He took a long drink from his glass before he went on. "He seemed to like you."

"I don't think there was anything special about *me*, he was just...lonely or something."

"Lonely?"

"Yeah, I guess."

"He seemed to have a hard time keeping his hands off you." Vic rattled the ice around in his glass. "But I guess when you wear a dress like that you must want that kind of attention."

"I didn't *want* anything from him."

"So why didn't you tell him to leave you alone?" His voice was completely unruffled.

"Well...I didn't want to cause a scene."

"Oh, sure. Let the guy do whatever he wants as long as there's no scene."

"Just what are you trying to say, Vic?" I was ready to get into it, now.

He seemed to consider his answer before he said, "I'm trying to say I was jealous."

I dropped that anger so quickly I couldn't believe it didn't make a hole in the floor.

"Close your eyes," he said.

I wasn't sure what he had in mind but I didn't argue. His thumb grazed the corner of my left eye and then dragged down my cheek. I blinked as he pulled his hand away.

"An eyelash," he explained. We kept staring at each other.

"I wish you had one," I finally whispered.

"You don't need an excuse to touch me, Gloria."

I felt myself being pulled toward him and I thought I would simply die if I couldn't at least kiss him. "We should cool it tonight." I said, catching myself.

"Why's that?"

"Well, for one thing your wife's here—" I looked at him. "She suspects us."

"Suspects us of what?"

"Don't play games right now, Vic. I'm serious."

"Why don't you let *me* worry about my wife? I can assure you, there's no problem."

"When we were all together? With Willie and…" I glanced up at him, "and…and that reporter? She gave me a funny look."

"She didn't give you a funny look."

"I know a funny look when I see one and she looked at me like…like she knew."

"Gloria, trust me. There's nothing to worry about."

"That's easy for you to say. She's not going to shoot *you*."

"She's not going to shoot anyone."

A strand of my hair had slipped out of the French twist (no surprise there) and was fluttering around my neck. Vic reached for it and coiled it through his fingers.

"Vic, please." I pulled away from him.

"You seem so tense tonight." I leaned against the railing to keep from staggering. "Who did you come with?" he asked.

"A friend. From Dallas."

"Anyone I know?"

"No," I lied, turning away from him to look at the lake.

"Do you like cherries?" he asked.

"What?" I couldn't believe I'd heard him correctly, but when I glanced his way, he was fishing a cherry out of his glass.

"You like cherries?" He held it up to me.

"Vic, stop it." I glanced toward the main part of the terrace but no one was in sight.

"Come on. Open up." He held the cherry to my lips. I opened my mouth. He pushed the cherry in, shoving his index finger so far into my mouth that I thought I might choke. But I didn't. I closed my lips around his finger and sucked it as he drew it out.

"Maybe you're right," he said. "Maybe we should try to ignore each other tonight." He walked away, but I stayed where I was, until my rubbery legs returned to normal.

* * *

"Looked as if you were the Belle of the ball," Ian said when he finally caught up with me. It was almost eleven and I hadn't seen Vic for a while so I assumed he'd left early.

"Your mood hasn't improved any."

"Actually, it has." He slipped his arm around me and pulled me toward him.

"I see you found him." Jim Drury waved to us. "Got something for you," he said to Ian as he slapped his pockets until he found a business card, which he passed to Ian. When I craned my neck to read it, Ian pulled it just out of my view.

"He didn't say it was for you, did he?"

I missed the name on the card but whoever it was, worked for the railroad company.

"She was combing the place for you earlier. She said you'd know what it was about."

"Thanks," Ian said, slipping the card in his wallet.

"Sounds intriguing, doesn't it?" I said. "Was she pretty?"

"She wasn't bad."

I looked at Ian, but he ignored me.

"Speaking of intriguing," Jim said, changing the subject, "what's happening with Peddy these days?"

"Nothing. Did he ever respond to my quote?"

"Yeah. He said, 'What can you expect from someone whose IQ range is dull/normal.'"

Ian and Jim cracked up.

"What are *you* laughing at?" I elbowed Ian in the side.

"Oh, come on. It's so obviously not true. You're neither dull nor normal."

* * *

"Where are you from?" I asked. It had cooled some, so we had slipped out to the terrace.

"Fairfield County," he replied.

Frowning, I tried to place it. "That's not in Texas."

His laugh was sharp and almost embarrassed. "No. It's nowhere near Texas." I believe he would have dropped the subject there, but I kept squinting at him. "It's in Connecticut."

"How'd you end up here?"

"Just needed a change, I guess."

"Now you need another change?" I said.

"What do you mean?"

"New York."

"Ah. Yeah. New York."

"You sound less than enthusiastic."

"No. I'm enthusiastic. It'll make the folks happier."

"Because you'll be closer to them?"

"That's one way to put it." He leaned on the railing and looked toward the lake.

"Do you have any brothers or sisters?" I asked.

He tore his attention from the lights and glanced at me. "You're full of questions tonight, aren't you?" I didn't reply and after a while, he added, "No. I'm an only child. Can't you tell?"

I wasn't sure why I should be able to tell, but I decided not to show my ignorance. "You seem depressed," I said after another couple strolled past us and disappeared into the darkness.

"Me? No." He sighed. "I'm just…tired, I guess."

"We can go whenever you want."

He turned from the scenery and smiled a sad smile, before he bent down and kissed me—a sweetly intense kiss that scared me a little.

On the way to the hotel, he glanced my way and said, "Are you going to sleep with me tonight?"

Startled, I caught my breath.

"Because," he continued, "I don't want to get my hopes up and I'm kinda tired of begging."

Maybe if he hadn't put me on the spot, I could have been more spontaneous once we reached the room. But by forcing me to think coldly about the situation, as if it was some sort of lab problem, he made me realize that if it were up to me, I'd be spending the night with Vic. I really liked Ian and I wanted things to work out with us. But, God! I just ached for Vic. Somehow, under those circumstances, it seemed dishonest—in a way that mattered—to sleep with Ian. Precisely because I liked him so much. I knew this was something he wouldn't understand even if I were stupid enough to explain it to him.

By the time he unlocked the room I was a wreck. We stood there eyeing each other suspiciously.

"Ian?" I said tentatively.

"What?" he barked back.

"I don't know what to say."

"Then I guess there's nothing to say."

"Things are moving too fast, that's all."

"Too fast? Jesus! How often do we have to go out before—"

"You think you're *buying* me?"

"I *thought* you liked me." He tossed his jacket over a chair. Sitting on the bed, he untied his shoes.

"I do. I like you…a lot. I'm just—. I'm just confused."

"You're punishing me, aren't you?" He unbuttoned his shirt.

"Punishing you?"

"For Samara."

The unfairness of this stunned me. "Fuck Samara! But, I don't have to tell *you* that, do I?"

"No. You fucking don't. At least what I have with Samara is honest." He threw his pants over a chair and pulled down the sheets on his bed. "I'm tired. I don't have time for this shit." He crawled into the bed, and faced the window.

I turned off the light and slipped into the bathroom to change. Should I take my make-up off? It was much more obscene for a guy to see a girl without her make-up than without her clothes. That's why all female fundamentalists wore so much of it. But at the last YD convention, when I stayed up until three and fell asleep before I could take off my mascara, my eyes were swollen, itchy and bloodshot for days. Slathering on cleansing cream, I wondered if Vic's wife slept in her make-up. That would be one of the downfalls of being married to a guy that cute. That cute and that undomesticated. Like

Cosmopolitan said, there'd always be someone waiting. In his case, there'd be a line.

Was Penny always that perfect? Did she never belch, or, God forbid, fart? She must spend her life arresting odors: gargling, douching, deodorizing, freshening, perfuming, and no doubt, living on Tums. I never realized there were so many pressures in a marriage. I'd never survive married to someone like Vic. Of course, I'd get to screw him every night. Jesus, I couldn't imagine how great that would be. I glanced in the mirror. The cold cream on my face looked like spackling. I ripped off a couple of feet of toilet paper and wiped it off.

That's what they were probably doing while I scraped goo off my face. Thrashing around in some bed—two beautiful people, unable to get enough of each other. I could be thrashing around right now if I wanted to. Even with Ian being all pissy in the next room. He'd get over it. All I'd have to do is slip into his bed. I considered this as I brushed my teeth.

My gaze fell on his dopp kit. Since it was sitting there, open. It wasn't like I was breaking and entering or anything. Besides, he was the biggest snoop around. He'd probably already gone through all my stuff. Biting my toothbrush, I rummaged around: Right-Guard, a green toothbrush, Ipana toothpaste, Prell shampoo, Canoe aftershave, fingernail clippers, a brush, a razor, Noxzema shaving cream, a corkscrew. A corkscrew? Bufferin, a piece of string, three Bic pens, an uncancelled five cent stamp he'd ripped off an envelope, rubber bands, Coppertone suntan lotion, lipstick. *Lipstick*? I opened it. Bright red-orange. Well, at least it wasn't his. Redheads never wore red-orange. Only a tall, thin woman with long dark hair would have the confidence to wear that. Well, fuck him. He could just go to New York to get laid.

I couldn't sleep. From all the thrashing I heard in the next bed, I suspected that Ian couldn't either. At three o'clock, I whispered, "Are you awake?"

"Yes," he replied, sounding miserable, "You want to do anything about it?"

At four o'clock I was freezing. Ian's breathing was deep and even, so I assumed he was finally out. If there were any extra blankets in the closet, I couldn't find them. The control for the air conditioner was next to Ian's bed and I'd have to turn the light on to figure it out. I got back in bed and curled up in a ball, but that didn't help. Finally, I slipped into bed with him. I leaned my back against him and he curved himself around me, wrapping me in his arms and legs, but he didn't wake up. I fell asleep almost at once.

* * *

"How did you get over here?"

I opened my eyes. The room was bright and Ian was up on his elbow looking down at me. His erection was against my hip.

"I was cold," I said.

He kissed my neck, causing my shoulder blades to pull toward each other. "You're not going to back out now, are you?"

There was no way I was backing out. He tugged at my nightgown and I sat up to pull it over my head. His hands caressed my shoulders and when I turned toward him, a muscle in his cheek tensed. His reaction to my body excited me. And I have to admit that it also made me feel very...powerful, and that excited me even more. For a big guy with such a volatile personality, he was very gentle. There was nothing about his physique that was soft, but his skin was as smooth as marble, except, of course, he was very warm. We kissed and touched and admired each other as if we had been together for years. When he finally entered me, he did so slowly and sweetly, as though afraid I might break.

"Jesus! Gloria, you're so tight," he said.

His hair tumbled down, tickling my nose and cheeks. I scooped it up in my hands and pushed it back. His eyes were closed, his brow knitted, his mouth open as if to cry out. Vic had had that expression. Maybe I did too. Interesting that people looked distressed when they were having such a good time.

"This isn't going to last long," he predicted, and no sooner had he said that than it was over. He rolled onto his back panting. "I'm sorry," he said.

"It's okay." I moved his way, wrapping myself around him. My body felt charged, as if an electric current were racing through it. It surprised me that I didn't make little electronic noises each time I moved.

"First time's always a bummer, isn't it?" he said.

I kept my mouth shut and nuzzled against him as if trying to bore a hole into his side. He swallowed me up in his hug and buried his face in my neck.

"Just give me a couple of minutes, okay?" he said.

"Okay," I said and waited. For more than a couple of minutes.

He crawled down the bed toward the television. He was more of a news addict than I and it was, after all, Sunday morning, but screw that. I tugged at his arm, pulling him back.

"Wallace is on *Face the Nation*. You interested?"

"Not in that," I said.

It seemed unladylike to behave so desperately, but, as if responding to a mandate of its own, my body climbed on top of his. The heat from his groin made me whimper and I started moving against him. He forgot Wallace as he clutched my back. When we finally made love, I though I might explode. As I reached that point of no return, I had such a vivid sense of Vic that I almost called out his name.

"You know who you've always reminded me of?" He said after a minute or two. He had a silly grin on his face so I knew he wasn't going to say Brigitte Bardot or Sophia Loren.

"If you say Tweety Bird, I'll never speak to you again."

That smile slid right off his face. "Oh," he said.

"You were going to say Tweety Bird, weren't you? I'm twenty years old!"

"No I wasn't. I was going to say…something else."

"Like what?"

"Like…The Roadrunner."

He snapped on *Face the Nation*, but a commercial was on: Joe Namath shaved to "The Stripper." When the show resumed, Wallace was spewing his usual hatred. I crawled to the foot of the bed, and flicked off the set.

"He pisses me off."

Ian lunged for the television, but I grabbed his arm and jerked it away, trapping it with my body. He tried to drag it out from under me, but I held on as tight as I could, so he tickled me. Shrieking, I rolled away from him. Wasting no time, he stretched toward the tube. I jumped on his back, monkey-like, wrapping my arms around his neck and my legs around his waist and then leaned backward, pulling him on top of me.

"Goddamnit, I'll show you!" he twisted away and pinning me down, sucked on my neck. I laughed so wildly that my sides ached, leaving me weak and exhausted. I gave up, but he had lost interest in *Face the Nation*.

"You're on the pill, aren't you?" he whispered as he eased himself on top of me.

"Actually, no."

"What do you mean, 'no'?" He pulled away and scowled.

"What does 'no' usually mean?"

"Well, in this case it means you're really stupid!"

"I like you, too."

"Are you kidding, Gloria?"

"No. I like you."

"Don't pull that shit on me. Are you or not?" I shook my head. "So, what are you using?"

"Well, I guess...nothing."

"What do you mean 'nothing?'"

"Well, I—"

"What if you got pregnant? Jesus!" He fell on his back and stared at the ceiling.

I had considered getting birth control pills after I slept with Vic, but I couldn't bring myself to call Dr. Hart and ask for them. He was from the Stone Age and I'd been seeing him since I was a baby. He never recovered from my pierced ears. If I asked him for birth control pills, I was sure he'd keel over, dry up and hollow out like a dead fly on a window sill. If, by some miracle, he did survive, I worried he'd call my mother and tell her what a Jezebel her daughter was. So I had put it off. Besides, I wasn't even sure I'd see Vic again. *And* the pill wasn't all that safe: it could cause blood clots or cancer. Plus, and this was what struck fear into the hearts of all Texas girls, it made you *gain weight.*

"I know that asshole probably doesn't use rubbers," Ian went on, "so what were you thinking?"

I leaned over him, believing my body against his would distract him. He caressed my back and his voice lowered.

"What were you thinking this morning?"

When I kissed him, his arms tightened around me, and his breathing became deep and even. "We can't do this now," he said, but he made no effort to stop.

"I want you, Ian," I whispered. I was toying with him. It made me hot, enticing him to ignore his better judgment.

"Gloria," he moaned when he could get his tongue out of my mouth long enough to speak, "this is really stupid."

"Please, Ian." All his integrity and reluctance vanished. Clearly, I had the instincts of a whore.

* * *

"I lead a charmed life," I said later.

I did, too. No one knew better than I how my good fortune was undeserved, but no matter how close I got to quicksand, I never got pulled under. At least not for long.

"You think you're so special nothing bad can happen to you? I've got news for you. Something bad *has* happened. You just don't realize it yet."

"Why do you bring him up every fifteen minutes?"

"Why? Because it bothers me that you're fucking him."

"I didn't realize we were going steady. I don't think Samara realizes that either."

"You can be a real bitch. I'm not claiming any exclusive rights. You want to fuck other people, by all means fuck your brains out. It just bothers me that you're fucking *him*."

"Ian! You care." I wiped an imaginary tear from my eye. "I'm…I'm so touched."

"You know what? Fuck you! Just fuck you! I'm taking a shower." He slammed the bathroom door so hard that the picture on the wall rumbled a little. This was kind of fun.

I was feeling very sexy and decided to slip in the shower with him, but when I tried the bathroom door, he'd locked it. This cracked me up and I slid to the floor laughing. When he left the bathroom, fully dressed, I was still sitting there in the hall.

"Why did you lock me out of the bathroom?" I asked.

"I want nothing to do with you until you're on the pill."

Jumping up, I followed him into the bedroom. As he turned on the television, I slipped my arms around him and nuzzled my face against his back, "That might be months."

"Well, then I want nothing more to do with you until we can buy some rubbers."

"Seems to me if I was going to get pregnant today, the damage has already been done." He sighed loudly as he turned toward me.

"Are you having fun, Gloria?"

"Actually—" I started giggling before I could finish.

"Well, if you don't care, why the fuck should I?" He grabbed me and pulled me down to the bed with him. I was all over him. "Just tell me one thing," he said.

"What?"

"Why *aren't* you on the pill?"

"Jesus! I'll see someone when I get back. Okay?"

"That's not what I'm asking. Why would you hop in bed with someone like—with anyone, really—and not?"

"Because I didn't know I was going to sleep with him until it…until it just happened."

"But why weren't you on the pill anyway, for Christ's sake?"

"Because there wasn't any *reason* to be." This confession did not win the *Good Housekeeping* Seal of Approval I expected.

"Are you saying Davis was the first guy you slept with?" It was as if I had told him my favorite meal was rat stew.

"Yes."

He blinked several times. "I could have lived very happily without that piece of information." He climbed off the bed.

"What does it matter whether he was first or tenth? Someone had to be first."

"Thanks, Gloria. I didn't understand that. I feel much better now." He threw his suitcase on the bed and started tossing things into it.

"Would you have felt better if I'd said he was twentieth?"

"Yes."

"I don't understand you."

"Apparently not. Let's get moving. I need to get back."

"Well, I have to take a shower first," I shouted, stomping to the bathroom, "and I'm going to lock the fucking door."

"Don't bother," he said. "I'll meet you in the car."

It crossed my mind that he might abandon me, but when I stepped outside, there was the yellow VW. Ian even got out of the car to open the hood, but he didn't speak. Neither of us spoke for about twenty minutes. This was becoming a ritual.

"Know what pisses me off?" he finally said. I knew I didn't want to hear this, so I said nothing. "The guy is such a fucking operator! When I covered the Legislature, we used to watch him. He'd be sitting on the Senate floor and he'd see some babe in the gallery. And he'd just look at her—kind of the way he watched you at the airport. He'd just bead in on this chick for ten, fifteen minutes. Then, when he left, she'd be waiting for him. He didn't even have to fucking *look* for her. She'd be there, panties soaking—"

"All right, Ian, that's enough."

"Okay, okay, I'm not going to say another word about it."

I didn't care if he never spoke again and I really resented that I'd slept with him. Besides, he could be making this up. Why should I believe him?

"Do you ever talk?" he asked, bringing me to attention. I glared at him. "I mean do you ever have a conversation? You know, other than just hot talk." I looked out the window and pretended he wasn't even there. "Does he know anything about you?" We drove a few miles. "So, does he?"

"Does he *what*?"

"Does he ever *talk* to you? I mean other than saying, 'drop your pants,' or 'spread your legs,' or 'suck my dick'."

"You are really pissing me off!" I resented Ian's need to cheapen my relationship with Vic.

"I would bet the family farm that he doesn't even know how old you are?"

"You'd lose."

"And that—other than what you've read in his brochures, and what I've been good enough to tell you—you don't know anything about him."

Neither of us had a thing to say the rest of the trip until, just before we reached Dallas, Ian pulled into a drug store.

"I want some gum. You want some gum?"

"Sure," I said. "And I could use some Preparation H."

He slammed the car door; he glanced over his shoulder and smirked. I felt a rush of affection for him. The Roadrunner! I laughed to myself. When he returned, he tossed a package of spearmint gum and a box of condoms in my lap.

"Somebody has to look out for you," he said.

* * *

Monday morning I asked Veronica for the name of her doctor. She told me it would take a while to get an appointment, but since she had a six-month stash of birth control pills in her drawer, she offered to cover me for a few months. She explained that I should start taking them five days after my next period. All I had to do was wait for my next period.

* * *

"Gloria Warren," I shouted into the phone.

Though I got to work on time, I'd been hanging around in the hallway gabbing with Mr. Sweet when my phone rang so I had to sprint to catch it. Lonnie Mossman was not in yet and it would be just like her to call, trying to learn I was late for work so she could give me grief. Cradling the receiver between my ear and shoulder, I tossed my handbag under my desk and flipped on the typewriter, hoping its hum would assure her I was hard at work.

"I want to see you."

Vic's voice was unmistakable. I closed my eyes as my hand flew to my mouth. I'd stayed awake hours the night before sorting things out. I knew Ian was telling the truth about Vic and while it was the last thing I wanted to know, it was probably worth knowing. I realized that if *I* hadn't spent that night with Vic, someone else would have. It was that simple. He just wanted fresh meat, and I'd been eager to be the virginal sacrifice. I was embarrassed by all the fantasies I'd had about him and what it would be like when we saw each other again at that party.

"Maybe...maybe, you know, this isn't such a good idea." I couldn't believe how hard it was to get that out.

"What isn't a good idea?"

"Us." The office was gearing up.

"Since when?" His voice was like dark honey.

"I don't want to get hurt."

"Sounds as if I'm the one about to be hurt."

"Right." This was perhaps the funniest thing he'd ever said.

"You think I don't have feelings?"

"Oh, I think you have lots of feelings."

"Was that a put-down?"

"I don't think we should see each other anymore."

"You don't mean that."

"Yes, I do." I toyed with the paper clips jumbled in a glass bowl next to my calendar.

"What have I done to deserve this?"

I had to clear my throat before I could speak. "I heard things about you this weekend."

"Who told you that?" He laughed, after I repeated Ian's claims. He seemed amazed.

"A reporter."

"Why would a reporter say such a thing?"

"He...he suspected there was something between us. He was trying to warn me."

"It sounds as if he were trying to get to first base with you. I'm surprised you fell for such a trick."

"It wasn't like that at all," I lied.

"Come on, Gloria."

"Maybe not everyone's like you."

"Trust me. The guy was trying to seduce you. It makes no sense otherwise. Maybe he saw us talking and took a chance. But he was after you, not me. Anyway, it's not true. Or it's at least a gross exaggeration. I've been with other women, but not to the extent that your little reporter friend implied." He suspected Jim Drury, since he'd seen us together and since Jim was short.

"Your wife is beautiful."

"She's exquisite."

"So why do you do this? And please don't tell me she doesn't understand you."

"My wife understands me better than anyone."

"Then what?"

"She doesn't like sex." I dropped the paper clip chain I was making back into the bowl and grabbed the receiver with my hand.

"Why would you marry someone who didn't like sex?" Lonnie Mossman arrived and walked by, oblivious to the world.

"She did once. She doesn't now. At least, not with me."

"You're lying!" I sat very erect as if I might have to evacuate the building any minute.

"What purpose would it serve for me to make this up? Would the woman I'm trying to keep, be impressed that the woman who knows me best prefers to sleep alone? Hardly says much for me."

"Why does she stay with you?"

"She likes the life."

"Why do you stay with her?"

"Politicians don't get divorced." When I didn't say anything, he grabbed the conversation. "You looked beautiful at the party. I could hardly stay away from you." I heard him rustling papers in the background. "So, did you drive back that night?"

"Ah, no. No, we stayed in Austin."

"Oh, really? Where?"

"I...I think it was the Holiday Inn."

"Oh, sure. I know where that is. So, did you sleep with this guy?"

"There were two beds in the room." I felt my armpits get sticky.

"There were two beds in the room you and I had. That's not what I asked you. Did you sleep with him?"

"No," I said.

"You didn't?" He seemed surprised. "He just stepped in the room and said, 'I'll take this bed, you can have that one'?"

"Well, yes. Sort of."

"And that was that?"

"Pretty much. Why are you grilling me like this?"

"Am I grilling you?"

"It feels like it. I feel like I'm on trial."

"You feel guilty?"

"I didn't say that. I told you we didn't sleep together, but if we had, I don't think you really have any business—"

"No, I don't have any right to object. You're correct. But now it sounds as if you're saying maybe you did sleep with him."

"I didn't say that. Why are you doing this?" His jealousy was turning me on a little.

"Is he a homosexual?" he went on.

"No." I snapped, laughing a little at the idea.

"You seem pretty sure of that."

"I am." I made a mental note to avoid criminal lawyers in the future.

"How can you know?"

"Well, because he isn't. Because he dates women."

"And he had no interest in having sex with you."

"No. I don't know. Maybe."

"Well, did he or didn't he?"

"He offered—"

"He *offered*!" Vic mocked. "You mean he said 'If you want to get laid, I'll see if I can get it up?'"

"Not exactly."

"But he was available?"

"I guess so. Yes."

"But you didn't sleep with him?"

"That's right," I said with conviction. I had repeated the lie so often that I was starting to believe it.

"Why? You like sex."

"I...Just because."

"Because why, Gloria?"

"Because...he wasn't you." The best way to get someone off your back is to give them what they want. Neither one of us spoke for some time.

"I want to see you." His voice was smooth and seductive and I felt delirious.

"Vic. Jesus!" I whispered. "When I talk to you, I get confused."

"Confused isn't what you get. But, even so, that should tell you something."

"It's just. My life is getting complicated—"

"And mine isn't? You think it's *easy* for me?"

"I don't know. Maybe you do this all the time."

"I *don't* do this all the time. How could I possibly do this all the time? I have a family, a law practice, a political career. How much time do you think I have to run around the State keeping my stable in order? Jesus! Would you believe me if I said you were the only woman I'd been with in three months?"

I barked out a laugh and then caught myself, waiting for him to repeat the claim. But he didn't.

"Fly down here tonight," he whispered.

I was so shocked that I couldn't speak.

"I'll have a round trip ticket waiting at Love Field."

"I have to work tomorrow."

"You'll be home by eleven."

"That doesn't give us much time together."

"It's better than nothing."

"Why don't you just take a cold shower?"

"I've been doing that all weekend."

"You want me to fly down there, have sex with you and fly back home?"

"That doesn't appeal to you?"

It's hard to be indignant when you're drooling, so I agreed. Besides, with all this Hunter business, maybe I needed to talk to a criminal lawyer.

* * *

Lonnie Mossman was distant all day. Whenever I looked into her office, she was having serious phone conversations. Something was definitely up. At noon, I tapped on her door.

"Yes, Gloria?"

"I'm going to eat at my desk today. Want me to bring you anything from the café?"

"No. I have a meeting downtown. In fact, I might not make it back here this afternoon." She folded up a legal-looking document and slid it the skinny middle drawer of her desk.

"Is everything okay?"

She smiled a quick, insincere smile as she locked her desk. "Sure. Everything's fine."

When I returned with my sandwich, Lonnie was just leaving. She was so agitated that she didn't even respond when I said, "have a nice day".

I looked up the number for Clearance Tyson, Attorney at Law. "I'm double-checking on the time of Mrs. Mossman's appointment today," I said.
"One-thirty," the receptionist replied.

* * *

The hands of the clock never moved so sluggishly as they did that afternoon. It was a good thing I'd finished my files because I couldn't have focused on policy numbers if the end of the war depended on it. Rather, I thought about Vic. About his face, his voice, his chest. But mostly I thought about kissing him.

Vic didn't kiss like the boys I'd dated. Mistaking enthusiasm for technique, they either smothered or drowned me, stirring up more anxiety than passion. Even Ian didn't kiss like Vic. He kissed fine, don't get me wrong, just not like Vic.

Eventually five came, and by six, the plane was taxiing on the runway.

* * *

Thirty minutes later, the plane touched down in Sumner, a small, rural town of twenty thousand, roughly seventy-five miles southeast of Dallas. The terminal was one large room with a ticket desk to the right and a conveyer belt system for baggage on the left. Since I had no luggage, I simply walked into the building and out again.

Vic's white Impala was at the far end of the deserted parking lot. I tried to seem relaxed as I walked toward it, but the closer I got, the more I picked up steam until, by the time I could see him, I was practically running.

"Hi," I said, leaning in through the passenger's window.

He had thrown his jacket in the back and had the sleeves of his white shirt rolled up, exposing his still-tan forearms.

"Get in," he replied. His voice was edgy and cranky. He did not smile.

"What's wrong?" I asked as I slid into the car.

He gave me an annoyed look before he placed his arm across the seat and squinted out the rear window. His eyes, only a shade away from unnerving in the best of circumstances, were downright scary. God, what a sexy guy he was!

"I just don't think it's smart to advertise that I'm picking you up."

For a man whose skin was chapping from so many cold showers, he didn't seem all that fired up to see me. Hardly glancing my way, he eased out of the airport parking lot.

"Where are we going?" I asked.

"Good question," he grunted.

"You know, Vic, you *asked* me to come down here."

"What's *that* supposed to mean?"

"You're sort of acting like I'm imposing on you."

"You having your period or something?"

He studied me coldly for a moment and then returned his attention to the highway. I could feel my temper wanting to act out. "You seem in a foul mood," he added.

"Jesus! I was in a perfectly fine mood until you started biting my head off. Are you mad at me about something?"

"Should I ever invite you down here again, say 'no,' okay?"

"Don't worry. Just stop the goddamn car and I'll walk back to the fucking airport. I wouldn't want to put you out any more than I already have!"

He didn't respond, didn't stop the car, didn't even look my way. He just kept driving. I crossed my arms over my chest and glared at my feet. When I glimpsed up, we were on an unpaved, deserted road where barren, rocky hills jutted up menacingly. I cut my eyes toward Vic and he returned the glance but said nothing.

The tires crunched over the winding gravel path as we jerked up a hill. After several minutes of dusty, bumpy driving, we turned off the road and stopped in a secluded area between two trees and amid high-growing yellow weeds: a place where mass murderers might meet to exchange anecdotes around a campfire. After he cut the engine, he slid the seat back as far as it would go. We both sat at our sides of the car, looking straight ahead as if we were in an elevator.

"What a mouth you have on you," he said.

I wanted to say, "Fuck yourself," but I just kept quiet.

"Come here," he whispered, reaching for my arm, and my stomach levitated like a table at a seance.

"Don't touch me," I snarled, jerking away from him. He ran his finger up and down my arm and I resented that I was mellowing. "Don't you think you owe me an apology?" I snapped.

"I'm sorry."

"For what?" I challenged.

"For whatever you think I've done."

"You really piss me off."

"Goodness." He placed his hand over his heart as if shocked. "I thought you were such a sweet little girl."

"Guess we both miscalculated things." I caught him peeking at his watch. "Am I keeping you from something?" I grumbled, realizing this behavior was exactly what *Cosmopolitan* warned against.

"We don't have much time. You want to spend it bickering?"

"*I* didn't start this."

"Didn't you?"

It occurred to me to get out of the car and walk back to the airport, but this was a spooky place, even in daylight. Though it was early for the mass murderers, I could imagine swarms of poisonous snakes, stinging scorpions, tarantulas and daddy longlegs hovering outside the door, ready to pounce on anyone foolish enough to step outside. While I glanced around, I caught him checking the time again.

"If you have such a pressing engagement, why don't you just take me back to the airport?"

Of course, it would have killed me if he had. What I wanted was an excuse to get over my annoyance with him so I could rape him. But he chose to make matters worse.

"You think I flew you down here to show you the scenery?"

"Oh! How stupid of me." I reached for my handbag. "Let me take care of that."

Vic crossed his arms over his chest and tensed a muscle in his cheek as I retrieved my checkbook and scribbled out a check for the amount of my ticket. Just to piss him off, I made it out to Vic and Penny Davis and next to "Memo" I wrote, *For services not rendered.* I waved it in his face, but his eyes were blazing at mine, so I added, "You have a joint account?"

His gaze flicked to the check and then back to me. I could tell he was seething and that felt very satisfying to me. Also—and I guess this is a little sick—it really turned me on.

"That's very funny, Gloria."

I got tired of holding the check, so I stuffed it in his shirt pocket. "So you don't lose it," I said, patting the pocket like a kindergarten teacher sending a note home.

"Hey," he whispered, changing his tone. "We don't want to fight, do we?"

He leaned ever so slowly toward me so that when our lips finally brushed, that was all it took. We kissed like that—not touching except for our mouths—for some time. As he scooted toward me, the leather seats crinkled and for some reason that noise made my stomach float. He told me to kneel on the seat and then he reached under my skirt and pulled my pantyhose and underwear down my legs. It was a clumsy operation that required my changing positions three or four times before everything slid off my feet.

"Whoever invented pantyhose should be strangled by them," he said as he unbuckled his belt and unfastened his pants. Heaving his hips off the seat, he fumbled awkwardly before he was naked from the waist down. I had a sort of sinking feeling.

"Come here," he said, pulling my arm toward him.

When I got closer, he put his hands on my hips and directed me to straddle him. He took my bottom lip between his and sucked it as he entered me and in spite of the lack of fanfare, I felt a wave of intense pleasure and warmth that was almost painful. We both groaned at the same moment. However, I soon realized this was not a great position for me. I felt gawky and graceless as I tried to find my rhythm. Clearly, he had his complaints, too, because suddenly, sighing an exasperated sigh, his fingers dug into my behind so that he could control my movements. He became more forceful, gasping and grunting. I watched a tiny spider make its way up the outside of the car's window. I regretted flying to Sumner.

I'd heard jokes about women faking orgasms, but I never believed it would be something I'd ever do—certainly not with Vic. But I did. It gave me a cheap, guilty feeling I'd never had about sex until then.

Seconds after my performance, he clutched me to him and began thrashing around to such an extent that we almost slid to the floor. Then it was over. He dropped his head back against the seat and closed his eyes while he caught his breath. A thin layer of sweat covered his face and the hair around his temples seemed matted and dark. When he opened his eyes, he smiled.

"That was great," he said, easing me off his lap onto the seat next to him. "I brought some towels," he said twisting toward the back seat.

"Towels?"

He retrieved two identical, frayed dishtowels. They were dingy white with faded yellow and blue sailboats landlocked across the boarders. He cleaned himself off with one as casually as if he were brushing breadcrumbs off his lap. I looked away: this was not something I cared to witness.

"Here," he said passing the second one to me.

"That's okay," I said. "I'm fine." I would have rather died.

"You sure?" he asked, frowning.

"Yeah."

He shrugged and tossed the towels into the back seat before reaching for his slacks. I watched him struggle into his clothes, a sense of loneliness settling in around me.

"Can't you find your stuff?" he asked when he noticed I hadn't moved.

I nodded and reached for my twisted pantyhose. As I untangled them, I became aware of his stare.

"Everything okay?" he whispered.

I nodded again and, resting my right heel on the car seat, I stuffed my toes into the bunched up nylons in my hand. When I got it up to my knee, I changed feet.

"I had planned to take you to my office," he announced. He was leaning against his door. "There's a...big sofa there. Even a shower."

He rubbed his thumb over his bottom lip and paused as if he thought I might have something to say about that. I hunched over my left foot, my gnarled pantyhose digging a groove in my right thigh. "Unfortunately, at the last minute, my partner decided to work late. He has a big case tomorrow."

I leaned my weight against my shoulders and lifted my hips so that I could pull my stockings in place. They twisted hopelessly around my legs like stripes on a barbershop pole.

"Gloria, I didn't mean for this to be so crude. I'm sorry if—. Well, I'm just sorry."

"It's pretty here," I said, not believing it for a minute.

"You think so?" He seemed relieved. "I always thought it was spooky. In high school, everyone came out here to neck, but I was always too scared of the place. Maybe I was just scared of the girls." The idea struck me as preposterous and made me giggle. He leaned my way and kissed me on the neck before he whispered, "We still friends?"

Involuntarily, I rubbed my face against his as he brushed his lips over my cheek. "Have we ever been friends?" I asked.

"Well, you know what I mean."

We kissed sweetly for several minutes, our tongues occasionally barely touching. And then he pulled away, tapped me on the shoulder brotherly and said, "We better get you to the airport."

"My plane leaves at ten." It was barely eight.

He leaned against the steering wheel and pinched the bridge of his nose with his fingers.

"I have to be somewhere at nine," he confessed. His eyes caught mine briefly before he looked away. "We're having some work done on our house and the architect is bringing preliminary plans by." He raked his hand through his hair. "I didn't know when we spoke earlier."

He started the car and began the descent downhill. It seemed to take no time to reach the airport, even though neither one of us spoke a word the whole way. I was pretty sure we wouldn't be seeing each other again and felt surprisingly numb about that. But, as we were pulling into the terminal, I realized I'd never asked him about Hunter. Vic stopped by the entrance without cutting his engine.

"I...I need to talk to you about something," I said.

"Can you make it quick?" he asked, checking his watch for the hundredth time.

"Never mind, Vic. You got what you wanted, that's all that counts." I reached for my door, but he stopped me.

"You know, you could drive me nuts! First, I resent the implication I'm somehow coercing you to have sex. From where I'm sitting, it seems like a fairly mutual interest. Secondly, you *know* I'm in a hurry. I didn't plan it that way, it just happened. If you had something you wanted to discuss, you should have brought it up earlier."

"Fine!" I shouted and opened the door. He reached across and pulled it to.

"What do you want to ask me?"

"It's nothing."

"Are you sure?" he said, practically sighing with relief.

"Absolutely."

"Then I have to go. I'll call you sometime," he said.

I knew he'd never call again and as angry as that made me, the reality was that I needed some advice. I didn't open the door. Instead, I watched a ticket agent make her way to the counter.

"I may be in some trouble," I blurted out.

He turned off the car and twisted toward me.

"You pregnant?" To his credit, his expression did not change.

"No! At least, I don't think so. But, no. That's not it."

"Then what?"

"I may go to jail." I started biting my nails. "I did something...really terrible."

"Did you kill someone?"

"Of course not."

"Did you steal something?" Vic reached over and pulled my hand away from my mouth

"No!" I trapped my hands between my knees just to keep them out of the way.

"Then what?"

"I think I committed perjury."

"Perjury? Did you testify in a trial?" I shook my head. "Before some federal hearing?"

"No, of course not."

"What did you do?"

"I lied to the FBI."

"Under oath?"

"No. Just, you know, over the phone. I reported a crime that never happened."

"That's not perjury."

"It's not?" I looked at him as if he had just lugged me from a burning building.

"No. It's called intentional false reporting and they can certainly nail for you that. Just depends on whether they want you or not. Did it have anything to do with radical behavior?" I shook my head. "Even accidentally?"

"No. It wasn't about politics."

"Are they harassing you?"

"They don't know it was me."

"Oh, well, Jesus!" He waved his arm dismissively. "What's the problem, then?"

"What if they find out?"

After I explained everything, he said, "How long were you on the phone?"

"Less than a minute."

"So they couldn't have traced it and they don't record casual calls: you're home free."

"But see, an innocent person went to jail and I'm the only one who can get him out, because it was just a joke that backfired. But if I admit that—"

"You reported this guy thinking he was innocent, but in fact, he wasn't. So, what difference does it make?"

"If everyone I know who smoked a joint got arrested, I wouldn't have any friends."

"Still, it's against the law."

"If you were my lawyer, what would you tell me to do?"

"If I were your lawyer I'd tell you to keep your mouth shut. You don't want the Feds to know you lied to them. Should they ever want to get you, they can do it with that."

"Well, thanks," I said, reaching for the door handle.

"Gloria?" I froze. Something about the gravity of his voice made the hairs on my arm squirm.

"What?"

"Are you on the pill?"

I hardly moved for ten seconds and then I glanced over my shoulder, locking eyes with him. "Of course," I replied.

Neither of us looked away: two natural liars locked in combat.

"Is that true?" he asked.

"Of course," I repeated.

Determined not to be the first to break the eye contact, I kept him in my sights until my eyes were brittle from lack of moisture.

He twisted the key in the ignition, signaling my dismissal, so I cracked the door open.

"I'm not sure when I'll get back to Dallas," Vic said.

"I know," I said.

Fighting with my pantyhose so that I wouldn't walk like a crab, I hurried into the terminal. Once inside, I turned and saw his brake lights twinkle as he slowed before entering the intersection outside the airport. Ironically, just then I felt him trickling down my leg. I watched the road long after his car was out of sight. Then I went to the ladies' room to clean myself up and to rearrange my stockings. It was eight-forty-five: I had an hour and fifteen minutes to wait in the world's most boring airport. Ah, the glamorous life of a jet set call girl.

I waited thirty-five minutes and then I walked to the wall-mounted pay phone next to the janitor's closet. A bloated directory swung from a chain and I thumbed through it until I found Vic's listing. Dropping a coin into the slot, I took in a deep breath before I dialed. A woman answered. It occurred to me to hang up, but I didn't.

"A long-distance call for Senator Davis, please." I held my nose so I'd sound like an operator. I waited while she called him to the phone.

"Yes?" he said.

"It's Gloria." There was utter silence on the other end. "I…I just wanted to remind you that you have a check in your pocket."

Not waiting for his response, I pushed my fingers against the phone's cradle rest, ending the connection.

Boyfriends had dumped me before. Just about all of them, actually. And while it was always depressing, it was usually my ego that got chipped. I agonized about what he'd say behind my back, resented that I'd bought him an expensive Christmas gift, kicked myself for not pointing out more of his faults when my opinion mattered, or worried I'd run into him when he was with a girl and so was I. But I'd never felt grief before. No one like Vic would come my way again. My life had peaked at twenty.

* * *

At four in the morning, I decided I might as well get up. Staggering into the bathroom to brush my teeth, I gasped when I saw that my gritty eyes were practically swollen shut and my skin resembled pink tapioca. In the kitchen I wrapped ice cubes in a frayed blue washcloth. Throwing myself on the sofa, I switched on the radio and pressed the ice pack to my face. The news was on. Someone from the district attorney's office was ranting that the Supreme Court's Miranda decision would end law and order: "We might as well make crime legal."

After a while, I returned to the kitchen and heated water. In the cabinet I found some Oreos, so I took a fistful, along with my coffee, to my desk. The sun was just climbing over the apartment complex across the street. It sent out a red-orange aura for as far as I could see. I watched it disintegrate before my eyes to a bleached-out blue. It didn't take that long.

The *Morning News* was outside the door. Ian's story about the Governor's race started on the front page and continued on page three. Photographs of six candidates dotted the article. Of course, Vic's was one of them. He smiled right at the camera, confident that he'd come out looking fine. Maybe I was reading too much into it, but though the article seemed objective about the other candidates, it turned hostile when it focused on Vic. On page seven, there was a snapshot of Lady Bird arriving in Austin. Ian's piece on Pete Thornton was in the Metro Section but it had no mention of the John Birch Society or the Klan. Once I finished reading, I turned back to Vic's picture. I cut it out and hid it between stacked-up envelopes in one of my desk drawers.

By six, I lost interest in moping so I left for the office. The main entrance wasn't opened until seven-thirty, but I knew I could get in through the delivery door of the adjacent café.

There was a creepiness to the empty office that I found exhilarating. Sometimes when I came in early (usually to do political work) I wouldn't turn the lights on. I'd just let the sun filter through the blinds and cast odd slanting shadows up the walls and across the floor. Each step I took echoed so that it sounded as if another person was following me. A distant, mechanical hum was the only other sound.

I don't believe I started out with devious intentions. I just wanted to get out of the apartment and there was nowhere else to go. But once I was there, the spookiness of the place made my blood sizzle a little. I pretended I was Emma Peel from *The Avengers*, spying for my government; risking my life in my tight, sexy jumpsuit with my glass of expensive, imported champagne.

I walked the parameter of the office, pretending I wasn't sure where the microfilm might be, but in no time I was in Lonnie's office. I tried her middle desk drawer with the same illogical optimism that makes people using pay phones to search for returned coins after their call has gone through. Like them, I was disappointed. Grazing the back of her file cabinet with my fingers, I located the keys hanging from a stick-on hook and opened her desk. The document was right there. I was just going to peruse it—learn what was going on. But it was impossible to read—much less digest—the legalese in the time I had, though it was clear that Lonnie was a defendant. It was forty minutes before starting time, but the front doors would open soon and people would trickle in much earlier. I had fifteen minutes of guaranteed privacy.

The Xerox machine took forever to warm up, then there was the obligatory paper jam, but I managed to copy the sheets and return the original to her desk and the keys to the hook before anyone arrived. I resisted studying the pages at my desk and instead crammed them into my bag.

"What happened with the dirt on Thornton," I asked when Ian answered his phone.

"Editor wouldn't touch it."

"Too bad."

"Yeah. Of course you and your pals could always try writing letters to the editor about it. Maybe the information could get out that way."

That's what I was doing when, at ten-twenty-five, my phone rang.

"Hi," he said.

I froze, the point of my pen ready to cross the "t" in fascist. I tried to think of something to say, but I didn't want him to suspect how grateful I was to hear from him.

"I did some checking," he continued, "and it looks as if even when an informant recants a statement, the authorities don't release prisoners. So it wouldn't serve much of a purpose for you to come forward. Except to get yourself in hot water."

"Vic?" I said, as if only just realizing who had called.

"Where is this guy being held?" I was afraid I might cry if I spoke, so I kept quiet. "Hello? Anybody there?"

"I…I don't know."

"Probably in the Federal facility at Seagoville. What's his name, I'll see what I can learn."

"If you ask questions, won't people wonder why?" I didn't want him involved in something seedy. I also didn't want trails leading back to me.

"I have friends there. It'll be unofficial."

"His name is Hunter Callihan."

"I'll get back to you." He was about to hang up.

"Vic—?" I called out.

"What?"

"Thank you."

Lonnie Mossman entered the office so I started scribbling on a piece of paper as if I were taking down information from someone. I was able to scribble for quite a while before Vic spoke again.

"Thanks for reminding me about the check," he finally said.

"Sure." So that was it.

Lonnie stopped by another supervisor's office and shut the door. They carried on an intense discussion. Vic and I lapsed into an awkward silence and I felt pressured to say something. Anything.

"Did you see the sunrise this morning?" I asked.

"The sunrise? No."

"It was, you know, really pretty."

"I'll be in Arlington next weekend." His voice was forceful, as if he were addressing a crowd. "Penny will join me Saturday, but Friday I'll be alone." He paused. When he spoke again, his voice was softer. "Unless you want to meet me."

"Sure." I almost stepped on his words. I didn't dare risk making him ask twice.

Lonnie Mossman hid away in her office all morning, which was great because I had a lot of political work to do. Election of officers was scheduled for the next YD meeting and I needed to get the notice out by the end of the week in order for the results to be legal. Our newspaper ad had netted us thirty-five new members, bringing our total to three hundred and ninety-eight. Of course, our roster was mostly on paper—folks who wanted to support the organization or who had wanted to get me out of their office when

I'd stopped by to ask them to join. But most of them had no patience for or interest in our activities. We had a core of thirty who did virtually everything and we had little in-fighting. Since no one else had the time or inclination to be President, and because I had done a pretty good job, I was running unopposed. These things were always worked out ahead of time. The agenda would include: a) Introduction of New Members, b) Election of Officers, c) Allotment of Funds for Newsletter and d) Endorsement of Candidate for State Office at the State convention.

I was getting away with so much personal stuff that I started feeling guilty. At three, when it was time for my soda and peanut break, I tapped on Lonnie's door.

"I was just going to get an RC. Want anything?"

Smiling wearily, she replied, "No. Thanks, though." She returned to her work, but I stayed where I was. "Was there something else?" she asked, looking up.

"Is everything okay?"

She studied me for a moment before her eyes strayed to her pencil cup. When she glanced back up, her professional smile was in place. "Yes, everything's fine."

On the bus ride home, I pulled out the Xeroxes. Once I adjusted to the legalese, which was similar to that used in political resolutions with a lot of "wherefore's" and "the party of the first part" and all that kind of garbage, I realized it was a child custody battle. Lonnie's ex-husband, Theodore, was trying to get their daughter, claiming Lonnie was unfit due to immoral and depraved behavior. Was he kidding? I gazed out the window and watched people scurrying along the sidewalk. Suddenly, and with startling clarity, my mind flashed back to the photos under Lonnie's blotter. "Love, Lisa," the photo had said.

* * *

When I reached the apartment, Veronica and Jo Beth were stringing dayglow hot-pink crepe paper across the living room.

"Hi, Gloria," Veronica cried. "Jo Beth's givin' me a little party. Come help us decorate." She tossed a roll of crepe paper my way.

"A party?" I didn't mean to sound disappointed.

"Ta celebrate her new fame and fortune," Jo Beth sneered. "You don't have ta stay, if ya have somethin' better ta do."

Bowls of Fritos, potato chips, pork rinds and onion dip sat on the table, while plates of Snicker's bars, cut into bite-sized chunks, complete with toothpick handles, studded the end tables next to the sofa. On the kitchen counter was what appeared to be a Barbie doll in a hoop dress. But on closer examination, I saw that it was a dome-shaped cake with Barbie plunged into its middle. Intricate white curlicues overlaid the cake's mint green icing, making the skirt appear lacy. Piped icing also covered her boobs so that it looked as if she wore a strapless gown. The doll had auburn hair, pulled up into a fat ponytail. Its arms extended stiffly forward, beckoningly, so that they wouldn't smooch up the skirt.

"Wow!" I said. "Where'd you find this cake?"

"Jo Beth made it."

"You *made* this, Jo Beth? Where'd you learn to do this?" I asked, turning the cake around to study it from all angles.

"I just taught myself," she replied casually, but I could tell my admiration pleased her.

"Jo Beth invited some folks from the club and a couple of guys from the television station," Veronica said.

"That technician I invited—wow—what was his name?"

"Rusty."

"Yeah, Rusty. What a hunk. I see a guy in a work belt and boots and my bra just unsnaps itself."

"Oh, Jo Beth," Veronica scolded, "You're bad."

"That's what you said about loafers and no socks last month," I reminded her.

"Well, yeah. That, too."

"When is everyone getting here?"

"In about five minutes," Jo Beth responded.

"That doesn't give me much time."

Against my better judgment, I glanced toward the mirror: my hair was so limp and mangled that it drooped in clumps and my ears stuck through the shafts, giving me that Minnie Mouse look everyone admires. What make-up I'd put on that morning had vanished and my dress looked as if I had just taken it out of an envelope.

"Is Rusty married?" I overhead Jo Beth say.

"I believe he's divorced."

"Is he seein' anyone?"

"I hardly know him, Jo Beth."

"Well, if he shows up with someone, there's always that new bartender."

"Just be careful you don't catch anything…again." I said re-entering the living room, pulling my wig into place. "There are only so many times people'll buy that toilet seat story."

"I will not dignify that with a response. Junior used ta say, 'virtue is simply a lack of opportunity.'"

"Hold it, Gloria," Veronica said, running her hand under the base of my wig, tucking in wayward strands. "Ya got hair hangin' out all over the place."

"There they are," Jo Beth shrieked as the doorbell rang. She climbed down from the chair where she had been standing. "Would you get that, Gloria? I have to freshen up."

I spent most of the next thirty minutes passing for an invisible doorkeeper. About thirty people showed. Some were from the club, some from the television station, one was a cop who had stopped Jo Beth for speeding, and another was a bus driver she'd wanted to get to know better. Veronica had invited her producer, costume designer and choreographer and a few close friends from *A Stretch Over Thyme*.

To my horror, one guest turned out to be Bob Love, the private detective Veronica had hired. He was a short, beefy guy in his fifties whose arms not only looked too short for his body but also stood out, away from his sides even when they were just hanging. His hair, which he slicked back to accentuate his receding hairline, was the color of a pencil eraser. When he talked, his head bobbed and weaved as if he were persecuted by low flying objects. His wife was probably in her early twenties. She had a practiced, vacuous expression and, except for the fact that she had more teeth than necessary, she was attractive.

"This is my roommate, Gloria. She's a politician," Veronica said as she introduced me. She pronounced it "polly-tician."

"Does that mean you run those little machines?" Bob Love's wife asked me.

"Machines?" I said.

"No, honey. That's polly-*graph*," he explained, dodging a miniature meteorite on his left. Turning toward me he added, "You know, lie detector machines," as if *I* were the one with only a brain stem.

"Remember," Jo Beth said as I was trying to escape the Loves, "As soon as Rusty arrives, you point him in my direction, girl."

The door flew open and a guy who looked like a fullback for The Cowboys burst into the room.

"All you squares!" he shouted, "Out!"

He scanned the room as if equipped with "square radar." His gaze stopped at me—I believe I was the only one not smiling at him—and he frowned before he pointed his finger at my face and said, "I'm watchin' you, girl." Then he barged into the kitchen, threw open the refrigerator and helped himself to a bottle of beer, which he opened with his teeth. As he spit the bottle cap into the sink, he said, "That's just a little something I learned at hairdressing school." Tossing his head back and holding the bottle a good two inches from his mouth, he poured the entire contents directly down his throat.

"Never could stand the taste of beer," he hollered, as he wiped his mouth with his sleeve and burped a watery belch.

Jo Beth laughed this high-pitched, phony laugh and with an overly limp wrist, swatted his arm as if to say, "You naughty boy."

"Who the hell is that?" I asked Veronica.

"Ronnie Jim Baxter, but his professional name is Mr. René. He's a hair stylist at Neiman's."

"They let someone like that work at Neiman's!"

"He's an artist. Women love him 'cause he's such a man."

I looked up. He was scratching his privates. "Yeah, I see what you mean."

Once the word got out that I was a polly-tician, people started complaining to me about their gas bills and speeding tickets. At one point, when I was speaking with an older woman from the television station, Bob Love and his wife joined us.

"If you ask me," the woman said, "the best thing the city fathers have done is fund that opera company."

"Ah couldn't agree more," Bob Love said, nodding vigorously three times to the left. "I got me front row seats for openin' night."

"You like opera?" I asked, a little astonished.

"Can't stand it," he said.

"Oh, honey, do we have ta go ta the opera?" his wife whined. "I just hate it."

"Well ever'one hates it," Bob Love assured her, "but it's good for you. Kinda like castor oil." He waved his hand in front of his face as if trying to bat away a swarm of gnats.

"All that screechin'," she went on, "Who knows what they're sayin'? Sometimes I think they're not even speakin' English."

He grimaced, for the first time embarrassed by her. "Come on, honey, 'course they're speakin' English. Don't be stupid."

A war cry from across the room interrupted us. Mr. René had spotted the Barbie cake. Leaning into it, he licked the icing off Barbie's breasts and then yelled out, "What do you know, a topless cake." Everyone around him tee-heed politely. "Let's make it a topless party!" he cried, ripping off his shirt.

Any appetite I had soured when I viewed Mr. René's pale, slack chest. As if what little good taste he had was in his shirt, he dashed from woman to woman, quickly squeezing their breasts and identifying whatever fruits or vegetables they brought to mind. "Pear." "Orange." "Cantaloupe." "Prune." "Turnip." "Apricot." "Grape." "Watermelon." "Carrot."

The women giggled good-naturedly as if to say, "Boys will be boys." A couple of them swatted at his hands, but no one seemed scandalized. As he approached me, I stared him down. I wasn't sure what I planned to do if he touched me, but I was sure I'd do something. Sensing this, he halted just before he reached me. Pointing his finger at my face again he said, "You know, this party's no place for squares." I kept glaring at him and after a moment, he announced that he needed another beer. Spinning around, he hurried to the kitchen where he performed his famous hairdressing school trick one more time.

"What do you think of this Barbara Jordan?" Veronica's producer said as we both reached for pork rinds. "Looks like she might get herself elected down there in Houston."

"Hope so," I said.

"Yeah," he replied, a tone of resignation in his voice. "Guess it had to happen sooner or later. I just wonder what it will do to social events in Austin now."

"Rusty hasn't shown yet?" Jo Beth interrupted.

"Jo Beth, I wouldn't know Rusty if I stepped on him and had to get a tetanus shot."

"Trust me. You'd know him," she said, turning and swishing out her flippy skirt as if she were Loretta Young or something.

The word had circulated that not only was I a polly-tician, but a liberal one, at that. Now folks approached me cautiously with a mixture of apprehension and curiosity on their faces.

"What do you think about these legal aid clinics they're setting up all over the State?" Veronica's choreographer asked.

Before I could answer, the cop butted in. "If you ask me, public defender's office is good enough for the criminals of Texas. I've seen the sort of scum we bring in and believe me, it's downright Christian of us to even give 'um trials."

"Ever'body? Ever'body?" Jo Beth called out from across the room.

There was so much chattering that no one heard her. She whispered something to the bus driver who was standing next to her. Grabbing her around the knees, he hoisted her to his shoulder.

"Hey, ever'body?" she cried out. Gradually, the room hushed. "We're gonna cut the cake now."

A rebel yell erupted from Mr. René's depths, as he hurried to the Barbie doll and started repeating, "I gotta get me a piece of that. I gotta get me a piece of that."

Expertly, Jo Beth started slicing the cake and distributing it to those who lined up. Mr. René made it clear he wanted the slice closest to Barbie's crotch. As Jo Beth approached his territory, he started panting and drooling and finally he yelled, "I don't mind telling you, I'm hard!" When Jo Beth handed him his cake, he actually sniffed it and shouted, "Mmmm Mmmm! I'd like to put my gun in her holster."

"You'd probably fall out," I said.

He jerked his head toward me. There was dead silence.

"Well, that was uncalled for, Gloria," Jo Beth hissed as she slapped a piece of cake on my paper plate. Everyone else looked at me as if *I* had been the one out of line.

As I walked off, Mr. René said, "What is she? Queer or something?"

After that, no one wanted to talk to me, so I decided I would bag the party and slip into my room for the duration. I was halfway there when someone knocked. Though tempted to ignore it, I whirled around and saw Jo Beth snap her head first toward the door and then toward me. She gave me a wide-eyed, outraged expression. Figuring it would be less irritating to simply get the door than to put up with her bitching, I stomped across the room and opened it. What could only be Rusty was there. He had left his work belt at home, but he still wore his boots and his curly brown hair and green eyes would make just about anyone gasp. He leaned against the wall with his thumbs hooked in his belt and his fingers pointed toward his IQ.

"Hi," he said, with a slightest come-on in his voice, and I could tell right away that he was, indeed, high. The whites of his eyes were blood-soaked and his head seemed to bobble around on his neck as if it might roll off at any moment. "I'm lookin' for this girl. Let's see...her name is Sue Beth or somethin' like that..." He scratched his head and looked at me sleepily as if he had no idea what he had just said.

"Jo Beth?" I asked.

"Yeah, that's it." He cuffed my chin. "You're pretty smart. For a girl."

He laughed good-naturedly, but I was feeling less generous than usual. I spotted Jo Beth. She was watching us, but just as I was about to point her out, she turned around and tried to appear preoccupied. Placing one high-heeled foot on our coffee table, she pretended to adjust her stockings—a thinly veiled excuse to expose her leg.

"Over there," I said, pointing. "She's the one with the semen stain on the back of her skirt."

Once I reached my room, I called Ian, but there was no answer. Then I called Herman: he was out. I was about to try Greg—he hadn't paid his phone bill and they were threatening to cut off his service, but it was worth a try. Before I could dial, however, there was a tap on my door. When I peeked out, I was astounded to see Mr. René standing there, his shirt on and buttoned up.

"Can I come in?" he asked.

"No way." He walked in anyway: I left the door open.

"I got the feeling you and me got off to a crappy start."

"No!" I said.

"I'll level with you: you' re not that bad. It's just you're hard. If you're not careful, you're gonna look like a dried up prune long before you should. You need to soften up. Get some class."

"When I'm ready for class, I'll certainly look for you."

"I was fixin' to suggest that. Why don't you come see me?" He whipped out one of his business cards and passed it to me. "Professionally. I could do wonders."

"I can't afford Neiman's." I handed his card back to him.

"We could work something out." Instead of taking his card, he slipped his hand over mine, forcing my fingers to grip it. "You know, I'm not really like this. Like I was out there." He stepped closer as if he might be thinking about making a pass.

"Really?" I dropped his card on my dresser and stepped out into the hallway.

"No." He followed me. "Women kind of demand it of me."

"Hey! We're fixin' ta go club hoppin'," one of the girls shouted as she headed for the door. "Wanna come along?"

Mr. René didn't appear to hear her.

"Because of my profession. If I act sensitive and artistic, they'll think I'm a fairy."

"A fairy or an asshole, huh? A tough choice."

Ignoring that, he continued, "The Texas Association of Hairdressers and Cosmetologists is having their annual formal next month—the Hair Ball, we call it. If you go with me, I'll do a complete make-over. Free of charge. You'll look like a million dollars."

"I'm not interested in going anywhere with you," I replied.

"I'm going to the clubs," he said. "Wanna come?" I shook my head. "I didn't think so. You're a square. No one's ever gonna marry you."

"Well, thank God for that."

* * *

Though in bed by eleven, I was wide-awake until early morning thinking about Lonnie and this Lisa woman. I'd never know any lesbians before—or at least if I did, I didn't know they were lesbians. My mind wondered to, of all things, Dorothy Samuels, this girl from junior high. Everyone made fun of Dorothy: she was short and bony, had frizzy brown hair and wore glasses thick as coke bottles. She was in my English class and once we had an assignment to write a composition about the person who had most affected our lives. Dorothy wrote about this summer camp counselor—a college girl—who'd recognized that Dorothy had musical talents and taught her to play the piano. Because Dorothy had an incredible ear, she was able, after a short while, to play popular songs after she'd heard them only three or four times. When she returned home, her parents told her they could not afford lessons, much less a piano, so nothing came of her talent. But Dorothy ended her composition by stating that she would always love that counselor.

Our teacher, a woman who had pursed her lips in disapproval so often that she had lipstick rivers running into her nostrils, called Dorothy's parents. No one knew what she said, but that night Dorothy's father beat her so severely that an ambulance was required. When she returned to class, Dorothy was even more ostracized and was the object of vicious jokes. Like everyone else, I avoided her. Eventually, she quit coming to school. I never saw her again.

As I lay there, I thought of all the small gestures I could have made that might have helped her survive those months. Little things that would have cost me nothing.

At three, I almost dozed off, but something popped into my mind and woke me. After I flipped on my lamp, I hurried to my closet. The black dress I'd worn in Austin was pushed to the far side. I pulled it out and searched the pockets. Agent Parker's card was still there. I tucked it into my wallet, crawled back into bed and slept like a puppy the rest of the night.

It was surprisingly easy to wake up the next morning. I was so psyched that I could hardly wait to get to work. I called him first thing.

"I have a favor to ask," I said. Lonnie was safely tucked away in her cubicle. No one else paid any attention to me.

"I'll see what I can do." I could practically see him smirking to himself.

"Don't you have access to those computers with everyone's criminal records in them?"

"Why?" Suspicion crept into his voice.

"Would you run a name through and let me know what turns up?" It was a long shot and I expected an outright refusal.

"You gotta be kidding!" he laughed. "That's not exactly kosher, you know?"

"You wouldn't have to send me documents—just tell me if there's anything—."

"Why would I do this for you?"

"Maybe you'd want me in your debt?"

He was quiet for a moment. "How far in my debt would you be?" He was going to do it!

"Pretty far."

"Next time I'm in Austin, would you come down?"

"Maybe."

"It'll have to be better than maybe."

"Okay, then." It was hard to say which of us was slimier.

The first thing I learned when I got into politics was that folks would do amazing things for you, if you just asked. The fact that I was female and young helped. But people with power were eager to use it, especially if it involved low risk and potential payoffs. As for my promise to Agent Parker, I could outmaneuver him when the time came.

* * *

The bowling-for-peace thing was that night, but I almost missed it because I ran home to take a nap and when Herman stopped by the apartment to pick me up, I was as unconscious as a vagrant on a park bench. It took him so long to rouse me that he almost left, assuming I'd gotten a ride with someone else. When I opened the door, confused about everything, Herman took one look at me and gasped.

"Aren't you going bowling?" He asked.

"Bowling?" I said. "Oh, shit. I fell asleep. But I'm awake now. Let's go."

"Wouldn't you like to comb your hair first?" he suggested.

* * *

Bowling turned out not to be my natural sport, pretty much like all the rest of them. The Draft Information Center reserved six lanes and each had four or six bowlers. Herman and Margaret were on my lane but Greg was supervising, so he wasn't bowling. Most of the participants were college-types who thought they or someone they loved would soon need the DIC's services.

The first time I bowled, my ball flew halfway down the alley before it landed with a window-rattling thud. Then it meandered ever so slowly toward the gutter. The second time this happened, a guy from the next lane explained that I should try to roll, rather than toss, the ball. This did work better—once or twice my ball nicked a pin or two just before it jumped the track—and I started racking up points. By the end of the first game, my score was twenty-nine and I felt pretty good about that, until Greg showed up.

"Twenty-nine, Gloria! How could anybody bowl twenty-nine?"

"They keep slipping in the gutter," I explained.

No shit," Greg said. "We're not going to get a cent off you. Where's your pledge sheet?" I showed it to him and after a moment, he said, "How'd you get Lance Wallace to pledge?"

"He's kind of a friend."

"Shit! He's got money and he pledged a lot. No one else got pledges over a quarter. Now, he's gonna get off paying a token. Who's this Earl Sweet?"

"One of the executives at my office."

"Well, shit, Gloria, this really stinks!"

"I didn't know it would be this difficult. Maybe I'll do better in the next two games."

"You sure as hell will! 'Cause I'm gonna bowl for you."

"Is that fair?"

"The system's not fair, Gloria. Move over."

* * *

"When you come to Austin," Agent Parker said during his call the next afternoon, "don't wear any underwear."

"I never do." I love to do shit like that to jerks who think they're shocking me. When he returned to Austin, I would tell him I was undergoing treatment for gonorrhea.

"Took me a while, but I did find something interesting. The guy's fairly law-abiding except for one weakness. I don't know if it's what you want—"

"What did he do?"
"Bigamy."
"Bigamy?"
"Yep. First wife lives in Salt Lake City—maybe Mormons. Then he marries wife number two in Tulsa. She finds out about Number One and sues him."
"What happened to Number One?"
"Still together, I guess. That's all I have."

* * *

"Hello? Is Theodore Mossman there?" I asked the woman who answered the phone.
"No, he won't be back until this weekend."
"Oh. So, he'll be there this weekend?"
"That's what I said." A bitch.
"Where is he now?"
"He's on the road! Who is this?"
"I'll call back."
Now my problem was how to get the information to Lonnie without telling her I broke into her desk. I hung around the office after everyone left and, using Lydia Chavez's typewriter (I'd read enough detective novels to know typewriters could be traced), I composed an anonymous letter to Clarence Tyson. Then I dropped it in the outside mailbox.

* * *

Situated between Dallas and Ft. Worth, Arlington was a bit of a trek. Busses ran from the depot in Dallas every hour and made stops at the hotels and Six Flags Over Texas. I caught the six o'clock bus, which reached the hotel at seven-thirty.

When he opened the door, he was wearing only a pair of gray slacks. The hair on his chest sparkled with beads of water. It was thick and golden and, at his abdomen, it tapered to a narrow strip that crawled suggestively into his pants. He had a small white towel draped over his shoulders and slender streaks of foam remained on his cheeks. I tried to just look at his face.

He wiped off the shaving cream and then flipped the towel over his head and around my neck, pulling me to him. When he kissed me, I swear to God, and I know this is corny, I swooned.

"A month alone with you. That's all I ask." Then he stopped abruptly. "Oh! Before I forget. I have some news. Hunter Callihan is a small time loser. He has a string of petty offenses, but nothing big enough to be of interest. The Bureau's embarrassed that it made a federal case out of a little grass, especially since there's doubt as to whether it even belonged to him. They want to make a deal—have him go away quietly. He'll get a suspended sentence, but that's all. You can relax."

Before I could relax, however, he nuzzled his face against my neck. His cheek was smooth and cool and smelled of soap. He grazed his lips over my face before he said, "I'm going to be in Dallas in two weeks. I'm speaking to the Texas State Teachers Association. Think you can save that date for me?" As he said this, he kissed me all over my neck.

"Jesus!" I whispered, "are you kidding?"

He chuckled as he pulled back and looked at me. Stroking his fingers lightly over my face, he said, "You're awfully pretty."

Embarrassed, I laughed. "I'm hardly pretty, Vic."

"*I* think you're very pretty." I laughed again and couldn't quite look at him. "Would I be spending all this time with you if I didn't think you were pretty?"

"Maybe, you know, you…like me, or something." Our eyes locked. My heart pounded expectantly. Suddenly, he walked away. I sagged against the wall.

"Hey," he called back to me. "I bought you a gift." He walked to the bed and retrieved a beautifully wrapped package. "Go ahead. Open it."

It was a small, square box and I expected to find something like a scarf inside. Instead it was a pink camisole, so sheer that even folded over several times, you could have read the fine print of a legal document through it. I was mortified to feel my face turn red.

"I love it when you blush," he grinned.

"I never blush."

"Sure you do. That's what I first noticed about you."

"It was not."

"At Love Field. I glanced at you and you started blushing and I said to myself, 'Davis! That young girl wants to sleep with you.'"

Had I heard him correctly? "I did not blush because you *glanced* at me."

"No. You blushed because you were having wicked little thoughts."

"You were leering at me!"

He threw his head back and laughed. "Come on, Gloria, I was hardly leering at you. Give me some credit. I can see why you might think I'm a dirty old man, but I do have political sense. I've always known you don't impress the voters by leering at girls young enough to be your daughter."

"You *stared* at me."

"I *glanced* at you."

"And you kept looking at me."

"I did: I was flattered. I decided to play with you a little, so I kept glancing over to see if you'd blush again."

I thought back to that night at Love Field. I'd been taken with him the moment he appeared, but—.

"Try it on." His voice brought me back to the present. "See if it fits."

While he tossed himself on the bed, propping his hands behind his head, I lifted the slip out of the box and started for the bathroom.

"Hey," he called after me. "Where are you going?"

"I. I was going to change."

"Why do you have to go in there?" I stood where I was. "Surely, you're not shy around *me*?"

"It's just—. It's a little embarrassing."

"What have you got that I haven't seen?"

"Nothing. I guess. But—"

"So there's no problem." A look of impatience flickered across his face. For the first time ever, I wished I was more like Jo Beth. "Gloria, why complicate this? It's just another way to be intimate. It's as if we were married and I'm watching you get ready for bed. Is that such a big deal?"

"Do you watch your wife get undressed?"

"I used to."

"Like this?"

"What do you mean 'like this'? She'd get undressed, sometimes I'd watch. I can't believe I take such sass from you."

"How come you never take your clothes off for me?"

"I did once. You chose not to watch. However, if that's what you want, all you have to do is ask."

Okay, I was being stupid. This was not that big a deal. After I untied the bow at my waistline, the wraparound dress fell away. Though I could feel Vic watching me, I avoided looking at him. I quickly removed the rest of my clothes and posed with my arms up in the air, like an acrobat.

"Very nice," Vic said and kicked the camisole toward me. I slipped it over my head and stood at the foot of the bed.

"Come here," he said. But I didn't move.

He scooted toward me and sat on the edge of the bed. His hands resting on my hips, he pulled me so that I was standing between his legs. He stared at me the way he had when we first met and it caused my stomach to flutter. Then he shook his head so slightly that had I not been staring back at him, I would have missed it, and he sighed a very deep sigh. The fluttering spread to my thighs and my chest and I felt lost and lightheaded. I slipped onto the bed and as I reached up to kiss him, he leaned back until I was lying across him. I had forgotten how thrilling it was to feel his chest against mine. My leg eased over his and the fabric of his pants scratched my inner thigh. My whole body, under the flimsy camisole, seemed oddly soft and fragile, as if it might split open at the slightest pressure. He closed his eyes while I kissed his cheeks and neck. His arms rested by his side passively, but I could feel his heartbeat against my breast and I knew he was not as relaxed as he appeared. For a while, the only sound in the room was our breathing, which was so deep and slow and in sync that I could visualize an oxygen balloon in some operating room filling and emptying, filling and emptying.

Finally, he slid his hand up my leg, under the slip and over my bottom as he whispered my name and I wondered why it was only men whose hearts gave out in such situations. I pulled back and studied his face. His eyes were hooded, his skin was flushed and his slightly open lips appeared swollen. I ran my fingers across his mouth and he clamped his teeth over one of them.

"You're so beautiful," I said, moving my fingers down his cheek, over his throat and to his chest. He stared back at me, neither flattered nor embarrassed by the compliment.

I looked at his chest as my fingers trailed through his hair. He twitched, tightening the muscles in his abdomen when I reached his stomach, where the hair narrowed. I followed it with my finger. To his navel. Into his pants. My fingers grazed the top of his penis and his body jerked as he gasped. I unfastened his waistband and unzipped his fly. After I pulled his pants to his knees, he hooked his heels into them and, peeling them off, he hurled them to the floor. My hand slipped around his penis and he moaned. I wanted to kiss him there, though I had never done that and wasn't sure exactly what to do. He seemed to know what I was thinking, because he ran his hand up my back to my neck and pushed my head forward.

Then the phone rang. A terrible jarring ring. I almost screamed and we both jumped forward, looking at the black piece of plastic as if it were a person who had suddenly barged in, which I guess it was. After the second ring, Vic rubbed his hand over his face and sat up.

"I have to get this," he explained.

He took a deep breath and let it ring once more before grabbing the receiver.

"Hello?" he said and after a half second pause, suddenly moved away from me to the other bed. "Penny! Where the hell are you?" He glared my way. "I thought you weren't coming until tomorrow."

My heart thudded so hard that I could barely catch my breath.

"A surprise? What's that?" He snapped his fingers at me and with his thumb indicated that I should be getting out. I fumbled around, trying to find my clothes while he stepped into his pants, hugging the phone with his shoulder.

"I'll come to the lobby and help with your luggage."

With difficulty, I threaded the sash of my dress through the waistband opening.

"Why not?" Vic watched me solemnly. "You sure? Okay, it's ah—" He checked to see how far along I was, I assume trying to decide if he needed to stall. Since I was slipping on my shoe, he sighed, "Four fifteen. Great! See you in a minute."

"Jesus!" He shouted. "We gotta get you out of here. Take the stairs. She's seen you."

I was about to leave, when he spotted the camisole lying across the bed.

"Shit! Don't forget this."

He crammed the slip and the wrapping paper inside the box and smashed on the lid. Though it spewed tissue and ribbons, he shoved it into my arms. As I was about to step into the corridor, we heard the unmistakable ping of the elevator.

"Shit," Vic whispered and shut the door quickly.

"It can't be her already," I suggested.

"Get in this closet just in case. I'll check the hallway." Slats on the door allowed me to see his feet. He opened the door and after a moment said, "Okay. I believe it's safe."

I pushed the closet open but before I could escape another elevator pinged and Vic held a hand up to stop me. We waited like that for maybe ten seconds until:

"Daddy! Daddy!" a child's voice called from down the hall. The last thing I saw before I pulled the closet shut was Vic slumping against the doorframe.

"Regina! What a big surprise." Through the slats, I could see him squat to lift her and I heard loud smacking noises as they kissed each other. "Mommy didn't tell me she was bringing you."

"It's your surprise!" Regina yelled.

"It sure is," Vic replied. I took very slow, deep breaths hoping to steady my stomach. "What made you change your plans?" he asked.

"I missed you, too." Penny kicked her shoes across the room. "Traffic was awful."

"Where's Danny?"

"He stayed with your mother. He has a game tomorrow."

"So, why did you come early?" he asked again, almost rudely.

"Well, we hardly see you anymore, so I said to Regina, 'Why don't we surprise Daddy and show up a day early.'" They both moved into the main part of the room. "Did we interrupt something?" she asked and I felt my stomach fall to my feet.

"Ah, no! I just...took a little nap," he mumbled.

"Doesn't look as if it was a particularly *restful* nap." She seemed almost flirtatious.

"Don't be silly, Penny," he snapped.

"Yeah, Mommy. Don't be silly."

"That's right, Regina. Isn't Mommy being silly?"

"Yes," Regina agreed.

"And mommies should never be silly in front of children, should they?"

"No!" Regina laughed.

"'Cause children might act silly, too, and then what?"

"I don't know," Regina said after some thought.

"We'd have a mess," Vic answered.

"I wasn't being silly," Penny replied and her voice seemed to gloat. "I just worry that Daddy's working too hard, trying to satisfy all the voters."

"Mommy, Mommy, look at the pretty bathroom!" Regina ran around with that pent-up energy kids have after a long trip. She explored the room as if it were a toy store, and she got dangerously close to my hiding place. Suddenly, Vic's legs came into view as he leaned against the closet door.

"Let's go downstairs and get something to eat," he said.

"We got Big Boys," Regina answered.

"We ate on the road," Penny confirmed.

"Well, I'm starving. Come with me while I get something."

"Now that I'm here, I'm not moving. Get room service." The television flicked on. "How'd the press conference go?"

"Okay, I guess."

"You lack your usual confidence."

"Had the feeling one of our old friends in the press was setting me up."

"Why's that?"

"He kept asking about integration. Must have mentioned it three times."

"What do you think he was up to?"

"Beats me. I'm sure we'll find out, though."

"Daddy? Can we go swimming?"

"Sure, honey. Wanna go swimming, Penny?"

"It's almost her bedtime."

"But look at her, she's wired. A swim would tire her some."

"Yes, Mommy. Yes, Mommy."

"Tomorrow, Regina. I'll take you swimming when Daddy's at his boring ole meeting."

"So, let's get something to eat. I'm starving. Besides, I need a drink."

"Call room service."

"I hate eating in the room. I spend most of my life in hotel rooms. Besides crumbs get all over—"

"I have to pee, Mommy."

"Daddy's right there. He can take you."

"No. *You*, Mommy. You!"

"Regina," Penny moaned, but she walked the little girl into the bathroom. Vic followed and shut the door behind them.

"I'll go get us some ice," he called to them.

He opened the closet and room doors simultaneously and jerked his head to indicate I should beat it. I blasted into the hall and rushed for the stairway, not even glancing back at him.

Careening down all four flights, I clutched the gift box against my chest as if it were a life preserver. When I reached the lobby, I spotted the ladies' room and made a beeline for it. Not bothering to lock the stall door, I fell to my knees and threw up into the avocado green toilet.

No telling how long I sat there. It didn't matter. I had no place to go here and no money to get there anyway. Eventually, I made my way to the sink and I splashed cold water on my face. Opening my purse, I counted the five dollars in my wallet. That was enough to take the bus back to Dallas, but since the busses had stopped running, it wasn't an option. Sometimes hotels provided limousine service to airports. Hiking my purse over my shoulder, I peeked out into the hall. The coast was clear. As I was about to leave, I glanced over my shoulder and spotted the now-crippled-looking box Vic had given me, lying on the floor where I'd dropped it. I opened it and looked at the lingerie. Then I closed it back up, crumpled the box in half and shoved it into the silver, bullet-shaped trash can under the paper-towel dispenser.

The receptionist told me that the hotel did have a limousine service for twelve dollars and that the next one was due in thirty minutes.

"Will they take a check?" I asked.

Each time the elevator pinged, I gasped and jumped around. I'm sure she believed I had just been upstairs stealing jewels from the hotel guests.

"Yes, if you have one credit card and a driver's license."

"I have a library card."

"I don't think they'll take that."

"Can *you* cash a check for me—for just seven dollars?"

"Are you a guest in the hotel?" She eyed me suspiciously

"No. I was visiting a friend."

"If your friend will vouch for you." She lifted the phone.

"No. No. That's okay. I'll think of something."

I stepped outside. It was a clammy night. The hotel was in an industrial-looking, roll-up-the-sidewalks-at-five area. The doorman tipped his hat as I passed. I considered hitching a ride, but the surroundings were so dark and deserted that it gave me the creeps.

"Is there a diner or something around here?" I asked.

"We have a restaurant in the hotel," he replied.

"I know, but—"

"Go to the street, turn right and about a mile and a half down the road is a Jack-in-the-Box. Can I get your car for you?"

"No. I'll...I'll just walk."

It was as dark out as the circles under Nixon's eyes—no streetlights or anything. The sky was clear, but there was only a new moon. A dirt path skirted the street and beyond that was a wooded area. When I had walked for about ten minutes, a banged up car passed me, slowed and then backed up until it was next to me. Two guys were in the front seat.

"Need a lift?" the passenger said. Ignoring him, I sped up.

"Where you going?" he asked. I was in no man's land. The hotel was too far away and the Jack-in-the-Box wasn't even in view yet. Everything else was dead.

"Hey, stuck-up! You need a ride?"

I was afraid to look toward them for fear they might have a gun. As long as I didn't see it, it couldn't intimidate me.

"What are you doing out here all by yourself?" he asked. "It's not very safe. You should probably get in with us before some thugs try to pick you up." I prayed for a police car.

"Ask her if she wants money," the driver said.

"My friend wants to know how much you charge."

"Piss off!" I said, though I knew I should just keep quiet.

"She said it's free," the passenger said.

Every news story I'd read about mutilated rape victims ran through my head. I considered the wooded area, wondering if I should chance it.

"Hey," he called again. "Why don't you get in the car? We'll take you to this party."

I kept on walking, but they stayed even with me. I could see lights ahead and assumed the Jack-in-the-box was getting close.

"I sure would like to fuck you."

My clothes were soaked from the heat, the exertion and the terror. My mind churned to devise a plan should one of them get out of the car.

"I have a twelve-inch dick," he said.

No other cars were in sight. Nothing. They carried on a hushed conversation, which I couldn't hear, but when the passenger said, "Pull over," that was my cue. I zigzagged toward the trees but my heels kept sticking in the ground, preventing me from gaining much speed. I had no idea if they were following, but even if they weren't I couldn't stop until I tripped. I crawled behind a large tree and peered out toward the highway. They were just pulling away: another car had happened by, scaring them off. I watched until both disappeared. Concealing myself among the trees, I made my way parallel to the highway until I reached the Jack-in-the-Box.

The three diners gawked at me when I entered. The attendant directed me to the pay phone toward the back of the restaurant. I called Veronica—she didn't have a car, either, but maybe one of her friends could come get me. Even Jo Beth, maybe. The phone rang and rang until I remembered that she had gone to visit her mother. Jo Beth was out, too. Greg's phone was disconnected. Herman Tedley didn't answer. Billy's name crossed my mind, but what would he tell his wife? Finally, I called Ian.

* * *

"Feldman," he answered, as if he were still at work.

"Ian?" I said.

"Hello! Anyone there?" he barked.

"Ian, it's me. Gloria."

"Hi." His tone lightened up. "You sound funny. You okay?"

"Are you busy?"

"Not now. I just got in. What's up?" An edge of concern wedged its way into his voice.

"I have a huge favor to ask, but promise me that if you're busy or you just don't want—"

"Gloria. What the hell's going on?"

"See, I'm kinda stranded someplace and I don't have any money—"

"Where are you? I'll be right there."

"No. I don't want you to pick me up. If I took a cab to your house, could I borrow the fare?"

"Gloria, where are you? I'll give you a lift."

"Well, see, I'm kinda far away."

"Like where?"

"Like Arlington."

"Arlington…Street? Avenue? Boulevard?"

"Arlington, Texas."

"How did you end up in Arlington with no way to get home?"

"It's a long story. I can pay you back when the bank opens Monday. Or I can give you a check." There was a long silence.

"Where are you? I'll be right there."

"No, really, Ian. That's not why I called. I just need—"

"Where the fuck are you, Gloria?" He seemed madder than the occasion required.

"I'm at a Jack-in-the-Box."

"Any particular one?" Sarcasm dribbled from the receiver.

I gave him directions. After I hung up, I slipped into the ladies' room. I was a mess. Leaves and grass poked out from my hair and my dress had a tear under the arm. Something black smudged my right cheek. I cleaned myself up as much as possible and then ordered some coffee while I waited for Ian.

It took him an hour and fifteen minutes. He pulled into the empty parking lot like the Tasmanian Devil, screeching his brakes to stop the car. Stepping out, he slammed the door so hard that I couldn't believe the little Beetle didn't roll over and curl up. He exploded into the Jack-in-the-Box and stood by the door glaring at me, his head cocked to the side and his thumbs hooked in his pants' pockets.

"Get in the car," he ordered.

He held the restaurant door for me, but did not rush over to open the passenger's side of the car. Before I had shut it, he threw the car into reverse and I almost went through the windshield.

"Put your seat belt on." The car squealed onto the highway. He drove recklessly, or as recklessly as you can in a Volkswagen, and he never looked my way.

"Look, I'm sorry I bothered you," I said after about ten minutes. "I called everyone else I knew first. You didn't have to drive all the way out here. I was happy to take a cab."

"You think that's what the fuck I'm mad at?" he shouted.

"I have no idea what you're mad at." He stopped the car so quickly that I flew forward and were it not for the seat belt I would have surely become human confetti.

"What the hell are you doing?" I screamed.

Turning the car sharply to the left, he crossed over the grassy island separating the eastbound and westbound traffic and started back in the direction we'd just left.

"Ian! Have you lost your mind? What are you doing?" He sped down the highway until we pulled into the hotel parking lot.

"*Now* do you know why I'm mad?" he asked.

What could I do? He had the goods on me; he was mad as hell. Seemed to me I had four choices. I could have lied, but he'd have seen through it. I really don't believe people should lie unless they know they can get away with it. Or, I could have looked him in the eyes and said, "Yeah? So what?" But I wasn't willing to suffer the consequences of such a line in the sand. I could have been sensitive, honest, and rational: just laid it all out on the table. I gave this serious thought. I could have said, "Look, Ian, I really care for you. You're my best friend. In fact, there are times when I think I love you, but God! I just can't get enough of Vic." Call it women's intuition or something, but I doubted that would produce desirable results. In the end, I had only one option: I cried. This was not totally manipulative: I am not a person who can cry at will. In fact, I've spent so much of my life faking a cavalier attitude that I have to be pretty strung out to fabricate even sniffles, but so far this had been one bitch of an evening and once I gave myself permission to do it, I was out of control.

"Shit," Ian whispered under his breath, while I let loose with these gut-wringing sobs that were so nauseating even I was turning against me. We sat there, not speaking, until exhaustion calmed me down.

"So what happened?" he said finally, chewing on the cuticle of his thumb. "Was he planning to have a threesome? Or did his wife show up?"

"I don't know what you're talking about?"

"Don't you? Vic Davis is staying here for the weekend."

"How do you know that?"

"Because the asshole had a press conference here this morning. And he's meeting with some Tarrant County business leaders tomorrow. And he—and his wife—are attending a Chamber of Commerce dinner tomorrow evening." His foot tapped restlessly on the floor. "And you? You had no idea?" I stared straight ahead. "You just happened to be walking the fucking streets on a lonely stretch in Arlington, an hour and a half from your fucking apartment, with no fucking money and no fucking car and you had no fucking idea that your fucking boy friend was just a fucking block away? Fuck that."

"Nice vocabulary."

"Why didn't you ask him for money?" There was no question about his implication. I tried to hit him, but he blocked my hand.

"I'm not the guy you should slap." He started the car and we drove back in silence. As we were pulling off the ramp into North Dallas, I turned toward him.

"Do you hate me?" I asked. We traveled two blocks before he answered.

"Sometimes."

When he stopped in the Saracen parking lot, I sat there for a moment.

"Would you—" I started and he looked at me for the first time since we'd left the hotel, "Would you like to come in for a while?"

"No," he said.

A tipsy couple, holding hands, made their way past the parking lot toward the club.

"I'm sorry," I said, after a while.

"Sorry about what?" He was looking out his window and biting his thumbnail.

"Sorry if I disappointed you." He didn't respond but he also didn't insist that I get out, so I assume he wanted to talk things out. "Under the circumstances, I'm deeply touched that you picked me up."

"I would have done it for anyone."

"Well, I'm grateful that you did it for me. I was…It was a spooky area."

He looked at me for a long moment before he turned away again.

"I don't know what would have happened if you hadn't. But if I had suspected that you could have been hurt, I would have walked home. And I'm not just saying that."

"Yeah. Well, it's late. You better go in. I'm tired."

"Are you sure you don't want to come in?"

"Positive!"

"Okay. Ah...goodnight."

He didn't walk me to the door, but he stayed in the parking lot until I was inside the apartment. Then he drove off.

I didn't bother turning on the lights. Instead, I went to the refrigerator to see if Veronica had any booze. A bottle of rum rattled around in the side compartment of the door. The phone rang. Eight times. There was no one I wanted to speak to, so I ignored it. I couldn't find a clean glass, so I washed out an AFL-CIO mug. The rum scalded my throat all the way down. And it tasted like shit. I screwed the cap back on and returned the bottle to the refrigerator. The phone rang again. This time I watched it as if I thought it might *do* something. After six rings, the caller hung up.

Even though it was only ten-thirty, I felt weary and decided to go to bed. I fell asleep immediately. Then I remembered I hadn't brushed my teeth, so I got up and went to the bathroom. As I stood before the mirror, my tooth felt strange and when I touched it, it fell out in my hand. Amazed, I looked in the mirror and sure enough, there was a big space where the tooth had been. I touched another and it just crumbled away. When I moved my jaw back and forth, I could feel my teeth shattering like icicles. I spit the pieces in the sink.

The phone rang and I sat up, startled, in bed. Panting, I ran my tongue over my teeth, relieved to find I wouldn't need dentures. By the time I was able to distinguish reality from nightmare, the phone stopped ringing. I couldn't fall back asleep. It was midnight.

I crept into Veronica's room, but her bed was empty. The latest *Cosmopolitan* was on her dresser. "How Passionate Are You?" was the title of a test on page 84. What the hell. I found a pencil on my desk.

> *"When you write him a letter, do you (a) use thin tissue paper to remind him of your negligee; (b) print SWAK on the envelope in fuchsia ink; (c) spray it with Intimate Cologne; (d) all of the above; (e) none of the above.*
>
> *"When you invite him for dinner, do you: (a) use a white tablecloth to remind him of a bed; (b) serve phallic-shaped foods such as asparagus, parsnips and carrots; (c) Dab Chanel No. 5 on the light bulbs; (d) all of the above; (e) none of the above.*
>
> *"When you serve him his favorite chocolate cake with chocolate icing, do you: (a) straddle his lap as you feed it to him;*

(b) scoop the icing off with your finger and rub it over his lips; (c) intentionally drop some on your blouse and ask him to wipe it off; (d) all of the above; (e) none of the above.

I could see where this was heading—So far I'd picked "e" three times—so I stopped. Besides, I never realized it was such hard work to get men to think about sex. The phone rang. Who would call at one-fifteen? Only a pervert. My eyes darted from window to window. What if those creeps somehow figured out where I lived? The phone rang again and I jumped. After the fourth ring, I decided it could be Veronica calling to say she wouldn't be home. I lunged for it, but got a dial tone.

Thinking about those two guys made me furious at Vic. It was as if I were simply a tie he had wanted to wear that night and when he saw it had a stain, it caused him only momentary disappointment to toss it in the trash. I hated him. What a bastard he was! I should have just opened that closet door when Penny showed and let him handle the consequences. He certainly hadn't worried about my consequences. I could have walked out and say, "Next!" like I was a receptionist in a doctor's office. God, I wished I'd done that just to see the look on his face.

Jesus! What if that kid hadn't had to pee? They would have found me, and then what? It would have been horrible enough to face Penny, but the kid! How loathsome would I have felt? Penny would know immediately what was up, but the kid would probably stare at me and then at Vic and then at me, knowing something was wrong but having no idea what it was. And from then on, Vic would have despised me. Like it was all my fault.

Absentmindedly, my hand went to my ear and I almost stopped breathing. My earring was missing. Shit! I jumped off the sofa and checked myself in the mirror. Both earrings were gone. I closed my eyes and tried to visualize where and when I'd taken them off. In his bathroom? No, I never got there. On the night stand? Maybe. Jesus! Penny was sure to find them. I felt sick. I stumbled back to the sofa; my hand was shaking. Then I spotted them. On the coffee table where I'd dropped them when I first got home. Besides, what did I care if Penny found them? Too bad I *hadn't* left them in his room.

How could I have let him screw things up with Ian like that? Ian was a million times better. Granted, Vic was gorgeous. And sexy. And brilliant. And important. But he was also married and selfish and mean...and I was pretty hung up on him.

Times like that you appreciate girlfriends. Someone who'll put things in perspective. Veronica was an expert at that. In our junior year, I was accidentally nominated Baseball Princess. Shock waves shook the whole school. Unfortunately, I beat out a cheerleader by one vote. That afternoon I went to the soda shop across from school—a place I usually avoided because it was the bastion of the in-crowd, and I always felt out of place there. But on that day I was there for some reason. I must have planned to meet someone there because I was by myself in one of the booths when some popular girls sauntered in and sat right behind me. One of them was Yolanda Madigan, the head of the pep squad. Earlier in the year, she'd kicked me off the squad because I missed practice every time Kennedy had an afternoon press conference.

"Janis got beaten for Baseball Princess!" one of them said, loud enough for me to hear.

"No!" Yolanda cried. She was always brown-nosing the cheerleaders because she hoped one day she'd be one herself. "Who got it?" There was a silence while I suppose one of them pointed toward me. "You're kidding!" Yolanda all but yelled. "*Janis* is cute."

Mustering every ounce of dignity I had, I left the soda shop as if I hadn't heard a word. I considered resigning—what did I care about that princess shit anyway? But Veronica talked me out of that. Of course, I wasn't crowned Baseball Queen; I came in last, but there was a half-page picture of me (and the other princesses) in the yearbook and it surprised me how proud I was of that.

Yolanda Madigan got married two days after graduation. She asked the entire cheerleading squad to be her bride's maids and you would have thought the event was going to be on by *the Ed Sullivan Show* the way everyone prattled about it.

I saw Yolanda at Preston Center last December when I was Christmas shopping. We didn't speak. She was pregnant, pushing a screaming and not particularly attractive baby around in a stroller. She did not have that glow of pregnancy you hear men talk about so much. Rather, she seemed doughy, harassed and angry and a good ten years older than me. I resisted a fleeting urge to forgive her.

* * *

Around two, there was some commotion at the front door and then Veronica entered. She flicked on the living room lights and gasped when she saw me sitting there by myself.

"Gloria, you scared the pee willie out of me!"

"I couldn't sleep," I said.

She knelt in front of me and held my hand as she peered up into my face. "You and that reporter have a fight?" she asked.

Once Veronica dated a married man—an oil executive—who showered her with gifts, the parting one being his partner, who simply showed up in his place. She wouldn't have been critical. But I'd never mentioned Vic and it seemed too complicated to go into now, so I just let her believe this was about Ian which, of course, it was.

"Go ahead and cry," she instructed with the authority of a Revlon make-up consultant, and on cue, I did. "Get it out of your system. Things always seem most depressin' this time of night. By morning, it'll be better. Not perfect, mind you, but better. When you're ready to talk, I'll be right here."

She filled the tub with some of her expensive milk bath and ordered me in it. She also gave me a sleeping pill.

* * *

I was as unconscious as a morgue stiff, when a chorus of sirens sped past the apartment, shaking me from my pharmaceutical coma. I tried to get up, but my head felt like a medicine ball and my eyes refused to focus. With effort, I staggered to the window and spotted some commotion about a block away. I almost fell to the floor pulling on my jeans. After I washed my face and brushed my teeth and sort of combed my hair, I made a cup of instant coffee and stumbled out the door. The early morning air was hot and muggy, making everything a little tacky.

A supermarket delivery truck had jackknifed across Harlow Avenue, and though there were no injuries, things were a mess. The cab had twisted onto its side while the trailer had pitched up and dangled in the air. Produce had bulldozed the rear doors and eggs oozed around with ketchup, mustard, A-1 sauce and just about anything imaginable. The combined odors on such a steamy day didn't help my wooziness. Cameramen and photographers were on hand and locals—still in their robes—rubbernecked the damage.

Ian was there. He didn't cover metro news, but since he lived a block away in the opposite direction, he probably heard the confusion, too. As I watched him, he spotted me, but then looked away, pretending he hadn't. I decided to confront him. He was unlikely to yell in a crowd. Slipping around, I was able to sneak in from behind. Standing to his right, I tapped him on the left shoulder, the way kids do, and when he turned that way, I said, "hi." He jerked toward me, but then pivoted back to the wreck.

"When this is all over, grab a couple of eggs and I'll make you an omelet," I said.

He turned toward me, with a look that could peel fresh paint, and was about to say something captivating, like "fuck off," when he stopped himself. His shoulders sagged as he sighed. "Jesus, Gloria."

"What?" I asked, confused.

He slipped a finger under my sleeve and said, "Your shirt's on wrong-side-out."

"Oh," I said, "I know that. There's a stain on the other side."

"You need a keeper." He started to walk away.

"You interested?" I said, following. It was risky striking out like that so soon after a brawl, but what the hell, I was so far down, I might as well line up all the rejections at once.

"I was. Once." He stopped and with both hands on his hips surveyed the wreckage.

"But not anymore?"

"No. I don't think so."

My chest tightened up a little. "So, I guess we're not going to the movie tonight?" I asked. "I hear *Virginia Woolf* is fabulous. I'd hate to miss it." His eyes narrowed but he said nothing. "Maybe I'll see if Veronica wants to go. Now that Hunter's in jail, she's around more."

I couldn't believe I was babbling like that. Once I managed to shut up, Ian turned away and watched the clean-up crew sweeping glass and goo into big dustpans.

"Well," I said after a deep breath, "you know where I am if you change your mind."

Veronica was still asleep when I got back. After I showered and dressed, I left a note telling her where I'd be and caught the downtown bus. Since I was feeling a little hungry, I stopped at a donut shop and had breakfast.

Lance had told me he'd be in his office Saturday and that I should stop in sometime between ten and three to collect the bowling money. He was a partner in a large firm that handled mostly labor-related cases. Though spacious, the offices lacked the rich trappings generally found in legal offices.

His secretary told me he was on the phone but had said I should go on in. I peeked in his door and knocked lightly on the frame. He waved me in with the two middle fingers of his left hand. A cigarette dangled from his mouth and his eyes squinted against the lingering smoke.

His blue-walled and burgundy-carpeted office was large and neat. There were framed photographs of Lance shaking hands with political figures as well as diplomas, cases of law books, and oil paintings of typically Western scenes: horses reared up amid dusty clouds; Mexican adobe houses; aging cowboys with scored faces and sagging shoulders. Over his desk was a plaque that read: "Forgive and Remember."

I eased myself into one of the leather chairs facing his desk and waited. He hunched over a legal pad scribbling notes, his cigarette jumping up and down as he spoke, sending smoke signals to the Indian village hanging across the room. In no time, I was able to figure out that he was lobbying for his latest cause: to remove the "illegitimate" designation from birth certificates of children born out of wedlock.

"The way I see it," he said, "we shouldn't be conferrin' titles on people who haven't earned 'um. Know what I mean? Just not American. There are lots a self-made bastards out there and I think 'hell, they've worked for—they should get that recognition. Every possible chance.' But these little kids. Shit. What have they done but had irresponsible parents?"

A framed picture of a woman sat on his desk. She had light brown hair and a make-up-free face full of freckles. She parted her hair down the middle and simply let it hang on either side of her head. She wore a plain white blouse with a Peter Pan collar and a navy blue cardigan over that. Although she was attractive, she was so unglamorous that it was hard to picture her with a guy as flashy as Lance.

"Gloria, darlin'," he said when he hung up, "you must be wantin' some money." He grinned at me as he reached inside a drawer and withdrew a checkbook. "What're the damages?"

I pushed my score sheet toward him and looked at the floor so we couldn't make eye contact. He picked up the page and studied it.

"Now, Gloria, darlin', you tryin' to tell me that you bowled twenty-nine the first game and then two hundred and sixty-five the second and two hundred and eighty the third?"

"Yeah, well. You know. It took me a while to, ah, get the hang of it and all."

"I been bowling for years and I never broke two-fifty. You must be a real natural at this."

"Yeah, I guess so," I said, glancing toward the painting of the despondent cowboy.

"Let's see," he said, studying the figures, "I don't have near enough fingers to add this." But he started writing the check anyway. "They'll probably make you the poster girl for this," he said, ripping the check out and passing it to me. It was for five hundred and seventy-four dollars. I couldn't look at him when I said thank you.

"Hey," he said. "Ya got two dollars on you?"

"I think so."

"Sign this. It's a petition urgin' folks ta write in Estelle Harris for Dunlop's old seat. We're gonna take out a full page ad in both papers."

"That's a great idea," I said, as I signed my name and then rummaged in my handbag for money.

"I think the least you could do is take me out to lunch since I can't afford the price of a burger now." He stood and started pulling on his jacket.

"Okay," I said, grateful for some penance. "It'll just have to be a place that takes checks."

Grinning, he walked over and offered me his hand. "Let's see what we can find. Maybe we'll luck out and spot a lobbyist."

We ended up at the Cro-Magnon Bar and Grill, an all but deserted, dingy hang-out for area lawyers. Grabbing an out-of-the-way booth, we sat opposite each other. The table had menus, salt and pepper shakers, a silver napkin dispenser and a bowl of peanuts. After glancing at the grease-spattered menus, Lance hollered for Lucille, the waitress to take our order.

"Do you take checks?" I asked when she reached our table, but Lance whacked me on the head with his menu.

"I was kiddin' you," he said.

"No. I'd like to buy you lunch," I said.

"Feeling guilty about somethin'?" he asked, grinning back at me, but before I could answer, he ordered a steak sandwich basket and a beer. "What sounds good to you?" he asked.

"Just a Coke," I said. "I had a late breakfast."

As Lucille walked away, Lance followed her with his eyes, or rather followed her butt. I wondered if Vic did shit like that. Was this something they learned in legislator school? Thinking of Vic, I wondered if it even crossed his mind that I might be dead in some field.

"Can I ask you a personal question, Lance?" I asked, pretending to admire the napkin dispenser.

"Sure can."

"All these women you fool around with…" I glanced up; he grinned. "Do you ever, you know, *like* any of them?"

"I love each and every one of 'um." He placed his hand over his chest, "My goddam heart is just brimmin' over with love."

We locked eyes momentarily before I rolled mine in disgust. I should have known better than to expect anything from him. Luckily Lucille arrived with our drinks. My Coke was in the bottle and not a glass so I grabbed a fistful of peanuts from the little dish and dumped them in the bottle. Lance watched—he had a curious expression on his face.

What?" I said, as I took a long swig from the Coke.

"Gloria, honey, I thought you were smarter than that."

"Don't knock it till you've tried it," I said, passing my soda to him. He ignored the bottle and fished around in his shirt pocket until he extracted three loose cigarettes. After selecting one, he returned the other two. Then he found some matches in another pocket, ignited one with his thumbnail and lit the cigarette.

"Which of my colleagues you sleepin' with?" He looked as if I'd told him I had cancer.

I paused, the Coke halfway to my mouth. "You're kidding, right?"

"I'm serious as a broke down dick."

"Even if that were true, which it isn't, why does the idea depress you so much?"

"Why? Because I like you. I don't want to see you get hurt."

"Why assume I'd be hurt?"

"Because if I'm right, and you're screwing around with one of my colleagues, he's probably married and I don't believe you're ready for that."

"How do you know what I'm ready for?"

"Don't forget, I've known you for years, honey. You have too many romantic notions—"

"I can't believe you think I'm *romantic*. That just shows how little you know me."

"You think you're in love with this guy?"

His question so surprised me that at first I couldn't answer.

"There is no guy," I said.

"Yeah, but are you in love with him?"

"If you think sex is so horrible for women, why are you always trying to inflict it on them?"

"Because with me, it's great." He grinned for a moment and then leaned toward me and lowered his voice. "I don't think sex is horrible for women. But there's sex. And there's sex: one of 'um nice and romantic and the other one's—" He squinted and shook his head slightly as if trying to pick tasteful words. "The other one's just goddam fabulous. I only wish you'd started out with the nice and romantic kind."

"How do you know I didn't?"

He looked at me while he inhaled a lungful of smoke. "I hope to hell you did."

Lucille plopped his sandwich before him. He didn't watch her walk away this time. Instead, he took two more drags off the cigarette and then ground it out in the ashtray.

"*Is* he married?" I looked up but didn't answer. "Gloria, darlin' don't you know there's only one thing a married man's lookin' for?"

"What's that?" I casually shook my Coke as if the conversation were only of mild interest.

"Somethin' different."

He picked at his food. I felt guilty that I'd ripped him off *and* depress him in the course of an hour. To cheer him up, I let loose with one of my more dramatic belches. Startled, he glanced up at me, somewhat outraged.

"You start lightin' your farts, we'll part company."

He ordered another beer, checked his watch and retrieved another cigarette.

"Why do you carry them around loose like that?" I asked.

"Tryin' to cut back. Only give myself ten a day. It's early to be down to two. This may have to be a special day."

After he paid the bill, I reached in my handbag and located his check. "Here," I said, handing it to him. "I didn't bowl those last two games."

"My momma didn't raise an idiot, darlin'," he said, passing the check back to me. "Keep it. If it keeps one kid out of this chickenshit war, I'll be worth it."

On my way to the bus stop, I passed a dingy store near the bottom of Elm Street. The crammed front window displayed so many stuffed animals that I could hardly take them all in. I'm not really a stuffed animal person, but one of them caught my eye. The bear was about eight inches tall and wore a crumpled blue trench coat. He had a notebook in one paw and chomped on a cigar. The brim of his hat was bent up and across its front was a square sign that read, "Press." Since it was only three dollars, I decided to buy it. And since it was only fifty cents to get it gift-wrapped, I did that, too.

I got off the bus two stops early and planned to just leave the gift by Ian's door: I didn't think anyone would steal it. But, when I spotted his car in the parking lot, I decided to knock.

"Is it your birthday?" I asked as if nothing were wrong.

"No." He seemed surprised to see me.

"Is it some sort of Jewish day?"

He smiled and shook his head.

"Is there anything special about today?"

"Not so far."

"Ah, well!" I opened the shopping bag and presented the gift. "Now there is!" He looked at it and then at me. "Go ahead," I said. "Take it."

"Is it a bomb?" he asked.

"You'll never know until you open it." He didn't take it so I reached for his wrist, lifted his arm and wedged the box between his elbow and his side. "You don't have to open it now." I felt a little foolish, so I decided to cut my losses. "Well, see ya," I said, starting to leave.

"Hey!" he called out after me. I glanced back. He leaned against the doorframe. "You wanna go to a movie tonight?" he asked.

"Which one?" I asked, taking a step his way.

"I don't know: *Virginia Woolf*?"

"It's supposed to be really good," I said.

"Well, you wanna go?"

"If you want to."

"What is this: eighth grade?" We both smiled. "I'll pick you up at seven."

"Okay," I said and couldn't wait for him to shut his door so I could click my heels. But as I turned to leave, he called out.

"Listen, Gloria." I stopped and pivoted back toward him. "And I *mean* this," he said all serious now, "I find out you're still meeting him, you'll never see me again. Not even to explain."

"It's over."

"Yeah." He started toward his apartment. "See you at seven."

It was four by the time I got home. Veronica looked up from the sofa where she was thumbing through a magazine.

"See, I told you things would be better in the mornin'," she chirped. "Where you been all day? You must've left at the crack of dawn." Before I could answer her, she jumped to her feet. "Oh, Gloria, I almost forgot. Some guy's been called for you."

My stomach tumbled a little. "Who was it?" I asked.

"He didn't leave his name, but he was so rude! When I told him you weren't here, he chewed me out. 'What do you mean, she's not there? Where the hell is she?' I said I wasn't your keeper but that you must have gotten up awfully early. Then he sorta calmed down and said, 'So she got in last night?' and I said 'yeah' and he asked what time and I said I didn't know, but that you were here when I got home at two. Then he slammed the phone down without even sayin' thank you, good-bye, bite my butt, or anything. He called a few more times and always seemed put out when I told him you still weren't home."

My earlier anger with him melted. Just like that. I sat in my room and just smiled to myself. In spite of my oath to Ian, I was already rationalizing seeing Vic again. And yet, I knew that was crazy. Some things you just know aren't going to pay off.

I stayed at Ian's that night because I worried Vic might call and I needed some time to think before I spoke with him again.

* * *

When Ian's phone woke us at eleven, I freaked, believing somehow Vic had tracked me down. It took a full minute for my pulse to return to normal.

"Feldman," Ian barked into the receiver. "Yeah? Yeah," he said.

He hopped up and hurried to his desk where he grabbed a notebook and started taking frantic notes. Once, he glanced at me and grimaced, as if I were an extravagant purchase he suddenly regretted.

"How many signatures?" he asked and paused a second. "And his is there?" He scribbled some more. "Thanks." He slammed the phone down and then lifted it again, dialing a number he knew by heart.

"Hank! Feldman. How much time do I have?" He reached for his pants, which he'd tossed over the bed, and pulled them on. "I just got confirmation on that story—" His shirt was on the floor. "It's practically finished. I just need to add this new stuff and—" He stepped into his shoes, not bothering with socks. "I'll be right there." Banging the receiver down, he turned to me. "I need to run down to the paper."

"You want me to come?" I mumbled, dreading the idea of getting up.

"No. Get some sleep. I'll be right back."

No sooner did the door click shut than I was up. I crept to the front door and listened until I heard the VW putt-putt down the street. My hand trembled a little as I hooked the chain lock. I figured I had at least an hour.

He had one of those desks with all the cubbyholes and each opening spewed junk: receipts, notes, scribbled phone numbers, flyers, extra keys, a bottle of black ink, name-dropping matchbooks.

There were magazines, stacks of books with ragged slips of paper poking out from between pages, spiral notebooks, bloated from use, and folded back to the next clean page. I flipped through a couple, but Ian's handwriting was impossible.

There were four drawers—two on either side. The upper ones contained writing supplies: white bond, letterhead for the *Morning News,* a "From the Desk Of Ian Feldman" note pad, envelopes, pencils, pens, erasers, and rubber stamps. I fanned through the papers and envelopes, but there were no photographs stashed away.

The bottom drawers had files. On the left side, the tabs read: Expenses, Investments, Martha's Vineyard, Real Estate. There were also files for taxes from 1960 - 1966. Pretty dull stuff. Except I'd never heard him mention anyone named Martha before, so I glanced through there. But it was nothing—just about some house in Massachusetts.

The other side had his political stuff. Phone directories for the state and national legislatures; background information on various issues—AFL-CIO, Communist Plot, Conspiracy Theory, Counter-culture, Education Bill, The Establishment, The Farm Workers, Governor's Race, Highways, Minimum Wage, Miranda, Natural Resources, Open Housing, Vietnam. Manila folders for ten candidates stood behind the divider entitled Governor's Race. Vic's was missing.

His closet was the size of a small room. Clothes hung on one side, while built in drawers banked the other. Shoes ran along the floor. There were two storage boxes, one on top of the other. I opened one and the smell of mothballs made me gasp. Woolens. The drawers just held routine stuff.

A shelf ran over the hanging clothes. An intriguing box to the far right called my name, but it was clearly too large for me to pull down. Oh, I could probably get it down; getting it back would be the problem. I got a chair from the dining room and when I stood on it, I was able to peek in. There was a trophy, a huge beer stein and some other garbage. Next to the box was a photo album. I pulled it down and carried it to the bed.

Black, triangular corners held each photograph in place. The first few pages seemed to be from his college days. A younger Ian, sporting a (gasp!) flattop, posed with friends, at football games or parties. There were shots of formal events—in each, Ian escorted a different girl wearing a strapless, tulle gown with a hoop skirt.

I nearly stopped breathing, however, when I came across an eight by ten of Samara. Her ballerina's bun was so tight that my eyes watered sympathetically. She wore a white tutu and stood on the toes of one foot while the other leg extended up behind her, over her head. She *was* a dancer. "To Ian. All my love, always. Samara." Her handwriting, of course was flawless. *She* didn't have trouble keeping her sentences straight without lines; *her* letters didn't shrink progressively across the page, as if the effort of expression had worn them out.

The next page covered a party. Ian was in a navy suit; Samara, an orange dress. In the first one, they beamed from behind a table crowded with gifts. Next was a group shot: two older couples, obviously their parents, joined them. Ian's mother was gorgeous, with cinnamon-colored hair tumbling beyond her shoulders. His father was almost as tall as Ian and was handsome except that he seemed too serious. Samara's parents could have been movie stars. The last picture was a close-up of Samara. Her smooth, dark hair hung around her like a veil, and blended so perfectly with her olive skin and brown eyes that she looked color-coordinated. Her teeth seemed too perfect to be real. She was so beautiful that at first I didn't notice the purpose of the pose. On her left hand, which she held up, she wore an enormous diamond ring.

The following pages were like a montage from some sappy movie: Ian and Samara on a bicycle built for two, dancing at a party, riding on a ski lift, enjoying family dinners. Then the scenery changed. Ian was in Texas; his hair was long. He must have taken most of the pictures because he wasn't in them. But there were lots of girls—most of them were attractive, but not all. He had clearly photographed every woman he'd ever encountered. Except me.

There were no photographs on the next few pages but the little black triangles that once bordered them were still in place. And that was it. I flipped through the blank pages to see if he had tossed the missing pictures between them, but he hadn't. I was staring at the wall trying to figure out why someone would remove photographs, when the front door crashed against the chain, almost causing my heart to stop.

"Hey, Gloria!" Ian yelled. "Let me in."

I flew into the closet and, holding the photo album over my head, hopped up on the chair. Unfortunately, I lost my balance and stumbled to the floor.

"Gloria, you awake?"

"Coming," I shouted. Shit. The album fell open and Samara's 8 X 10 came unhooked from two of the triangles. My hand was shaking so much that it took forever to slide the corners back in place. Finally, I got that squared away and managed to return the book. Now I just had to calm myself down and get the chair back into the dining room.

Wouldn't you know he had the door open as far as possible? There was no slipping the chair past him. He'd know what I'd been up to. The only thing more humiliating than getting caught was acting like you cared. I pushed the door shut and unlatched the chain.

"You get scared?" he asked, stepping inside. When he spotted the chair, he smiled. "I believe you're the most devious woman I've ever known." He smiled, confident there had been nothing to find.

"Why didn't you tell me you were engaged?" I demanded.

"Because I'm not." He sobered slightly.

"I saw the pictures."

"I was. I'm not now."

"You still see her."

"We're friends."

I waited for him in bed while he brushed his teeth. "I knew the second I left you'd snoop around," he called from the bathroom. "I just knew it. It's kinda satisfying, really, when you realize your instincts are that sharp, you know what I mean?"

When he joined me, he put his arm around my waist and pulled me to him like a spoon. He was dozing within minutes.

"What happened?" I finally said. Ian jerked as if a fire alarm had just gone off.

"Wha—" he mumbled.

"With you and Samara. What happened?"

"Christ! Can this wait?"

"No."

"We broke up, what do you think?" He snuggled down into his pillow again. I sat up and turned on the lamp by my night table.

"Oh, no," he moaned.

"She's beautiful."

"Yes. She's beautiful, she's talented, she's Jewish, she's sophisticated, she's smart, she's fun, she's rich, she's a great cook, a terrific hostess, and a good friend. She's close to perfect, if you want to know the truth."

"Not like me."

"She's nothing like you. Jesus."

That pretty much said everything, so I turned off the light. I could feel Ian mentally drumming his fingers.

"I didn't mean it like that," he whispered. "For all of her perfection, I found Samara just a little boring."

"So you broke up with her?"

"No. I didn't have the nerve. I postponed it. We were just twenty-three. I said I needed some time, wanted to try something different, live somewhere else. So, instead of going to Columbia, I moved to Austin. After a while, we broke up."

"Why?"

"I *told* you—"

"No, but what was your excuse? You couldn't have said 'I find you boring'."

"You can be such a pain in the ass," he said, sighing heavily, "I got involved with someone else. Big time. So when I went home for Thanksgiving, I told everyone."

"Samara must have been upset."

"I believe she knew something like that was going to happen. She handled it much better than my parents."

"They were disappointed?

"They were livid. Not so much because I dumped Samara, but more because they disapproved of—. Of…ah, the new woman."

"Why?"

"The three M's: married, mother and Methodist. And she was five years older than me—They made it clear they never wanted to meet her. Even if we got engaged."

"She was *married*?" Ian and I had more in common than I thought.

"Yeah. Well, her marriage was a catastrophe almost from the beginning. I happened to come along at a time when she'd had it."

"How'd you meet her?"

"At a party. She was with her husband, but he never paid much attention to her. I was in kind of a funk over several things: Samara, my job—I was on the outs with the paper's political editor. I was in no mood to party. I was drinking a beer and brooding off in a corner, when someone said, 'Maybe it would help if you talked about it.' She was…gorgeous and with no more encouragement than that, I told her all about Samara. 'If you have any doubts at all,' she said when I'd finished, 'then marriage is a mistake. It's often a mistake even when you're completely confident it's the right thing.' I explained that Samara was close to perfect, and she said, 'I know all about perfect,' and glanced across the room toward her husband.

"The next day, she phoned me at the paper and asked me to have lunch with her. Before lunch was over, I was in love. A month later, she left her husband. We talked about getting married as soon as the divorce was final."

"What went wrong"

He sighed and stared off into space for a while. "They got back together. For the kids."

"Do you ever see her?"

"When I was in Austin, I'd run into her occasionally. But now that I'm here—"

"Do you still...love her?"

Ian glanced my way. "I *care* about her. But, we weren't really right for each other." He rolled over on his side, facing me. "That was a long time ago," he said as he kissed me. I put my arm around his waist and noticed that the small of his back was sweaty.

"Ian?" I said, a little later, when the lights were off and we were both into our own thoughts. "How come you've never taken any pictures of me?"

From the corner of my eye, I saw him turn my way, a puzzled expression on his face. He didn't move for a moment and then he got out of bed and walked into his closet. When he returned, he was screwing a flashbulb into a camera.

"Okay," he said aiming it at me, "say cheese."

"Not now, you jackass," I shouted as the flash exploded.

"Oh! I think you had your eyes closed," he ejected the spent bulb and twisted in another.

"Ian! Put that goddam camera down," I shrieked as I hid under the sheets. He took four pictures of me as a lump in the bed before he turned out the lights and climbed in next to me.

"I can't wait to see how those turn out."

"You're such a jerk," I said.

* * *

On Monday evening, I bounded out of Freedom Mutual with the other low-level employees, whose main goal in life was to spend not one second longer than necessary in the office. To outsiders, we must have appeared as if we were escaping a building engulfed in flames. No sooner had I negotiated the front steps and started down the sidewalk to the bus stop, then I heard a car horn toot behind me. While there was no reason in the world I should have expected such a signal, I glanced back without slowing my pace. When, a second later, I registered what I'd seen, I screeched to such an abrupt halt that four people careened into me, scattering mayonnaise-smeared Tupperware containers and pocket books all across the pavement. I was grateful for the commotion because it gave me a moment to adjust to the shock of seeing Vic's car by the curb.

"Where can we go?" he asked, once I eased into the seat next to him.

I shrugged.

"Your apartment?"

I shook my head.

"Should I get a room?"

"No!"

"We need to talk. You don't have any suggestions?"

I shook my head.

He started the car and I watched his hand move from the ignition to the steering wheel. The tendons running to his fingers were huge. He had recently adjusted the Speidel band of his watch, exposing tiny, diagonal indentations around his wrist. The long, golden hair on that inch or two of visible arm lapped in one direction as if combed in place.

I wished I could have watched us make love. Not because I was some sort of sicko, but because I'd have liked to have seen his hands touch me; liked to have paid attention to how he looked when we kissed; liked to have watched the muscles in his back contract when he reached for me. I forced myself to look away. There was a nickel on the floorboard, to the right of the gas pedal. From where I sat, the upside-down Thomas Jefferson looked shockingly like a penis.

Vic parked at Bachmann's Lake, close to Love Field. I counted how many times his engine pinged while cooling down. He was watching me but when I glanced his way, he looked out the front window.

"I feel terrible about what happened," he said. His mouth was tight and his shoulders heavy. His remorse pushed a rush of warmth through me that was so intense I thought I might cry. Luckily, a plane flew over. When the noise subsided, he asked, "How'd you get home?"

"A friend picked me up."

"Your reporter friend?" I nodded. "At the hotel?"

"Down the street."

"Was he curious about why you were there?"

"Actually, he wasn't."

"I was off-guard when Penny called—" Vic continued after a while. "You had me so worked up and then she was downstairs. I wasn't thinking. When Regina showed up—Jesus." He covered his eyes with his hand. "It would have been really nasty, if they'd found you there. I just wanted to spare you that. Spare us all that."

"I understand. It's okay."

"No, but it's not okay. Because, see, I forgot where we were. I thought you could just slip out and get home and it wasn't until you left that I realized—When I got back in the room with the ice, it hit me. I gave Penny some lame excuse before running to the lobby to look for you. I wanted to get you a room, or pay for a taxi or something. But you'd vanished. I called your number until Penny got suspicious. I told her I was trying to set up appointments: I planned to hang up when you answered: I just wanted to know you got home."

The second hand on the dashboard clock jerked from one moment to the next.

"Don't you have anything to say?"

"No," I said.

"I want you to say something. Anything."

"I thought I'd never see you again."

"I can't believe you'd want to."

"At first...that idea upset me. Maybe because I just didn't want it to end like that. But when I thought about it, I realized there were worse ways it could end. And it has to end eventually, you know?"

"What are you saying?"

"I guess I'm saying maybe it would be better if you didn't get in touch with me again."

"I don't blame you for hating me—"

"I don't hate you. I'm not even angry. You're a married man with a public life. I never imagined anything would come of this. But I need to stop seeing you now."

"Gloria." He reached out and stroked my cheek with the back of his fingers. I had to struggle not to close my eyes. "Don't do this to me."

"Please, Vic. This isn't easy."

"Then why do it?"

"When I was in that closet? I was really scared—"

"That'll never happen again. I promise."

"Scared Penny would find me. Scared of what she'd say to me or about me. Scared of being involved in a scandal." As I spoke, my stomach knotted painfully. "Scared she might even kill me—"

"Gloria—" he put his arm around me and pulled me to his shoulder.

He was wearing Aramis. When I looked up, I saw his jawline, his cheek, a tiny pulse in his throat, and what I wanted more than anything at that moment was to touch him; to rub my face against his; to kiss him. I moved away.

"But I was also scared I'd hurt her. Jesus! She's never done anything to me."

"We won't hurt her, Gloria."

"It's not as if, you know, you and I *care* about each other or anything." My voice quivered a little.

"We don't *care* about each other?" He looked at me as if I had asked for his left testicle to press in the dictionary along with Veronica's wrist corsages.

"Well, I mean…it's really just…sex, isn't it?"

"Is it?" He glared at me. "You believe I'm some pathetic guy who has to take advantage of a twenty-year-old because my wife's lost interest in me? I've got news for you, Gloria. If I just wanted to get serviced, all I have to do is step out on any sidewalk in this great country of ours and snap my fingers."

It took me a moment to catch my breath after that, but only a moment.

"Don't be so modest, Vic. You're a good-looking guy."

"You can joke, but women like me. I could have sex every night with someone different, probably for the rest of my life."

Was this a warning? Or just an observation? Had I been put in my place? Or flattered? It didn't matter: every insecurity I had reached for a weapon.

"I wanna go home," I said.

"You don't get what I'm saying, do you? I don't *want* casual sex. I don't find it satisfying." I rolled my eyes. "Okay. Once in a while it's hard to pass up, but it's not what I want."

"Vic, I'm really tired."

"I don't care that you're tired. I'm goddamned exhausted and I still have a long drive."

"Things always have to be your way, don't they?"

"You think I'm having it my way now? You think I *want* this? Running around like an idiot for a…for a teenager?"

"I'm twenty."

"My ten-year-old son is closer to your age than I am. Jesus! Believe me, if I had it to do over again—" He stopped himself. Our eyes locked.

"Are you saying you regret this?" I whispered.

"I'm saying it was a big mistake."

My chest felt as if it caved in like a rotting jack-o-lantern. I blinked rapidly to clear up my vision and turned toward the lake.

"Then why did you do it?"

"Because I saw you and something happened."

"Was that fair? To me?"

"Probably not." He exhaled. "I'm a bastard. Is that what you want me to say?"

"It doesn't matter what you say."

"Since we've established that I'm some sort of heartless plunderer, why don't we examine you? Why did you agree to go to my room? You weren't *that* innocent."

"You...you seduced me!"

"And no one had ever tried that before?"

"Of course guys had tried that before—"

"So why me? Why give it all up for an old man with a wife and kids? You're smarter than that."

"Because I couldn't...*not*." We stared at each other.

"Something happened, right?" he whispered.

"I guess so." I was afraid to look at him for fear that 'something' would happen right there at Bauchman's Lake. Instead, I concentrated on the nickel, trying to guess its date.

"In the interest of complete honesty, I didn't plan to see you again after that first time."

I wondered how the nickel found its way to the gas pedal. Was it Vic's or Penny's? Or did one of the kids drop it one afternoon when they'd gone out for ice cream. Danny—was that the boy's name?—was probably flipping it on his thumb, when it fell. Maybe he tried to retrieve it, but got yelled at for getting in the way while Vic was driving.

"As great as it was, you were just too young. You might find this hard to believe, but I'm not fascinated by young girls."

Or maybe the nickel fell out of Penny's purse after she'd gone grocery shopping. She was in too much of a hurry to close her handbag and when she had to brake suddenly to avoid hitting a kitten, everything spilled. She thought she'd gathered it all up, but she overlooked the nickel, or maybe she didn't. Maybe she didn't think it was worth her effort. It wasn't important. What *was* important was that I wasn't Vic's girlfriend or lover—I was just a mistake. And that was all.

"Then you ambushed me in Austin. I was furious when I saw you there."

"Furious?" My insecurities tested their weapons: slipped bullets into the chambers, rubbed their thumbs across the blades of the machetes, toyed with the pins on the grenades.

"At first, I had this crazy notion that you were there because of me. That you were *pursuing* me. But then I realized you couldn't have just shown up: someone had to invite you. And that pissed me off even more. I was curious to learn who your date was. More than curious. Every time I looked your way, a different guy had his hands all over you."

"No one had his hands all over me!"

"Well, it seemed that way. I decided I had no use for you. But when I saw you go out on the terrace, I followed. And once we were alone, Jesus! The air crackled. It was all I could do not to throw you over one of those tables. So I told myself, 'Davis, you better just screw this kid and get her out of your system—"

"Well, that's the most romantic thing anyone's ever said to me," I cut in. He wasn't just putting me down: he was wrecking the memory.

"I'm not trying to be romantic. I'm trying to be honest."

"I've always believed there was something to be said for lying."

My whole purpose had been to make myself obsolete. I thought he kept seeing me because he liked me, but he'd only wanted to get rid of me. From the very beginning. And I couldn't wait to help him. God, I felt so humiliated. I knew I was going to cry and I would have given anything—anything—to avoid that.

"Gloria." His voice had a distinct I'm-trying-very-hard-to-be-patient quality to it. "The last few days have been a real bitch. Not just because of you, though you were certainly a factor. I'm tired, I'm irritable and perhaps I'm not being articulate, but—"

"Oh, I think you're being very articulate."

"Would you let me finish?" He slouched in his seat and pinched the bridge of his nose. "I could lie to you, Gloria. I could tell you I fell in love when I first spotted you. I can tell those kinds of lies without even blinking. It's much more dangerous to be honest."

"I don't need your honesty. In fact, it's the last thing I want." Whenever I inhaled, my breath caught. "You're off the hook. I'm not angry: you don't have to feel bad. I got home okay. I can take care of myself." Pathetically, revoltingly, I started sobbing before I finished.

It made me so angry to degrade myself like that, that I cried even more, those humiliating gulping sobs that make everyone sick. To my surprise, he didn't even seem to notice. He'd probably seen a million women cry—an occupational hazard.

"I want to be honest with you, Gloria. I want you to understand that." He looked at me with detached compassion: as if I'd just lost on *Queen for a Day* and was going to have to continue washing my family's underwear in the stream that ran alongside our trailer park. "I'm trying to explain to you why I don't want us to stop seeing each other now."

"You've made that very clear, thank you." He wasn't quite through with me yet. God forbid he should leave the table before stuffing himself. I started sniffling and rummaging around in my handbag for a tissue. Vic reached in the back seat and presented me with a box of Kleenex. I ignored him, so he pulled one out and held it to my nose.

"Here. Blow," he said. I snatched it out of his hand and pushed his arm away.

"I'm not your kid!" I yelled. "I can blow my own damn nose." And I did. A repulsive blubbering blast that seemed to go on for hours. It was so demeaning that I started laughing. If that didn't get me out of his system, nothing would. I glanced up, expecting to catch him laughing or puking, but he just looked back at me with his masked expression. My insecurities took aim.

"I hate you," I said, climbing on my knees to face him.

"No, you don't."

"You have no idea." I was right in his face and I accentuated each word as I continued. "I'd rather have a child by Richard Nixon than ever even speak to you again."

We stared each other down until his eyes fell, almost imperceptibly, to my mouth, and I knew what the bastard was thinking: that all he'd have to do was kiss me and I'd flip over on my back. Because I worried this might be true—even now after all this honesty—I moved away.

"Gloria, if you're going to play games with the big boys—and I'm not just talking about sex with me—you probably should grow up a little."

"Look who's lecturing about growing up? You know what I think? I think deep down, you're not a very nice person." He looked directly at me and I knew he was trying to be intimidating, but I'd been around him too long for that. "You think you're so perfect that people should just put up with whatever you do and not ask questions, not be disappointed and not make demands. The only thing that's really important to you is you. No one else matters. Not me. Not Penny. No one." I waited, but he didn't respond. "I'm crazy about you," I said, and the resentment in his expression softened before he glanced toward the floor, avoiding me. "And you can't even tell me you like me. And you know why?" He looked back at me. "Because you have to protect yourself. Need to be able to say one day, 'Look, I never promised you anything.' or 'You knew what you were getting into.' Well, I *didn't* know what I was getting into, I only know I want out. Because even though I'm crazy about you, Vic, I don't think I like you."

His expression hardly changed, but I knew I'd scored. My need to hurt him had been overwhelming. It pleased me to realize that I knew where to strike. But almost immediately, I wanted to take everything back. He glared at me for a minute and then, in his incredibly cool way, he turned the keys in the ignition and started the car. A sense of dread crept through me. The napalmed bridge left me trapped forever behind enemy lines.

When he stopped at my apartment, he propped his left elbow on the window frame, feigning interest in the badly scratched Opal parked next to him. I sat there dazed for a second, thinking one of us should say something, but he didn't look my way. I opened the door and got out. My stomach ached so much that it was difficult not to double over.

"There's a nickel on your floor," I said.

He frowned as if I had said something terribly complex. I nodded toward the gas pedal and his eyes followed my lead, but the nickel held little fascination for him. Glancing into the rearview mirror, he shifted into reverse and waited for me to move away before he backed out. I stepped backwards and stood where I was, like a statue, not even blinking.

* * *

Veronica had left a note saying that she was visiting Hunter, so I rattled around the apartment. There were now six newspapers piled on my desk—two the hefty Sunday editions. Mechanically, I flipped through the pages neither digesting nor caring about the articles I skimmed. Then, on the front page of the Sunday *Morning News*, there was an article by Ian entitled "Davis Murky on Integration." It almost made me stagger: no wonder Vic was so weary. I was sure Ian was not quite coloring within the lines on this one. Granted, Vic was not as liberal as the rest of us, but he'd hardly be taken seriously by the left wing if he'd opposed something that important.

> *"In 1951, while attending the University of Texas Law School, Vic Davis actively opposed the integration of Delta Phi. Don Harris, now a successful lawyer in Kilgore, was one of three Negro students at the School. Delta Phi considered pledging him.*
>
> *"Initially this move had unanimous support. But when outside pressure came to bear on the house, a petition was circulated to stop the proceedings.*

"Asked about this at a recent press conference, Senator Davis stated that he had always supported integration. Once the letter surfaced, he was unavailable for comment.

"When contacted, several others who had signed the letter stressed the coercive tactics used by the alumnus and the administration and pointed out that theirs was the only fraternity at that time to consider such a radical move. If they reluctantly backed down due to official pressure, they should still be given credit for being ahead of their time."

My stomach ached so much that my back hurt. I worried I had an ulcer or cancer. However, when I dressed for bed, I found I had simply started my period. I should have been relieved, but I wasn't. While I was washing my face, Veronica burst into the apartment, squealing and dancing around.

"Hunter's gettin' out of jail this Friday," she screamed, flying into the bathroom and throwing her arms around me.

* * *

Throughout the week, whenever my phone rang, I bolted for it as if jolted by a cattle prod. But it was never Vic. Each time I told myself I'd quit expecting to hear from him, but then the phone would ring again and my hopes would elevate as quickly as my pulse. I considered the ultimate transgression—calling him. Though women could now vote, have careers, say "fuck" and "shit," and sleep around, it was still improper for them to call guys.

I never mentioned the integration article to Ian. It was a cheap shot and I couldn't believe he was proud of it. Perhaps once he realized I was not seeing Vic anymore he would ease up. The election was two years away: maybe he'd get this out of his system by then.

Tuesday evening, Greg and I arrived at the Records Building for the YD meeting. I carted past newsletters and brochures assuming that if any new members attended, they might want to see what we had been up to. To my surprise, all thirty-five showed up. To my horror, a thirty-sixth also surfaced.

"Hoyt!" I said, when I got control my gag reflex. "What a surprise to see you here."

"Well, it became apparent to me at that luncheon that what the YDs most needed was someone with a level head."

His tone was as icy as a Dallas office in August.

* * *

"The first matter of business is the election of Officers," I announced after I called the meeting to order. One of the new members raised his hand. I nodded in his direction.

"Don't you want to open with a prayer?"

"We don't usually do that," I informed him.

"I move we open with a prayer," another new member shouted.

"I second it," someone else called out.

I called for a show of hands and, sure enough, prayer won.

"Can I have a volunteer to lead us in a prayer?" I asked.

A straw-like guy leapt to his feet. Though he was about six-two, I had a good twenty pounds on him. His face was so narrow that it must have once been trapped in a vice, causing his beady eyes to trip over each other. In fact, he was an inch away from being a Cyclops.

"Dear Lord Jesus Christ, our savior and God," he started in.

Though I was standing right next to him, I glanced toward Greg and rolled my eyes—I had no concern about the prayer-leader's peripheral vision.

"Please guide and direct us this evening as we struggle to make decisions that will strengthen the Christian values of this great nation. Give us the courage to take righteous stands though they may be far from popular and may lead some to ridicule us for our fervor. Let us always keep in mind, that as crusaders in Your holy war, we must be willing to face sin and take the necessary action to combat it. Though always an uphill battle, we will struggle to get our licks in no matter how dark and dank the surroundings; no matter how slippery the slopes; and no matter how stiff the opposition. Amen."

I glanced toward Hoyt: his head was bowed reverently.

"Do we have nominations for the office of President?" I asked once services ended.

"Yes, Madam Chair," Herman said, "I nominate our current President, Gloria Warren."

"I second that," Greg said.

"Are there any other nominations?" I asked and was surprised when Hoyt raised his hand.

"I'd like to nominate Michael Noonan."

"Who the hell's Michael Noonan?" Greg demanded.

Michael Noonan, it turned out, was our resident minister. Hoyt smirked at me, but I resisted the urge to give him the finger. I glanced at Greg. We both knew who was behind this. The newcomers captured all the offices, voted to eliminate the newsletter, and declined to run anyone for state office.

Usually, after meetings, we'd all go out drinking, but no one was up for it. Once Greg dropped me off, I called Ian—both at his apartment and at the newspaper—but he didn't answer. Veronica was out, probably with Jo Beth. When I left the apartment, I wasn't sure where I was going: I just needed a walk. But I ended up at Ian's. He still wasn't home, so I waited on his front steps.

Eventually, the VW chugged into the parking lot. Minutes later Ian materialized, whistling to himself. He froze when he spotted me.

"What are you doing here? I thought you'd be out celebrating."

"There was nothing to celebrate."

He studied me, whipped out his keys and unlocked the door.

"Let me guess...LBJ's been awarded the Nobel Peace Prize!" He glanced my way. "No, I guess that's not it. One of your friends got arrested for not bathing." He held the door open, "You gonna come in or what?"

I stepped inside.

"We got voted out of office."

He stared at me for a moment before his gaze fell to the floor and then rose to the ceiling.

"Want a beer?" he asked.

I shook my head.

"Mind if I have one?"

I shrugged.

When he returned from the kitchen, he took my hand and pulled me to the sofa.

"God! I'm really sorry," he said once I explained what happened.

"Well, enough about me. What's new with you?"

"What makes you think there's anything new?" he asked jumping up and starting across the room as if the phone had just rung or something. Then, he stopped and turned toward me. "You want a beer or anything?"

"No. I'm fine."

"I think I'll have another beer."

"Is something wrong, Ian?" I asked when he returned.

"No, of course not. Other than your election, I mean. Everything's fine. Fine."

With his thumbnail, he shredded the label off his bottle. Curls of soggy paper surrounded the bottle like confetti.

"Gloria?" he said, still hunched forward over the coffee table. "There's something I need to tell you." He glanced my way. "I was going to call you the second I got in—" He flopped back against the sofa and sighed. "I heard from the *Times* today. Looks like I'll be moving to New York in September."

"Congratulations," I said, trying to smile. "At least one of us has something to celebrate. That's why you were so…cheerful. Earlier."

"Actually, when I first got the call, I was ambivalent. Not about the *Times*. About leaving Dallas. About leaving you."

We sat there on the sofa, our elbows resting on our knees, our eyes focused on some nothing thing in front of us. I wanted to say something encouraging so he would know I was happy for him. Instead, I just sat there.

"Then I had this idea." He seemed nervous. "I thought maybe you'd move to New York with me."

"Me? In New York? What would I do there?"

"I'm sure you could find a better job there than what you have here."

Now it was my turn to stand up and walk across the room. He followed me.

"Gloria, listen to me. I have contacts in the city. A family friend is a producer of *The Huntley-Brinkley Show*. Wouldn't that be more exciting than Freedom Mutual and the YDs put together?"

"Where would I live? Isn't New York expensive? I couldn't even afford to move."

"You could…you could live with me. If you wanted to. If you didn't, I'd help you find a place—even help you with the rent until you were, you know, established." Our eyes met but after a moment, he looked away. "Maybe," he continued, "Maybe, this election was divine intervention. Maybe the gods are saying, it's a good time for a change."

"I'd be nobody in New York," I said.

"Yeah, but everybody's nobody in New York."

* * *

When I got back to my apartment, Veronica and Jo Beth were flipping through bridal magazines.

"How'd the election go?" Veronica asked.

It was a routine question and she expected a routine answer. I considered saying fine: Jo Beth was the last person I wanted to share this news with. But I knew I'd look even more pathetic if I lied.

"I lost," I said.

"*Lost*?"

"We all lost. The club was taken over by some new members."

"Well, can't you...*sue* or something?" Veronica shouted.

"No. There's nothing I can do."

"Did you have any idea—"

"No. It was a complete surprise." I fell into a chair and tossed my leg over the armrest.

"Ya must feel like a little piece of your soul's been ripped right out," Jo Beth whispered. "It's the surprise that hurts so much," she went on and I couldn't believe this ditz was getting philosophical. "When Junior left, I believed we were so happy. It was Dusty's birthday. I used ta give her these great parties, ya know? Would cut sheet cakes up into animal shapes and decorate them with colored icing and candy and coconut and then I'd make matching little clay figurines for the kids who came. We always planned the parties for the weekend, so Junior'd be around. I remember that morning at breakfast as if it was yesterday. I said, 'I'm thinkin' about having Dusty's party next Saturday.' 'Do what you want, darlin'," he said, 'I won't be here.' 'Well, ya have ta be here,' I said, 'You're her daddy!' And he said, 'Well, Ah'm tired of bein' a daddy.' I near dropped my teeth! 'Ah'm tired of bein' a daddy, and ah'm tired of bein' a husband and most of all, Ah'm just tired of bein' here.' And that was that," she said, turning away, suddenly interested in the doily under our side-table lamp.

"Jesus!" I said and we all sat there, stunned, as if Goldwater had just been elected President.

"I believe what I did wrong was I let Dusty become too important and I ignored Junior. If only I could live that time over again. Maybe we'd all still be together if I could do it right this time."

A million put-downs came to mind, but for the first time ever I didn't feel like beating up on Jo Beth.

* * *

I was a poor loser. A good loser would have maintained enthusiasm for the cause regardless of who was banging the gavel. But when I handed over the club files, I explained nothing. Since they had no interest in the newsletters, I kept all the back issues. And, most devious of all, I "forgot" to give them the list of dependable contributors. I had cultivated that list and Mr. Noonan could do the same for his administration.

I started watching *the Huntley-Brinkley show* regularly.

About the only positive thing in my life was Hunter's imminent release from prison. I was looking forward to seeing the jerk. And I made myself swear that'd I'd soak my tongue in acid before I'd smart off to him once he started hanging around again. Veronica considered having a party for him, but decided she wanted him all to herself. During their last visit, she'd told him about the baby.

"He needs time to get used to the idea," was all she said when I asked how he took it.

She was so nervous that morning that she almost went to work without mascara.

"I just have so much on my mind," she jabbered. "First, Hunter's coming home, then I gotta make plans pronto for the weddin'. And then—and here's the scariest part—I gotta back out of my contract with WDIP."

"Tell them you're pregnant. Surely they won't want you on TV with a pot belly."

"My contract says I won't get pregnant for two years."

"Say you were pregnant when you signed it but didn't know!"

"And have them think I'm loose or somethin'? No. I'll have to come up with somethin' better than that."

* * *

Friday I finished my files by eleven and sat with my hands folded on my desk, hoping someone would notice I was under worked and promote me. But Lonnie hardly looked my way.

After work, I went to Chandler's, the men's shop where Billy Anders worked. I wanted to buy Hunter a present, but I knew I couldn't trust myself to get him anything nice. I asked a salesman to call Billy to the floor.

"I need to buy a gift for someone, Billy, but I don't—"

"A boyfriend?"

"Ah. No. My roommate's boyfriend is...having a birthday and I wanted to get him, you know, something."

"How much you want to spend?"

"I don't know. Not much. I don't really like him."

"Cologne? Cuff links? A wallet?"

We settled on a tie/handkerchief set. I'd never seen Hunter wear a tie, but I really liked the set. It was paisley in shades of blue, yellow and green.

"Seems sort of a shame to blow your nose on this," I said, fingering the handkerchief.

"You don't blow your nose on it," Billy said, outraged. "You wear it in your breast pocket, showing, like this."

He stuffed it into his pocket, leaving just the corner peeking out. Vic was the only person I knew classy enough for that. I also bought a bottle of Aramis. Billy waited with me while the clerk wrapped my package.

"What's this I hear about the YD elections?" he asked.

"Yeah. Bummer, huh?"

"Well, you'll get it back. Just wait. Need a ride to hear Vic speak Friday?" he offered.

"Uh, no. Thanks, though."

The clerk had handed me the gift, so Billy tapped me on the shoulder and started for his office.

I reached the bus stop just as my bus pulled away, so I had twenty minutes to kill. I stepped inside the newsstand on the corner and browsed through some magazines. A new publication, *Up and Coming* billed itself as the progressive magazine of the Sixties. I thumbed through it. On page twenty-three, there was a picture of a woman sitting on a bench with her legs sprawled open. A man, on all fours was next to her with his head under her skirt. I quickly flipped the page. "In Defense of Child Pornography" was an editorial I didn't even bother to skim. A little later there was a full-page headshot of a beautiful woman who was delicately picking something off her tongue with her thumb and forefinger. "How to remove unwanted hair" was the caption at the bottom of the page. Scenes from an orgy, where all the women were wearing these uncomfortable-looking leather outfits went on for six pages. I was a little repulsed. Though I'd never admit this to Greg or some of my other political friends, it wouldn't bother me if they censored some of that shit. I carried the magazine to the counter and paid for it.

When I got to the apartment, Veronica was alone in the living room.

"Where's Hunter?" I asked.

"I wouldn't know. Went down there this mornin'...thought I'd give him a ride home. I guess she got there first."

"I'm sure he'll get in touch with you...as soon as he can. I'll make us some coffee."

As I scooped instant coffee into two cups, someone knocked at the door.

"Maybe that's Hunter," Veronica whispered. "How do I look?"

"You look beautiful," I said.

"My hair's smooth?"

I nodded.

"No rats showin'?" She glanced in a mirror. "I need lipstick."

"Forget lipstick. Get the door." I felt absurdly excited.

She hurried across the room and threw open the door. We both gasped when we saw Bob Love instead. At the sight of the private detective, all of my nerves frayed. I knew why he was there. Somehow, he'd discovered I was the informer. My hand was shaking like someone with the DTs and when I tried to pour the boiling water into the cup, it spilled all over the counter.

"Why, Bob! What are you doin' here?" She gave me a what's-all-this-about look. I stooped behind a counter pretending to search for a dishtowel, but really just wanting to hide.

"Hah yew?" He stepped into the apartment and twitched his head three times.

"Just fine and you?"

"Ah'm fahn." He cleared his throat before he continued. "Ah wonder do you have any information concernin' Hunter's whereabouts?"

I peeked up. This wasn't about me.

"Well, he lives over in Tanglewood—"

"Used to," he cut in. "The place's been cleared out."

Veronica looked toward me for some sort of denial. I sprang to my feet.

"Cleared out?" she gasped.

"At approximately ten A.M., his wife picked him up—"

"She's not his wife!" Veronica shouted. "I've told you that a million times."

"Well, whatever. Anyway, she picked him up. At 10:30, some new information came to my attention and I went by his place to talk to him about it. That's when I discovered that they had disappeared."

Bob Love glanced quickly toward the back room as if he might have seen Hunter race past.

"Disappeared? Well, there must be a mistake. I…I mean, where would he go? He can't leave town—"

"He's skipped bail!" I called out.

Both Veronica and Bob Love turned toward me and then looked back at each other.

"I'm sure he'll turn up. Maybe they've moved to a cheaper apartment. *Or*, maybe they've split up. Did you check around? I bet that's it! They broke up and he's lookin' for a new place." Veronica actually jumped up and down with uncontrollable glee.

"He's skipped bail on *your* money!" I said. "What a snake! What a low…"

"I'm sure that's what it is, Bob. And I'm sure I'll be hearin' from him real soon. And you can bet I'll get right in touch with you just as soon as I do."

"The guy has no decency." I knew I should shut up, but I was so relieved to have dodged solitary confinement, and moldy bread that I couldn't help it. "Skipping bail. Jesus!"

Bob Love's head jerked up and down, right and left as if the circuits in his brain suddenly went bananas.

"Gloria, would you please just shut up!" Veronica shouted.

Trying to butt out, I returned to my coffee making. My hand steady now, I was able to pour the water into the cups without swabbing the counter.

"Ah have reason ta believe he's left the area. Now if he *should* get in touch with you..."

I got a spoon and stirred both cups, adding a little milk to each.

"Why does everyone just *assume* the worst about Hunter? Just what makes you so sure he's left town—"

"Number a things. His wife—girlfriend—didn't show up for work today. Called in sick. And the kid's not in school." He shrugged his shoulders repeatedly like a rhino trying to ward off irritating birds.

"What kid?" Veronica and I both froze.

"Their son. They have, let's see, an eight-year-old boy who goes to St. Gregory's Elementary School—"

"A son!" I was outraged. "Well, that figures. God! I knew I was right about him."

"Just let me know if ya hear anything? Cops don't know yet, but it's only a matter of time. Then things'll get smelly."

"You can bet we will!" I volunteered. "He should hang!"

"I'll let ya know if anything turns up," he said as he turned to leave. I sipped my coffee but it was still hot.

"Oh, Bob?" Veronica stopped him. "What was the new information you wanted to talk over with Hunter?"

"It concerned the informer."

My heart pulled its own plug.

"Did you find out who it was?" Veronica asked.

"No. Nothing like that. But it was a female. Just wanted ta see if he had any eye-dears as ta who it might be."

My cup exploded into a trillion pieces as it hit the floor. Veronica and Bob whirled around toward me: my eyes locked with hers. I knew she knew. She stood at the door long after Bob Love had vanished.

"I'm so stupid," she said. "All this time I was paying a detective and the answer was right here."

"I should have told you. I wanted to, but I just couldn't find the right time. I never wanted this to happen."

"And what did you want ta happen?"

"It was just a joke."

"A joke?"

"Just a silly joke. I never thought he'd be busted. I only wanted…I don't know what."

"And now he's gone."

"I know you're angry."

"Yes, I'm angry."

"You should be."

"I am."

"But don't you see now. I was right about him. He would have stayed with her anyway. They have a son! That wouldn't have changed."

"But now there's another baby. And he *loves* me. It could have worked out."

"I'm really so sorry."

She walked across the room and sat in a chair, crossing her legs and placing her arms carefully on the armrest. "You could go ta jail for this," she said calmly.

"I know," I said, looking at the floor.

"I guess your fate's in my hands. Just like mine was in yours before."

"I guess it is," I said.

Neither one of us moved for what seemed like fifteen minutes. Then, as regally as a queen, Veronica walked to her room. I got the broom out of the hall closet and swept up the shards and slivers of the broken coffee cup. Using an envelope from my desk as a dustpan, I managed to scoop the mess up and toss it in the trash. Then I sat on the floor, my back resting against the refrigerator. A banging at the door shattered the silence. Hoping it might be Hunter, I scurried over to open it, but it was Jo Beth.

"Where's Veronica?" she shouted. "Is Hunter here?"

I pointed toward her room and Jo Beth scooted toward it. An ugly scene would surely take place once she knew the latest. But she hadn't been in there five minutes before someone else knocked. I prayed it would be Ian but like a nasty infection jumping on a festering wound—there was Hoyt.

"Well, now I know why none of my calls were returned."

"What do you want?" I blocked his entrance to the apartment.

"Not you, that's for sure. Where's Ronnie?"

"She's gone." I tried to shut the door but at that moment, Veronica rushed out.

"Who's there?" she asked, clearly expecting Hunter. She stopped.

"Hoyt!" In an instant, her practiced, gracious, beauty-queen smile masked her disappointment.

"When ya didn't return any of my calls, I thought you must of forgotten what a charmin' rascal I was." He barged his way in, shoving me to one side.

"What calls?" she asked and they both glowered at me.

"Well, that's okay, darlin', you can make it up to me if you'll join me for dinner tonight."

"Tonight? Well, I don't know. This has been a really bad day. I wouldn't be very good company."

"You wouldn't have to be company at all. Just lookin' at you would be enough for me."

"Oh, God," I groaned, which caused Veronica to sear me with a look of hatred.

"On second thought," she said, "it might be good for me to get out of this apartment."

"Then it's settled."

Hoyt put his arm around Veronica just as Jo Beth rounded the corner. When she spotted Hoyt, she looked as startled as if she'd found her first gray hair.

"Junior! What're you doin' here?" she said.

"Junior?" In spite of everything, I laughed. "*This* is Junior?"

"Why, Joey, I didn't expect ta..."

"No, I guess ya didn't."

"Jo Beth," Veronica started, moving away from Hoyt and fixing him with an accusatory stare as if he'd just belched in his underwear, "are you sayin' this is your..."

"You bet your bippy it is."

"—husband?"

"Ex-husband," Hoyt corrected.

"I thought you left Dallas!" Jo Beth said.

"I did. But I came back."

"And ya didn't even let me know? Just for old time's sake?"

"Now, Joey, I always intended to—"

"You said we were still friends!"

"I don't feel too good." Veronica touched her stomach.

"Look, Joey. I'm beginning to feel like a fart trapped in a blanket, if ya know what I mean?"

"Such a way with words." I couldn't pass that up.

"How long have ya been back?" Jo Beth asked.

"Not long. I came back to go to law school."

"You'll make a great lawyer." Her hurt expression turned to veneration. "What year are ya?"

"Third."

"Third?"

"Well, just *startin'* the third."

And ya never had time to call me? Not even to ask about Dusty?"

"How *is* Dusty?"

"Fine. Gettin' big. Ya wanna see her?"

"Love to. Love to."

"How about tomorrow?"

"Ah. Can't tomorrow, Joey. Gotta study, you know. But, listen. We'll set somethin' up."

"Sure." Jo Beth smiled.

"I think I should just be headin' out for now. Look, I'll call ya, Joey, and we'll straighten this out."

After Hoyt escaped, no one could think of anything to say. Finally, Veronica sighed heavily.

"Jo Beth, I'm sorry. I didn't know."

Jo Beth tried to smile. "I took back my maiden name—Taylor sounded better than Whitehead."

"Are you okay?" Veronica coaxed.

"Oh, sure. I got over him a long time ago."

"Maybe I'll go lie down. I feel real tired."

Veronica shut the door to her room and Jo Beth and I just stood there as if we'd accidentally stepped in quick-drying glue.

"Well," I said after a bit, "Wanna go to a movie with me?" Jo Beth seemed startled. "I need to get out. Thought I'd go to a movie. You wanna come with me?"

"I don't feel like fightin' tonight, Gloria."

"Neither do I. I'll even pay." Jo Beth regarded me while I leafed through the newspaper. "Something light, I think. Funny. We both need to laugh."

"Do ya think we should leave Veronica alone?" she asked, glancing toward the shut door.

"Yes, I think she might like that," I replied. "Here we go," I said, turning the paper back to the movie section. "*That Darn Cat*. Hayley Mills. Supposed to be cute. About a Siamese cat that solves a police case. What do you think?"

"Well, okay. Maybe a movie would be good."

"We need to get going. It starts in thirty minutes."

She picked up her handbag and as we were walking out the door, she turned toward me. "You know, I always thought maybe you had a real nice streak in you, Gloria, but I'd never wanted to hurt your feelin's by pointin' it out to ya."

* * *

After the movie, I went to Ian's and stayed there until Sunday. I worried about Veronica, but I couldn't face her. When I finally returned, she'd gone. At least she and her clothes had. She left a note saying she'd be with Jo Beth until she could find another place and asked that I forward her calls. Luckily, not many people stopped by because every time there was a knock at the door, I freaked, thinking it was the FBI. No doubt I would need a lawyer, which I couldn't afford. Greg might know one of those storefront guys. Or, maybe this was a good excuse to call Vic. Maybe he'd help. Or maybe he'd just refuse to take the call. In the meantime, all I could do was worry.

I lost my appetite, which was just as well, since money would soon become an issue. I couldn't afford the apartment by myself and there was no one who'd agree to live with me. There were cheaper places but it cost money to move and most apartments required a hefty security deposit. We'd paid our rent through August 15, so I had until then.

The logical thing was to move in with Ian and then move to New York. But, after all the time I'd logged in Texas, meeting the right people, learning the issues, making a name for myself, could I leave? Just because I couldn't afford my rent? New York! Jesus. It was too big and too cold and too dangerous—neighbors actually watched while a guy stabbed a woman on the street. That would never happen in Texas: ten people would have pulled out rifles and perforated the bastard. And probably the woman, too. But they wouldn't have just watched.

Hunter's gift was still in the bag, sitting on the sofa where I'd tossed it. I had forgotten the Aramis. I pulled out Vic's picture and dabbed Aramis all over it, careful to let each drop evaporate completely before adding another: I didn't want to disintegrate the newspaper. Once it dried, I pressed the picture to my face.

Also on the sofa, still in its bag, was the copy of *Up and Coming* I'd purchased at the newsstand. I flipped through it until I found a subscription form. The first thing I did was check the "bill me later" box and then I looked up Michael Noonan's address in the phone book.

* * *

Lonnie Mossman took two personal days early in the week. I called my friend at the courthouse that evening and learned that her husband had dropped the suit. She returned on Wednesday, her old interfering self. I don't know why I thought things would be different; she had no idea I was even aware of her problems, much less involved in them.

"Don't you have anything to do, Gloria?" she asked when she spotted me sitting idly at my desk. I could tell she expected me to jump or faint at being discovered.

"No, ma'am," I said nonchalantly.

"What about your folders?" She casually opened the top one.

"I'm finished."

She waited for an explanation. "With all of them?"

"Yes, ma'am."

Not that she didn't believe me or anything, but she set her papers down on the corner of my desk and systematically checked each of my files.

"You got these this morning?"

"Yes, ma'am."

She glared at me with thinly veiled fury. Then she picked up her papers, spun around and walked off. It was hard not to smirk. Thirty minutes later, she called me into her office. When I got there, she was leaning back in her chair, her legs crossed to the side of her desk.

"Since you are clearly too smart for the rest of us at Freedom Mutual, I'm going to expand your responsibilities. Starting today—now, in fact—I expect you to do whatever odd jobs I have." She tapped the top shelf of her in/out box, which was overflowing with tissue carbons. "You can start with this filing."

On Thursday, the day before Vic's speech, I resented hanging out in Lonnie's office: What if my phone rang? Maybe he thought we still had a date Friday. If I saw him, maybe he would help me with the Hunter business. I kept Lonnie's door open and whenever a phone rang, I strained to hear if it was coming from my desk. But, by that evening, I had to come to terms with the fact that Vic had not been bluffing when he left me, and though it was best to be out of such a troublesome relationship, I missed him. I really missed him. I saw Ian constantly and at times I was sure I was in love with him. But no day passed that I didn't take Vic's picture out from between those envelopes and just look at it and smell the Aramis.

On Friday, I dawdled over my folders so I could hang around my phone as much as possible. During my lunch hour, I caught a bus downtown and window-shopped at the stores around the big hotels, but I never ran into him. And no one called. I wondered if he thought about me while he sat in his room: maybe he even dialed half my numbers and then hung up. I told myself that if the phone rang and the caller hung up when I answered, I'd know it was Vic wanting to hear my voice. But no such call came. By four-thirty, I was furious with Vic. I refused to sit around being miserable all night knowing he was in town. I called Ian.

"Wanna come over for dinner tonight?" I asked.

"Can't," he said, "I have to cover a meeting."

"The teachers' thing?" I asked.

"Yeah." There was a long pause before he spoke again. "I'm surprised you're not going."

"How about after?"

"Then I have to write it up."

"It could be, you know, a late dinner," I said.

Ian arrived around ten, and I was grateful for his company. He didn't mention the meeting or Vic, but he brought a gift that he'd wrapped in grayish tissue paper so wrinkled that I knew he'd gotten it out of a shoebox. One of the corners was ripped where he had pulled the paper too tight; he'd taped over the tear. In place of a ribbon, he had stretched green rubber bands around it. Across the tissue paper he had written, "To Gloria, I love you, Ian."

"Nice wrapping job," I said.

"Are you being sarcastic?" he said. "Look at this!" He slipped a finger under the rubber bands. "I could have used brown ones! I made a special trip to the drug store for these."

"Why am I a little reluctant to open this?" I laughed, cutting my eyes toward him.

"If you don't want it," he answered, grabbing it, "I'll give it to one of my other dates. They don't have such phony airs."

"Okay. I apologize."

"Forget it. You lost your chance."

"If you don't give it to me, I'm not going to feed you." He considered this.

"What do you have?"

"Steak." He looked at the gift and then at me, wrinkling his face in exaggerated concentration.

"And what else?"

"Salad."

"Any dessert?"

"Chocolate cake with chocolate icing." He tapped his thumbs on the gift as his eyes scanned the ceiling contemplatively.

"Homemade or store bought?"

"Homemade." He handed the gift to me.

"From a mix," I added once I had the package.

"Oh, you hussy!" he shrieked, outraged. "Give that back." He lunged for the package, but I jumped out of his way, laughing while I shredded the paper. I already knew it was a framed picture. Affecting modest apprehension, he waited for my reaction. It was a picture of me, though only he and I would know that since his sheet completely covered my head.

You're such a jerk," I said, whacking his arm with it.

"You should see the one in my office. Everyone wants to meet you."

I used a white tablecloth and served asparagus as our vegetable, but I drew the line at perfume on the light bulbs. *That* struck me as stupid.

"Ian," I said as he inhaled his food, "Does this table cloth remind you of anything?"

He frowned. "What?" I've never known anyone who liked to eat as much as he did.

"The table cloth. This *white* tablecloth. Does it remind you of anything?"

He studied the tablecloth, chewing thoughtfully, before he looked at me. "Like what?"

"Like anything!"

"I dunno. Maybe."

"*What* does it remind you of?"

He shrugged. "A ghost?"

"A ghost?"

"Well, hell! What does it remind you of?"

"It's not supposed to remind *me* of anything."

"Gloria, are you having…some…female, you know, activity? Right now?"

"Female activity?"

"Yeah. I heard women sometimes go nuts when—"

I grabbed a fistful of chocolate cake. "I'll show you female activity—" I walked over to him and smeared the cake in his face. He pushed himself away from the table defensively. I stepped over him, straddled his lap, sat down and kissed him roughly on the mouth, smearing the cake and icing all over our faces. At first, he tried to push me away, but then he gave in.

"Mm," he said, licking his lips, "you've never tasted better." Grabbing more cake, I smeared it in his hair.

"Shit!" he yelled and stood up, dumping me to the floor.

"You're such a loser!" I said. "Don't you know what a white table cloth is supposed to remind you of? Of a bed. Of sex."

His dumbfounded expression combined with his chocolate face and the clumps of cake clinging to his hair made him seem ridiculous. I laughed so uncontrollably I couldn't get up.

"You look like shit," I said.

He picked up the rest of the cake and started toward me.

"All right," I warned. "Put the cake down."

He knelt beside me and, lifting my shirt, dumped the cake on my stomach. Then he carefully arranged my blouse back in place. I was screeching so hard that I worried the neighbors might call the cops. Ian lowered himself on me, squishing the cake all over the place.

"You're right," he said. "That tablecloth really turns me on." We made love right there on the floor, the chocolate cake making repulsive sucking noises when we moved.

It took hours to clean up the mess. Not only was the carpet a disaster, but our clothes were so disgusting that I had to change and run to the basement to wash them in the machines. Ian, of course, had nothing to change into, so he draped a sheet around himself toga-style.

"What does this sheet remind you of?" he asked, as I cleared the table.

"A dining room table," I said.

"That's exactly what it reminds me of, too," he said. "So where's dessert?"

"You ruined dessert, you pig!"

"That was all you had?"

"That cake was enough for twelve people—six if you were one of them."

"And to think I spent a fortune on that frame," he said.

* * *

Once Ian left the next morning, I tore through the *Morning News* to read his account of Vic's speech. The second I saw the headline, I was furious.

DAVIS STAND ON EDUCATION COLORED BY LOBBYISTS' GIFTS

Speaking here last night before a group of educators, State Senator Vic Davis (D-Sumner) reiterated his liberal-sounding agenda for education.

"Texas is one of the wealthiest states in the Union, yet we are close to the bottom of the heap in per-pupil expenditures," he told the enthusiastic gathering. Referring to the fact that three-fourths of the State's gas tax goes to highways while only one-fourth is allotted to education, he argued, "I cannot believe this is the priority of our citizens. But the establishment, which is clearly more interested in fast cars than fast minds, has consistently rejected any change in this ratio."

"Davis detailed how during his tenure in the Senate, he tired unsuccessfully to change this equation. "Let's go fifty-fifty," he told the cheering crowd of four hundred. "Surely the minds of children are more crucial than another cloverleaf intersection in the Dallas industrial district."

But the Senator's speech was not without its detractors. "Why not ask him who pays the rent on his bachelor pad at the Driskill Hotel?" asked an unidentified source. After some probing, it was learned that the railroad lobby provides his Austin apartment.

The possibility of a conflict of interest arises when one considers that Davis serves on the powerful State Affairs Committee whose duties include the building and maintenance of Texas highways. Since competition between truckers and the railroad is fierce, some question that this pro-education appeal is an attempt to disguise his debt of gratitude to the railroads.

I tried to rationalize Vic's behavior, but then I realized he'd disappointed me. I had come to terms with the idea that he wasn't perfect. I wanted to believe he was, but of course, that wasn't fair. No one was. And if you were dynamic and powerful, there would always be those who'd want you in their debt. And they'd always have something: if not money, then women, or committee assignments, or invitations, or introductions, or tips, or fame. There were limitless possibilities, and everyone has a price. I hated to think how cheaply I'd sell out. Maybe I already had. Would I be supporting a man who worried about Communists, supported the NRA, and had avoided taking a stand on the war, if I didn't have something to gain from his success? What moral peak did I stand on?

Veronica's room was spooky. Her vanity mirror had pictures taped around the border. The tangled tassel from our high school graduation hung on one corner, while a green plastic Hawaiian lei she got at the New Year's Eve party where she met Hunter, hung on the other. Stacked *Cosmopolitans* stood by her nightstand. I sat on her bed and glanced out the window. It was a beautiful day. I should do something: even hang out at the pool. But I just sat there.

Ian was working the weekend: the Republican Party was having a mini-convention in town, which he had to cover. Saturday would be shot, and he was vague about whether Sunday looked any better.

But Vic was not vague. Surely, now, I had to accept that I'd been replaced. Maybe he'd replaced me last night. Maybe he spotted some kindergarten teacher, fresh out of college, with porcelain skin and an apricot-blond ponytail, sitting at one of the front tables, going over her folder of bulletin-board pictures carefully clipped from some inspirational magazine and he used his penetrating stare to lure her to his room. Maybe they were still there banging their brains out.

I looked in a mirror. God, what had he ever seen in me? I was certainly not his type. He liked perfect women who, by their mere presence, reinforced that he was perfect, too. Thank God he never met Veronica: I would have been history even before I was an event.

I pulled my hair away from my face: it was my real problem. It just hung there, this mousy, limp mess, with nothing to do. When I released it, it fell around my face as if exhausted by the effort of moving. Without thinking, I grabbed Veronica's cuticle scissors and chopped off a segment just behind my temple. It did this amazing flip right over my ear. With the section in front of it hanging there, I looked like someone out of *Asher Lev*, a novel I'd read about Hasidic Jews. All I needed was a black hat. The idea struck me as so hilarious that I cut the other side and then searched around Veronica's room for a hat. She had an old cowboy hat, so I put it on. God, it just cracked me up. These two stringy things hanging in front of two pitiful flips.

When I realized what I'd done, I had trouble catching my breath. I ripped the hat off and stared at myself. Clearly, I was cracking up. Soon they'd send me off to this snake-pit kind of place and I'd be there with the other nuts—only their hair would look fine.

"Jo Beth," I shouted into the phone. "Can you come over? Something terrible's happened."

"What is it, honey?" she said when she arrived minutes later. Then she stopped dead. Before she could activate whatever section of her brain controlled sensitivity, she burst out laughing. "My God, girl! What have you done to yourself?"

"Jo Beth! What am I going to do?" I wailed.

"Now, now, honey. It's not as bad as all that. Let me look at you." She circled me several times to take in the entire crime scene. Finally, she said, "It's gonna have ta all go."

"Can you do it for me?" I pleaded.

"I think you've done enough amateur work on yourself. You need to see a professional."

"I went to that place on Lovers' Lane once." At my desk I searched for the Yellow Pages. "What's the name of that salon?"

"Know what?" Jo Beth started, "You need Mr. René." I was speechless. "He's a true artist. 'Course he might not be hot on seein' ya after the way you acted. But, tell ya what. *I'll* call him and see if he'll do it for me."

"How much will it cost?"

"A fortune and he probably can't see you today. Saturdays are impossible."

Mr. René was double-booked until Saturday evening, but he agreed to make a house call Sunday. He told Jo Beth that even before my self-mutilation, he viewed me as the ultimate artistic challenge. He'd show up around eleven with his supplies and he wanted a six-pack of Lone Star Beer, five hot dogs, a can of Cheeze-Whiz, and two packages of Hostess Snowball cupcakes (white and pink). He'd do it for nothing, but I had to relinquish all control and agree to before and after shots for his portfolio. I started to object, but Jo Beth, suddenly a beacon of reason, intervened.

"What could he possibly do that'd be worse'n this?" So I agreed.

* * *

Late that afternoon, the phone rang six times before I bothered answering.

"I looked all over for you last night," Julia said.

"Last night?"

"At that horrible teachers' thing."

"Oh, well, I was sort of busy."

"Did Vic mention that I asked about you?"

"I haven't spoken to Vic...in a while."

"Ah. That explains things."

"What do you mean?" Had she seen him with someone else?

"I went to that moronic meeting because I was hoping to see you. When I read that he was speaking, I was sure you'd be there drooling."

"Why were you looking for me?"

"I'm having this brunch and I was hoping you could come."

"A brunch?"

"Yes. My friend, Pamela Newton, will be here. Our first husbands were partners. But now she's single and has given up on marriage as the gateway to happiness. Says she can live very happily without some man. Who can't? Acting like they have the cure for everything sagging there between their legs. So, Pamela's given up the good life and *works*, can you believe it? As a speech writer for William Proxmire—ever heard of him?"

"The Senator from Wisconsin?"

"Exactly. Oh, I'll have to tell her you knew of him. Anyway, she'll be in town and I wanted to have a little girl-party and it occurred to me that you'd enjoy meeting each other. Most of my friends would rather shop at Sears than discus politics. I'm afraid Pamela will find us quite tedious. I thought you could help. When she gets tried of hearing about divorce settlements, diet pills, and sagging tits, you could talk about voting, or whatever it is you people talk about."

"Julia?" I asked once she filled me in on the party. "What did...when you spoke to...ah?"

"I asked him how I could get in touch with you and at first, he pretended not to know who you were. So I said, 'You know, that cute little child you've been screwing.'"

"Jesus, Julia!"

"Well, that loosened up his tongue, as well as his bowels, I imagine—though if looks could kill! He's *very* sexy when he's mad, don't you think? Anyway, I couldn't remember your last name and he's the only acquaintance we have in common and I'd just sat through endless drivel about the dignity of teachers. I mean *really*: they want summers off! Anyway, I didn't have the time or patience for his bullshit."

"Did he say anything?"

"You mean like, 'Send her my love,' or something like that?"

"No. I mean…anything."

"He just said, 'Her last name's Warren and she lives on Carlisle.' Then he moved on."

"Was he—? Did he seem…to be *with* anyone?"

"Oh, poor child. A man like that? He's only ever with himself."

* * *

All day Saturday, I watched television. In the afternoon I occasionally got off the sofa and change channels, but by evening I just left it where it was and watched whatever was on until, at some point, I fell asleep. Before dawn, the paperboy dropped the *Morning News* outside and the clap it made woke me. A snowy test pattern shimmered on the TV. My back and neck ached from sleeping on the sofa, which had butt dents and surfacing wire coils. I worried that I would walk like Quasimodo the rest of my life.

In the city section of the paper, there was a picture of Peddy with Michael Noonan.

DALLAS YDS TO AVOID FARM WORKERS RALLY

> *Michael Noonan, newly elected President of the Dallas County Young Democrats, announced that the Executive Committee of the organization voted to boycott the much-publicized Austin rally supporting the Valley Farm Workers.*
>
> *"Anyone who believes Texas farmers can afford to pay their seasonal help minimum wage is simply naive and anti-business. There are many employment opportunities in our great State and if the farm workers feel they are not being treated fairly, they are welcome to seek other positions. That has always been the American way."*
>
> *The YDs also expressed dismay at the fact that Robert Kennedy would be the guest speaker at the event, a direct slap, Noonan says, at President Johnson. Noonan stressed his belief that the Communist Party has heavily infiltrated the labor movements in general and the farm workers in particular.*
>
> *The Dallas County YDs plan to hold an alternate rally and picnic in Guywyler Park from noon to three and have already*

enlisted the support of numerous local businesses. Downtown movie theaters will offer free popcorn on that day to any patrons who wear LBJ buttons, and the Acme Television and Appliance Center will give a free shotgun with every purchase of a matching washer/dryer combination.

I poked around my desk until I found the page from the phone directory with Peddy's number. Confident that he'd still be asleep at six on a Sunday morning, I dialed, let it ring twice and hung up. At six-thirty, I called again. At seven and again at seven-thirty, I got busy signals.

After I finished both papers, I tied a scarf around my head and walked over to the Seven-Eleven to pick up Mr. René's sustenance. I was too young to buy beer, but luckily there were still some bottles left over from Veronica's party.

He arrived at eleven-fifteen, loaded down with two suitcases and a briefcase. With flair, he arranged them across the coffee table and snapped them open. They contained scissors, straight razors, shavers, shampoos, conditioners, hair sprays, boxes of hair color and permanents, rat tailed combs, brushes, a pale pink Snow White hand-held mirror, blue curlers, pink clips, bobby pins, hairpins, plastic aprons and capes, small white towels, a Brownie camera, a bonnet hairdryer, and several beauty products I couldn't identify.

He studied my hair with an expression that combined anger, outrage, and revulsion, as if he'd eaten half a sandwich and only just noticed that the bread was green with mold.

"I can't deal with this on an empty stomach," he said. "Where's the beer?"

I pointed toward the refrigerator and after he poured the beer down his throat, he opened one of the Hostess Snowball cupcakes and swallowed it in two bites. Dragging a stool from the kitchen, he patted the seat, indicating I should sit, while with his other hand, he dug lodged cupcake from between his cheek and gums. He snapped an orange plastic apron open and slipped it over his head before tying it around his waist. Then he grabbed the yellow plastic cape and billowed it over me as if he were making a bed. He took six photographs of me from all angles, going out of his way to catch me at unflattering angles.

"Can I have that mirror?" I asked, pointing to Snow White.

"Shut up," he replied.

He circled me slowly, occasionally pulling sections of my hair out, glancing at the ends and whistling or muttering under his breath. This went on forever and my back, which was still suffering from the sofa, was about to give out. Finally, he retrieved a straight razor and a small comb—the kind you can buy from vending machines—and started combing and snipping.

"I don't like short bangs," I said. He didn't trouble himself with a reply.

I kept trying to cut my eyes downward to see how much hair was accumulating on the floor, but the second I moved my head, Mr. René would sigh this long-suffering sigh. When he finished cutting, he took a hot dog break. He had no interested in the rolls or mustard I had set aside for him. Rather he just ate five hot dogs raw and then swallowed another beer.

"Can I peek now?" I asked.

"I'm not finished." His belch lasted for the whole sentence.

From one of his suitcases, he pulled out what appeared to be a badly stained bathing cap perforated with a million tiny holes. He stretched this over my head, pulling my eyes into a frozen surprised expression and cutting off all circulation to my brain.

"What's this for?" I asked, but he just whistled some tune to himself and ignored me.

With something that resembled a crochet needle, he hooked and then viciously pulled strands of my hair through the holes in the bathing cap until I must have looked like I had just survived the electric chair. My eyes watered so badly that I had to blow my nose.

In the kitchen he mixed horrid-smelling chemicals and than slathered the concoction over my head. I sat there silently while he grabbed the Cheeze-Whiz and seated himself on the sofa to watch television—alternating between religious services and cartoons. He kept squirting the Cheeze-Whiz directly onto his tongue until it was empty. Then he pulled me off the stool, led me to the kitchen, ripped the bathing cap off and washed my hair.

"This is a foolproof haircut," he said as he led me back to the stool. "You don't even have to comb it. Just shampoo every day and it will fall in place by itself." He did this little fingering thing that hairdressers always do and then squirted hairspray on a few strategic spots.

I took a deep breath before I accepted the Snow White mirror. Once I built up my nerve, I glanced at my reflection and almost passed out.

"Oh, my God," I shouted. "I'm bald!"

It was the most bizarre haircut ever. My bangs were very long, practically hanging into my eyes, and were jagged. I had what looked like long, pointed sideburns in front of each ear and longish tendrils curling down my neck, but other than that my hair was as short as an Eagle Scout's. I reached up to touch it, but there was nothing there. He had done something to my color. It was still a light brown, but it seemed to glow.

"Trust me," he said. "You look a million times better. Like a kewpie doll."

"I never wanted to look like a kewpie doll in my life."

"It's your look. Guys will be crazy about you *if* and I mean this, if you follow two rules." He took the mirror from my hands. I was in such shock that he had to pry my fingers loose. "First, you come see me every three weeks for a shape-up."

"How can I afford that?"

"You can't afford not to. Cuts like this turn on you if you don't show 'um who's boss."

"What's the second rule?"

"Keep your mouth shut."

Mr. René took ten photographs, begging me to smile, but I couldn't. Then he left, taking the cupcakes and beer with him.

Calcium! Wasn't that what *Cosmopolitan* said would make your hair grow faster? Not wasting a second, I walked the three blocks to Target. I couldn't find the vitamin's section so I stood by the pharmacy desk until the gray-haired man in the white coat looked up from what he was doing.

"What can I do for you, young lady?" he smiled so widely that I worried his face might split.

"Can you tell me where the calcium is?"

"I'll do better than that. I'll get it for you." He stepped from behind his counter and led me to the vitamins. "What dosage do you need?" he asked.

"I have no idea, but strong, I think."

"Why are you taking it?" he asked, as he studied the specifications on three bottles.

"For my hair."

"You have such pretty hair. Is this your secret?"

Was he making a joke? "Uh, yeah, I guess it is."

As I was leaving, another man rushed over to open the door for me, smiling broadly as I passed.

* * *

Ian was free at eight o'clock Sunday night. He picked up Chinese food and stopped by for me.

"Wow!" he said. "What'd you do to your hair?"

"Do you hate it?" I asked, trying to retract my head between my shoulders, turtle-style.

"No. It's great. I love it!"

* * *

"What were the Republicans up to?" I asked, as we ate the Chinese food in his apartment.

"They want to woo people like you." I'd never seen anyone eat with chopsticks before.

"Like me?"

"Liberal Democrats."

"Are they nuts?"

"No. It makes sense. They want to persuade the liberals to vote Republican so that the Republican Party wins enough seats to become viable. Then, they figure, the conservative Democrats, who are really Republicans, will jump ship and you guys can run your own party."

"You mean the Democratic County Chairman might support Democratic candidates?"

"Could be."

"Speaking of which, did you see this?" I tossed the article about the YDs in his direction.

"Of course."

"Jesus! It's almost sacrilegious, isn't it?"

"Well, there's no law saying the YDs have to be liberal."

"Well, aren't *we* broad-minded?"

"Actually, not *we*, just me."

"Hey, what's wrong?" Ian asked a little later when he caught me staring off into space.

"Oh, nothing. I just really wanted to see Bobby Kennedy. Now I can't even go."

"What do you mean, you can't go? Anyone can go!"

"It won't be the same. Besides, everyone would be talking about me."

"Right! Bobby Kennedy comes to town and all anyone can worry about is you."

"I'm *not* going."

I took my plate to the kitchen and scraped the glazed carrots and green peppers into the disposal.

"But that's stupid. You gonna abandon the farm workers because Noonan won the election?"

"No. I'll go to Floresville next weekend."

"Floresville?"

Floresville was John Connally's hometown so organizers had scheduled a full-day stopover on the steps of city hall. Speakers, folk singers, and rock bands were schedule for well into the night. A wealthy benefactor invited out-of-town supporters to camp out on his lawn.

"No one important's going to be there," he said, digging into the food carton for a lone bean sprout.

"Well, then I'll fit right in."

* * *

Everyone at work gushed about my hair and I was feeling a little better about myself until Lonnie announced that that she wanted me to re-alphabetize her Rolodex.

"It's gotten a little messed up," she explained.

However, after I spent an hour on it, I realized it was in perfect order. Next, she asked me to type new labels for all of her files: the old ones were getting hard to read. After that, she had me inventory the supply closet. I was beginning to hate every minute I spent in the office.

Twice I sauntered past Mr. Sweet's office to see how far along his secretary was. She was huge but didn't have that tongue-hanging-out look that they get just before they deliver.

* * *

Ian had been speaking with real estate agents in New York for weeks and suddenly several pieces of property in his price range came on the market. He made arrangements to fly to the city the week following my trip to Floresville, hoping to combine five days of apartment hunting with a visit at his parents'.

Do your parents know about me?" I asked.

I was flipping through his record collection, looking for something to play. He was lying on the floor next to me.

"Of course."

"What do they think?"

"About what?" He put his hand around the back of my neck and pulled me to him.

"About me, stupid!"

"They've never met you."

"And if they do, what will they think?"

"They'll think you're gorgeous," he said.

Leaning over me, he kissed me lightly and then, pulling me closer, he kissed me again. During the past few weeks, Ian had become even more attentive—almost clingy. He was always touching me: my shoulders, my arms, my knees, my hips. Sex had gotten better and better with him and while it wasn't heart-exploding like with Vic, it was sweet and tender.

"I'm serious. Will they be mean to me?"

"Of course not! Why would you say that?"

"You said they refused to even meet your last girl friend."

"Ah, but she had kids. They were worried the family coffers would be raided by renegade toddlers who wouldn't understand the first commandment: 'Never touch the principle.'"

"What?" I said, laughing.

"Never touch the principle."

"What about the Vice Principal?" He eased himself on me, unbuttoning my blouse.

"If the topic comes up, better keep your mouth shut."

"What does your father do?" I asked a little later when we were sorting though his books.

"My father? He's a thoracic surgeon."

"What's that mean?"

"It means he's rich."

"And your mom? Does she work?"

"She's a housewife. Into charities. What about your folks?"

"My father's a gardener."

"A gardener? You mean a landscaper?"

"No. A gardener. He has a small business. He takes care of gardens for people like your father. You know, mows, weeds, fertilizes, plants, rakes."

"Oh."

"And my mother is a secretary at an elementary school."

"Am I ever going to meet them?"

"I don't think you'd have much in common."

"We have you in common."

* * *

July Fourth was the kick off for the general election and the State Fairground's Automobile Building was the site of a Democratic Party shindig. Political organizations, lobby groups and causes rented booths in order to answer questions and distribute information to interested citizens. Starting at noon, there was an ongoing Texas barbecue as well as dancing, contests and speeches. The Midway would be open as usual and fireworks in the Cotton Bowl would start once it got dark. Both liberal and conservative groups participated. I'd volunteered to staff the candidates' booth for three hours that afternoon. It was the first time I'd surfaced since my overthrow, and I was a little self-conscious.

I got there at two and immediately noticed that the Young Democrats had their own display. We'd considered the possibility six months earlier, but didn't have the funding to rent space. Their exhibit was startlingly professional-looking, with red, white and blue bunting stretched over the top like a canopy. An unfamiliar girl was organizing pamphlets and literature.

"Hi," she said, smiling.

"Hi," I replied and scanned the material on the table.

"Can I help you with anything?" she asked.

"No. I'm just looking around."

"If you'd like ta join, I have applications right here," she said. Either my haircut had radically changed my appearance or I was even more of a has-been than I thought.

"I'll think about it," I said.

In addition to the applications, there were LBJ bumper stickers and buttons, a brochure explaining the domino theory, a pamphlet from the Chamber of Commerce bragging how Dallas was an almost perfect city, and a stack of slate cards. It was routine for the Party to print up slate cards once the primary and run-off elections were over, so that less involved Democrats would know how to vote. However, as I studied the cards, I could tell right away that something was wrong. Not one liberal candidate appeared.

"Hey," I said to the girl, "I don't see Lance Wallace's name on this card."

"Who's he?" she asked.

"He's one of the Democratic candidates."

"Well, we're not supportin' all of 'um. Just the ones on this card."

"But you have to support all of them," I said. I turned the card over: it originated in Peddy's office.

"Why?"

"Because they're Democrats and you're a Democratic organization. It's one of the rules."

"Not our rules," she informed me.

Stuffing the card in my handbag, I made a mental note that I would contact the State YDs and see if this was censurable behavior.

The first person I spotted as I left the YD stall was Peddy who was leaning against the NRA booth talking to Charlotte Flynn. I hadn't seen her since I'd swiped her minutes at the convention. I considered slinking away, but I refused to give him the satisfaction of knowing I felt out of place. Besides, I wanted to underscore that I had nothing to feel guilty about concerning the missing minutes, so I walked right over to them.

"Republicans not doing anything today, Peddy?" I asked.

"I imagine they are: they're a patriotic bunch. What are you doing here?" he replied, tearing his gaze from Charlotte. "Someone shave your head for being a communist sympathizer?" Peddy asked.

Ignoring him, I glanced down at the literature. "Teaching Children About Firearms" was a brochure advocating target practice in public school starting with the first grade. Bumper stickers claiming, "When guns are outlawed, only outlaws will have guns," and, "Fight Crime: Shoot Back," were everywhere. "Here's My Equal Rights," was the title of a pamphlet that showed a housewife waving a jewel-encrusted pistol in her right hand.

"Gloria used to be president of the Dallas YDs," Peddy told Charlotte," but just recently it was taken over by some responsible young people."

"Responsible for what?" I asked.

"Just responsible. You know, law-abiding."

"You mean they support segregation and the bombing of civilian villages in Vietnam and oppose paying decent wages to working Americans? Stuff like that?"

Peddy tolerated me the way one tolerates commercials in the middle of a favorite television show. "Some day, if you ever grow up, you'll realize issues like those are a lot more complicated than you think."

"Why don't you explain them to me, Peddy?"

"I don't have time for or interest in educating you."

"Well, not today. I can see you're busy pushing guns and all, but next week or next month."

"I'll never have the time or interest, Gloria, because you know why? I don't like you." He turned to Charlotte and tried to resume their previous conversation.

"You could explain why we don't need Social Security or Medicare or how Black children learn more in dilapidated, segregated schools, or why only educated people should be allowed to vote, or—"

"Maybe you didn't notice," he spoke through clenched teeth, "our conversation is over."

"That is, unless you just don't know. Then it would be a waste of my time to find out your reason was just that you wanted the status quo, or because rich people stood to lose money if things changed—"

"I don't have to put up with you anymore, Gloria. You know why? Because you're nobody now."

That got a little close to the bone, and while I don't think I revealed that he'd scored a point, I decided the fun was over.

"You'll be one yourself soon, Peddy. Then maybe we can have lunch or something, you know, at some place that only serves leftovers." I turned and walked away.

As I was making my way to the candidates' booth, I spotted Lance Wallace and Chick Flower leaning against a stall as if preventing it from toppling over was their committee assignment. As I approached, they stopped talking and stared my way and I knew that when I passed, they would turn and watch me walk away, commenting on what I had or didn't have. Out of the corner of my eye I could see them smirking as I got closer. Operating under the mistaken impression that I could embarrass them for their immaturity, once I passed, I swiveled my hips as if I were a waitress at the Carousel Bar. Rather than put them in their places, this simply made them hoot and holler as if they were drunken football players who'd just won the championship. I whirled around and gave them the finger. Just as I reached my booth, they caught up with me.

"Where'd you get that sexy do?" Lance asked.

"Where do you get most haircuts?" I snapped.

"I see we're a little grumpy today," Chick said.

"Did you see the YD booth?" I asked.

"Pretty snazzy, huh?" Lance said.

"Drop over there and check out their slate cards. You won't be so impressed then."

"Why's that?"

I passed the card to Chick. Lance looked over his shoulder.

"Hey, I don't see your name here, Wallace." Chick said.

"Why those chickenshit bastards!" Lance said.

"Yew just hide in the bushes and watch. I'll solve the problem," Chick said. He ventured toward the barbecue vender and lined up. Lance glanced at me. We shrugged and then lost interest.

"Hey," Lance said, "I hear you're seein' Feldman?"

"Yeah. What about it?"

"Nothing. He's a good boy."

"Yes, he is."

"Last time I saw you, I worried you were gettin' in over your head somewhere." He held my glaze. Vic had taught me something: I kept my expression blank. "Guess I was wrong."

"Guess you were."

"Well, I'm relieved. 'Cause I had a feelin' I knew who it was—" I started straightening up the brochures. "And believe me, honey, he's way outta your league."

"Nice picture," I said, holding up Lance's campaign pamphlet.

"You like it?" he asked. Flattery is the surest way to change a subject.

"Yeah, it's great. You know, if you acted halfway normal, you'd be a pretty cool guy."

"Gloria, darlin'. That's the closest thing to a compliment you've ever paid me."

I examined the pamphlet to see what else was there. It was the usual stuff: endorsements from Ralph Yarborough and the President of the AFL-CIO, not to mention praises from other members of the House underscoring his legislative capacities. But I was taken aback when I read, *much* to my surprise, that he was an Elder in his church.

"You're an Elder in your church?" I asked, outraged.

"Hell, yeah. You have a problem with that?"

"Seems a little hypocritical to me."

"How's that?"

"Well, Lance, aren't you, like, sleeping with half the state? Isn't that a sin or something?"

"It's all in how you look at it. You're right. The Bible says adultery is a sin. But it also says that you must not hide your candle under a bushel. Lota women in Texas would think it'd be a sin if I didn't screw around."

"Watch this!" Chick called as he passed with a plate of barbecue.

When he reached the YD booth, he started flirting with the girl working there. Hiking a hip on the table, he chatted away until suddenly he gestured dramatically and the plate landed in the slate cards. Both he and the girl jumped toward the box and started sopping up the gooey sauce. Eventually Chick lifted it up and, after a brief exchange, walked off with all the cards. Once out of her range, he tossed them into the trash. When he returned to our booth, we both applauded.

"I told her I'd clean 'um up and get 'um back to her in an hour or so," he informed us.

"She's gonna be lookin' for ya," Lance warned.

"She's gonna be lookin' for Pete Thornton. That's what I told her my name was." Laughing, Lance clapped him on the back. "You owe me one, now," Chick said to me.

"I'm not running for office. I'd say the liberal candidates owe you something."

"Maybe that's even better. No offense."

"Chick's fixing ta run for speakership," Lance said.

"So I heard. Will you be opposed?" I asked.

"Damn straight! But I'll give 'um a fight. That's where I thought you'd come in." I looked at him blankly. "Folks tell me you're real clever. Got a way with phrases."

"Not really," I said after a pause, believing he was setting me up.

"I thought maybe we'd get a nice picture of me holding up a gavel and you could come up with some catchy slogan to go under it." He held his empty beer bottle upside-down by the neck as if it was a gavel and struck a posed. Lance snickered.

"People gettin' sick of seein' you holdin' on to your gavel all the time," he snorted.

"Damn!" Chick shouted, as some residual beer soaked his shirtsleeve. "I need me another beer."

"Make it three," Lance called after him. "You want a beer, don't you?"

"I don't drink," I said.

"You Baptist?"

"No."

"I am."

"I can tell."

"I don't drink, play cards or screw standin' up."

"Yeah, I know," I said, groaning. It was an old joke. "Too much like dancing."

"Maybe after the fire works tonight, you and me could get together and come up with some good slogans for my campaign." Chick was back with the three beers. He and Lance took long swigs of theirs.

"Can't." I said quickly. "I have a date."

"Well, then tomorrow. Or next day. Come by my office. Around six. Everyone'll be gone then."

"Don't have a car," I said.

"Speakin' a cars," Lance said leaning in toward me, "I got me a new red MG."

"What's an MG?" I asked just to annoy him.

"A sports car. Convertible."

"Wow," I replied, in as bored as voice as possible.

"If you'd like, I'd give you a ride around the block."

"Can't. I'm working."

"Ole Chick'll watch things while we're gone, won't you?"

"What's that?" Chick asked. He was leering at some woman across the way.

"I said you'd hold down the fort here while I take Gloria out for a spin in my MG."

"Depends on how long you plan on takin'."

"An hour or so. We're just going to go around the block."

"Only takes five minutes to go around the block," I cut in.

"Well, maybe we'll stop by the lake and I'll let you look under the hood—"

"Or in the back seat," Chick added.

"Ain't got no back seat in that car," Lance pointed out.

"So, I guess you'll be perfectly safe," Chick said, winking.

I leaned back in my chair and glared at them. "You know," I said, "I *have* a boy friend."

"Well, hell! I gotta wife and two girl friends! I ain't askin' ya to the prom. I'm just asking if ya wanna take a goddam ride in my goddam MG. That's all. 'Course, if you wanted to, you could probably talk me into neckin' a while. Especially if you're as clever as they say."

"Really? And I always heard it took money to get you to do anything." I just made that up, but Chick doubled over laughing.

"Hey, Lance," Chick said, sobering slightly and slapping his friend's arm: something important was about to transpire. "See that broad over there in the gray shorts? I think I'm in love."

We all studied her for a moment. She was tall with dark hair and while she was certainly attractive, I wouldn't say she was a knockout. However, she was clearly too good for Chick.

"Nice legs, don't you think?" Chick asked.

"Yeah. Big ass, though."

"I like big asses!"

"Well, then knock yourself out." They watched her. "Wait a minute!" Lance shouted. "You know who that is?"

"No, do you?"

"She's that bitch from the railroad lobby. The one that spilled the beans about Davis."

My antenna shot right up.

"What'd she say about Vic Davis?" I asked.

Chick glanced around, surprised to find I was still there, but Lance stared at me and I was sorry I'd expressed any interest in Vic.

"She blabbed some pissant story 'bout how the lobby provides him a free apartment in Austin," Chick said. "Failed to mention how she provided herself free of charge, too."

"*She* had an affair with Vic Davis?"

I couldn't help myself. Lance kept staring at me, but I glanced toward the woman. She looked prettier now. She was maybe twenty-eight. Her skin was ruddy, as if she had acne scars, but her oval face and almond-shaped eyes were very attractive. Chick and Lance were both right: she had long, shapely legs, but her hips were slightly out of proportion to the rest of her body.

"Vic Davis don't have affairs," Lance informed me, giving each word equal weight. "He just lets off steam occasionally."

"But," Chick continued, "she thought it was an affair. Kept dropping by to get serviced, until she found him with someone else. And the excrement hit the ventilator, as they say."

"How long ago was this?" I asked, feeling a little queasy.

"Oh, shit. I donno," Chick said. "Year ago."

"She's a lady carries a grudge big as her ass," Lance said.

"Maybe she did the right thing," I said.

They both looked at me as if I were speaking Vietnamese.

"Should he accept an apartment from the lobbyists?"

"You know how goddamn much they *pay* us?" Lance hollered. "Four hundred godamm dollars a month! And if that's not bad enough, every two years, we gotta interrupt our jobs for four to six months and live in Austin."

"Almost everyone has some sort of creative housing arrangement. We have to."

"The citizens of Texas wanna undercut the lobby's influence, pay the legislators a decent wage. Hell, it's hard to even keep yourself in whiskey for four hundred a month."

We glanced back at the woman in the gray shorts. She walked over to a group of men. After she said something to them, they all sobered up and, one by one, drifted away, leaving her there by herself.

"Supposedly that little indiscretion cost her her job. Got deee-moted to assistant editor of the newsletter. Locked away in the basement; hardly sees the light of day."

"Serves her right," Chick snorted. "Why do good lookin' women have to be such cunts?"

The woman in the gray shorts acted as if nothing had happened and in spite of my jealousy, I felt bad for her.

"I might still have my way with her," Chick said, keeping the woman in sight. "Rough her up a little. She deserves it."

"Whatever turns you on."

They started to walk away.

"Hey, Chick," I called out to him.

"What's that, honey?"

"I just thought up your slogan."

"See," he said, nudging Lance while glancing toward his prey. "I told you she was clever. What is it, darlin'?"

"Under this picture of you and the gavel we write, 'To hell with the chitty-chitty, let's get on with the bang-bang!"

"Now that's a great slogan," Lance said. "I think I'll make me a T-shirt out of that one."

"Yew two enjoy yourselves. I got me a score to settle." With that, Chick headed off for the woman in the gray shorts.

"Aren't you going with him?" I asked Lance.

"There are some things a guy has to do in private," he told me. But, after a moment, he ambled off toward them anyway.

A commotion at the far end of the building signaled that someone important had arrived and for a maniacal moment, I wondered if it might be Vic. It was unlikely he'd spend the Fourth away from his home district, but who could predict what an ambitious man might do. I kept squinting toward the noise, but admirers surrounded the celebrity and I couldn't' tell who it was.

"You look busy." I whirled around; it was Willie.

"I'm bored. What are you doing here?"

"Escortin' the man," he said, nodding toward the horde.

"Which man?" I managed to say, my heart racing.

"Who else? Ty Whittaker."

"*Ty Whittaker*?"

"Jesus. You have no idea what a toll this is taking on me."

"I thought you resigned."

"I did. But, a guy's gotta work and he offered me more money." We glanced toward Whittaker, who was pestering Lance Wallace.

"I thought Vic Davis wanted you for his campaign?"

"He doesn't have a chance. Not this time. If I sell out, it's gotta be for a winner."

"Why doesn't he have a chance?"

"Too unknown. Too much baggage."

"Willie! Willie!" An agitated Ty Whittaker rushed toward us.

"Ty, have you ever met Gloria Warren?"

Ever the Southern gentleman, Whittaker, set his emotions aside and smiled charmingly toward me. "Well, no. I do not believe I have ever laid eyes upon this young lady."

"Gloria's president of the Dallas County Young Democrats."

I started to correct Willie, but decided what the hell.

"Is that right? The Young Democrats have been amongst my most loyal supporters and for that I will always be grateful."

"Thank you," I said, glancing down to avoid his eyes.

"But Willie!" Suddenly he was churned-up again. "Lance Wallace says he knows of a barber that's open."

"Goddamnit, Ty. I told you. We don't have time. You got a press conference in an hour and if we don't leave soon we're gonna be late. Your hair's fine! Goddamnit. Isn't it, Gloria?"

Prematurely silver and very thick, Ty Whittaker's hair was probably his best feature. He seemed like a politician sent from Central Casting. "It looks fine," I said.

"It's stickin' up," he insisted, patting his head.

"Where?" I asked.

"Here. By my cowlick. I'm self-conscious of my cowlick."

"I don't see a cowlick," I assured him.

"Here. Look." He knelt on the floor, giving me an aerial view. Willie leaned against my booth and covered his eyes with his hands. Two, maybe three hairs asserted their independence.

"Well, maybe it's sticking up a little, but Mr. Whittaker, you're so tall, who's ever going to see it?"

"Those danged right-wing reporters will aim the cameras so that's all anyone will notice."

"I can't believe they'd want to film with the cameras focused on the top of your skull," I said.

"It doesn't matter!" Willie shouted.

"That's easy for you to say," Ty replied, his voice cracking, "It's not your future—"

"It doesn't matter, because we don't have time to do anything about it!"

"Lance Wallace knows—"

"I don't give a fuck what Lance Wallace knows! We don't have time."

"You're sure?"

"I'm positive!"

"Really, Mr. Whittaker, I wouldn't have noticed if you hadn't pointed it out."

"Yeah, but you're not like these fascist news people. They're always looking for something to ridicule."

"They'll be much nastier if you're late than they will if your cowlick is sticking up," Willie said.

Dejected, he ambled back toward the crowd he'd left earlier.

"He had another vision this morning: she warned him about his cowlick. He spent the whole time on the plane studying himself in the bathroom mirror. The second we landed, he disappears and I find him an hour later in a phone booth, calling all the barbershops in the yellow pages. Of course, it's a holiday: no one's open, but does that stop him?"

"Well, you've just got—what?—two more years of this."

"Don't remind me. I'm already on antacids. I'm getting a prescription for tranquilizers next Monday. I found a gray hair the other day!"

"Why do you do it?"

"I believe he's going to be the next Governor of Texas," Willie said and sighed, as if resigned to the state's fate.

"Speaking of hair: notice anything different?"

"You do something different to your hair?" he asked.

"I trimmed it a little."

"Oh. Looks nice," he said. After a moment, he sighed again and continued, "Well, shit," he announced, "I better round him up and get started for the press conference."

"Good seeing you again," I said.

"Yeah," Willie said, but he wasn't paying much attention. He scanned the room. "Now, where the hell did he go?" he asked.

"He went back over toward Lance Wallace."

"Where the hell's Lance Wallace?" he asked.

We both perused the group across the way. Chick was there but Lance had vanished. I caught Chick's attention and waved him over.

"Willie's looking for Ty Whittaker," I explained. "Know where he is?"

"He just left with Lance Wallace."

"Left?" Willie shouted.

"Yeah. He said he needed a haircut before some press conference and Lance told him his MG could go a hundred and twenty miles an hour. Said he'd have him back here in no time."

"That's it!" Willie said, and with that he left the exhibition hall.

* * *

Ian arrived at four-thirty, and after stopping by to check in, he wandered around, tanking up on barbecue and laughing with politicians. Since I didn't have much to do, I kept an eye on him. When he ambled over to the woman in the gray shorts, I stood to get a better view.

"What you still doin' here, darlin'?" Lance asked. His tousled hair made him seem vulnerable and, for a bizarre moment, I found myself attracted to him.

"What happened to your hair?" I asked.

"Been tearing around in my MG with the top down." He combed his fingers through it. "Is it a mess?"

"Pretty much," I said, resuming my surveillance.

"Some girls tell me I look sexy this way."

"Really?" I said as if mildly surprised.

"What do you think?"

"I think you look like you with your hair wrecked."

"What the hell's so interestin' over there."

I pretended to straighten up my table. "Nothing. Where's Ty Whittaker?"

"He should be back here pretty soon, I imagine."

"I think Willie quit again."

"What makes you say that?"

"He was pissed that you two left. Guess they had a press conference or something."

"Hell, I got him there on time. Willie was at the station waitin' for us. Didn't seem mad to me. What're you watchin'?"

"Lance!" I practically shouted. "Can I trust you?"

He held up his right hand. "I've never gotten anyone pregnant yet. Except my wife."

"See Ian over there?" I grabbed his shirt and pulled him toward me so he could see. "Can you slip over there and let me know what's going on?"

"Now, why do you care about that?" he asked, eyeing me suspiciously.

"I'm just curious. Can you do that? And," I caught his arm as he started to leave, "can you do it without letting them know that's what you're doing?"

"You think I'm a Gomer?" he said, walking away.

Politicians are gifted eavesdroppers. Lance snaked his way toward Ian and then stopped next to him, slapped some guy on the back and started up a dialogue. While he appeared absorbed in his discussion, he positioned himself so that he was privy to everything Ian and the woman said.

"I don't believe we've met."

A grotesque couple in their early thirties interrupted my spying. The man was average-sized and wore a blue polyester suit with white over-stitching, accessorize with a brown Texas string tie, held at his throat by a metal longhorn. His hair was the color and texture of a thatched roof, too thick to part normally, making it resemble a bargain hairpiece. His eyes were so pale it was unclear if they had any color at all. His wife was a round-faced, dimpled, show girl with a pelvis-length tangerine skirt and a sheer off-the-shoulder peasant blouse that looked like the top of a baby-doll pajama set. Her eyelashes had the texture of barbed wire.

"I'm Pete Thornton," he continued, "and I'm running for State Representative."

His lips barely moved and the words seemed to slide out of his nose. The show girl smiled modestly, wiggling her shoulders slightly and sighing, as if to say, "isn't he wonderful?"

"Could I leave these pamphlets here?" He held out about fifty triple-fold brochures.

"Sure," I said, "I'll take care of it."

"That's very kind of you." He walked off in a stooped, tight-assed way, as if worried that a good bowl movement would leave him with nothing but a shell.

On the first leaf of his pamphlet, he listed his campaign promises: "cut taxes; reduce government spending; fight for states' rights; work to reinstate prayer in school; endorse separate but equal educational opportunities for all Texans; support our government during a time of war." The next page had endorsements from right-wing officials. Pictures of the Thorntons and their moon-faced, slobbering baby appeared throughout. His hobbies were bird hunting, praying, and duplicate bridge. He belonged to Young Americans for Freedom and Crisis Christians, and was co-founder of the White Christian Children's Coalition. Missing was any mention of the John Birch Society. But there was room to add that.

* * *

"They were just talkin' bidness," Lance said when he returned.

"I know that, but what were they saying?" I picked up one of Pete Thornton's pamphlet, blew on the ink so it wouldn't smear and then placed it in the finished pile.

"Well, they were tryin' to be discrete, but it wasn't hard to figure out. She's all upset 'cause her office knows she squealed on Davis and she wants Feldman to say she's innocent."

"Will he do that?" I opened another pamphlet, turned to the back page and started writing.

"Didn't seem so. What the hell you doin'?" he asked, leaning in to read my handwriting.

"Pete Thornton left off some crucial information." I handed him a completed brochure.

"Got another pen?" he asked, after he studied it.

* * *

Once my stint was over, Ian and I planned to hit the Midway. Outside the automobile building, a television crew was doing interviews, and photographers from both newspapers were taking pictures for the Sunday edition. As we headed for the rides, Estelle Harris' car arrived.

"Let's say hi to Estelle," I said, pulling on Ian's arm to slow him down.

Before we could reach her, however, Peddy rushed forward, opened her door and reached in to help her. Sensing a human-interest story, photographers snapped away and television cameras panned toward them. To everyone's surprise, once Estelle was standing, she turned on Peddy and whacked him across the face with her pocketbook. It was all I could do to keep from applauding until I realized how it would look on television. Swarmed by reporters asking why she smacked Peddy, Estelle simply replied, "Why don't you ask him?" They did, and of course, he said he had no idea: he had simply offered her a hand and she took offense. Perhaps she was one of the new, liberated women who resent gentlemen.

* * *

"Are you going to bail out that woman from the railroad?" I asked Ian as we sat in the Cotton Bowl and watched Roy Rogers' third cousin do rope tricks.

He leaned against the seat behind him and studied me for a while. "No," he said finally, "I'm not."

"Why not?"

"Because it wouldn't be right."

"But she gave you a story. Don't you owe her something?"

"I owe her confidentiality, which she got."

"But she stuck her neck out and now you could help her—"

"She did stick her neck out. But not because she wanted justice: she hoped to hurt someone. I'm frankly stunned you're defending her. We met at that party in Austin and she said she had a story that might interest me. When I realized what it was, I warned her that she was taking a big risk, but she insisted she didn't care. There's nothing else I can do for her."

The fireworks lasted forty-five minutes and as we were leaving, we stumbled on Lance carting a toddler on his shoulders.

"You ever met my son? This is Tommy. Tommy, can you say hi to these people?"

"Hi," Tommy said, and buried his face in his father's hair.

"Is your wife here?" I asked.

"Nah. She hates loud noises."

"You ever get to the bottom of the Estelle Harris thing?" Ian asked.

"Oh, hell yes. Didn't you hear? Estelle won't utter a peep, but this kid was standin' next to the car and claims Peddy ran up, opened the car door and said, 'Come on you old bitch. We're gonna cram your Pinko record right up your ass tonight."

* * *

The next day both papers ran pictures of Estelle swatting Peddy. However, neither gave explanations. Even Ian had been unable to affect the outcome. The evening news ran the footage repeatedly, while bewildered commentators speculated. Three days later there was a citizen's editorial on the evening news in which a man lamented the growing hostility of Blacks and cited Estelle Harris as an example. With such a breakdown of respect and human decency, he said, no wonder we were having an unprecedented number of race riots across the country.

* * *

When I flew into San Antonio Saturday morning, it was already ninety degrees. I regretted not wearing shorts, but since I was flying I felt I needed to dress up a little. Instead, I wore a short wrap-around skirt and a sleeveless blouse. I'd made a FLORESVILLE sign and I wasn't thumbing for ten minutes before someone picked me up and dropped me right in the middle of town. Because I was so early, I found a close-up spot under a shade tree.

By eleven, about five hundred people—mostly college kids who were there, no doubt, for the folk singers and parties as much as for the labor movement—crowded around City Hall. Since everyone I knew was going to Austin, I didn't expect to see anyone familiar, so I brought a book along to read until things picked up.

Soon, I was surrounded by scantily dressed college kids acting wild and cool the way they do when they're in public, convinced that everything they say is so clever, folks for miles will want to hear. The group closest to me was so distracting that I kept peeking up over my book at them. Though there were eight of them spread over an orange Indian-print bedspread, two dominated. A monumentally homely guy—about nineteen—was the self-appointed wit and sage. John was short and had stooped shoulders, a raging case of acne and overactive saliva glands. Whenever he spoke too fast—which was all the time—or laughed his mule-like bray—which he did whenever he wasn't talking—the spit that wasn't watering the lawn collected in the corners of his mouth like soapsuds in a defective laundry machine. Only one of the girls was attractive. Terri was tall and shapely and wore a plunging halter-top and cut-offs so short they showed butt cleavage. Her frosted hair was short but puffy. She had enormous, expressive eyes, which she overworked, and crater-like dimples. Either she had too much energy to sit or, more likely, she was trying to display her body for those unfortunate souls seated farther away.

I was grateful when the Farm Workers finally arrived. A small Mexican band led the way and was so infectious that the crowd clapped to the beat while cheering the marchers. Terri, of course, stood and danced so that everyone would know she was also coordinated. A Catholic priest, a union organizer and a local official expressed their support of the movement and the crowd yelled and applauded. As the last speaker finished up, he said:

"And now it gives me great pleasure to introduce a young man who flew all the way here from Sumner."

I glanced up. There was Vic.

"A man who is increasingly mentioned as a candidate for governor in 1968. I am proud to introduce to you the Honorable Vic Davis, State Senator from Sumner, Texas."

Though I was one of probably three people there who had any idea who he was, a roar exploded from the crowd as he stepped to the microphone. Terri shot to her feet.

"Oh, my God!" she shouted. "Is he tough or what?"

While Vic waited for the applause to die down, Terri and her friends pledged undying support for his gubernatorial campaign.

"I want to direct my words, not to the supporters of this noble march, but to the marchers themselves," Vic said, and everyone cheered as if this were profound. "It is a great honor to stand before you on this most historic day. For all its wealth, Texas has more people in the poverty bracket than any other state in the union and this will not change until a minimum wage bill is passed. And when such legislation is enacted, it is imperative that the farm workers be included. I am humbled by the dedication of those of you who have spent the summer walking from Brownsville to Austin. As your slogan so aptly states, 'All we want is justice.'"

He then slipped into what sounded like impeccable Spanish. The crowd became frenzied. Though the throng was primarily Anglo, and had no idea what Vic said, they took their cues from the Chicanos among us and screamed encouragement. As he finished his speech, he raised his arm and gave the clinched fist salute. "Viva la Huelga. Viva la raza!"

I was as proud as if I were his mother. Even Ian would have been impressed, I believed. Many of us, touched that he could and would speak in the language of the marchers, became teary-eyed. I felt a rush of affection for him; not lust, affection. Affection and respect.

Terri's squealing, however, broke my trance. She jumped up and down and screamed as if she were at a Beatles concert. Then, just to corrupt the entire mood, she turned to her friends but announced to all of us: "I'd go down on him in a minute."

"Terri, you're so oral!" John chided, rolling his eyes and stroking his chin professorially. "Just get yourself a pacifier." He brayed and sprayed at his own wit.

"I bet you this guy can be had," Terri announced as she watched Vic shaking hands with the other dignitaries. She had her hands on her hips and a determined expression on her face.

"Give me a break, Terri," one of the others said. "He doesn't have time for you."

"Come on," Terri shouted. "Let's head him off."

Vic squeezed through the crowd, shaking hands, smiling and chatting. Terri and her entourage elbowed through to the sidewalk where they could intersect him. Just to nourish my masochism, I watched. When he neared, Terri rushed forward, threw her arms around his neck, and kissed his lips. He disentangled himself and smiled as he moved on. She stood to the side, screaming as if she'd won *The Sixty-Four Thousand-Dollar Question.*

I decided to fly back early.

There appeared be no taxis in Floresville, but I was sure I could hitch a ride. As one of the folk singers led the gathering in "We Will Not Be Moved," I made my way to the parking lot and waited for the rally to break up. Since most folks were staying for the parties, only a few headed for their cars.

"Anyone going to the airport?" I asked each group until finally a businessman from San Antonio said he would drop me off.

"Are you in love with this Vic Davis like all the other young girls seem to be?" he asked me once we were on the highway.

"Yeah. I guess so," I replied.

I just missed the late afternoon flight and there wasn't another until eight-thirty, so I plopped down in the lobby. I had my book but I couldn't concentrate. Instead, I just watched people come and go.

Suddenly I realized I was looking at Vic. Had been for some time. He was alone in line at the Braniff counter, checking in. He had no luggage: he must have just flown in for the rally. While I was confident he wouldn't see me on his way to his gate, I didn't want to risk the remote possibility of a humiliating encounter. If he looked my way, and then ignored me, it would kill me. If he spoke to me, pretending there had never been anything between us, it would make me furious. And if he tried to seduce me, it would screw me up; but if he didn't, it would crush me.

Across the lobby was a ladies' room. I could stay put there long enough for him to pass. The ticket clerk was helping him, so it was a good time to split. However, when I tried to stand, I found that my legs had adhered to the plastic seat. It was like trying to pull away from a butt-sized suction cup. On the third try I jerked myself forward so hard that I knocked over a pedestal ashtray, it's clang reverberating throughout the airport. Fighting the urge to glance his way, I darted off to the restroom.

Overheated and flushed, I splashed icy water on my face and neck. There were no chairs so I just paced back and forth until I was sure he'd had time to move on. I cracked the door and peeked out: he was standing right there. We stared at each other for a moment before I pushed the door open and walked out like I was normal.

"I *thought* that was you," he said, glancing toward the toppled ashtray. "I was about to have someone check on you. Are you ill?"

"Ill? No."

"You were in there so long. I worried you were sick."

"Oh. No. I'm fine, I guess."

"You did something to your hair," he said as if he noticed it was different but, even though I was practically bald now, couldn't quite figure out what it was.

"I had it cut."

"You sure did." He put his hand gently on my shoulder and turned me around so that he could see the back.

"It'll grow back out. Someday." I mumbled.

"It's very pretty. Makes you look sophisticated." He grinned, as if teasing a toddler.

"Is that funny?" I asked.

"Well, if I had to pick a word to describe you, 'sophisticated' wouldn't rush to mind."

"Oh," I said and looked down at me feet.

"Do you think I just insulted you?" he asked.

"No. Everyone wants to be a hick."

"I didn't call you a hick."

"It's OK," I shrugged.

"No. It's not okay. Listen, when you get home, look up sophisticated in the dictionary. Then you'll understand."

"Sure."

"Will you do that?"

"I said yes."

"What are you doing here? In San Antonio?"

"Ah…I was at the rally in Floresville."

"You were?" He smiled.

"Yes. I…I heard your speech."

"What'd you think?"

"I was impressed."

"Were you?"

"Along with everyone else."

"Why didn't you say hello or something?"

"Well, you seemed—. I mean, I didn't have time. I had to get to the airport and all."

"What time's your flight?"

"Oh, not for a while. I…I missed the earlier one."

"You hungry?"

"Hungry?"

"I'll buy you dinner."

"Well, when's your flight?"

"In twenty minutes. But there's always another one. Wait. I'll go change it now."

Obediently, I stood were I was while he trotted back to the ticket counter and charmed the attendant into switching his flight. As I watched him, my chest tightened up and my throat constricted. Please, God, please don't let me cry. I'll quit swearing, I'll go to church, I'll even quit torturing that asshole, Dexter Peddy. Just let me get through this with some dignity. I stopped short of promising to give up sex. Dignity was only worth so much.

* * *

"I'm just delighted to see you," he said.

He ushered me down the hallway toward the departure gates until we reached a small, dimly lit bar. The waiter seated us against a wall toward the back of the nearly deserted room. Menus stood between the napkin holder and the salt and pepper shakers. Vic handed me one and then studied his. I watched him. Sensing this, he glanced up at me.

"What?" he said, an amused expression on his face.

"You speak Spanish."

"Yes."

"I didn't know that."

He smiled and returned to his menu. "Don't get the chili here, it'll kill you."

"Are you, you know, fluent?" He lifted his eyes to mine.

"Didn't I sound fluent?"

"Well, what would I know? You sounded great, but—"

"I'm fluent. The burger's your best bet. Wanna beer?"

"I'm, you know, not…old enough."

"Oh," he said, glancing away. "That's right."

"How have you been?" he asked, once he'd ordered two burgers, a coke and a beer.

I just nodded. He reached over and took my menu out of my hand and gave it back to the napkin holder.

"Why are you leaving the rally so soon? I understand they have all sorts of things planned for the evening."

"Well, I was going to stay, but I changed my mine."

"Why?"

"I didn't know you were going to be here."

His casual smile eased into a confused expression. "Are you changing the subject?"

"No, I guess not." Someone passed by in the hallway and called out a greeting to the waiter, who waved back. "How come *you're* not staying? You'd be the star."

"I never stay for the parties."

"Really?"

"That surprise you?"

I shrugged.

"I'm interested in politics, Gloria, not mischief."

"It's odd that I know so little about you, you know, considering." I picked up a tent sign on the table. It advertised a drink called Santa Ana's Downfall. "You're very secretive."

"Secretive?" he laughed. "It's impossible to be secretive in politics."

"I know almost nothing about you."

"What is it that you feel you need to know?"

"If I asked you something personal, would you tell me the truth?"

"I wouldn't lie to you."

"What does that mean?"

"It means I reserve the right not to answer at all."

"Never mind, then."

"Why does that offend you?"

"Because I'd tell you anything about me and you've never—"

"One of these days you'll learn that knowledge is power. You *shouldn't* tell people just anything they want to know. You never know when they might use it against you."

"You think you can't trust me?"

"Actually, I believe I can. It's just a rule I have. But try me. What do you want to know?"

"And your answer won't be affected by what you think I want to hear or by what you want me to think?"

"I'm beginning to feel a little uneasy. *If* I answer, I'll tell you the truth." He locked eyes with me: a dare.

"Do you sleep around a lot?"

His expression did not change at all, but I had surprised him. I could almost see his mind calculating a non-answer. Then he said simply: "No."

"I guess we should define 'a lot'," I said reaching for the tent sign again.

"No. We don't have to define anything. I know exactly what you're asking me. You're asking me if I'm on the prowl all the time and I'm telling you, no, I'm not."

"Well, then why does everyone think that?"

"Because at one point in my life, I was."

"When was that?"

He laughed. "Now you're getting into the area where I might not answer."

I studied the tent sign though there was still only one sentence to read. Vic took it away from me and put it back where it belonged.

"Why is it so important to you?"

"I know it's over with us. And that's okay, really. Ah. It's better, you know, for both of us, but—"

"But what?"

"Sometimes I feel, you know, foolish. I never knew what I was to you—not that I had to be much, you know? But I hear things. About you. And sometimes I see things."

"See things? Like what?"

"Like you with women."

"What's that supposed to mean? You see me with women, you see me with men."

"You're different with women. You flirt with them."

"So?"

"And I saw that woman kiss you. This afternoon."

"Which one?" he asked. Then he stopped and looked down at the table. "I'm sorry."

"That's sort of what I mean. How many men would say 'which one?' when someone said, 'I saw that woman kiss you today.'"

"Is that my fault? I give a speech and as I'm leaving silly girls rush over and kiss me. You think I *want* that? I'm a serious politician, Gloria. I'm considering a run for Governor of one of the largest states in the Union. How beneficial is it to have women throwing themselves at me? Last week, in Houston, some girl tossed a bra at me! In the middle of my speech! Jesus!

How do you instill confidence with that shit going on? Luckily the press is only interested in serious news, because, believe me, something like that could turn a candidate into a joke!"

"Are you involved with someone now?" He leaned back in his chair and casually looked over his shoulders.

"No," he said.

"I know it seems crazy, but I want to know the truth."

"You *do* know the truth."

"Because, it occurs to me that maybe…maybe I was nothing. To you. Maybe I could've been anyone. And you know, hey, I'm broad-minded. I can live with that. I understood the situation all along. But…I'd rather *know* than speculate."

The waiter arrived with our food and we sat by silently, not looking at each other, until he left. Vic doctored his hamburger with ketchup and hot sauce, but I wasn't hungry. He took a gulp from his beer and I watched his throat move as he swallowed. He placed his glass on the table but continued to hold it. I could tell he was looking at me, but I avoided his gaze.

"Well, I feel magnificently crummy," he said. I resisted the urge to apologize. "I'm going to give you enough information to ruin me. Would you like that?"

"I would never hurt you."

"I believe that. Obviously." He was quiet for a while as if trying to figure out where to start. "Have you ever noticed, Gloria, how bad things happen in clusters?"

"No."

"Well, they do. Once something horrible happens, brace yourself, there's more to come."

"I lead a charmed life," I said, still clinging to that belief.

"So do I," he replied and finished his beer. He held up the empty glass until he caught the attention of the waiter, who nodded and hurried off to fetch him another. When he set the glass back down, he tapped it rhythmically with his index finger before he finally exhaled a long, irritated breath.

"My career took a downward spiral a few years ago. I crossed the Establishment. I was young. Idealistic. Arrogant. Sure of myself. I know better than to do something like that now, but back then, it appeared as if it would pay off. Then it backfired."

"Is this the Kennedy thing?" I asked.

"How did you know about that?"

"Someone told me. A while back."

"After Kennedy died, the Establishment came after me. I'd worked for years to pass a bill that would extend the Interstate to Sumner: it would have made a huge difference economically to my district. Connally vetoed it. When I was up for re-election, he handpicked my opponent, convinced my top financial backers to drop me, and made three visits to my district to campaign against me. I'd never even had an opponent before that. It looked as if I were washed up."

The waiter returned with the beer. "Is something wrong with the hamburgers, sir?" he asked Vic as if I were not there.

"No," Vic assured him and then raised his eyebrows to me.

"No, they're fine," I said. To prove it, I took a bite. Placated, the waiter vanished. Encouraged by my example, Vic started eating. "But, you won that election—" I prodded.

"Yes, to everyone's surprise, I ended up with sixty-three percent of the vote." He sighed as if exhausted. "But, when things looked most bleak, Penny got involved with another man. I don't mean she had an affair: she got *involved.* In all fairness, I wasn't that easy to live with. I wasn't home much and when I was, I was distant. Grumpy. Plus, during my glory days, there'd been a few women. And though I never promised these women anything, more than one of them told Penny I wanted a divorce. I didn't.

"As I've told you before, Penny understands me. Probably more than any other woman could. In some ways, she's a lot like a man. She knows what she wants and she's ruthless."

"What does Penny want?"

"What we all want: power. And I'm her ticket. She was willing to put up with a lot. And she did: God knows we all bruise. But I stepped over the line that separates forgivable human frailties from fatal transgressions when my career got into trouble.

"She wanted a divorce. Took the kids and moved out—Regina was a baby." He stared off into space. "After a few months, she came back. Not because she loved me so much, but because I was the father of her children and the life I could offer—though crumbling at the time—was more appealing than her alternative. Don't let her looks fool you—Penny's a shark."

"And so you took her back?"

"She held all the cards. I even agreed to her terms. In public, we were the perfect couple. At home, we had separate rooms." He leaned back in his chair and stretched his long legs out diagonally under the table, crossing his feet. I could reach down and touch his ankle if I wanted to.

"I hated her," he went on. "There was no way I could hurt her—you have to have emotional leverage for that. So I settled for humiliation. I can be a real bastard. Thank God for double standards. The more women I seduced, the more admired I was, but Penny...Penny couldn't get away with much. As long as she stayed the long-suffering wife, she could garner some sympathy. 'Poor Penny,' women would whisper, but they smiled my way when they said it. She got tangled up in the net she threw over me. And I wanted her to starve there."

"I thought you said you didn't sleep around."

"I don't. Not anymore. Not like that. For a while, I blighted the state. No one was off-limits. They didn't even have to be attractive. Then one night I was with a woman—a friend's wife, a tedious woman—and I thought 'this isn't much better then jerking off.' And I stopped, but the stories about me didn't. In the recent past, I've only been with three women."

"Who were they?"

He laughed and I assumed he wasn't going to tell me, but then he did. "The first was a secretary in the DA's office. She'd always been good to me about passing along information—nothing unethical, you know, just overly considerate. When she filed for divorce, I gave her some ammunition. Her husband golfed at my club: bragged a lot. After the divorce, she invited me to lunch. To thank me. She thanked me for about six months."

"And the second?"

"Was an actress at the Sumner Theater Center. Penny and I had season tickets. We agreed to host a fundraiser at our house and the actors all came. I told her I was a fan, that I thought she was very talented and pretty. She told me she was frigid. Right there in my kitchen. Out of the blue. Jesus! What was I supposed to do? A cry for help like that?"

We both laughed. "Was she?" I asked.

"No. Of course not."

"What happened to her?"

"What happens to all actresses: she moved to California."

"Do you ever hear from her?"

"For a while." He picked up the tent sign and read about Santa Ana's Downfall. "And the third was a scruffy kid I was very fond of. But the relationship was too threatening for both of us. So it ended before it started."

I watched the waiter approach two men who had just arrived. One of the men must have told a joke because they all laughed. The waiter seated them several tables over from us. They ordered martinis and while they waited for their drinks they studied the menus.

Vic was not being entirely honest: What about the woman in the gray shorts? And the woman she caught him with? When he seduced me, he'd considered it a one-night stand. Surely, there were others.

I glanced back at the new arrivals. Following my lead, Vic watched too. When the waiter brought their drinks, they both ordered the chili. We looked at each other and laughed.

"If they're on your flight, sit as far away from them as possible."

It was the first time I'd heard Vic make a joke, particularly something off-color. And that made me laugh even more.

"You…still seeing that reporter?" he asked.

"Well—" I started and then stopped myself. I'm not sure what I was going to say, but I knew it was something that would encourage Vic. And even though I wanted that—more than wanted it—I knew it was a mistake. "Yes."

"You want anything else?" Vic asked, signaling for the waiter. I shook my head.

"What happened to the man?" I asked, while we waited for the check. "To Penny's—"

"He's around. He's one of those noble, idealistic pricks. Penny had to choose. He wanted to marry her, not just screw her. Though I believe she has occasional flings, I'm certain he's out of the picture."

I walked him to his gate and waited until it was time for him to board.

"What if Connally opposes you in sixty-eight?" I asked.

"He won't. We have a deal."

"A deal?"

"I remain neutral on the war; he stays out of my race. They believe I could influence young people—probably just because my hair's long—and they don't want me stirring things up any more than they already are."

"So you sold out?"

"The only people who don't sell out, are those that don't have anything to offer. Once elected, I can do and say whatever I want from a position of immense power and influence."

When they called his row, he turned toward me and extended his hand. "Take care, Gloria," he said as we shook hands.

"You, too," I said, but he was already halfway up the ramp.

* * *

I read a book once—I can't remember its title, but it was one of those old books with stilted language and dated views: I didn't like it much. It was about a man who could have one wish. He took some time to think of what this wish might be and while he was thinking, a voice or something kept saying, "Wish for happiness. Wish for happiness." Since I didn't finish the book, I don't know if that was, in fact, what he requested, but I recall thinking that happiness might be the last thing I'd wish for.

For one thing, how would you even *realize* you were happy if you weren't occasionally sad? Or lonely? Or depressed? Or anxious? Or defeated? If parts of you hadn't been bloodied, or scarred, or scraped, or broken or mangled: your leg, your arm, your heart, your spirit? How could you laugh—how would you even *know* what was funny—if you hadn't done your share of crying? If there wasn't this deep, dark cesspool of misery swirling around inside you, puddling like crude oil, waiting to be tapped into so it could gush out? How could you enjoy life, if you hadn't occasionally—for however briefly and insincerely—considered ending it? And wouldn't people who were *always* happy, like those who were *always* depressed, be tedious and unproductive? Why do anything? If you had nothing to overcome, or prove, or rectify, had no scores to settle or debts to pay, no skeletons to hide, no humiliations to pick at, no need for revenge, no old boy friends to punish, no high school tormentor whose nose was begging for a pile of shit, no desire for personal glory, no yearning for power, no craving for money, no longing for fame—what would you do all day, but sit around and smile?

Though Vic's absence had always hurt, I had adjusted. In the beginning, my attachment to him was shallow: he impressed me because he was so handsome and powerful and, of course, such a fabulous lover. I missed all of that, but really, there wasn't much more. After seeing him in Floresville and talking to him in the airport, I felt a respect for and a closeness to him that I'd never known earlier and I regretted that it hadn't been part of the equation all along.

* * *

The next morning, I walked to Ian's and tapped on his door. There was no answer, but his VW was in the lot so I knew he was home. I banged louder and eventually he opened the door, looking puffy and groggy. He wore the bottom half of red plaid pajamas and, in spite of his size, he reminded me of a kid.

"What are you doing here?" he asked, digging at his eyes with his knuckles.

"I came back early."

He stepped aside so I could enter the apartment. The drawn curtains made the room unnaturally dark compared to the bright sunshine outside.

"How come?" He shuffled into the kitchen and filled his electric percolator with water.

"Why else? I missed you."

He gave me a look and said, "yeah, right."

"Once the rally was over, I decided to just leave rather than hang around all by myself. No one was there."

"No one?" His back was to me as he searched through a cabinet, so I couldn't read him.

"Well, Vic Davis was there."

"So I heard." He found the coffee and started scooping it into the basket of the coffee pot. "What'd he have to say?"

"He spoke in Spanish."

"You didn't talk to him?"

"No. Even if I'd wanted to, it was so crowded…" I didn't feel I had to come *that* clean.

"Well, he's one shrewd politician, isn't he?" Ian plugged in the coffee pot, which instantly started rumbling.

"Why do you say that?"

"Astute move: going to Floresville instead of Austin. In Austin, he'd be up against the big time, but in *Floresville*! I guess he was quite a star."

"The crowd loved him. Even you would have been impressed."

"Oh, I'm *always* impressed with Vic Davis." Ian retrieved a skillet from a lower cabinet and put it on a burner. Then he opened the refrigerator. "Want some eggs?" he asked.

"No. Thanks."

He tossed a square of butter into the skillet and as it melted, he swiveled the pan back and forth to coat it.

"I didn't know he was going to be there," I said, feeling a little defensive.

He glanced over his shoulder at me. "I believe that," he said as he cracked the eggs over the skillet. "Though when I read the wire yesterday, I wondered."

* * *

During the next week, we spent almost all of our free time together since he was leaving that following Monday for New York. After work, I'd stop by my place to check the mail and glance at the newspaper before I'd gather up whatever I need and walk over to his place.

Vic got fabulous press for the Floresville appearance. A *Times Herald* editorial praised his sensitivity to the Chicano population, saying wasn't it time a Texas politician finally bothered to learn the second most used language in the state? I clipped the articles on Floresville as if they were about me and put them in a folder that I buried under some standing files in my desk.

In Thursday's mail, I got a letter with no return address.

> *Gloria, I'll be in apartment 8-D of the Turtle Creek Village Condos next Tuesday from 4:30 until 9:30. If you're having second thoughts, as I am, it would be wonderful to see you.*

His handwriting was disappointing. He'd used a ballpoint pen and the loops of his L's and E's were blobbed with ink. His letters were neither neat enough nor sloppy enough to be distinguished. Every word was legible but they were tiny and undramatic. I wished he'd signed it. People usually had flair with their signature.

I read the letter once and quickly threw it away in the brown paper bag under the sink.

After I grabbed what I'd need to take to Ian's, I locked up and hurried down the street. About a block away, I slowed my pace until finally I stopped altogether. I was running late and Ian might worry if I didn't show up soon. Still, I turned around and headed back to my apartment. Once inside, I tossed my clothes on the sofa. It took me a while to locate the dictionary, which I'd squirrelled away in the bottom drawer of my desk.

> *Sophisticated: 1) made wise or worldly wise by education, experience or disillusionment; not naive; 2) Pleasing or satisfactory to the tastes of sophisticates; 3) altered from the natural or simple; 4) impaired or debased purity or genuineness; 5) deceptive, misleading; 6) complex or intricate. Difficult to understand.*

The letter was still there—the only thing in the brown paper bag. I pulled it out and glanced at it because I couldn't remember if it started out "Gloria," or "Dear Gloria." Then I threw it away again.

The next morning, when Ian flipped on *The Today Show*, the big story was from Chicago. Someone had mutilated a group of nurses in their apartment. God, I hated hearing shit like that. The lone survivor, hid under a bed while the assailant strangled and stabbed her roommates. She hadn't risked crawling out until daylight. Then she climbed on the fire escape and screamed for help. They had a composite picture of the murderer.

"You're going to be late," Ian warned. He was ready to leave and I hadn't even dressed yet. I glanced at the clock. I couldn't possibly make my bus. "If you hurry, I'll give you a ride."

"What must it have been like for that woman who lived? " I asked once we were in the car.

"Pretty grim, I imagine."

"Lying under that bed for hours, imagining what the room must have looked like with mangled bodies and pools of blood everywhere. And not just any bodies, but the bodies of your best friends." I felt queasy.

At a red light, Ian studied me a moment before he said, "It was Chicago. Not New York."

"It could have been New York."

"It could have been Dallas."

"I don't think so."

* * *

Ian had to cover a meeting that evening, so we agreed that I'd wait at my place until he could drop by. I found myself glued to the television. So far there'd been no arrest in Chicago. No telling where the creep was by now.

When a commercial came on during the evening news, I strayed into the kitchen and stared at the cabinet under the sink for a while before I jerked it open and retrieved Vic's note. I wouldn't see him, but I wanted to save the letter, like a souvenir. After reading it a couple of times, I hid it next to his picture.

* * *

The morning of Julia's brunch, I woke up regretting that I'd make the commitment.

"Do I look okay, Ian?"

I was a wreck. Now that I didn't have access to Veronica's wardrobe, I had to rely on my own dreck. Ian said when in doubt, be as subtle as possible, but he wasn't from Texas. We finally settled on a white and beige pantsuit. It wasn't my favorite, but it was polyester, so it wouldn't wrinkle.

"You look great."

"I don't look fat?"

"How could you look fat?"

"Is this lipstick okay?"

"It's fine."

"It's not too bright? I feel like I'm all mouth."

"You are."

"I'm serious! Can't you tell I'm nervous?"

"Jesus, Gloria. This is a whole new side to you. You actually give a shit."

"These people aren't like us, Ian."

"How's that?"

"They're rich and sophisticated."

"Hey! I went to Harvard, babe!"

"You know what I mean. What if I drop my doughnut on the floor?"

"I don't think you'll be having doughnuts."

"What if I have to pee a lot? Sometimes when I get nervous—"

"Then ask if you can use the restroom."

"Why do I even bother trying to talk to you?"

"Just because Julia's got money, doesn't mean she's not a regular person. She likes you or she wouldn't have invited you."

Ian drove up to Julia's brick mansion, via the white stone circular driveway.

"I wish you had a better car," I said, eyeing the Cadillac and Thunderbird parked next to the four-car garage.

The front door was the size of a cathedral's, only more ornate, with what Ian called art nouveau carvings along each side. Shrubs and flowering plants formed geometric designs in the space inside the circular drive.

"Ian, I have a strong feeling this is a mistake," I said.

"Mistake? What kind of mistake?"

"I woke up this morning *knowing* something terrible was going to happen here."

"You're just nervous. It'll be fine."

"You ever watch *The Twilight Zone*?" I asked.

"*The Twilight Zone* is fiction."

"No, it's not. They tell you at the beginning it's based on truth."

"But they don't tell you how much truth, do they? For instance, if a show is set in Minneapolis, well, Minneapolis does exist, but the rest is fiction."

"Ian, I *know* I should skip this."

"Get out of the car."

"Once I had this premonition that something was wrong with my parents. I called them every Saturday and it was only Thursday, so I tried to put it out of my mind. But I couldn't. Then when I called Saturday, I found out my dad was in the hospital. *Had been since Thursday.* See what I mean?"

"No."

"I don't feel good about this, Ian."

"Everything will be fine."

"If something happens, it's your fault."

"Fine. I'll take full responsibility. Now, get out."

An older woman in a sky blue dress with a starched white apron opened the door. The foyer looked like the lobby of a hotel. A massive oriental rug covered the terra cotta tiled floor. An oversized staircase loomed straight ahead and then split and curved both to the right and the left. Asian-looking vases, bigger than me, held trees on either side of the room.

The maid steered me to an airy living room. The interior wall was a pale rose while the exterior one was a series of sliding glass doors. A rose and olive-green striped sofa dominated and three rose print chairs surrounded an ornate coffee table. A fireplace for giants took up the north wall, while five steps leading up to a dining room defined the southern end of the room. Three women, all in their thirties, all impeccably dressed, sat in the room, but Julia was missing.

"You must be Gloria," one of the women said. She had thick, sandy-colored hair that hung straight to her shoulders and wore a black sleeveless shift with pearls around her neck. "I'm Pamela Newton."

She held out her hand to me. Though less glamorous than Julia, she had a warmth that immediately put me at ease. Her green eyes crinkled when she smiled her slightly crooked smile and her lean oval face had the ruddiness of an athlete.

"Julia's on the phone, but she'll be back in a minute. Do you know everyone?" Her arm extended toward the others. I shook my head. "This is Tess Ruffino," she said indicating a slightly plump, platinum blond whose high, fat French twist resembled a white tornado. She nodded toward me.

"We've heard so much about you," Tess said. "I feel as if we already know each other."

"Really?" What did Julia know about me other than that I was sleeping with Vic Davis?

"And this is Rhonda Bridges, the best interior decorator you'd ever hope to meet." Rhonda combed her blondish-brown hair close to her face, in defiance of popular styles. She wore a multi-print sundress, made of some gauzy fabric that swayed when she moved.

Before I could acknowledge her, Julia breezed into the room. Taking the Cleopatra thing a little far, she had tiny beads threaded through her hair so that she jangled like a charm bracelet. She wore a vivid red-orange, polished cotton jumpsuit with an oversized rolled collar and large cut-out circles on each side to expose the indentation of her waist.

"That was Penny Davis," she chirped. "She was calling from the Highland Park Village. I guess she made a wrong turn. She should be here shortly."

I wondered how much *The Twilight Zone* paid for stories.

"Gloria!" Julia shouted, just noticing me. "You're here. I didn't hear the bell." She placed her hand softly on my shoulder as if to steady me. "We have a surprise, Gloria. Pamela invited her school chum, Penny Davis, to join us. I only just found out myself. But the more the merrier, don't you think? My! What have you done to your hair?"

"Penny Davis?" I whispered.

"You look beautiful," she said, covering for me. "Look at this face!" she said to the others. "Is she all eyes or what?"

The others mumbled agreement.

"You know Penny Davis?" Pamela asked, her eyebrows arching.

"Ah…" I started and looked toward Julia.

"Have you ever actually *met* Penny, Gloria?" Julia asked.

"No. Not really," I muttered.

"Julia tells me you're involved in politics," Pamela said. "Penny's husband is thinking about running for Governor."

"Yes. I've been with him…I mean, you know, when he's given speeches in Dallas and I didn't have anything else to do, which hasn't been all that often, you know, maybe—. Actually, just once. That's right. Just once." I realized I was rattling as if I'd downed about six diet pills, but I couldn't stop myself. "I only saw him once. At the airport. There were, I don't know, maybe fifty other people there, so I didn't, like, *speak* to him or anything. Moderate, right? And then I left. By myself. I'm liberal. I'll probably support, you know, that fool, Ty Whittaker."

"Gloria!" Julia interrupted. "Why don't you come with me to the kitchen so I can get you some champagne." Once in the hallway, she called her maid and requested a drink for me.

"I don't usually drink. I'm afraid it will make me sick."

"Well, this isn't a usual situation, is it?" she whispered as she slipped me the fluted glass.

"Maybe I should leave," I said, sipping the champagne.

"Nonsense! Everything will be just fine once you calm down a little. Here. Drink up." I drained my glass. "Feel better?"

"I hope I don't puke…I mean, throw up."

"Well if you do either, just avoid the Orientals." She refilled my glass and then slipped her arm through mine. "Let's get back to the others."

"Gloria is President of the Young Democrats," Julia said when we returned. I didn't correct her.

"It's so encouraging to find young people interested in party politics," Pamela said. "They're all so impatient now, not that there's not reason to be. Between the war and all these race riots, I'm sure it must seem as if the government is completely incompetent—"

"Julia tells me you're a speechwriter," I said, relaxing some.

"I write speeches, but I'm not a speechwriter. I'm a legislative assistant for environmental issues and when he needs an environmental speech, I write it, because it's my area."

"That must be awfully exciting," I said, impressed that I could carry on a conversation.

"It's hard work, but it is fun and I guess, at times, exciting."

"It just must be so satisfying to be able to influence someone who can *do* something."

Pamela laughed. "I'm not sure how much I influence the Senator: he's much more inclined to listen to his constituents. But, yes, of course, there are moments when I'm able to convince him to take a controversial stand on something important. I am fortunate to work for a man who is both courageous and intelligent. And when it turns out that the unpopular stand proves to be morally correct or even, ultimately popular, well that's as good as it gets."

"I *love* politics," I said.

"Have you ever considered moving to Washington?" Pamela asked.

"Yeah, I always assumed that's what I'd do. I even started a list of people I'd work for."

Pamela laughed. "Usually *they* interview *you*. But who's on your list?"

When I told her, she said, "I know people in those offices. If you decide you want to make the move, I could put in a word for you. In Washington, *who* you know is more important than what you can do."

"Well, I guess I'm not really considering that anymore," I said. "My...my boyfriend wants me to move to New York with him."

"New York is a wonderful, vibrant city. If I didn't love politics, that's where I'd be."

"I've never been there. Actually, I'm a little...uh...nervous about it."

"I have no doubt you'll enjoy New York. But don't make the mistake the women of our generation made. Don't sell yourself out for some man."

"Oh, I really like him—"

"I'm sure you do. But, what you have to worry about is, will you still like him years from now if you abandoned everything you want to make him happy?"

"And don't put him through law school or medical school, whatever you do!" Tess said.

The doorbell rang and I shot a panicked look at Julia.

"That must be Penny," Pamela said.

"It'll be fine," Julia whispered to me as she passed into the hallway.

Penny was breathtaking. Her hair fell loosely around her face and she seemed elegant in a white sleeveless blouse and pale pink straight skirt. She and Pamela embraced and exchanged the sort of greetings good friends do after a long absence. Julia introduced Penny and my heart thumped so hard as I waited for my turn that I worried the glass figurines on the mantle might jiggle off from the vibration. I put my champagne flute down because my hand was shaking so badly.

Penny did not clutch her heart and start yelling "Whore, whore!" when she focused on me. Instead, she said something almost as bad. She said: "I believe you know my husband."

"You have a husband?" I stammered.

"Vic Davis."

"Uh. Yes! I've heard him speak. One night—*evening* actually. *Early* evening, I heard him at the airport. Big crowd there. I left early. Alone. I had a date or something."

"Penny!" Julia intruded. "Have some champagne." Penny smiled gloriously at Julia and sipped the drink, but turned back to me immediately.

"But weren't you with Billy Anders when he drove Vic to Dallas after the convention?"

How I remained standing is a mystery to me. "Oh! Yes! That's right. I had forgotten. I was, you know, reading a book, so I didn't pay much attention. That's your husband, huh?"

Luckily Pamela distracted her and she turned, leaving me alone with Julia.

"Smooth," Julia whispered to me.

"I think I should go," I whispered back.

"And have everyone speculate why you left so soon? You don't want that. Not with this crowd."

Brunch was on a terrace overlooking the pool. Potted flowering trees lined the bricked patio, shielding us from the sun. Six metal chairs whose arms twisted into curlicues and who's thick lemon-colored cushions sighed when you sat on them, circled an oval, glass-topped table. Plates of exotic cheeses, breads and sliced fruits made up the first course. Somehow, the terrace was air-conditioned. I wasn't sure how Julia accomplished this, but as I sat there, gusts of refrigerated air grazed me. And though it was ninety degrees, I had goose bumps on my arms. Julia sat next to me, and Penny was across the table and to my left. I tried to avoid making eye contact, but twice I glanced up and caught her staring at me. Both times she quickly looked away.

"Has anyone kept in touch with Kiki Milford," Pamela asked?

"Oh, haven't you heard?" Tess asked. When Pamela shook her head, Tess continued. "Remember how she and her husband used to go to those wife-swapping parties? Well, Kiki was so self-conscious about being flat-chested that she had a series of silicone injections."

"You're kidding!"

"Ten altogether. You should have seen her! It was as if she had helium balloons under her halter. Everywhere she went she wore plunging necklines leaving her tits shimmering there like Jell-O."

"So what happened to her?"

"Well, she became the hit of the wife-swapping parties before she moved on to bigger things," Rhonda added.

"Such as?"

"Rumor is, she now runs a high-class call-girl service in Duluth, Minnesota," Tess said.

"Duluth, Minnesota?"

"Doing very well, too," Rhonda said.

"Well, more power to her," Julia exclaimed. "Her husband was a pig anyway. Acting like every woman he'd ever met couldn't wait to suck him off on the ninth hole at the Dallas County Club. Granted it was dark, but still."

"What happened to him?" Pamela asked.

"Oh, get this! He ups and marries this twenty-year-old."

My stomach knotted.

"You're kidding. He really *is* scum," Rhonda said.

In spite of myself, I glanced toward Penny. She was watching me, only this time she didn't turn away.

"Well, if it makes any of us feel better," Julia said, "I heard he gave her this new vibrator, supposedly for her complexion. You can fill it with ice or warm water and it gets rid of morning puffiness or tired lines—a real concern for twenty-one year olds, I understand. But the damn thing is shaped like an enraged cock, so one wonders."

Everyone but Penny cackled.

"Penny, I'm afraid my friends are a little raunchy for you," Pamela said, dabbing at the corner of her eye with her napkin.

"I can't believe he'd marry her!" Tess said. "It's one thing to screw around, but what could they *talk* about. She's probably barefoot and beaded and he's got his three-piece suits."

"Not to mention golf knickers," Julia added. "If you ask me, she's the one I pity."

"Have *your* eye on anyone these days, Julia?" Pamela teased.

"Not really," Julia sighed heavily. "Men tire me these days. All that chest-thumping every time you fake an orgasm. You'd think *they'd* faked it!"

"Still I think it's scandalous!" Tess boomeranged back to the earlier conversation. "These middle-aged men running off with teenagers!"

"It *is* outrageous," Julia agreed. "But in all honesty, it has only struck me as outrageous since I turned thirty. We can only hope the bastard ends up with that distasteful spraying problem my third husband had."

"Spraying problem?" Pamela laughed. "I'm afraid to even ask."

"We practically had to hire someone full-time just for the bathroom! Eventually, they put him in the hospital and cauterized the bastard. Well, the whining and self-pity that spewed out of that man. I mean, granted, no one wants people probing around that close to their brain, but, do you want to be cured or are you content to carry an umbrella with you every time you have to take a leak? 'Try having a baby,' I said to him. Not that *I* ever would, mind you, but really!"

"How many children do you have, Penny," Tess asked.

"Two. A boy and a girl."

"They must be beautiful!" Rhonda said.

"How could they not be?" Pamela cut in, reaching over and patting Penny on the arm. "Have you ever seen Penny's husband?"

"You know, I have yet to marry a handsome man," Julia announced, pouting slightly.

"Well, that's not true," Pamela said. "What about your first husband?"

"George?" Julia seemed outraged.

"Your *first* husband."

"Oh, him." Julia waved her arm dismissively. "I don't really count him. He was my high school boyfriend and we were madly in love."

"My first husband was handsome," Rhonda said, "and, no reflection on Senator Davis, but when it comes to gorgeous men—if you win, often you lose."

I glanced at Penny: she was looking down at her hands.

"That's the truth!" Tess added. "We get old and they get rugged-looking. And now with the sexual revolution and all this casual humping..."

"I'm sure Penny doesn't worry about Vic that way, do you Penny?" Pamela asked.

Penny glanced up and took in all the women before she answered. "Vic is very committed to his marriage," she replied.

An uncomfortable silence followed. I cleared my throat.

"Well, where would he ever find someone more beautiful than you?" I don't know why I said that: I'm not an ingratiating person and I really didn't want Penny's attention. The hypocrisy of my sensitivity was staggering even to me.

"Thank you," Penny looked directly at me, but she didn't smile.

"Why, Gloria!" Pamela said, "What a charming thing to say! You certainly have chosen the right field. Gloria is active in politics, Penny, did you know that?"

"I guess if I had thought about it, I would have realized that," Penny said.

Now it was my turn to look at my hands.

"You have such beautiful gardens, Julia," Penny said, changing the subject. "Do you do it yourself?"

"Goodness, no," Julia replied, lighting up a cigarette she'd stuffed into a sparkly holder. "I have help. I just say 'make it pretty,' and he does the rest. Do you garden?"

"Well, I try, but now with Vic thinking about a statewide race, I fear it's going to go to seed in no time."

"Oh, you can't let that happen! You don't want the voters to believe the experience is frazzling."

"Well, but it is."

Did I imagine that Penny glanced at me when she said that?

"Tell you what I'll do," Julia said. "As a contribution to your husband's campaign, I will give you my gardener. For six months. Free of charge."

"Oh, I can't agree to that."

"Nonsense. You'll *love* Carlos. Believe me, the man is a credit to his race."

At the mention of Carlos, I glanced at Julia, but she didn't seem to notice.

"I thought he worked in your stable," I said.

"Carlos does whatever is needed," Julia replied. "And he does it all expertly. Come!" she said, leading us toward the back yard. "This is what he did last summer. It's my favorite thing."

We followed her to a pond, which was about eight feet wide and six feet long and surrounded by flagstone. Brightly colored fish swam just under the surface and blooming plants bobbed on top. After splashing down a small waterfall, the water was collected in a tank and recirculated to the pond

"It has not been without its problems, though," Julia said. "Right after we stocked it, I came out here one morning and all the fish were belly up. Carlos decided it was the water temperature, so we played with that, restocked, and two days later, another wipe out. Finally, I called this fish expert. And he says, 'Lady, I tank you've had an orgasm in the water.' I was impressed with his power of observation until I realized he meant organism. He gave us some chemicals and everything's been perfect since."

The gurgling of the waterfall spoke right to my bladder and once I built up my nerve, I excused myself to use the restroom. Inside, the maid directed me to a room off the den. The bathroom actually had artwork on the walls and, across from the sink, there was a locked cabinet displaying jewel-encrusted eggs that were so elaborate—almost tacky—that I couldn't keep my eyes off them. I spent quite a while in there examining them through the glass, and when I finally left, Penny was in the hallway, waiting for me.

"I've been wanting to have a word with you," she said. "Privately."

My mind raced to concoct a believable lie that would buy me survival time. A glance at the glass wall in the adjourning room revealed that the others were still touring the gardens.

"I believe that you've been seeing—" she glanced over her shoulder to assure herself no one else was nearby, and I knew I was seconds away from puking. "Ian Feldman," she all but whispered.

"Well, as I said, I've been to a couple of his speeches—" I stopped. It was like I'd had a small stroke. I heard the name she'd used, but it was as if she'd slipped into gibberish. "Who?" I asked.

"Ian Feldman. Aren't you seeing him?" She kept glancing around, as if she were as edgy as I was.

"Can we sit down?" I asked. She led me to the living room and while I collapsed, exhausted by the relief, in an overstuffed chair, Penny perched on an ottoman, her bony knees resting against each other.

"The reason I'm asking," she began at once, "is I'd like you to give him a message."

"Oh, sure." I'd do anything, I was so grateful she wasn't pumping me full of bullets.

"Would you tell him to ease up on Vic." She folded her hands in her lap and studied them. "He's been giving him a hard time lately," she continued. "I'd like it to stop."

I sat there with my mouth open for sever seconds before I managed to say, "I have no influence over his work. If I made such a request he'd just—."

"I don't want the request to be from you. Tell him it's what *I* want." She eyed me meaningfully for a second or two. "Can you do that?"

"Sure," I whispered, still slumped back in the chair, seemingly unable to move.

* * *

When Ian arrived, I was waiting in the driveway. I don't remember how I excused myself from the others or even what they were doing. I just remember standing there, watching the yellow VW approach.

"Looks like you survived," he said as he opened my door.

"I guess." I climbed in and fastened my seat belt, but Ian lingered there next to me.

"What's wrong?" he asked.

"What makes you think something is wrong?"

"You seem—I don't know—strange. Pensive."

"Pensive?"

"Thoughtful. Like you have something on your mind."

I shrugged and after a second he shut the door and got in on his side.

"What do you say we grab an early dinner and catch a movie?" he said as he started the car.

I shrugged. "Whatever," I said.

"You hit it off with Julia's friend?"

"Yeah. I guess." I could tell he was watching me, but I kept looking straight ahead.

We stopped for a red light by a Chevrolet dealership that was having a promotional sale. Clowns with helium balloons waved to passing motorists. Ian reached over and stroked my hair.

"Hey," he said, "Wanna tell me what's bothering you?"

"Ian?"

The clown beckoned us to come inside.

"What?"

"The older woman you were in love with—. Was her name Penny Davis?"

Our eyes locked. A car honked impatiently and Ian shifted into first as he glanced up to confirm that the light was green. It wasn't until he pulled the gears into fourth that he said, "Yes."

I didn't take my eyes off him for four blocks, but he resisted any urge to look my way.

"Why didn't you tell me?"

"I don't know," he said, checking the mirror before changing lanes. "I guess to protect her."

We passed a billboard for Lone Star Beer that had a real waterfall cascading down its length. Occasionally, kids threw things into the mechanism, such as laundry detergent or dye.

"Her? Or you?" I whispered as I watched the pink water splash at the bottom of the sign.

"What's that mean?" His voice was defensive.

"Sort of answers a lot of questions, doesn't it?"

"Such as?"

"Everything was to get back at him for keeping her."

"That's not true."

"You admitted that you looked me up because of him. You took me to that party in Austin so he'd see us together. Or, was it to distract him? So that you could be with Penny."

"Your overactive imagination's getting the best of you."

"Is it? There was a time at that party when I was looking all over for you and trying to avoid her and neither of you was anywhere around. Were you with Penny that night, Ian?"

"I spoke to her, but that's all."

"Privately?"

"Yes."

"I see."

"She's a friend, Gloria."

"So I'm the only party in this who had no idea?"

"Do you feel you're so much better off now that you know?" he snapped.

"No, I certainly don't feel better off, that's for sure. What else are you keeping from me, Ian?"

"What the hell is *that* supposed to mean?"

"Well, there was the time Samara came to visit—"

"I knew you were going to throw that up to me!"

"How many more surprises do I have to look forward to?"

"You know, I've taken some shit off you, too."

"I guess it's good we're facing all these problems. Before we do something stupid."

When we reached Carlisle, I told Ian I wanted him to drop me off at my apartment. Without saying a word, he drove to the Saracen but once he parked, he followed me inside. He stood by the door for a moment and then collapsed onto the sofa.

"How'd you figure this out anyway?" he asked.

"She was at Julia's." His eyes widened. "She gave me a message for you." He didn't say anything. "She wants you to ease up on Vic."

I walked to my room and changed into some shorts and a tank top. When I returned, Ian was where I'd left him. We stared at each other for a minute and then I turned away and pretended to read something on my desk. A second later, he was beside me.

"Gloria, this isn't such a big deal. When I first started seeing you it was because of him, but that hasn't been the case in a long time. Would I ask someone to move in with me just to piss off that jerk?"

"How can I believe you now?"

"You *know* you can believe me."

"Vic was more honest with me than you were."

"I can't believe you'd say that."

"I know you don't want to hear anything positive about him, but he was always kind to me. And he made it clear he didn't want to hurt Penny. He even admitted he loved her."

"That's was just to keep you at a distance."

"You don't know shit, Ian."

"If he loved her, what was he doing balling you?"

"He wasn't *balling* me."

"Yeah? What would you call it?"

"We made love."

"Dream on, Gloria." I slapped him and, as if I was the one who had just been hit, my eyes watered. “You still care about him, don’t you?” he said, rubbing his cheek.

“We’re friends,” I said, imitating him.

“Bull*shit*!” He shouted. “You may be many things to him but friend is not one of them.”

“And what sort of things do you think I am to him?”

“You’re a notch somewhere and you, and all the others, are his assurance that he’s irresistible. And while you’re daydreaming about him, he’s not giving you a second thought.”

“Have it your way. I don’t give a shit what you think.”

“He’s married, he has kids. He lives with a woman who hates him. His career is everything. He craves adoration. He wants power. And he doesn’t care who he hurts to get it. He has a million you’s in his life. Penny’s a hell of a nice lady. Look how her life’s turned out.”

“She could leave him. She could leave him and have you in a second, I bet.”

“That’s not true. Not now. You have to know that.”

“I don’t know anything about you, Ian. I’m not sure I even want to.”

He stood and walked to the door. “I’ll call you when I get back from New York.”

“Don’t bother.”

* * *

Chicago police wasted no time arresting Richard Speck, a loner (aren’t they all?). People who knew him said they couldn’t imagine him hurting a fly. Funny. Wasn’t that what Norman Bates said about himself at the end of *Psycho*? Give me a fly killer any day. The startling news, however, was that Richard Speck was from Dallas. He could have been someone I’d bought groceries from or hitched a ride with.

* * *

The Turtle Creek Village Condos were four blocks from my apartment. The lobby had a security system that required visitors to call the appropriate apartment for admittance. Before I could dial his suite, an elderly man inside triggered the mechanism for me, so I didn’t alert Vic that I was on my way.

When he opened the door, his inquisitive expression turned briefly to surprise before he smiled.

"Gloria! I wasn't sure you'd come."

He was even more handsome than I remembered and my heart started pounding as I looked at him. He wore a dark blue suit and a white shirt, but he had taken his tie off. He looked very lawyerly. Ian once told me that when Vic went to trial, he tried to stack the jury with women because he knew they'd always support his client.

He led me past the tiny galley kitchen to the elegant living room, which was dominated by a brown leather, tufted sofa and a chrome and glass coffee table.

"What do you think of the place?" he asked as he strolled over to the sliding glass door. He pushed it open and a gust of hot air whirled through the chilly room. We stepped out onto the terrace and admired the view of Lee Park below.

"It's lovely," I said. The sun was making a direct hit and within second we both had sweat necklaces, so we slipped back into the apartment. The place really was incredible: everything was color coordinated and tasteful: even the pictures on the walls had the same hues as the furniture. What was most noticeable, however, was the complete lack of clutter. Not only was it spotless, but not a single item sat on a counter top that would give any hint about the person who lived there. Even the closets, I noticed later, were virtually empty.

"Who lives here?" I asked.

"A friend."

"Oh."

"A *guy*. A lawyer in town. He doesn't exactly live here. Just uses it for business." Vic indicated the sofa. "Here. Have a seat. You want something to drink?" he asked, slipping into the kitchen.

"No, that's okay."

"I have iced tea, soda. Let's see..." He opened a cabinet. "Scotch, bourbon, gin, rum…just about anything."

"I'm fine. Thank you."

"I need a drink." He returned to the sofa with a squat glass and a bottle of Southern Comfort. He poured some into the glass, drank it and then he poured some more before screwing the cap on the bottle.

"Well," he said, as he leaned over and kissed me. "How've you been?"

"Fine. And you?"

"Busy." He kissed me again and started unbuttoning my dress.

"What does he think you're doing here?" I asked.

"Who?" he frowned, confused.

"The guy who owns the place. What does he think you're doing here?"

Vic laughed robustly and then resumed fiddling with my buttons. "Oh, I don't think he spends much time worrying about that."

"Does he know about me?"

He stopped what he was doing and looked at me. "No. Of course not."

"I mean...what was your excuse for, you know, borrowing the place?"

"We're writing an article together. For a legal publication. I've set aside Tuesdays to work on it. I have political business in Dallas, too, so I just spend the day here. He gave me his key so I'd have a quiet place to work." He watched me a bit. "Feel better?"

"Oh, I wasn't—I didn't—I was just curious, that's all."

"We could meet here again next Tuesday. If you wanted. He slipped his hands around my back and unfastened my bra. "Would you like that?" he whispered.

I fumbled with his buttons until I could peel away his shirt. "Yes," I said.

He pulled me against him and I felt wildly excited as I heard his heart thudding. While I kissed him—his lips, his cheeks, his eyes—he struggled awkwardly with his slacks until he had them down to his knees. Then he pulled the skirt of my dress up to my waist, slipped my panties to one side and slide into me. I felt a wave of heat flow through my body as if an electric blanket covered me.

"God, I want you," I groaned.

"Well, you have me," he replied, not understanding.

When I reached an orgasm, I cried and after that I was as limp and clingy as a piece of cooked spaghetti. After a moment or two, Vic sat up and started untying his shoes.

"You know," he said, "I've only made love twice with my shoes on. And both times it's been with you." Once his shoes and socks were off, he leaned over me and kissed me while he pulled my dress all the way off. "There's a perfectly good bed in the next room," he said.

The bedroom was almost as large as the living room and as I entered it, the white fuzzy rug lapped up and tickled my ankles. There was a four-poster king-sized bed covered in an emerald green, velvet spread. Vic whipped the comforter and the top sheet down to the foot of the bed. The sheets were green satin and cold against my skin, but Vic was there instantly, warming everything up.

At some point, I must have fallen asleep because suddenly he was sitting beside me. He had his slacks on and was holding his shirt. His hair was wet. The slant of the fading sun suggested it was getting late.

"I'm going to have to go soon," he said.

A hollow loneliness caused a metallic taste at the base of my tongue. I started to slip off the bed, but when I pulled back the cover, I spotted whitish smears on the satiny fabric and felt ashamed. I lay down stiffly on my back and pulled the top sheet up to my neck.

"What was he like?" I asked, focusing on a cobweb glinting from the corner of the ceiling.

"Who?"

"The guy Penny got involved with," I whispered.

"He was a prick."

"He must have had some good qualities." The web was empty: no captives mummified, no spider tending to business.

"You'd have to ask Penny about that." Annoyed, he stood, tucking his shirt into his pants.

"Did you know him? I rose up on one elbow and watched him as he hooked his pants, causing them to tighten briefly over his lower back.

"Why are we talking about this?"

"I just wondered what you thought of him."

"Not much." He walked toward the window and looked out at the view.

"I mean, if he hadn't gotten involved with Penny, what would you have thought of him?"

"I wouldn't have thought of him at all."

"So, it was just that you were jealous."

"What did I have to be jealous of? I won, didn't I?"

"But was it worth it?"

"It's always worth it to win."

"Even if you don't want the prize?"

"Winning is the prize."

Vic walked me to the lobby, saying he wanted to pick up a newspaper before he left. As we passed the newsstand, he glanced over my shoulder and his attention shifted so completely that I assumed he was witnessing a crime. I spun around.

She had platinum hair that hung so perfectly to her shoulder blades that I was sure it was a fall. Her hot pink and orange pantsuit consisted of hip huggers and a dangerously tight halter-top. Her face was not that attractive. She had tiny eyes smeared with dark eyeliner and her complexion bragged of past acne. But, somehow, I doubted men held that against her. I turned back to Vic who was as frozen as if he'd spotted Medusa.

"Well. Bye," I said, smiling, as if ignorant.

He glanced down at me and smiled. "Yeah. It was just great seeing you again."

"Yeah," I said.

He patted me on the arm and started, energized it seemed, for the newsstand. I walked toward the door, not daring to look back.

* * *

When I got home, I sat cross-legged on the sofa and stared out the window, watching the sky ease from twilight to night. Every time a car passed, bouncy lights played around on the wall. I can't remember ever feeling lonelier. I missed Veronica more than I could have imagined. And I appreciated Ian in a way I hadn't before. Whenever I thought of Vic, I couldn't help but see the expression on his face when he spotted the platinum blond in the newsstand. Vic, I guessed, would just always be Vic. It was stupid of me to assume he'd treat me any better than the woman he'd loved enough to marry.

It took me forever to fall asleep. When the phone rang at two, I though it was a fire alarm and jumped out of bed, staggering around looking for my robe. Once my brain kicked in, I lunged for the phone, knocking the receiver to the floor.

"Yes?" I said, into the earpiece. My nerves twittered from the pandemonium.

"Gloria?" Jo Beth sounded distant. I righted the receiver. "It's Veronica. She's in the hospital."

* * *

It took me an hour to get to St. Catherine's because not many cabs operated so early in the morning. Jo Beth met me at the entrance. Veronica was still in recovery.

"I called you just as soon as I got her squared away," she said.

"Thanks. I appreciate that."

"It was terrible, girl. I was sound asleep and Veronica started screaming in the next room. I swear ta God, I thought Richard Speck was in there *killin'* her."

"What'd you do?"

" I called the cops and got me a knife. It took all my courage ta walk inta that room."

"I bet!"

"And then, God! All that blood! And Veronica was hysterical! It must have taken five minutes for me ta figure it out what happened. Then the cops came. They called an ambulance."

"What are they doing for her?"

"A DNC. Ta make sure ever'thing came out."

A nurse with a shower cap on her head and booties on her feet materialized. "Are you Miss Lloyd's friends?" When we nodded, she went on. "Miss Lloyd is just fine. She's sleeping. If you want, you can come back during visiting hours—at nine-thirty."

"Could we just...look at her?" I asked.

The nurse hesitated, then relaxed and sighed. "Just for a minute," she said.

Veronica's room was a double but the other bed was empty. We crept in and stood at her feet. An IV bottle dangled from a pole next to her and a tube coiled its way to her hand where a mound of tape concealed the needle stuck in her vein. Her complexion was ashen, the skin under her eyes was gray and her blistered lips were almost blue. Her matted hair hung listlessly around her face. Even so, she was still beautiful.

* * *

"Too bad we don't know how ta reach Hunter. Maybe if he knew he'd get in touch with her. Cheer her up a little." We had slipped into the hospital cafeteria to order breakfast.

"He wouldn't care," I said.

"I know," Jo Beth sighed.

In the hospital shop we looked for gifts. Jo Beth chose a huge bouquet of yellow roses, but I wanted something more permanent. I settled on a music box. When wound, two wooden animals—a dog and a cat—held hands and danced to the song *Together*.

"Gloria?" Jo Beth said as we hung out in the waiting room. "When Veronica started screaming?"

"Yes?"

"And I thought she was bein' murdered?"

"Yes?"

"I considered slippin' out the window. Goin' ta get help, I told myself, but really, just wantin' to get away." She was crying. "Guess that makes me a horrible person."

"I think it just means you're human, Jo Beth."

I knew I should call my office and tell them I'd be late, but I just couldn't face a showdown with Lonnie. When visiting hours finally arrived we agreed that Jo Beth should go in first and then, if Veronica felt Okay about it, I would see her. I expected the worst, but when Jo Beth came out, she said Veronica would see me.

She was staring out the window when I came in and didn't look my way even after I said hi. I put the gift on her tray and stood at the foot of her bed.

"Are you okay?" I asked.

"Not really," she said.

"No. I guess not. It was a stupid question." In daylight the room was stark and depressing. "I'm sorry about the baby."

"Are you?"

"Yes. I'm sorry about everything."

Glancing toward the door, I saw two nurses wheeling a gurney down the corridor. It held a tiny old lady whose mouth gaped open and who had tubes running from every part of her body. The nurses stopped, exchanged instructions and then pushed the gurney into the room across the hall. "One, two, three," one of the nurses said, and at that point they lifted the woman off the gurney and slid her onto the bed. I turned back toward Veronica when she cleared her throat.

"I wanted you ta know that I won't turn you in ta the authorities," she said. A warm sense of relief spread through my arms and legs. "What you did was wrong—criminal even—and you deserve ta be punished. Even more'n Hunter, and me, and the baby. But, unlike you, I can't find it in myself ta send anyone ta jail. But, Gloria," she continued. "I don't ever want ta see or speak ta you again. I hope you will respect that." Before I could respond, she went on. "I'm tired now, Gloria. I'd like ta go back to sleep."

"Sure," I said, lingering by the door. "Well, bye."

When she didn't answer, I slipped out.

* * *

I got to Freedom Mutual around ten-fifteen and Lonnie Mossman summoned me to her office before I could even turn on my typewriter.

"You're late," she said as if I might not have realized that.

"Yes ma'am. I had to take a friend to the hospital—"

"Why do I have trouble believing that?"

I was too weary to argue with her so I just sat there looking at the green marbleized pencil cup on her desk.

"It's obvious, Gloria, that you haven't had much sleep. You look like the devil. What'd you do? Party all night and then oversleep?"

The pencil cup had thick black veins running through it. I'd never noticed that before.

"You're going to have to learn some responsibility if you want to make it in this world, Gloria. You're going to have to think about something other than yourself for a change. As of this moment, you're on probation. One more slip up and you're out of here. Understand?"

"Yes Ma'am."

"Do you have anything to say for yourself?"

"No. I think you just about said it all."

* * *

That evening I called Jo Beth to see how Veronica was doing but there was no answer. She was probably at the hospital. I played Solitaire for three hours. Ian had not called the entire week.

Each day seemed endless. Lonnie continued to think of projects for me: I expected her to hand me a toothbrush and some Comet and send me to the bathrooms. Each evening I watch the news and learned of yet another race riot. Since the Fourth of July, there had been six eruptions across the country. I thought back to the black woman on the bus: if I had been in her position, I'd have probably felt like torching something. If she had been my mother, I'd have burned down a city.

The day after Veronica's miscarriage, Jeanette (Mr. Sweet's secretary) swelled up and doctors ordered her to stay off her feet for the remainder of her pregnancy. While I had nothing against Jeanette—didn't even know her, in fact—the news delighted me: now, maybe I'd get that promotion and, like high school, Lonnie could become merely a bad memory.

Rumors flew through the office that there would be an in-house promotion before the end of the week and that interested workers should submit applications with the Personnel Office ASAP. Since I knew I was Mr. Sweet's choice, I wasted no time getting mine in.

During the week, I found myself meandering past Mr. Sweet's office several times a day. Often he was interviewing women from the steno or typing pools. I always waved and he would nod back, but he never rushed out to talk to me or stopped by my desk. On Friday I panicked. I felt betrayed that he had ignored my application. Even if he'd found someone more qualified, we were friends and he owed me an interview at least.

On my way back from the soda machine during my afternoon break, I noticed a woman from the Claims Department sitting at Jeanette's desk, arranging the drawers to suit her. I watched her for a while and then glanced toward Mr. Sweet's office. When our eyes met, he quickly looked down at his papers. I was halfway to my desk when I decided to confront him.

"Gloria!" he said, all smiles, like it was a social visit. "Come in. Have a seat."

"I was just curious," I said, "about why you didn't even call me in for an interview."

"Sit down," he said more seriously. "You know you're one of my favorite people around her. But, this is a demanding job, and I require someone more…well, professional."

"When have I not done my job?" I asked, sipping my Coke.

"It's not that you don't do your job, it's that you seem to have other priorities."

"That's because I have a lot of time on my hands—because I'm fast and efficient."

"I have no doubt that you're under-utilized where you are and I think Lonnie should probably transfer you to the typing pool where you'd be more challenged."

"Typing pool? You think the typing pool would *challenge* me? I can type ninety-eight words a minute. The requirement for the typing pool is forty-five."

"Ninety-eight words a minute? That's a lot. That's—"

"Faster than you can talk, Mr. Sweet. And if you'd bothered to look at my application, you'd have known that. I've been publishing a newsletter for two years—I can write better than most of the executives here. And, just in case it was ever necessary, I can take shorthand."

"I've always known you were an exceptional young woman. Tell you what. I'll put in a word for you in Personnel. Next thing that comes along—"

"You could have at least considered me. I thought we were friends." The backs of my eyes burned.

"We *are* friends!" he called out to me as I headed for the door. "It's just—"

"Go to hell," I said, as tears welled up in my eyes.

I sprinted back to my desk. I didn't care if they fired me. In fact, I wished they would. It was only three o'clock, but when I reached my desk, I flicked off my typewriter, picked up my handbag and left without saying a word to anyone.

* * *

Once I got off the bus, I ran the entire way home. I was so out of breath—so *outraged*—by the time I reached the apartment, that at first, I didn't notice anything. Then I realized something was terribly wrong. Initially, I believed I had somehow entered someone else's place and was trying to figure out how my key had worked; was even wondering if we all had the same key, only we didn't know it; was nervous that at any moment the real tenants would rush out from the bedroom and shoot me for trespassing.

But no. There was my desk, my sofa, my stereo. There was the only mirror that belonged to me. There were all the LBJ buttons resurrected and scattered around. But that was all that was there. Veronica had moved. The chairs, the television, the coffee table, the posters, the plants, the appliances and the phone were gone. Her room was empty, except that the lei was lying on the floor. I felt as barren and as vacant as a boarded up building. I'd managed to lose everything that mattered: Veronica, the YDs, Ian, even that stupid job.

The weekend was endless. There was nothing to do; no one to talk to. I tried to read, but kept reading the same paragraph over and over. I sorted through my forty-fives and played depressing songs to cheer me up. I found "Gloria." G-L-O-R-I-A and broke it. I managed to first batter it with a shoe and then crack it in half by bending it against my bookcase until it snapped. Then I lost interest in my records.

Saturday, it seemed unhealthy to stay inside all day. Ian was due back Sunday—thought I had no idea when—and things might improve then. I just had to get through Saturday. I took a bus to Preston Center. The mall was bustling. As soon as I got there, I knew I didn't have the energy to spend money, but I forced myself to look around. I walked in each store, went up and down the aisles, and then left. Then I caught the bus back home.

* * *

"Hi, honey," Jo Beth said, dropping by that evening. "I wanted ta make sure you were okay."

"Veronica moved out."

"I know. Rusty'n me helped her. Hope ya don't, you know, mind."

"How is she?"

"Physically, she's fine. Just fine."

"Is she depressed?"

"They say it's hormones, but what do those guys know. She's depressed 'cause she lost the last thing she had of Hunter. It'll take a while. Hey," she said, slapping my arm, "I thought maybe you'd let me take you out ta dinner tonight. You know, ta sorta pay you back for being so sweet about Junior'n all."

"Oh, thanks, Jo Beth, but…I already ate," I lied.

"Well, then a movie! How about a movie?"

"I'm kind of tired and, you know, Ian'll be back tomorrow. I'll just go to bed early."

"You sure?"

"Yeah."

* * *

Sunday we had thundershowers on and off all day. After I read the papers, I walked to Ian's but his car was not in the lot. At six, it cleared up and I stepped outside to get a better look at the faint rainbow that faded in and out in the sky. It was so hot and muggy that wavy steam rose from the cement. It seemed Ian should be home and I worried that he wasn't going to come by, so I walked to his place again. His car was still gone.

That evening I threw a pillow on the living room floor and lay there listening to the radio. I was afraid I wouldn't hear him from my room should he knock later that night. At three, I woke up, turned off the radio, and moved to the bedroom.

A lawnmower outside my window woke me at nine-thirty: I had forgotten to set my alarm. At first I thought perhaps my clock was wrong, so I called the operator.

"Can you tell me the time?" I asked.

"Nine-thirty-three," she replied.

I slammed the phone down. A shot of adrenaline surged through my body. I kicked back the sheets and raced to my closet, but by the time I got there, inertia took over. Stumbling to the kitchen, I made coffee. There was no way I could face my office. If I'd had a phone I would have called in sick, but I didn't, so what could I do? At noon, I walked to Ian's—it was stupid; he'd be at work. I peeked in his windows to see if I could tell whether he was back or not, but I couldn't.

It was three-forty-five, when he finally stopped by.

"Your phone's been disconnected," he said, as if accusing me of something.

"When did you get in?" He seemed taller than before.

"Last night. What happened to your phone?"

"It was Veronica's. She moved. Why didn't you stop by?"

"It was after midnight. All your lights were out. You office told me you didn't work there anymore."

I don't know why that surprised me, but it did. "I guess not," I said.

After a moment, he reached for my hand and laced his fingers through mine.

"I missed you," he said.

"Ian," I said, "I've done a lot of thinking while you've been gone and I've decided that if you still want me to, I'll move to New York with you."

"Hey! That's great." He threw his arms around my waist and swung me in a circle. "I believe—" He put his hand on his chest. "I really believe you'll love New York. If you just give it a chance."

"I'm sure I will."

"You seem depressed."

"It's been a hard week."

"It's always hard to make changes."

"Know what bothers me most?" Ian shook his head. "Most of my life, I've felt like I didn't belonged here. In school, I was always on the outside: no great student or athlete or beauty. Too sarcastic to be popular. It wasn't until I got into politics that I felt people liked me. Even the Republicans, when I was hanging out with them, went out of their way to do nice things for me. I seemed to have a knack for all the ends and outs and I loved it. And even though I was still like a freak or something, I felt successful. Important. When I walked around downtown, people knew me. They'd call out: 'Hey, Gloria, how you doing.' Sometimes important people: judges, politicians, even business people. Occasionally folks I didn't even know would stop me and say, 'I saw you on television last night, didn't I?' I don't believe that will happen in New York."

"I can't argue with that."

"I think the reason things went so well for me was that people were fascinated that I was a kid. They'd include me in things—meetings, strategy sessions. When I was eighteen, I got seated next to Ramsey Clark at a fundraiser dinner. At twenty, I'll be just like everyone else."

We went to a Chinese restaurant where Ian babbled about New York as if he was the Chamber of Commerce. There was a play on Broadway—*Cabaret*—that he wanted to see, and an exhibit at the Metropolitan Museum that couldn't be missed. Yes, New Yorkers could be obnoxious, he said, but once you understood them, like Texans, they were endearing.

"Here's a story for you," he said. "Last Wednesday it rained like crazy—had been raining all night. I got up early 'cause I needed to visit this guy in Long Island. To get to Long Island you have to take this toll road. So, I get to the road, pay my toll and then drive maybe ten feet and there's a barricade set up. I roll down the window, 'What's up?' I ask the cop. 'Road's closed,' he says. 'Flooded out.' So I have to make a U-turn and leave."

"Did you get your money back?" I asked.

"Gloria, this is New York. I had to pay the toll again to get out! Know what's worse? The same guy took my money. Just walked to the other side of his booth and without batting an eye held out his hand for the toll."

"That's outrageous," I said, but I couldn't stop laughing.

"No. It's just New York."

I stayed at Ian's that night. He'd put a deposit on a place in New York and had taken pictures of it for me. It was a narrow red-brick townhouse with black shutters and a black wrought-iron fence enclosing the handkerchief-sized yard. There were four floors but each had only two or three rooms. The bedroom was on the top floor and over that was a roof top where we could picnic or sunbathe or just hang out—like in *West Side Story*. There were large windows, chandeliers, fireplaces and beautiful woodwork.

It was good to be back with him: there was coziness to our relationship that I'd never had with anyone else. I could do a lot worse than move with him to New York. For all I knew, the City could turn out to be a marvelous adventure. I'd never break into politics there and I wasn't sure that even if I could, I'd want to. I understood Texas politics—the rules, the craziness, the players, the limits. It was my heritage. I was sure there'd be a whole different set of parameters in the East. And I suspected it would be a little boring by comparison.

Curled around Ian, listening to his slow, even breathing, I knew I didn't want to see Vic again. Clearly, I didn't have the concrete skin necessary for a relationship with him. Vic did like me: I believed that. But once, at least, he must have *loved* Penny. I had a lot of respect for her: at what point did she say, this has nothing to do with me, so I'll ignore it? How did you ignore it, though? I thought back to that drive from Austin to Dallas. She was right there when Vic climbed into the back seat with me. She must have known. Known that he hadn't sat back there because it was the choice seat. Known, as he did, that I'd already been snagged.

* * *

On those evenings when Ian had to work late, I packed boxes—mostly YD stuff. My parents said they'd store them in their garage until I wanted them back. There was a scrapbook I had put together after the Assassination, which contained every newspaper and magazine article I had come across. I flipped through it quickly before I closed it up and put it in a box. On top of the scrapbook, I threw all my old newsletters and YD files. As I was sorting through folders, I uncovered the Floresville articles. I scanned them briefly, debating whether to toss them or store them. Finally, I reached in the envelope drawer and withdrew Vic's picture and the letter he sent to me about the apartment and put them in the file. Then I put the file in the box and taped it down.

I still thought about Vic, though I had stopped looking at his picture. Around dusk every evening, I wondered if he realized it was over. Had he ever tried to contact me again? I felt guilty that I hadn't been honest with him. While I didn't flatter myself by thinking this would devastate him, I didn't feel good leaving things hanging either.

Kelly Girls worked out pretty well. Because of my skills, I got plenty of calls. I went to a different office each day and, since I was a stranger, everyone was helpful. The pay wasn't bad either. I actually made more than I had at Freedom Mutual

On Monday, my temporary position sent me two blocks from Freedom Mutual's offices. During my lunch hour I walked to El Chico's and ran smack into Lonnie Mossman.

"Gloria!" she said, astonished. "How are you?"

"I'm fine," I answered, hoping the hostess would seat one of us soon so I could avoid a lecture.

"Are you alone?" she asked, glancing behind me.

"Uh. Yes, ma'am," I replied.

"Would you care to join me?"

"Oh, well—" I started, but she interrupted me.

"I'd *like* for you to join me." She smiled.

"Sure. I'd, you know, love to."

My booth had a cigarette burn on the seat, which caused the brown leatherette to pucker outward, making it seem as if someone had shot a bullet through it. I made a mental note to avoid sliding across the seat so that my nylons wouldn't become a secondary victim. Though Lonnie looked jovial as she studied her menu, I knew it was only a matter of seconds before she'd start her lecture. Feeling a little like a kid sent to the principal's office, I decided to take the initiative and get things over.

"I'm sorry," I said, "about how I behaved. I know I should have called. I didn't mean to—. Didn't mean to quit, actually. It's just...I had some problems, you know, and I kind of fell apart or something. I'm sorry."

"Actually, I wanted to apologize to *you*, Gloria." Her bronze nail polish glittered in the light as she folder her menu and placed it on the table. "For riding you the way I did. I don't blame you for—. In fact, when you didn't show up and didn't call, I tried to contact you, but your phone was disconnected. I even stopped by your place. Twice. Is everything Okay now?"

"Yeah, I guess."

"Where are you working?"

"Uh. For Kelly Girls."

"I'd hire you back. I mean Freedom Mutual would if I recommended it—in a much better position. There's something in Personnel. If you're interested."

"Well, I'm leaving Dallas. Texas. Soon. That's why I didn't get a real job."

"I see." She reached for a soft tortilla, slathered it with butter and rolled it up in a tube. "I had some...difficulty myself not long ago. I have a child—"

"Really?" I said far too quickly and Lonnie Mossman smiled as she bit into the tortilla.

"I suspect you knew that, somehow."

I didn't say anything.

"I suspect we owe you a great deal."

Stunned, I glanced up.

"I put everything together after you'd gone and I worried, when you didn't show up at work, that I'd never get to thank you."

"Put everything together?"

"My lawyer got an anonymous letter. At first, I was so delighted with the break that I didn't question my good luck. But later, I asked to see it. The stationery had Freedom Mutual's watermark on it. I knew right away who sent it." We regarded each other. "I can't imagine how you got that information—how you even knew about my case—"

I looked out the window.

"And I suspect I'd rather not know. But thank you."

"You don't have to thank me."

"But I want to. And I want to say something. You always drove me crazy. I believe you know that. Everyone under me played by the rules, but you never did and that irritated me. You were my sharpest employee and I had big plans for you, but I felt you had to be broken first. I didn't mean to be malicious. I thought I was helping you. Does that make sense?"

"Sure."

"Anyway," she opened her purse and pulled out a checkbook, "I want to give you something. We'll call it a severance package." She wrote out a check for three hundred dollars.

"Oh, I can't take this," I said pushing it back to her. She stopped my hand.

"It would mean a lot to me if you would." Something in her expression seemed almost pleading, so I put the check in my bag.

* * *

"Goodness! She looks great doesn't she? It's so excitin' seein' someone ya know on TV, don't ya think?"

Jo Beth had invited me over to watch Veronica's premiere on television. I had declined a job assignment that day and Jo Beth simply called in sick. She was spiffed-up in a green floral mini-dress.

"Ronnie's like in the movies. Nobody one day and the next, she's famous. And that apartment of hers! Can you believe it? Oh, you haven't gone over there yet. You should see it, Gloria. Why, you can see all of Dallas from her bedroom! They don't just have a club there: they got a beauty salon, a restaurant and even some shops! Right there in the lobby. I always get real dressy whenever I go over." She showed off her dress to me. "We're havin' lunch there. You know this dress cost me three days' salary?"

"It's nice. Colorful."

"That's why I bought it. Colorful. She looks okay, don't ya think?"

Veronica looked fabulous. Her leotard was one piece and looked as if someone had simply painted a series of random, psychedelic curlicues across her body.

"Yeah. She looks great. Is she still depressed?"

"A little. That Hunter! Not even so much as a letter! You were sure right about him, girl." We watched silently for an interval, before Jo Beth said, "Hey, guess what? I'm takin' Dusty to a dude ranch this weekend.

"That's great!"

"I thought you'd think so. She's a neat kid."

"I know."

"I sorta thought she was the reason things didn't work out for me'n Junior. But now, I believe he's the reason it didn't work out for me'n her. Oh!" She clapped her hands and rolled her eyes. "You won't *believe* what happened! Remember that drawin' I sent off last month?"

"That 'Draw Me' thing you found in the match book?"

"Yeah! Well, I heard from 'um. And guess what! They liked it and have accepted me for their correspondence program. They're even givin' me a partial scholarship."

"How much will it cost you?"

"About $600 when you include books and supplies, but accordin' to their literature, it'd be well worth it."

"I don't think artists make much money…"

"Most of 'um don't, but for $8 extra, they include a book on marketin' your work, and a list of galleries and businesses who are lookin' for new talent. Think I should give it a try?"

"I don't know, Jo Beth…"

"Oh, here comes my favorite part. Can you believe she's that limber? I tell ya, that right there's the main difference between me and Ronnie. Yessir. She's something else."

Veronica, sitting on the floor with her legs straight out in front of her, stretched down, gripping her ankles with her hands, and simply rested there as if this were not only natural, but also comfortable.

"We've been together since we were kids," I said, feeling suddenly lonely.

"That's funny! That's exactly what I said ta Junior when he walked out. Ya know what he said? He said, 'The petals gotta fall off the roses sometime.' Are you cryin'?"

"I'll be okay."

"Just cuz she's moved doesn't mean you can't still see her. I mean it's not like she's left Dallas or somethin'. Give her time. She misses you. Ya know that music box you gave her? She has it sittin' right in her livin' room."

"She does?"

"Yeah!"

"It'll never be the same."

"But it could be somethin'. Oh!" Jo Beth applauded as the show ended. "She was wonderful, wasn't she? Things are really beginnin' ta happen for Ronnie. Ya know what? I think I'm gonna do it! That art school thing. Hell, it's only money. And even if it doesn't work out, it'll give me somethin' ta look forward to. I always dreamed of bein' an artist. If ya don't try, ya never know, do ya?"

"I guess not."

"That's the real tragedy—never knowin'."

"Yeah."

"You ever had a dream, Gloria?"

"A dream?" Vic flashed into my mind. "No. Not really," I said. Then I added, "I used to think I wanted to move to D.C. Become a force in politics. But I've outgrown that."

"Well, honey. I guess I'll spray my hair one last time before I go meet Ronnie. Do ya want me ta say anything to her for ya?"

"No. There's nothing to say."

When Jo Beth left, I walked back to my apartment. It was so hot outside that the cement radiated through my shoes causing my feet to sweat and swell.

I was in the middle of packing when at three-fifteen someone rang my doorbell. I assumed it was Jo Beth reporting on her luncheon with Veronica, so when I opened the door, and saw Vic standing there my heart flopped around like a fish on the floor of a boat. He glanced at me and then at the liquor boxes strewn around the apartment.

"You moving?" he asked, scratching his chin with his thumb.

"Vic!" I said, self-conscious that I was wearing ratty sweat pants and a tee shirt. He, of course, looked like an ad for Brook's Brothers.

"What's going on?" He stepped into the apartment and closed the door behind him. His expression combined confusion, disappointment and outrage.

"My roommate moved, so I, ah, have to find another place to live. I can't afford to stay here."

He stayed by the door and seemed as uncomfortable as I felt. "I called your office. They said—"

"Yeah. I kinda quit."

"So what are you doing? For work?"

"Kelly Girls. For a while."

"You need any money?"

"No! No, I'm, you know, fine."

"You find a new roommate?"

I tried to look innocent when I said, "Yeah, sort of."

"Well, give me the number there so I can get in touch with you." He reached in his breast pocket and pulled out a pen.

"Actually, Vic, I'm...ah...leaving Texas."

His eyes widened "When?"

"Soon."

"Where will you go?" He snapped his ballpoint shut and hooked it back on his shirt.

I shrugged. "Does it matter?"

"I guess not. Away is away." He walked to the sofa and sat down. "So, you're just running off?"

"Well, there's not much left for me here."

He studied me for a long while and then nodded and looked away. "I see."

I managed to bite an entire thumbnail down to the quick before he glanced back.

"Tell me: if I hadn't stopped by here today, would I have ever found out about this?"

"I would have called you. Before I left. To explain."

"Let me just get all this straight. You lost the YD election; you quit your job; and then your roommate moved out. So now, because there's *nothing left for you here*, you're going to just pack up everything and hit the road. Is that right?"

"Sort of."

"Aside from the fact that I find that *terribly* flattering, I am perplexed at what you hope to accomplish. Believe me, there've been a million times I've wanted to run away. But that's not how you overcome disappointments. You just eyeball the bastards and say, 'You're not getting the best of me.' You have to be willing to fight for what you want. I thought you were tougher than that."

"Probably, I should level with you," I said, blinking wildly and glancing around the room as if I were addressing a crowd. "I'm going *with* someone."

He raised his eyebrows.

"A...a guy." I concentrated on picking at my thumbnail until I was able to make it bleed.

"Your little reporter friend?" he said after he cleared his throat.

"Yes. Except...except he's not so little." I glanced up at him quickly, looked away and then glanced back.

It took him a moment to register what I'd just said, but once he did, he gawked at me as if I had just offered him the head of a puppy for lunch.

"Feldman?" He said, amazed. "You've been seeing that prick, Feldman?"

I nodded.

"For how long?"

"For as long as I've been seeing you."

He leaned back on the sofa and seemed to deflate a little. "Feldman and I have...a history."

"He told me."

"Well, it all makes sense now, doesn't it? All this digging around in my past—" He stood and paced the room. "I just thought it was right-wing Dallas, but there was a little conflict of interest going on here, wasn't there? And you knew it!" He pointed his finger at me. "You knew it and you never warned me. I would have handled things differently, if I'd had some kind of warning—If I'd known what I was really being criticized for. You could have warned me. You could have at least warned me."

"Ian wasn't after you because of me. He hates you because of Penny. Not me. Anyway, he's leaving, so you won't have to worry about him anymore."

"And you think you're going with him?"

"Yes."

"No. You're not."

"You have nothing to say—"

"I have a hell of a lot to say about that."

"He's...He's talking about getting married."

"Well, that's ridiculous. You're too young to get married."

"How old was Penny when you got married?"

"Twenty-three, and that was too young. You *want* to marry him?" He sounded as if he couldn't imagine this was possible.

I shrugged. "I could do worse."

"Most people get married because they're in love with someone."

"I care a great deal for Ian."

"Are you in love with him?"

I nodded. "I think so." I whispered.

"Well, then. Congratulations!" He walked wearily toward the door. I followed.

"Not that it changes anything, but I want you to know that I did—*do*—care about you. That I will be sad to lose you—not just for the obvious reasons, but because I've enjoyed knowing you. You touched me, somehow."

He reached for the doorknob, stopped and pivoted back to me.

"You're right," he said. "You could do a lot worse than Ian Feldman, but he doesn't really deserve you." He smiled, but only with his mouth. Then he walked toward me and touched my cheek with the back of his fingers. "I guess this is good-bye," he said, as he leaned down and kissed me.

Though our lips barely touched, we had trouble breaking off the connection. My stomach floated and my knees felt watery. Finally he pulled away, but neither of us moved. I had to tell myself to open my eyes. Someone whispered: "I *love* you," and I realized it had been me.

What followed seemed to be happening to someone else. It was as if I were watching some terribly tragic and romantic movie that had nothing to do with me. I saw me slip my arms around his neck and kiss him. I saw him kiss me back. Saw us make our way to the bedroom.

After, we lay there—his arm around me, my head resting on his shoulder. He picked up my hand and kissed me first on the palm and then the wrist and then the inside of my elbow.

"When I was a young boy," he started in, "maybe eleven or twelve, I came upon my mother in our backyard. We had several acres of meadowland behind our house and at that time of the year, it was full of blue bonnets. Like a field of blue velvet. I stood beside her watching the flowers, but she seemed to be in a trance, unaware that I was nearby. We just stood there for, God I don't know how long, and then she said, 'Victor, promise me one thing: don't ever turn your back on love.'"

For a moment I was speechless. It was the first piece of his life he'd volunteered. For no reason. It was kind of a Hallmark Moment. He watched me, clearly expecting a response.

"Well," I said, clearing my throat, "*She* certainly created a monster."

He looked at me blankly and I worried that I had wrecked things. But then he threw his head back and laughed out loud. I laughed, too.

"That was *really* funny," he said.

"Well, yes. I have my moments."

He continued to chuckle, but eventually that depressed me.

"Why did I ever let you back in my life?" I whispered.

"Gloria, you couldn't possibly consider moving away with this guy—marrying him even—if you have such strong feelings for another man. Granted I have a special interest here, but do you think it's fair to him?"

"He's a great guy," I said. "I don't know what to do."

"You have to end it."

"I don't think I can do that to him."

"Sometimes it comes down to personal survival. People get hurt all the time. We all have to have a commitment to ourselves. Because the reality is, you're the only person who has your own interest at heart. Maybe you don't know exactly what you want right now, but I bet it's not marriage and I bet it's not New York. Nothing good comes without a price—a *high* price. Believe me, life is not easy."

"There's no possible happy ending for this," I said after a while. "For us."

"Maybe. But there's more to 'this' than 'us'. You can't spend your life avoiding situations *just* because they might or might not be painful. Otherwise, some day you'll wake up and realize you've had no life at all."

I thought about Ian and how much fun we had together and about the beautiful apartment and life he was offering me. Maybe I didn't have the same obsession for him that I did for Vic, but I knew I could be happy with him. For a long time. We were friends and wasn't that more important than anything else?

"I'm going to go with him, Vic. It's the smartest thing for me to do."

"It's dishonest. Some day you'll resent each other for it. I can get you a job, Gloria. In Austin. With the railroad lobby or one of the State departments. I even have a friend—a classics professor at UT—who's going on sabbatical and wants a house-setter. He'll pay someone to stay there and take care of his cats and plants. One word from me, it's yours. When the session starts up, I'll stay there with you. Penny never comes to Austin anymore."

"I'm not just leaving to get an apartment. I care deeply for Ian. And he loves me."

"But you love me."

"And how do you feel about me?"

"I can't believe you'd ask that."

"Why? You never tell me anything. I never even know if I'm going to see you again."

"I take incredible risks to see you—"

"Do you love me?"

"I don't know what love is anymore, Gloria. I only know that if you left, I'd miss you."

There was a knock at the door. I jerked toward my clock and saw that it was after six.

"What am I going to do?" I asked, panicked.

"Tell him the truth."

"I can't do that."

"A clean break is less painful than a compound fracture."

"I'll handle it my way," I said, slipping out of the bed and grabbing my sweatpants.

"You're going to make a big mistake."

"Well, it'll be *my* mistake." Once I pulled on my tee shirt, I opened the bedroom door. "Promise me one thing?" I glanced nervously at Vic sprawled across the bed. "Don't make an appearance." I couldn't read his expression. "If you—" I started to say love, but decided not to push it right now. "If you care for me at all, please do me this one favor." Still, he said nothing. I slipped out and shut the door, pulling it until it clicked.

"What took you so long?" Ian asked.

"I—. I was asleep." I avoided looking at him.

"Grab your stuff and let's go to my place. I got steaks—"

"Go on. I need to get myself together a little. I'll walk over in a few minutes."

"You sure?"

"Yeah. I'll come over in an hour or so."

Something rustled in the back room. Ian didn't seem to hear it.

"I went to the liquor store and got some boxes," he went on. "Want me to get them out of the car?"

"I'll get them later," I said, kind of pushing him outside.

A door opened. Suddenly, Ian froze, staring at something over my shoulder. Even his hair seemed to turn white. I didn't look back. I knew what he saw. He spun around and left. I didn't even call out to him: what was there to say?

I eased the door to and turned around. Vic was leaning against the wall, his arms crossed over his bare chest, his pants fastened, but his belt hanging loose.

"I can't believe you did that," I whispered.

"Then you know me less well than you should. Did you think I wouldn't fight for you?"

"Is that what you were doing?"

My eyes shifted to the mirror. To my horror, I hadn't changed at all. There were no oozing sores, no wrinkle ruts, no bald patches. My mouth hadn't sagged into a cruel expression; my eyes hadn't narrowed to sinister slits; my skin hadn't clouded; my nose hadn't sprouted a wart; my earlobes hadn't tripled in size. In fact, if I didn't know me, I would have thought, "what a sweet-looking person."

It made me sick. Literally. I rushed to the bathroom and puked until I thought maybe I'd break a rib. Exhausted, I slumped to the floor. Somehow the toilet flushed; when I squinted up, Vic was standing over me. I didn't even care that he saw me in such a repulsive state. He sat next to me and wiped my face with a damp, cool washcloth, then held a small glass of water to my mouth.

When I woke, much later, I was alone. It was dusk. It seemed like my head had cracked open over my right eye. My tongue felt swollen, my lips scorched, my throat raw—as if I had swallowed a handful of razor blades with a glass of ammonia. The apartment was empty.

I turned on the shower and while I waited for the water to heat up, I brushed my teeth twice. I stood under the spray until it cooled down. Physically, that did wonders. I was so thirsty I could hardly swallow and suddenly craved ginger ale, thought I knew I would have to settle for water since I hadn't been shopping in weeks.

When I entered the living room, I spotted Vic unpacking groceries in the kitchen. A six-pack of Seven-Up was on the counter. He stopped what he was doing and looked at me, but neither of us spoke. After opening two cabinets, he located the glasses. Reaching for the tallest one he glanced back at me.

"Thirsty?"

The ice trays were cemented to the freezer wall and he had to bang one several times with his fist to dislodge it. He held the tray under running water until the cubes swam loose. Then he filled the glass with ice and opened a soda. It fizzed wildly. We both watched the foam die back down enough so that he could add more Seven-Up. When he handed it to me, tiny sprays of soda shot out of the glass like a miniature water fountain and when I drank, they hit my nose, making my eyes water. Gasping, I drained it all at once, and Vic refilled it for me.

"Are you hungry?" he asked. I shrugged. "I'm a great cook. I bought the ingredients for Spaghetti with Marinara Sauce. Old family recipe. Pasta's good for your stomach."

"You're Italian?" I asked, feeling a little lightheaded.

"My mother was."

"Funny, you don't look Italian."

"Northern Italians are often blond. But my father's Anglo-Saxon."

"Do you speak Italian?" My legs felt rubbery so I walked over to the chair and sat down.

"You bet."

"Anything else?"

"Deutsch!" he said. I frowned at him. "German. And some French."

"You must be really smart."

"Didn't you know that?" he laughed. "I learned most of them when I was a small boy—we lived in Europe a while. Kids pick up dialects easier than adults. Want more Seven-up?"

"Yes." I held out my glass. My hand shook so he steadied it with his own while he poured.

"You need something to eat. When you're sick like that, your system gets all screwed up." He didn't ask for help, didn't even ask where the pots and pans were. He just rummaged around until he found what he needed. "If you want," he shouted out to me, "you can sit on one of these stools and I'll share my secret recipe with you."

I made my way to the stools and watched as he chopped onions, garlic, carrots, celery and tomatoes like a chef. After he splashed oil into a skillet, he dumped the vegetables in. The aroma was intoxicating. When the vegetables were cooked, he added tomatoes and two cans of tomato sauce and then reduced the heat.

"This needs to cook a couple of hours, so I got us some antipasto."

He opened cans of artichokes and olives and then sliced pepperoni, cheese and bread and arranged them on a platter. I was starving.

"Think you can handle some vino?" he asked, uncorking red wine.

Occasionally through the hours that we sat there first eating the antipasto and later the spaghetti, I worried about Ian; wondered what he was doing; puzzled over whether I should call him later. But each time he crossed my mind, I chased the thought away. Once, when I pictured him sitting, depressed, in his living room, staring out the window, I felt overcome with grief.

"Feldman will be okay, Gloria," Vic said, as if reading my mind.

"How do you know?"

"Because he and I are a lot alike."

"He loved Penny."

"I know."

"He must hate you."

"Well, that's mutual."

"But," I said, "he probably hates me more."

Vic glanced my way before he drained his wine glass. He sighed heavily and looked back at me. "Probably," he said.

He stayed with me that night, which was not all that easy for him to arrange. He did not even attempt to have sex. I have no idea whether he was being sweet or just protecting a shaky investment. But I realized that as long as he wanted me, all he ever had to do was show up.

The early morning sun woke me. Ian was on my mind and the thought caused an ache so deep that I could hardly catch my breath. But, when I glanced toward Vic and saw him lying there, in spite of everything, I wanted him. I reached out and touched his chest. He opened his eyes and smiled at me.

"I think you're *so* beautiful," I whispered, rubbing my leg over his. Surely this could win me a position of honor in the Whores Hall of Fame.

"I know you think that," he replied.

We made love as urgently as that first time. Afterwards, I stared at a crack in the ceiling that ran from the overhead fixture to the far corner of the room. They'd paint the place once I moved out. It would be like new.

Before he left, Vic walked to the Seven-Eleven and copied the number of the pay phone in front of the store. "I'll call you there at three and let you know how soon we can get you moved. Everything's going to be fine. I'll take care of you." I could imagine my high school tormentor, Yolanda Madigan, eating her heart out.

* * *

I stayed in bed for several hours after he left and only got up then because I was hungry. Some leftover spaghetti had congealed in a plate by the sink. I ate that. I walked to Seven-Eleven, but Ian did not answer his phone, at home or at the newspaper.

At two o'clock—one hour before Vic was to call—I unlocked our outside storage unit and located the army footlocker I'd stowed there after we moved in. I packed whatever would fit into it. Everything else—my furniture, my stereo, my dishes—I'd just abandon.

My wig was on the dresser in its vinyl case. I tried it on and looked in the mirror. Somehow, it embarrassed me so I tossed it in the trash can by my closet.

As I was going through my desk, I came across Charlotte Flynn's tote bag. When I dumped its contents onto the bed, an envelope slipped out from between the pages of her *Robert's Rules of Order*. Curious, I picked it up. It was addressed to Charlotte with no return address.

> *Dear Charlotte,*
> *I count the days until we can be together again at the convention. These last few months without you have been unbearable. If only my wife weren't so dependent, I would leave her and we could be together forever. Until she drops dead or I become less sensitive, we must settle for these stolen moments together.*
> *Dexter*

It was the first sign of humanity I'd ever seen in Peddy. In his clumsy way he cared for someone else. For a moment I mellowed on him. But only for a moment. Too bad I wasn't still newsletter editor; I'd certainly print this. I could, of course, send it to Jim Drury. He'd get a good laugh out of it, but the *Times Herald* would never run it.

I found an envelope. The page I'd torn from the phone book was still around. There was only one person who'd care about this letter. Though I found my hypocrisy staggering, I addressed the envelope to her.

I wrote a quick note to my parents and enclosed my apartment key, asking if they would come by sometime before the fifteenth and pick up at least the boxes I'd packed.

At four-twenty, I caught a bus to Washington, D.C.

I slept a lot on the trip and I dreamed like crazy. The dreams were strange in that they were fleeting, almost always involved Vic, and, most bizarrely, were joyful. In one, I stood outside Titches Department store, waiting for a lift. Suddenly, Vic's car appeared and I was jubilant as I opened the passenger's door. In another, I was on a long escalator and as I glanced upward, I spotted Vic smiling down at me. Once, I woke with a start and stared right into the eyes of the woman across the aisle from me. From her expression, I had the feeling she'd been watching me a while.

"Is everything okay?" she asked.

"Yes, of course," I said.

It was in Hot Springs that I realized I was financially embarrassed. I'd left Dallas so quickly I'd failed to cash a check. Hadn't even thought of it. I had eight dollars. I was sure I'd be able to cash one once I got to D.C. If not, I could always call Pamela Newton. But I'd have to be careful on the trip. To avoid expensive food costs, I picked up four cans of Metrical and six candy bars in the little shop at the depot.

By the last leg of the trip I was weary, and plagued with doubts. I felt stale and oily, and when I touched my hair, it seemed both slick and gritty. It had been weeks since Mr. René cut it and he was right—it was turning on me. The section over my ear had gown out enough to stick out ineptly and the tendrils in the back and at the sides were now just droopy. It would be a while before I could afford a professional cut and who knows what another stylist would do. My back ached from sitting, and my muscles longed for activity. I was a refugee. I had no home, no job, no place to go, no one to talk to, a cloudy future, a past I wanted to forget, and no friends.

As we approached D.C., it dawned on me that I had no idea where I'd stay. I assumed there'd be hotels close to Capitol Hill, but I didn't *know* that. Didn't have a hint as to how much they would cost or whether there'd be vacancies. Didn't know how far the bus depot was from the Hill. I started biting my nails and I *craved* a hamburger: three days of chocolate is not as great as it sounds.

But, when the bus drove down Constitution Avenue and I saw the Capitol for the first time, I *knew* I had done the right thing. It was a beautiful day. The sky was the color of robins' eggs, and the white marble government buildings glittered in the sun. In a small park, blue salvia and dusty miller bordered red and yellow tuberous begonias. Above, hanging from black lampposts, baskets of orange and yellow lantana swayed in the breeze. It was such a contrast to all the cement of downtown Dallas. Washington was the most beautiful city I'd ever seen. Lady Bird had done a great job! I was proud to be a Texan.

Capitol Hill employees scurried around, carting papers and files, and I wondered which of them might become friends. I watched a woman take dication from an older man who barked instructions over his shoulder as they crossed the street. Three girls my age picnicked on the Capitol lawn. They had spread out newspapers to avoid grass stains, but seemed unconcerned about wrinkles as they sat cross-legged and hunched over talking and laughing. Two other women lingered by the stairs leading to one of the House Office Buildings, resolving some controversy before returning to their offices.

I smiled to myself; no one's hair looked all that great.

The End

Printed in the United States
33415LVS00003B/70-90

9 781413 760781